THE ELVES RAISED A SECRET CITADEL

It was delightful. It was vengeance, if only vicariously, and to this day, I regret that, dwelling alone in the barrens, I missed the beginning of it. Soon enough, though, I sensed a change in the world, and started investigating. I discovered dragons everywhere running amok, laying waste to their own dominions, slaughtering their chattels and protectors, and in their wanton, reckless bloodlust, leaving themselves vulnerable to their foes. I picked off several myself, when I had the chance.

I suspected the elves had unleashed some manner of curse, for of all the slave races, they possessed the most powerful magic. But if they were responsible, they'd covered their tracks well. Those I put to the question had no knowledge of it, and I couldn't approach the enchanters, diviners, and lords who might.

THE YEAR OF ROGUE DRAGONS

Richard Lee Byers

Book 1
The Rage

Book 11
The Rite

Book 111
The Ruin

Realms of the Dragons
Edited by Philip Athans

Realms of the Dragons 11
Edited by Philip Athans

Other FORGOTTEN REALMS Titles by Richard Lee Byers

The Haunted Land
Book I
Unclean
April 2007

Book II
Undead
March 2008

Book III
Unholy
Early 2009

**R.A. Salvatore's
War of the
Spider Queen**
Book I
Dissolution

The Rogues
The Black Bouquet

Sembia
The Halls of Stormweather
The Shattered Mask

THE RUIN

THE YEAR OF ROGUE DRAGONS

book III

Richard Lee Byers

THE RUIN

The Year of Rogue Dragons, Book III
©2006 Wizards of the Coast, Inc.

Cover art by Matt Stawicki

First Printing: May 2006
Library of Congress Catalog Card Number: 2005935516

9 8 7 6 5 4 3 2 1

ISBN-10: 0-7869-4003-4
ISBN-13: 978-0-7869-4003-5
620-95534740-001 EN

U.S., CANADA,
ASIA, PACIFIC, & LATIN AMERICA
Wizards of the Coast, Inc.
P.O. Box 707
Renton, WA 98057-0707
+1-800-324-6496

EUROPEAN HEADQUARTERS
Hasbro UK Ltd
Caswell Way
Newport, Gwent NP9 0YH
GREAT BRITAIN
Save this address for your records.

Visit our web site at www.wizards.com

For Mark

Acknowledgments
Thanks to Phil Athans, my editor;
to Eric Boyd for pointing me to useful references; and to
Ed Greenwood, for all his help and inspiration.

PROLOGUE

2 Eleint, the Year of Rogue Dragons (1373 DR)

A frigid wind, too cold for summer's end, whistled out of the west, making Stival Chergoba shiver inside his bearskin cloak. Pale, shifting lights danced across the night sky, resembling the green and purple radiance that sometimes shined in the north. Those western lights, however, were white and blue. The colors of ice.

The stocky gray-eyed ranger was on watch, so it was his duty to report the supernatural phenomena. He tramped to the clearing at the center of the sacred grove, only to discover that, as usual, he needn't have bothered. The thirteen druids had already sensed the coming attack and commenced preparations to counter it. Madislak Pemsk, the leader of the coven, a stooped old man with a blotchy bald crown, a beak of a nose, and a ratty brown robe, spoke a word of power and stuck the end of his staff into a pile of wood, whereupon the fuel burst into flame. A younger priest, blond and fair-skinned like Stival himself—and most everyone else in Sossal—put his lips close to the trunk of an oak and whispered. Eyes closed, movements slow and sinuous, a pretty female mystic in a brief, sleeveless tunic danced, saluting the cardinal points with a bronze sickle.

It's all right for them, Stival reflected. This is their kind of fight, and they all have something meaningful to do.

He didn't. He possessed his own mystical abilities, charms passed down from previous generations of scouts and hunters, but none that could influence the outcome of a struggle such as the one they faced.

What he could do, as his ivory-colored scale armor attested, was kill dragons, and that was what he should have been doing. White wyrms had done harm to Sossal for as long as anyone could remember, but never more than this year, when they'd all run mad at once. His homeland needed warriors to combat them.

But it also needed circles of druids to fend off the constant threat from the west, and the barons believed the spellcasters in turn required men-at-arms to guard them. So Stival had reluctantly gone where his masters bade him, while other warriors won renown—and the gold, land, and admiration of beautiful women that often accompanied it—confronting the dragon flights.

In years past, Stival had enjoyed such rewards himself, but squandered them all through various indiscretions. Accordingly, he needed more, but it seemed unlikely he would achieve them anytime soon.

Well, no point brooding about it. Not when he still had tedious, pointless tasks to perform. He stalked back to the edge of the wood, where he had a clear view of the terrain beyond, and the glowing sky above.

In time, a ghostly giantess coalesced from the rippling sheets of blue and silver phosphorescence. Since his arrival at Ironspring Grove, Stival had seen the apparition half a dozen times. But even so, he caught his breath, for the spectacle was one element of his current existence that hadn't come to bore him. Pale and slender, clad in a billowing gown with a plunging neckline, the phantom was perfect, beautiful even though her expression conveyed nothing of softness, humor, or affection—nothing, in fact, but cold determination and avidity. The druids insisted she wasn't a goddess, merely the image of a spellcaster like themselves painted large against the sky, but Stival still found it difficult to credit.

Her mouth moved, and her hands swept through mystic figures. In the center of the grove, the druids chanted counterspells. The wind gusted, continually reversing direction, cold one second and warmer the next. Branches rattled, and leaves tore free.

In an hour or two, the apparition would fade away, the winds would quiet, and everything would be as it had been before. It had happened that way without fail ever since the magical confrontations began, a decade before. Thus, though he remained alert, Stival swarmed up into the crotch of a blue-leaf tree and settled himself to watch the phantom without trepidation or alarm.

Then she looked down at him.

Or peered downward, anyway. She couldn't really be looking at him, because that wasn't actually her looming over the earth, just a sort of shadow. Even if it had been, she would hardly have noticed him any more than an ordinary person would spy an ant creeping in the dark a mile away.

Yet it was strange. She'd never stared downward before, and irrational as it seemed, he couldn't shake the feeling she was gazing straight at him. His guts believed it, even if his head rejected the possibility.

Then the phantom spoke to him.

Her soprano voice, dulcet and low, seasoned with a trace of the accent of some distant land, emerged from the howl of the freezing wind. Perhaps it had always been hidden there, and he just hadn't heard it until then.

No need for concern, she crooned. *Everything's all right.*

Some diminishing piece of him knew she was lying, but it wasn't the part in control of his tongue. He sighed away the breath he might have used to shout a warning and slumped as his muscles went slack and heavy.

Then, for the first time ever, he saw her smile. *That's good, my darling boy,* she told him. *That's very good.*

He smiled in return, and savored the contentment that came with her approval. Until he spotted the dark shapes silhouetted before her immense and luminous form like tiny stains on her dress. They were hard to make out amid the glow, especially with his mind blank and sluggish, but he'd spent too many years fighting wyrms not to recognize dragons on the wing.

It's all right, the phantom murmured. *The drakes are my children, too. They won't hurt you.*

For a moment, Stival was relieved to hear it. But his memories wouldn't let him slip back into lassitude. Though still a relatively young man, he'd seen too many folk fall beneath the dragons' fangs and claws. Like everyone in Sossal, he had abundant reason to hate and dread the reptiles, and *no one* could convince him they were harmless, not even—

He realized he was gasping as if he'd run for miles, and likewise shivering with cold. At some point, a crust of frost, a manifestation, perhaps, of the apparition's magic, had frozen over his garments and exposed skin.

What mattered, though, was that he'd shaken off the enchantment. He peered about and saw with a jab of fear that only he had been so fortunate. Most of his comrades had come to the edge of the wood, the better to watch the phantom, and covered in rime, they still stood motionless and entranced. Meanwhile, the onrushing wyrms had nearly reached the grove.

Stival snatched for the curved rothé horn hanging at his hip. One of the druids had fashioned the trumpet, and supposedly, its call could bolster a warrior's strength and courage.

Praying it would likewise break the phantom's mystical hold on his comrades, Stival pressed the cold brass mouthpiece to his lips and blew with all his might.

The horn blared. Men-at-arms stirred, then cried out as they realized dragons were nearly upon them. A few bolted. The rest frantically readied their weapons. Stival jumped down from the blueleaf, strung his longbow, and rattled off a charm. The reptiles, big as houses and pale as bone, touched down just beyond the edge of the wood, then lunged into the trees.

A crested, wedge-shaped head with a beaklike snout swiveled toward Stival. It cocked back at the end of its swelling, serpentine neck. Stival wrenched himself behind the blueleaf.

The blast of frost, the white's breath weapon, screeched at him. The cold pierced him to the marrow, but the tree shielded him from some of the effect, and the charm he'd cast, a protection against chill and ice, blunted the rest.

He jabbered a spell, nocked an arrow, looked around the blueleaf, and loosed the shaft. It hurtled straight at the reptile's silvery, slit-pupiled eye, but the creature twitched its head to the side and so saved its sight. Still, the missile stabbed deep into its mask. Thanks to his ranger magic, the white's armor of scale and hide had proved no more protective than parchment.

It roared and charged, the edges of its folded, upraised bat wings snagging branches and snapping them to shreds, its long strides shaking the ground. Scrambling backward, Stival kept shooting. His second arrow glanced off its scales. The third lodged in its chest, but didn't slow it down.

Stival tossed aside the bow and drew his broadsword, for all the good it was likely to do. The bards liked to sing about lone heroes besting wyrms in close combat, but he didn't know anyone who'd managed the trick in real life. To think that mere minutes ago, he'd been wishing for a battle against dragons. By the Forest Queen, what an idiot he was!

The white crouched, gathering itself to pounce. Then a volley of whistling arrows battered its flank. It pivoted toward the source of the harassment, and darts of green light pierced it. A dazzling, crackling thunderbolt blazed into its long, sinuous body and out the other side. The druids' protectors were all warriors and rangers, but a few were wizards as well, and two of these had assailed the wyrm with their magic. The creature collapsed and thrashed, crushing brush and saplings beneath it, nearly doing the same to Stival before he jumped clear.

He turned to grin his thanks to the friends who'd saved him from what had seemed certain death, then bellowed a warning instead. Because their own death was streaking in to take them from behind.

It was the biggest, hence oldest and strongest, white Stival had ever seen. But it was also something more, something that, until then, he'd hoped only existed in tales of horror and woe. Patches of slimy rot mottled its hide, and bone gleamed through rents in the skin. Its wings hung in tatters, and the sunken eyes glowed. It could only be a dracolich, a wyrm that had embraced undeath and in so doing, amplified its natural might tenfold.

Stival's warning did no good. His comrades had grouped together to coordinate their efforts and protect each other's backs, but the close formation doomed them. When the dracolich sprang in among them, it crushed half a dozen beneath its bulk, and only needed a heartbeat or so to massacre the rest. The gnashing jaws bit an archer in two. Snatching talons tore other men to fragments. Wings hammered, swatting the warriors beneath. The long tail lashed back and forth, smashing everything in its path, flinging broken bodies through the air.

The dracolich gave Stival a leer. A length of ice like a glittering spear materialized in the air before it, then shot toward the ranger.

Stival tried to dodge, but to no avail. The missile slammed into his chest and exploded, jabbing pain and chill through his torso and peppering his face with flying bits of ice. The impact threw him down onto his back.

He was still alive, however. His armor, charm of protection, and luck had saved him yet again. But he knew that if he wanted to stay alive, his only chance was to play dead. He lay still, and watched the dracolich through slitted eyes.

The dead thing cocked its head, regarding him. Terrified, he realized he was mad to think he could fool a dragon in that way. Their senses were too keen. It surely heard the breath whispering in and out of his nostrils, the heart pounding in his—

The dracolich whirled and bounded off. Either it had been too certain of its kill to really scrutinize the fallen man, or some more enticing opportunity for slaughter had lured it away.

Gritting his teeth at the pain of his injuries—he hoped they were only bruises, perhaps a cracked rib or two, and nothing worse—Stival clambered to his feet, looked around, and despaired at what he saw. As best he could judge amid the chaos, four wyrms had attacked the grove. The garrison likely would have fallen to such an onslaught under the best of circumstances. Denied the chance to prepare, they had no chance at all. They'd been lucky enough to kill one young-ish reptile, but the other wyrms were butchering them by the second. A white struck, caught a spearman in his jaws, and swallowed him whole. Conjured hailstones battered archers bloody, and a plume of pearly dragon breath froze several warriors in their tracks.

It was plain they couldn't hold. They could only hope to buy time for the druids to flee.

But, Stival wondered, would the priests do that? Intent on their rituals, their awareness focused on spirits and forces extant on other levels of reality, did they even realize the grove was under attack? Even if they did, they might not sense that dragons were responsible. In which case, they might head *toward* the danger to aid in the defense.

Stival blew the retreat on his trumpet, then shouted, "Fall back! Warn the druids!"

He whirled and ran. Others followed. On the other side of the battlefield, the dracolich snarled. The air birthed swirls of thick gray fog, masking everything beyond arm's reach. The cold vapor had a measure of solidity—when Stival plunged into it, it was like trying to push through wet blankets drying on a clothesline—and its touch covered the ground in slippery frost. With every stride, his feet threatened to fly out from underneath him.

He'd never reach the druids that way—not without more magic of his own. He recited one charm, then another, the ranger spells momentarily suffusing the air with the smells of earth and verdure. When he dashed onward, his stride was longer and quicker, and his balance more sure.

But still, the near-blindness hindered him. The fog resounded with the screams of men dying close at hand, and he tried not to think about the fact that, at that very instant, a dragon could be closing in on him, or he could be running straight at it, and he'd never know until it was too late.

Finally he burst out of the fog and sprinted onward. A handful of other men also made it out, and they pounded along behind him.

As he'd feared, the druids still lingered in the clearing at the heart of the wood, and were making preparations to join the fight. Madislak murmured a spell that sent a gray cast washing through his skin, as if it had turned to rock. Another druid sprouted quills from his left hand, while a third dropped to all fours and melted into an enormous wolf.

"No," Stival wheezed, his battered torso aching even worse. "Dragons are attacking. You need to run."

The priest with the spines on his hand frowned. "Leaving you warriors to fight alone? Absolutely not."

"You don't understand," Stival said. "One wyrm is a draco-lich, and none of them are reckless or stupid with frenzy. Somehow, they're cooperating with that bitch up in the sky.

It's bad, and you have to get away. In the days to come, the land will need you."

"He's right," said another warrior, speaking with difficulty, swaying on his feet. His right profile looked pallid and frost-bitten, and it was clear from the way he angled his head that the milky eye on that side was blind. "Most of the company have already died—"

The dracolich sprang out of the trees.

"Go!" Stival shouted. "Save yourselves!" He charged the colossal creature, and the other warriors, possibly all that remained of the garrison, did the same.

Attack a wyrm when you can come at its flank or rear, and scramble clear when it wheels to face you. Those were the standard tactics, but they didn't help . The dracolich was simply too fast and powerful. Its snapping fangs and raking claw attacks were too cunning to dodge, and invariably tore their targets to shreds. Indeed, even its stare was perilous. The swordsman with the ruined eye met its gaze and froze in position. Off balance, he fell, and the lich raised its foot high and stamped him to pulp.

At least, Stival thought, the druids were running. One caressed the trunk of a pine and vanished. Another read from a parchment, then shot down into the solid ground as if plummeting into a hole. Others shrank into the shapes of owls or bats and took flight. Someone conjured a mass of twisted, thorny brambles to hinder pursuit. Maybe at least some of them would get away.

One, however, wasn't even trying. Madislak brandished his staff and chanted, and Stival felt a surge of strength and vitality tingle through his muscles. Presumably the other sur-viving warriors experienced the same. Their sword and axe strokes, which had glanced off the dracolich's milky scales most of the time, started to penetrate more often.

It didn't matter, though. The creature kept right on slaugh-tering them. When Madislak shouted a word of power, blue and yellow flames exploded into being all along the lich's back, but died instantly, without burning it in the slightest.

The wyrm killed a spearman with a twitch of its tail, another man with a flick of its talons, and whirled toward Stival. As he tried and failed to stay ahead of the jaws and foreclaws, he saw that he and Madislak were the only ones left.

The dracolich leaped upward, snapping its wings to carry it higher. As it plunged toward the ground, Stival realized he didn't have time to dodge out from underneath. He shouted and raised his sword high, hoping that, as it crushed him, the wyrm would drive the blade deep into its own belly.

Then Madislak rattled off an incantation, and power burned through Stival's body. Wind shrieked and scooped him up as though he weighed no more than a feather.

It whisked him out from beneath the plummeting wyrm, then up above the treetops and into the sky. As he hurtled along, he saw that his form was vague and gray, though from the inside it felt as solid as before. He peered about and discerned the misty form of Madislak streaking through the dark alongside him.

Stival wondered if they could speak in that altered state, and decided it was worth a try. "You saved me," he said, his voice faint, ghostly, but audible. "Thank you."

"I hoped to save some of the others," Madislak replied. "But the dracolich killed them so quickly, and I knew the other druids needed more time." He shook his head.

"You did the right thing," Stival said. "You wise ones had to survive, to deal with that."

He gestured toward the phantom in the west. She was still smiling, a smile of hateful satisfaction, and as if in response to her delight, snow began to fall from the summer sky.

Zethrindor contemplated his kill and thought how strange it was to feel no desire to eat it. But the need and taste for meat had left him when he passed from life into undeath.

Fortunately, the exultation of slaughter itself endured, as did the joy of victory.

As far as he was concerned, he was victorious, even if most of the druids had thus far eluded him. He'd massacred their retainers, seized their place of power, and put them to flight. Not bad for what was only the initial move in the game he'd come to play.

Ssalangan came racing into the glade, cast about, realized the fight was over, hesitated, then turned toward one of sod huts where the druids had made their homes. Zethrindor hissed, and the living white cowered. The older wyrm would have had no difficulty establishing dominance even before his ascension. As a dracolich, with the others still awaiting their own transformations, his control was absolute.

"Mielikki's servants fled," Zethrindor said, "some in the guises of bats and night birds. You and Rinxalabax need to hunt them down. Hop to it!"

Ssalangan wheeled and scuttled away.

The dracolich doubted his minions would actually catch anyone. Human spellcasters were tricky, you had to give them that, and by and large, whites were less cunning than the general run of dragonkind. It was only with the advanced age Zethrindor had reached that they attained true wisdom and guile.

Still, it was worth trying. One never knew, the whites might prove lucky, and in any case, the effort would keep them away from the druids' possessions while Zethrindor looked for treasure. Perhaps, if he felt generous later on, he'd allow the other wyrms to scavenge coins, rings, and such from the bodies of the men-at-arms.

As he stalked toward the huts, he reflected that it would be nice to gain some sort of tangible benefit for himself. Sammaster had vowed that by transforming the various races of chromatic dragons—the whites, reds, blues, greens, blacks, and their lesser kin—he'd change the face of Faerûn itself. In the world to come, dracoliches would rule as emperors. As veritable gods.

It was a splendid dream, but so far, reality had fallen short of expectations. Shortly after Zethrindor's metamorphosis, Sammaster had prevailed on him to serve another. A mere human. Even when living, the white had never stooped to such an indignity, and naturally he had at first refused. But the undead wizard kept cajoling, promising it would only be for a little while and was vital to the success of all their schemes, until, in the end, Zethrindor grudgingly acquiesced.

Perhaps Sammaster imagined he'd agreed because he was grateful for his transformation, thankful to achieve power and immortality and to escape the eternal madness threatened by the Rage. Maybe, to some degree, he was. But it was also clear that the magician, though indisputably a benefactor to the wyrms he purported to worship, was likewise keeping secrets from them. The present situation was a case in point. Why did he think it important that the tyrant to the west have dragons to aid her? How was it relevant to his own grand design?

Zethrindor suspected knowing the answers to such questions might provide the key to ultimate power in the world to come, and he knew his best hope of discovering them lay in complying with the lich's wishes.

Even if he never did find out, his present endeavors still might prove worthwhile. Many a warlord had conquered in the name of a king—or queen—then found it expedient to keep the spoils of war for himself.

Starting small, for the time being, with the druids' possessions. Zethrindor stuck his head through the doorway of a hut and discovered an iron cauldron positioned beneath the smoke hole. Magic throbbed like a heartbeat inside the black iron. With the tip of a claw, he scratched a rune in the earth, beginning a divination to discover its purpose.

ONE

12 Eleint, the Year of Rogue Dragons

Floating on the breeze with Jivex hovering nearby, Taegan Nightwind scrutinized the riders approaching across the steppe. He assumed they'd spotted him and the faerie dragon as well. That was the trade-off a flying lookout represented. He could spot trouble coming a long way off, but might also serve as a beacon to lure it on.

Were the horsemen trouble, though? Some of the nomadic tribesmen were friendly to outlanders. Indeed, it was to confer with such folk that the black-winged elf and his comrades had come to Narfell, while the majority of Kara's "rogue dragons," better able to travel long distances and bear extreme conditions, sought the secret source of the Rage in even less hospitable lands farther to the north.

"Shall we take a closer look?" Taegan asked.

"Why not?" Jivex said. Sinking rapidly in the west, the sun had already softened from blazing white to bloody red, but the small wyrm's silvery scales still rippled with rainbows. "I doubt they'll dare to bother us, not once they recognize me."

Taegan smiled. "I suspect word of your prowess has yet to reach this remote corner of the world. Still, I imagine that with a modicum of caution, we'll fare all right."

Pinions pounding, the flyers beat their way closer to the riders. Essentially, the nomads looked like all the other Nars Taegan had seen since entering this wilderness of scraggly grass and wandering herds of reindeer. Armed with lances, bows, and scimitars, they were lean, swarthy, and wore their long raven hair pulled back into horsetails. Thanks to their proud bearing and fondness for gaudy clothes and jewelry, the barbarians bore a strange resemblance to the rakes of Lyrabar, one that had surprised and amused Taegan on first acquaintance. Each bestrode one of the hardy, long-legged Nar steeds prized throughout the northlands.

Still, it seemed to Taegan that something was different about that group, but at first inspection, he couldn't say what. But in the meantime he supposed the important thing was that they weren't making any hostile moves. Possibly they were too busy gawking. Avariels were rare everywhere, and faerie dragons were equally a marvel to the common run of men.

He swooped lower, and Jivex followed him down. "Hello!" Taegan called. "My friends and I are emissaries, bearing tokens from Dragonsbane, King of Damara. We seek information to benefit all folk, Nars included. To that end, we would very much like to speak with you."

The brawny, coarse-featured chieftain at the head of the procession pointed the tip of his lance at the patch of ground in front of him, signaling for the flyers to land. Taegan had received more gracious invitations in his time. Still, he furled his wings and dropped lower. Once again, Jivex followed his lead.

Then, from the corner of his eye, Taegan glimpsed a small, sharp-featured rider behind the chieftain lifting a polished ebony rod with gold caps on the ends. The avariel drew breath to shout for Jivex to beware, but by then, green and turquoise light was already swirling from the tip of the wand. The radiance spun and twined around itself, creating a pattern enthralling and numbing at the same time. All Taegan wanted to do—all he *could* do—was hover and stare at it.

But as his friend Rilitar Shadow-water had told him, it was hard to shackle the will of an elf, and from somewhere deep inside him there surged a wave of wrath and revulsion that enabled him to tear his gaze away from the seething lights. When he did, he saw that the riders had already lifted their short, deeply curved bows, and drawn the cords back to their ears.

He couldn't dodge so many arrows in any conventional way, nor did he have time to cast a spell. He lashed his wings and dived at the ground with every iota of speed he could muster.

The cloud of arrows thrummed over his head. At once, he tried to climb again, but gravity and momentum had him in their clutches, and it was no use. He slammed down hard—from the stab of pain, possibly hard enough to break an ankle—and fell forward onto his knees. At the same moment, he realized what had seemed odd about the Nars. They didn't have any children riding with them, nor any women save those who'd opted to follow the way of the bow and lance. They were obviously a war party, if only he'd had the wit to realize it.

But he could berate himself later. For the time being, he had to cope with the tactical situation. It had its good aspect—the riders in the front rank currently shielded him from the archers in the rear—and its bad: Those lead warriors were only a few yards away, and were even then aiming their lances and kicking their mounts into motion.

Taegan scrambled up. His ankle throbbed, but supported him. He still lacked sufficient time for a spell, so he simply yanked his sword from its scabbard, and the Nars were upon him.

He sidestepped one lance and beat another out of line with his blade. His second attacker—the chieftain—snarled and tried to ride him down. Taegan jumped left, and the tall chestnut horse thundered past, missing him by inches.

Only two Nars had charged straight at him. Had the rest attempted it, they would have collided with one another as they converged. But they wheeled their mounts to encircle him, and gripped their lances overhand to thrust and jab.

Fortunately, the envelopment took a few moments. Taegan could have used the time to cast a spell to whisk himself to safety, except that it would mean abandoning Jivex. He looked around for the faerie dragon, but couldn't see him anywhere.

Meanwhile, the Nars had nearly finished surrounding him. He snatched a loop of tanned hide from the pouch on his belt, twirled it through a mystic pass, and declaimed an incantation.

A lance leaped forward—but the Nar's aim was off, and Taegan didn't even have to twitch to avoid it. Thanks to his magic, the riders saw him standing a step away from his actual location.

It was a good defense, but not a perfect one. In a moment or two, clever attackers would figure out the trick and attempt to compensate, and meanwhile, even oblivious ones might strike with faulty aim, and spit their target by sheer luck. Taegan had to pivot repeatedly to keep someone from stabbing him in the flank or back. Doing his best to block out the pain in his ankle, he dodged, ducked, parried, and when practical, chopped right through the shafts of the long spears. Thanks to the enchantments Rilitar had cast on it, his deceptively slender elven sword was equal to the task.

He also shouted: "Jivex! Where are you?"

No answer.

The tribal wizard guided his mount into the ring of lancers. He no longer held the ebony wand. Apparently, since Taegan had resisted its power once, he thought it better to assail him with a different sort of magic. He shouted words in some grating arcane tongue and lashed his left hand through a triangular figure.

Taegan couldn't tell what effect the warlock intended to create. But he suspected it was likely to kill or cripple him, and that the subtle illusion that had thus far frustrated the lancers wouldn't hinder it in the slightest. Unfurling his wings, he gathered himself for a desperate spring at the magician. A sword stroke, even if it failed to connect, might rattle the Nar and spoil his conjuring.

Unfortunately, the nomads to either side of the wizard discerned Taegan's intent and angled their lances to protect their comrade. If the avariel made the leap, he would only impale himself on the tips of the spears.

A plume of glittering vapor swept upward from the ground and in an arc from right to left. Caught in the fumes, the mage, his protectors, and even their mounts swayed drunkenly. Smirking, chortling, the spellcaster broke off his incantation, from the sound of it just a syllable or two short of the conclusion.

Jivex popped into view. By making an attack, he'd forfeited the veil of invisibility that had shielded him before. The arrow stuck in his back, where one platinum butterfly wing joined the torso, revealed why he was crawling instead of flying.

Jivex scurried toward Taegan. Other Nars, who'd avoided a whiff of the faerie dragon's breath weapon, kicked their mounts forward and lowered their spears to stick him.

Jivex whinnied as if he were a horse himself, and most of the mounts shied. Taegan lunged at the one that kept coming, hacked the head off the rider's lance, then balked the steed with a slash to the shoulder. The animal screamed and floundered backward.

Jivex leaped onto Taegan's back and clung between the roots of his pinions. The avariel hadn't expected it, and the sudden weight sent a twinge of bright agony through his ankle and knocked him staggering.

"Stop clowning!" Jivex said. "Get us out of here."

Taegan began the spell, dodged one lance and parried another. Jivex stared and by dint of his innate magical abilities, produced coils of thin gray mist. When the stuff touched a tribesman or his mount, they faltered as if it had abruptly become difficult to remember what they were supposed to be doing.

Taegan reached the end of his incantation. The world shattered into spinning light, then formed itself anew. But the milling Nars were hundreds of yards away. Taegan threw himself down in the grass so the barbarians wouldn't spot him.

"Ouch!" said Jivex, still clinging to his back. "Be careful! When you fling yourself around, it hurts my wing!"

"As you're rending my shoulders," Taegan replied. "Was it truly necessary to sink your claws in?"

The dragon sniffed. "Don't whine so much. You sound like a hatchling."

Taegan sighed. "Hop off and let me inspect your wound."

Pavel scanned the darkening sky, looking for some sign of Taegan and Jivex, who'd flown off to the north, then descended behind a rise. According to Raryn, it had been to make contact with a column of horsemen. Pavel had no idea how the squat, ruddy-skinned arctic dwarf knew that, but had no doubt his friend was correct.

"Kara and I could go after them," said Dorn, standing beside the wagon, his enormous iron arm and leg black and vague in the failing light. "We could fly there in just a minute or two."

"But only if I take dragon form," Kara said. At the moment, she wore her more customary shape of a slender woman with violet eyes and moon-blond hair. "And if the Nars see a wyrm approaching, they're likely to panic."

"Particularly with an ogre-ish thing made half of metal

mounted on your back," conceded Dorn, but without so much of the old bitterness. Since he and Kara had become lovers, his capacity for self-loathing had diminished. "Still, if our friends are in trouble—"

"Here comes Taegan, anyway!" exclaimed Will, standing in the wagon bed amid the bundled gifts they carried to ingratiate themselves with the tribesmen. Curling black lovelocks framed the halfling's face, and his curved hunting sword, seemingly oversized for a member of a race the size of half-grown human children, hung at his side. "But where's Jivex?"

Raryn peered, blue eyes squinting beneath bushy white brows. "Taegan's carrying him. They did have trouble, and we'd best be ready for more." He removed his bow from the wagon and strung it with one smooth, seemingly effortless motion.

Taegan touched down, wincing as his feet received his weight, favoring the right one. He set Jivex gently on the ground, and the faerie dragon rewarded him with a hiss.

"Jivex needs your help, Master Shemov," the avariel said, "and afterwards, I'll be most appreciative if you can look at my ankle."

"Of course," Pavel said. He kneeled down to examine the dragon's wound.

Will ostentatiously turned away. "I won't watch the charlatan butcher another victim. My heart can't bear it."

"Quiet," snapped Dorn. He pivoted toward Taegan. "What happened out there?"

"About what you'd imagine," said Taegan. He sat down on the ground and massaged his ankle through his oxblood leather boot, which he still kept polished to a gleaming shine even after tendays on the trail. "We approached a few dozen Nars, not realizing they were a war party. They gave us some trifling trouble before we won clear."

The broadhead arrow had driven deep into muscle. Pavel knew his magic could mend the wound, but only after he extracted the shaft. "I need to cut this out," he murmured, "and it's going to hurt. It will help if you can remain still."

"Of course I can," the faerie dragon said. "I am Jivex, after all."

"Were the Nars hunting us in particular?" asked Dorn.

Taegan shrugged, a gesture performed by the gleaming raven wings as well as the shoulders. "I can't say. But now that they've found us, indeed, skirmished with a pair of us, I'm reasonably certain we'll see more of them. They don't seem the sort of fellows to leave a quarrel unresolved."

Pavel opened his pouch of surgical instruments and purified the steel scalpels, probes, and tongs with a pulse of conjured red-gold radiance.

"Where are they, then?" asked Will, scanning the horizons, his warsling dangling in his hand. "They must know where we are, if only by watching where Taegan landed, and those Nar horses are fast. It shouldn't take them this much time to gallop over here."

"I imagine Taegan and Jivex used magic to escape," Raryn said. "That may have convinced them to proceed with caution. To wait a while and make a night attack."

Pavel sliced into Jivex's shining scales. The faerie dragon hissed and stiffened, but true to his promise, kept himself from flinching. Fresh blood welled forth, filling the human's nose with its coppery tang. Kara took a step back, lest the scent enflame the frenzy caged in her mind.

"Well," said Will, "in any case, it's really not a problem, is it? Like Kara said, one look at her in dragon form, and they'll run. You should probably reveal yourself now, singer, before they shoot any more arrows our way."

"I could," Kara said, "but then we'd lose our chance to talk to them."

Will snorted. "I believe that bird has already flown."

"I hope not," Kara said, "because we've already conferred with the Adorabe, the Var, the Dag Nost—all the friendly tribes—and learned nothing. We must now find a way to question those without ties to Gareth Dragonsbane. Otherwise, our mission will fail."

"It might come to nothing in any case," Taegan said. "The savage Nars may know no more than the others."

"At the very least," said Pavel, without looking up from his work, "I'm reasonably certain Sammaster spent some time in Narfell. One of the inks he used to write his cipher—"

"There you have it!" said Will. "If the imbecile thinks we have something to learn here, we can be sure it isn't so." He chuckled. "Still, it would be nice to have some tidbit to chuck onto the table at the Feast of the Moon."

The seekers and their allies had agreed to assemble in Thentia on that date three months hence, to share their discoveries and formulate a final plan of action. If they had no new information, or too little to point them to their goal, then, soon after, the metallic dragons' psychic defenses would fall before the ever-burgeoning power of the Rage, they'd all go mad and remain that way forever after, and their ruin would mean death, suffering, and oppression for countless other folk across the length and breadth of Faerûn.

"It would indeed," said Taegan. He smiled at Kara. "What do you have in mind, radiant Lady?"

"Music," she said. "My magic will ensure the Nars hear the song a long way off, before they come close enough to begin shooting, and likewise enhance the charm of the music. Once they do venture near, sorcery will make me seem the most beautiful, virtuous, regal woman they've ever seen. The right sort of conjured light, playing around my person, will heighten the glamour. With luck, the total effect will cozen them into approaching us peacefully."

Dorn scowled. "I don't like it. You're talking about fixing all their attention on yourself, and such charms don't always work. It could be you'll wind up making yourself a nice, shining target in the dark."

Yes, Pavel thought, and while in human form, Kara is as susceptible to harm as any ordinary woman.

He drew the arrow from Jivex's wound, wiped the blood from the point, examined it, and found no sign of poison or death magic.

"I'm not inordinately enamored of the idea, either," Taegan said, "particularly since the Nars have a wizard of their own. It's possible he'll resist your enchantments, then do his utmost to free his comrades from your influence. On the positive side, however, if the barbarians do attack, their first effort will likely take the form of a volley of arrows. We have a spell to protect you from that."

"Too bad the elf who knows it lacked the brains to cast on me," Jivex muttered, just loudly enough to make sure everyone heard.

"What if the magician hurls fire or ice?" Dorn asked. "Do we have a charm to shield her from that?"

"Not with absolute certainty," Kara said. "But I know wards that will improve my chances."

"In addition," said Taegan, "Raryn and Jivex can see in the dark, and Kara has a spell to confer that ability on the rest of us. Some of us can spread out, hide, and monitor the Nars. With better chances," he added, "than they have of seeing us. If one of them tries to initiate hostilities, we'll spot it, and take him down at once."

Dorn shook his head, grotesque with the iron half-mask sheathing the left profile and the traces of puckered scar tissue peeking out from underneath. "No. It's too—"

Kara silenced the half-golem simply by giving him a smile. "A few nomads aren't that much of a danger, are they, compared to what we already faced, in Northkeep and the Monastery of the Yellow Rose?"

He hesitated, then growled, "No. I suppose not."

Pavel's imagination filled in the words his friend couldn't bring himself to say, at least, not in front of everyone: *It's just that I love you so much, I'm terrified of losing you, and sometimes it slips out.*

"But," Dorn continued, "we're going to be do this as safely as we can, and at the first sign of trouble, you transform."

Kara inclined her head and curtsied. "As my captain commands."

Pavel murmured a healing prayer, and his hand tingled

with warmth and crimson light. He pressed it against the gory cavity at the base of Jivex's wing. New tissue grew to fill the gap, and unblemished scales sprouted to seal the rawness over.

A skiprock ready in his sling, Will lay on his belly behind a clump of grass. Thanks to Kara's magic, he could see clearly for a few dozen yards, though colors mostly washed out to gray.

Wreathed in soft, shifting, multicolored light, the bard sang a ways behind him, near the seekers' horses, ponies, and wagon. The song's lyrics celebrated the joys of wandering far on horseback, and the bond between rider and steed. Infused with glamour as it was, it kept threatening to captivate Will as thoroughly as it was supposed to enchant the Nars. He had to keep wrenching his attention back to the task at hand.

Off to Will's right, Pavel lay in a depression in the earth. It wasn't much cover—the flat grasslands were miserly when it came to providing places to hide—but in the dark, perhaps it would serve. The lanky, yellow-haired priest cradled a crossbow in his hands.

Walking their horses with nary a whicker, a creak of tack, or a jingle of harness, the Nars began to appear at the limits of Will's vision. Like Kara's defenders, the barbarians had spread out, perhaps even encircling the outlanders completely.

But as they rode closer, the halfling saw reason for hope that they wouldn't follow through on their hostile designs. Bows and lances dangled, seemingly forgotten, in their hands. Some smiled childlike smiles.

Not all of them, though, at least not all the time. Certain Nars, those with the strongest wills and sharpest wits, most likely, periodically balked, frowned, blinked, or shook their heads, as if trying to cast off some manner of confusion.

The fellow who hesitated most often and seemed to be

struggling the hardest was a sharp-nosed runt with a black wand in his hand. He must be the magician Taegan and Jivex had mentioned. Will considered slinging a stone and knocking him unconscious, but decided against it. If the other Nars noticed their comrade had suffered an attack, that might break Kara's hold on them all by itself.

The mage muttered something to an ugly, hulking barbarian who was likely the chief. Will suspected it was a warning. Enthralled by Kara's vibrant melody, though, the leader didn't seem to hear. He just rode closer to the singer in her veils of shimmering light, and after a moment, the warlock's mouth stretched into a grin. He stuck his wand inside his boot and followed his companion.

This is going to work, thought Will. Dip me in pitch if it isn't.

Somewhere in the darkness, something squawked—or seemed to. With Kara's song amplified to carry over a distance, and infused with a power that made a listener want to attend to it and it alone, it was hard to catch other sounds. Will wasn't sure what he'd actually heard.

But he knew he'd heard something, because the warlock and some of the other Nars reacted. They reined in their horses, sat up straighter, looked around, and readied their weapons.

Kara responded by singing a soaring arpeggio so compelling that, despite himself, Will twisted around to look at her. He wouldn't have been surprised if every owl, reindeer, fox, and mouse on the steppe, or even the blades of grass, had done the same. Awash in golden phosphorescence, the bard appeared as beautiful as Sune Firehair herself. It seemed impossible that any of the Nars could escape her spell.

Until another outcry sounded, this one loud enough there was no mistaking the mingled screams of a horse and its rider.

Nar steeds were prized partly for their mettle, but the noise spooked them even so. They shied, reared, whinnied, rolled their eyes and tossed their heads, and their riders struggled to control them. The delight in the nomads' faces gave way to perplexity and fear. The magician hammered his temples with the heels of his palms, then shouted words of power, staccato and harsh as an axe chopping wood.

Will jumped up and spun his warsling. The skiprock flew as true as he'd expected, hit the warlock in the head, then bounced away without even rocking him in the saddle. Apparently the tribesman, prior to making his approach, had cast his own ward to armor himself against missiles.

The Nar bellowed the final word of his incantation. A ring of shimmering distortion expanded outward from his position. For an instant, as it swept over Will, his joints ached as if he were some withered ancient crippled with arthritis.

But the real problem was that the magic freed the other Nars from Kara's enchantments, as they demonstrated by clamoring in fury. The chief shouted orders, directing some of his men to attack the bard and the rest to help him find and kill the foe who was stalking them in the dark.

A dozen arrows hurtled at Kara, only to shatter uselessly against her willowy form. Will doubted the magic could withstand many more, however. Though no spellcaster himself, he'd spent enough time around such folk to know that every such impact chipped away at the invisible shield.

He didn't understand exactly how things had gone so wrong, but it seemed plain that he and his friends had no choice left but to fight. He slung a skiprock, and a rider toppled from his mount. Dorn or Raryn—Will didn't see where the attack came from—drove an arrow into another barbarian's chest.

Pavel, however, shouted, "No! Defend yourselves, but don't kill them!"

"He's right!" Kara cried. As a woman or dragon, she was beautiful, but midway through the shift from one to the other, she was a heaving, swelling thing vaguely sickening to behold. "Don't hurt—"

The Nar wizard interrupted her with a fan-shaped flare of fire that blistered her half-formed blue-crystal scales. She hissed and recoiled.

Pivoting back toward Pavel—who at some point during the last few heartbeats had conjured a halo of red-gold light around himself—Will said, "What's your idiotic idea this time?" Before the priest could answer, though, riders came thundering at them.

Arrows flew. Will dived onto the ground, and they streaked over him. But Pavel was no acrobat, and the halfling worried that his friend had been hit. When he looked around again, though, the priest was unscathed. His magical aura, buckler, and shirt of mail had evidently protected him.

Will could only pray to the Master of Stealth that such luck would continue, because the god knew, the prohibition against killing placed them at a considerable disadvantage. Nars charged, and he slung a skiprock. It cracked against one horse's head, rebounded to strike another's, and both animals toppled. The halfling hoped the riders had survived the spills.

Pavel shouted rhymes and swept his gold-and-garnet sun amulet through mystic passes. A black horse, the target of one spell, wheeled and galloped away, bearing its rider helplessly along no matter how he yelled and dragged on the reins. A second conjuration froze a nomad as if he were a statue, and his mount, sensing its master's incapacity, veered off.

But two attackers remained, and had nearly raced into sword range. Will tucked his sling back in his belt and poised himself for what he must do next.

A Nar charged him. The halfling somersaulted, dodging pounding hooves and a sweeping scimitar. That brought him alongside the horse's flank. He sprang, and just managed to grab hold of the rider's dyed leather garments.

It was a feeble hold, and while he fumbled for a stronger one, the Nar attacked him. The nomad couldn't use the scimitar to slash in such close quarters, but he could bash with the heavy brass pommel.

The blows hammered down on top of Will's head, splashing sparks across his vision. Refusing to let the jolts of pain paralyze him, he finally achieved a secure grip on the Nar's belt.

He snatched out his dagger and drove it into the horseman's thigh.

The shock of the wound made the nomad stop beating at Will's head for a moment anyway. The halfling then struck with the pommel too, smashing blows into the nomad's kidney and solar plexus. The Nar jerked and flailed. Will clambered higher up the horseman's body and landed a strike to the jaw, snapping the larger combatant's head back. The nomad's eyes rolled up in his head, and he toppled sideways, out of the saddle, carrying Will along with him. Will sprang clear, performed a shoulder roll, and swarmed to his feet without injury.

Well, without further injury, anyway. His head throbbed, and blood streamed down into his eyes. He wiped it away and looked around, just in time to see Pavel catch a scimitar cut on his buckler.

The force of the slash made the priest stagger a step, but failed to disrupt the rhythm of his incantation or the precision with which he flourished his medallion. When he reached the end of the spell, the Nar's eyes opened wide. He dropped his sword, hauled brutally on the reins, jerking his mount around, and rode away as fast as he could.

"Right," said Will. "Maybe I'd cheat and scare them away with magic, too, if I was too cowardly to risk a fair fight."

"Perhaps I'd fight as you do," Pavel said, "if, like you, I had no particular use for my head. Will you survive?"

Will explored his gashed scalp with his fingers. "I think so."

"A pity."

Pavel peered about, spotted a dark Nar mare with a white blaze and socks, and crooning to the animal in a reassuring tone, slowly advanced on it. The horse retreated. Pavel whispered a prayer and gripped his amulet. Though Will wasn't the target of the spell, mere proximity to the magic made him feel irrationally relaxed and happy, even as it seemed to dull the shouts, clash of metal on metal, and other sounds of combat stabbing through the darkness. Pavel eased toward the mare again, and she allowed him to swing himself up into the saddle. He rode to Will and hauled the halfling up behind him. Then he turned the horse to survey the battlefield. Will took the opportunity to do the same.

The Nars were brave, he had to give them that. Even Kara's shift to song dragon form hadn't scared them into breaking off the attack. Or perhaps, knowing they had another foe skulking somewhere in the darkness, they simply didn't know which way to run. In any case, they were fighting savagely, and still trying to avoid unnecessary slaughter, the seekers defended themselves as best they could.

Singing a fierce battle anthem with incantations threaded in, Kara fought a duel of spells with the Nar warlock. He battered her with a flare of jagged shadow that ripped one of her wings, and she responded with a wave of silvery light that seemed to have no effect on him.

Exploiting the prodigious strength of his iron arm, Dorn caught hold of a stallion's neck and dumped the animal and its rider onto the ground. Jivex dazed several attackers with a jet of his sparkling breath, Taegan, likewise on the wing, dodged a lance thrust and bashed his opponent with the flat of his elven sword, while Raryn parried a scimitar stroke with the shaft of his harpoon.

That was much as Will had time to take in before Pavel rode in the opposite direction from the battle.

"Aren't we going to help the others?" the halfling asked.

"They'll be fine," Pavel said. "If the Nars push her to it, Kara can slaughter the lot of them, all by herself. But perhaps we can spare her the necessity."

"How?"

"By stopping Brimstone."

"He's the one who attacked the Nars? How do you know?"

"Because I can feel him lurking somewhere nearby, as you'd feel the pangs of a broken tooth. Now stop blathering and look for him."

Brimstone, Will reflected. It made a certain amount of sense. Since he and his comrades traveled by day, the vampiric smoke drake couldn't journey with them. Accordingly, he was exploring Narfell on his own, but made contact with his partners periodically. They'd actually been expecting him to turn up for a while, and certainly the wyrm would have no qualms about massacring a company of Nars for any number of reasons.

Blood dripped down Will's face. He swiped at it, then caught an acrid smell of smoke and combustion, and spotted a long, sinuous shadow.

"There he is!" he said. "Swing left!"

Pavel tugged on the reins, and in another moment, Brimstone came into clear view.

Red eyes glowing like hot coals, ruby- and diamond-studded platinum collar gleaming, a couple arrows jutting from his dark scales, Brimstone crouched among the shattered bodies of horses and men, with one living Nar squirming helplessly beneath each forefoot and another flopping in his jaws, impaled on the elongated fangs. The vampire's throat worked, and he made a gulping sound, as he sucked his current victim dry of blood.

The mare balked at approaching the wyrm any closer. His features taut, Pavel simply dismounted and let go of the reins. Will had to jump off quickly to keep the horse from running away with him.

Pavel raised his amulet above his head. "You know," said Will, "Brimstone is our ally. We could try just talking to—"

Warm golden light shined from the sun symbol. To Will, it felt pleasant. But Brimstone squinched his eyes shut and twisted his head away until the glow faded.

He didn't recoil sufficiently to release his prisoners, though. Rather, he pulled the corpse from his fangs with a flick of his forked tongue, spat the body out, and sneered, in his eerie, sibilant whisper, "Sun priest."

"Let them go," Pavel said.

"Have you gone mad?" Brimstone asked. "I saw you lying in wait for the savages as Karasendrieth's music lured them in for the kill, and I decided to make your task that much easier by slaying some of them myself. Which is to say, I'm helping you."

"Well, actually—" began Will. The drake's shining eyes shifted to him, and despite himself, he faltered. Even for a seasoned hunter of wyrms and other dangerous creatures, there was something particularly horrible about Brimstone, something Pavel, Lathander's agent and thus a sworn foe of the undead, felt even more intensely.

Will took a breath and began again. "Really, we hoped Kara's song would lull the Nars into being friendly. We were only 'lying in wait' to protect her if it didn't work out."

Brimstone snorted, suffusing the air more strongly with the hot, bitter stench of his breath. "Be that as it may, they meant to kill you. They're enemies, and their deaths needn't concern you."

"You know," said Will, looking up at Pavel, "at this point, it probably is too late—"

"Quiet," Pavel rapped, without taking his unblinking eyes off the drake for even an instant. "Set them free, abomination."

"I weary of the blood of hobgoblins and yetis," Brimstone whispered. "It's poor stuff compared to the ichor of men. You have no legitimate reason to deny me this prey, and I intend to keep it. Be thankful I don't take your blood instead."

"Back away," Pavel said. He shouted the opening words of a spell. Brimstone bared his fangs and charged, hurtling forward with appalling speed.

Curse it! Will thought. Over the past several months, he'd dodged death at the hands of countless foes, only, it appeared, to perish under the fangs and talons of a creature at least nominally an ally. He slung a skiprock at the huge ruby in Brimstone's collar. It was supposed to be impossible for an undead dragon to wander far from his horde. Back in Thar, Pavel had conjectured that the choker contained the magic enabling Brimstone to break the rule, and that destroying it might thus slay the drake as well.

The missile hit the gem, but to no effect, and Will had no time to fling another. Already Brimstone loomed over his intended victims. Already he was pouncing into striking distance.

"Lathander!" Pavel shouted.

Yellow light, hotter and brighter, blazed from the upraised amulet. Brimstone screeched and balked, though his momentum almost carried him right over the human and halfling. Patches of his charcoal-colored scales burned away.

Will didn't think he'd ever seen his friend conjure such a fierce light before, but then, Pavel had changed. The struggle to end the Rage had put a hitch in his walk, etched new lines in his handsome face, and maybe strengthened his faith as well.

Still, though, the magic was insufficient. When the flare faded, Brimstone, blinking as though half-blind, his charred hide steaming, whirled back around toward the priest. His throat swelled, and his head cocked back at the end of his long neck, as he prepared to discharge his breath weapon. Pavel stood poised to try and dodge.

Will darted between the dragon and the human. "Sammaster!" he cried. "Remember him?"

Brimstone hesitated.

"You hate him more than anything, don't you?" Will continued. "That's why you're here, and why you need Kara and the rest of us, Pavel and me included. You'll never get your revenge without us."

The wyrm sneered. "You have an inflated opinion of your own importance. I suspect that if the two of you died here and now, the search would proceed without you."

Maybe, thought Will, but the important thing is, you're talking again instead of attacking. Your temper's cooling a little.

With an effort of will, he managed to turn his back on the drake and face Pavel. "And you," the halfling said, "you're acting just as stupid, though naturally, in your case, it comes as no surprise. Stopping the Rage is what's most important, right, and to do that, we need Brimstone the same as he needs us. By the Hells, he already rescued Dragonsbane and saved your homeland, didn't he?"

"I still can't stand idly by and watch him feed on human beings," Pavel said. "My vows forbid it."

"Fine," said Will. "You stopped him. Now let it go."

Pavel took a long breath. "Get out of here," he said to the wyrm.

"Someday," Brimstone whispered, "we'll finish our appointed task. Then you and I will enjoy the consummation we crave." He flexed his legs, spread his immense wings, and sprang upward.

Pavel watched the vampire, making sure he was really flying off, then strode toward the men Brimstone had held helpless beneath his claws. Scurrying to keep pace with the long-legged human, Will was amazed to discover the wyrm had managed to charge without trampling the Nars, and almost as surprised to see that one of the nomads was the chief.

For the moment, the horror of his ordeal and the miracle of his deliverance had wrung all the aggression out of him. He stayed on the ground, trembling, staring ashen-faced at his rescuers.

"It's all right," Pavel said, lifting the barbarian to his feet. "You're safe now, and I can help any of your people who are wounded. You just need to order them to break off the attack."

———— ❦ ————

Five Nars examined Dorn's iron arm, testing the sharpness of the talons and knuckle spikes. One accidentally gashed his finger. He grinned and held it up for his companions to see.

Unlike most civilized folk Dorn had encountered, the nomads didn't seem repulsed by the ugliness of his iron parts. Rather, they admired them as weapons. Still, he hated being the object of anybody's curiosity, and had to strain to bear it without discourtesy.

But maybe it was easier than it used to be. If so, he knew he had Kara's influence to thank.

Of course, most of his partners were exotic by Nar standards, but they all seemed to be tolerating the barbarians' gawking more comfortably than he. Preening, Jivex related stories of his battles against the wyrms, dracoliches, and demons that he had, to hear him tell it, slain more or less unaided. Taegan, meanwhile, displayed the particular blend of exquisite manners, wit, and swagger that had helped make him one of the most fashionable fencing masters in Lyrabar. The difference was, he no longer insisted on identifying himself as "an adopted son of Impiltur" or some such thing. He was willing to call himself an elf.

Not an avariel, however. As best Dorn could judge, Taegan's recent experiences had convinced him the elf race as a whole merited respect, but not his own winged offshoot of the family. If anything, the reverse was true. In the maestro's estimation, the avariels, due to some defect in their fundamental natures, had wasted centuries hiding like timid savages in the wilderness while their cousins raised splendid cities and perfected subtle arts.

Well, Dorn reflected with a fleeting, crooked twitch of a smile, if Taegan remained ashamed of his blood, it was too bad, but likewise his own affair. Malar knew, Dorn was about the last man on Toril to teach anybody else the trick of feeling easy in his own skin.

That might be why he disliked meeting strangers, and exchanging pointless blather with them before getting down to whatever business was at hand. But the Far Quey were like other Nars and barbarians in general. You couldn't rush through the exchange of courtesies without offending them.

Finally, though, the most important men in the raiding party were ready to sit down around a fire with Dorn and his comrades. Raryn fetched a jug of brandy. The Nars broke out a straight, spindly pipe as long as a man's arm and stuffed the bowl with the dried, ground remains of what was presumably a plant.

The nomads displayed a calm, proud demeanor. A newcomer wouldn't have guessed they'd recently tried to murder their hosts, or survived a clash with a creature out of nightmare.

Mibor, the chieftain, took a pull from the jug and passed it on. "We thought the night dragon was your ally," he said in a voice as deep and harsh as Dorn's own, "and that the bard meant to hold us helpless while it slaughtered us."

It was evidently as close to an apology as he intended to go. Maybe, since Brimstone actually was the hunters' ally—a fact they all had better sense than to emphasize—it was more than they deserved.

"We understand," Kara said, human once more, lustrous eyes catching the firelight. "But I only meant to give you the song as a gift, and to signal peaceful intentions."

Taegan grinned. "I attempted to convey the same thing. It seems the Far Quey are warriors of such valor, they find it difficult even to fathom such a message."

Dorn wasn't sure whether that worked out to a compliment or not, but Mibor accepted it as such, and inclined his head.

"When you and the little drake first flew over our head," the chieftain said, "you said you were looking for information, and that if we helped you, we would help ourselves as well."

"It's true," Pavel said, his hands and jerkin still smeared and speckled with the blood of the men he'd tended. "I imagine that over the past few months, you've at least heard about flights of dragons ravaging the land, even if you've been lucky enough to escape their attentions yourselves. A circle of metallic drakes and wise wizards has formed to cure the wyrms of their madness, but to do so, they must first recover certain secrets."

Mibor frowned. "Secrets known to Nars?"

"It's possible," Kara said, "you can at least point us in the right direction." She accepted the pipe, inhaled, held the smoke in her lungs for a moment, then puffed it out in a perfect blue ring. "Do the Nars have tales of a time when elves—folk like my friend here, but most likely without wings—dwelled hereabouts?"

Mibor shot an inquiring look at Shabatai, the small wizard, presumably a custodian of tribal lore as well as the Far Quey's spellcaster. Shabatai hesitated, and Dorn sensed that, like many a civilized arcane practitioner, the Nar disliked admitting to ignorance on any subject whatsoever. But at length he smiled wryly and said, "No. Once, powerful mages ruled this country. Our memory goes back that far. But they were humans, not elves."

"Do you have any mysterious ruins?" asked Will. "Preferably haunted, accursed, or riddled with mantraps. So far, that's been the pattern."

"The cities of the wizard-kings lie buried in the earth," Shabatai replied. "Once in a great while, someone finds a way down to one or another of them. But I know of none, and even if I did, the old lords were human, as I said."

"Still, they may have known the *Tel-quessir*," said Kara, "and left records in one form or another."

"Indeed," Taegan said, "but if our friends can't point us to one particular site, someplace associated with elves, dragons, or famed as a repository of ancient lore, I'm not sure how to proceed. It's late in the game to dig up Narfell at random."

"What about the Hermit?" asked a young Nar woman, her swarthy, sinewy forearms tattooed with lines of high-stepping horses rendered in white ink.

Shabatai snorted. "It's not an old town or fort, and has nothing to do with wyrms or elves. On top of that, if it truly exists at all, it's certain death to seek it out. Why, then, would we speak of it now?"

"Because," the female warrior replied, "if the stories my grandmother told me are true, it knows the answer to every question."

Will grinned. "It sounds like just our kind of trouble."

The ogre smashed Dorn's human leg out from under him, and he slammed down on the ground. Around the arena, the spectators who'd bet on the giant-kin cheered, while those who'd wagered on the half-golem boy clamored in dismay. Dorn tried to scramble back up, but his thigh was broken, with jagged bone sticking through the skin, and a burst of pain paralyzed him. Smirking, its long, bestial face studded with moles, the ogre raised its greatclub and swung at its opponent's torso. Dorn tried to roll and catch the blow on his armored half, but the weapon pulped flesh and shattered ribs. The huge creature hit him again. Again. Again—

Dorn's eyes sprang open. The pummeling, however, continued, though it was far less painful than it had been in the dream. He turned his head.

Kara had taken to sleeping nestled against his human side. At the moment, she writhed and flailed, trapped in a nightmare of her own. He shook her gently, she started to rouse, and he spotted Brimstone, his ember eyes glowing, looming over them. Dorn cast off his blankets, jumped up, and interposed himself between Kara and the vampire, iron half forward, vulnerable flesh angled back.

Brimstone sneered, revealing the long fangs at the front of his jaws and giving Dorn a whiff of his smoky breath. "Easy," he whispered. "If I meant you or Karasendrieth ill, you'd already be dead."

"Your presence poisons her sleep," Dorn growled, keeping his own voice low. "And anyway, you shouldn't be in camp. If the Nars see you talking to the rest of us, it could turn them hostile again." It was amazing that one of the sentries hadn't already noticed the huge reptile crouching in their midst.

"It's the Rage tainting her dreams," Brimstone said, "and my magic will keep each and every barbarian, the guards included, slumbering till dawn. Now help me rouse the others. We should talk." He turned, his tail swishing through the grass, and stalked away. He took care to step over the men sleeping around the dying campfires, and if he presently thirsted for their blood, nothing in his manner betrayed it.

Swallowing a spasm of loathing, Dorn lifted Kara to her feet. "Are you all right?" he asked.

"Of course," she said, "it was just a dream." But she avoided his eyes, and in so doing, proved Brimstone correct, for in Dorn's experience, only the Rage had ever made her feel ashamed.

"Don't be upset," he said, feeling awkward as usual when trying to give reassurance. "You're still sane."

"For now."

"For always. You know I'll look after you. Now come on. Pavel was sleeping over this way."

They found the priest snoring in the tattooed arms of the female warrior. By the time he pulled on his clothing, Brimstone had gathered the others by the wagon.

"So," hissed the smoke drake, "the Nars proved informative."

"We're not sure," said Will. His mouth gaped wide in a yawn. "Eavesdropping, were you?"

Brimstone didn't deign to answer the question directly. "I couldn't hear everything they said."

"Then you missed a diverting tale," said Taegan, running a comb though his black, silky hair. The bladesinger's comrades generally kept a certain distance from Brimstone, but as usual, Taegan lounged within easy reach of the drake's fangs and claws. "In the foothills of the mountains to the west, the hobgoblins breed like maggots in the belly of a dead cow. But there's one patch of land where they never venture. Thereon dwells a mysterious entity so sagacious as to approach omniscience. Alas, it's also thoroughly malevolent and reclusive—hence the appellation 'the Hermit'—traits that disincline it to share its wisdom with others.

"In times past, people in desperate need of answers used to seek it out," the avariel continued. "They carried treasures with them in hopes of striking a bargain. But only one ever returned, and as a warning to others, the Hermit sent him back with an affliction, an ungovernable craving for the blood of his kin. He wound up killing his entire tribe."

Will grinned at Brimstone. "Sounds like someone we know."

The vampire's eyes flared brighter. "I've killed the equivalent of many tribes."

"I have every confidence," said Taegan. "But have you heard of the Hermit? None of us has, not even Kara."

"No," Brimstone said. "But like the rest of you, I've never visited Narfell before."

"Many people across Faerûn," Pavel said, "have legends of all-knowing oracles, but it's questionable that any such seers exist. Even individual gods don't know everything, though perhaps they do in the aggregate."

Perched on the seat of the wagon, tail flicking, Jivex made a spitting sound. "We don't need the Hermit to know 'everything,' just how to wash the dirt out of my head."

"Fair enough," Pavel said, "but the details of the Nars' legend make me doubt the Hermit truly exists at all. Which is to say, it's possible some dangerous creature dwells in the hills, but it may not be a learned sage. Because, if it kills everyone who enters its territory, how would anybody ever find that out and pass the report along?" He frowned. "Though it's possible that over time, some of the tale has been forgotten, and the missing piece explains what seems nonsensical."

Will snorted. "Thank you, bookish idiot, that's very helpful. Say no with one breath, yes with the next."

Pavel sneered. "It's better to be able to think two contradictory thoughts than none at all."

"So," said Raryn, tufts of his silvery mane sticking out every which way, "it comes down to this. Maybe the Hermit is real, maybe it isn't. The only way to know is go look."

"If we think the trip worthwhile," Kara said, "and I do. I suspect we've learned all we can on these steppes."

"And 'all,'" said Will, "wasn't much. But we could swing south. Head toward the Great Dale."

Taegan grinned. "At least it would be warmer. We could enjoy another taste of genuine summer before the season passes away. But the one thing we know about the ancient elves' citadel is that it stands somewhere in the far north. We're more likely to find clues to its whereabouts if we poke around in the same vicinity."

"I agree," said Dorn.

"Sounds like we're all of the same mind," said Will. "Go hunt the Hermit, and if it turns out we're dropping our bucket in a dry well, we'll just have to hope Azhaq, Llimark, or one of our other partners finds the lost castle, or whatever the place turns out to be." He glanced toward the eastern sky, where black was beginning to lighten to gray. "No point trying to go back to sleep now. Want to start breakfast?"

"We're not done conferring," Brimstone whispered. "When you reach the hills, I'll start traveling with you. Obviously, that will require you to journey by night and rest by day."

"No," Pavel said. "It's too dangerous for us to have you lurking around all the time. You proved it by attacking the Nars."

Brimstone spat sparks and acrid smoke. "You traveled with me before and took no harm, and if the Hermit is as dangerous as the nomads claim, you may well need me."

Dorn turned to Pavel. "I don't trust the thing, either," he said, "but he can be useful. If he turns on us, you and I will just have to kill him."

Pavel smiled crookedly. "I'll hold you to that. Now, if you'll all excuse me, I have a sunrise to celebrate."

He walked a few paces away, to a spot where he enjoyed an unobstructed view of the eastern horizon, spread his arms wide, and started to chant. Perhaps he flashed a grin when the sacred words made Brimstone hiss, spread his dark gray wings, and fly away.

TWO

25 Eleint, the Year of Rogue Dragons

The hobgoblins had left signs, white stones arranged into glyphs on the ground and symbols hacked into tree bark, for those able to interpret them. Raryn could, but didn't need the warnings to sense the blight infecting the wooded hillsides, though most of the manifestations were subtle.

The trees weren't monstrously deformed, but a little stunted and twisted, and already dropping their leaves as if resigned to the advent of autumn. Night birds fluttered from limb to limb, and animals scurried in the brush, but not often, and when Raryn caught a glimpse of one, it had a starved and mangy look. The gray mist hanging in the air was similarly unsettling. The chill it carried couldn't bother him, but it felt slimy as well as wet.

Of course, even if a traveler missed all that, the horses' refusal to proceed beyond a certain point had been the final giveaway.

Yes, something inimical had taken root there. The question, though, was whether it was the Nars' Hermit or something less exotic. Offhand, Raryn could think of several creatures whose mere presence acted to corrupt the air, earth, and water in their environs. He and his partners sometimes earned their pay hunting them, and as often as not, it was Raryn's job to range ahead of the others, looking for sign, spying out the lay of the land, and making sure they didn't all blunder into danger in one clump.

He was performing the same function while Taegan and Jivex scouted from the air. With luck, somebody would spot something informative before they all probed too much deeper into this nasty place. It was giving him a headache.

He glanced back, making sure he wasn't outdistancing his comrades on the ground. They were at the limit of his night sight, but he had little trouble making them out.

Or at least, such was the case at first. Gradually, though, the fog thickened, until Taegan and Jivex swooped down to join him.

"If we keep flying," the avariel said, "we're liable to lose track of the rest of you. The mist obscures you."

"I suspect," Raryn said, "it's hiding something else, too. Because it can't be natural, coming on like this. The weather's wrong. We'll wait here and let the others catch up. We should all be one group again."

So they stood, turning, peering into swirling, billowing murk, listening to silence, for what felt like too long a time. Then, finally, shadowy figures appeared.

Raryn felt a jolt of alarm, but for an instant wasn't sure why. By the time he realized the advancing party didn't include a dragon in its true form, and that the enormous Brimstone with his luminous eyes ought to be visible if anyone was, Jivex was already flitting forward to greet the new arrivals.

"What kept you?" the faerie dragon asked.

No one answered. Instead, the white-haired thing masquerading as Kara snarled, baring its fangs, and pounced. As it attacked, some glamour fell away from it and its companions. No one could mistake the animate corpses for the bard, her friends, or anything alive. The stench of their rotten flesh burned in Raryn's nostrils even from several paces away.

Caught off guard, Jivex simply hovered as the Kara-thing lunged at him. Raryn nocked an arrow and let it fly. The shaft streaked under the little dragon to bury itself in his assailant's torso. Possibly more troubled by the enchantment bound in the point than by physical trauma, the creature stumbled and fell backward.

The other undead charged, and with a snap of his wings, Taegan sprang to meet them. He rattled off a charm as his sword darted left and right, and several phantom duplicates sprang into existence around him. Jivex whirled through the air, raking at the foes' crumbling faces and glassy eyes as he shot over them.

Raryn exchanged his bow for his ice-axe and advanced to join the melee.

The bloated, hulking thing that had impersonated Dorn bashed at him with the branch it was using for a makeshift warclub, and he sprang inside its reach to avoid the blow. He struck at its knee, half severing its lower leg, and the undead toppled forward. He stepped behind it, poising his axe for a chop at its spine.

But that move brought him face to face with the little Will-thing, lurking behind its ally. Maybe it was a dead halfling. The decay, some patches wet, others dry and crumbling, made it impossible to be certain.

It sprang at him with a rusty dagger in either fist. He swept the axe around in a block that barely succeeded in deflecting both stabs, then split the creature's skull.

As he strained to free his weapon, the Dorn-thing rolled over and reached for him. Taegan lunged, drove his point into its torso, and its upper body flopped back onto the ground.

"That's the last of these," the bladesinger said, "but there's still no sign of our friends."

"Then we'll have to go find them," Raryn said.

They hurried back the way they'd come, until they exited the fog nearly as abruptly and cleanly as if they'd stepped out of a house. Plainly, it was a creation of magic, and one of their comrades had cast a counterspell to scour a section of it from existence. It seemed evident, too, that the vapor must muffle sound, for since it no longer clogged Raryn's ears, he heard Kara's battle anthem, and other sounds of combat, clearly enough.

His missing friends stood in a circle with shambling corpses and floating, lunging shadows attacking from all sides. Brimstone and Kara— in dragon form—met the threat with spells and flares of their respective breath weapons. Pavel invoked Lathander's red-gold light. Will slung stones and Dorn loosed arrows when they had the luxury, but they mostly used their swords when one foe or another charged into striking distance.

"Kara!" Raryn bellowed. "We need a way in!"

The song dragon turned in his direction and spat a bright, crackling flare of vapor. It blasted some of the undead into oblivion and left others floundering in what sufficed them for pain.

Raryn, Taegan, and Jivex raced forward, across the ground she'd cleared. Though it wasn't entirely clear. A charred husk on the ground grabbed Raryn's ankle, and he had to jerk free. Another corpse-thing shambled at him, and he veered to avoid it. A wraith in the form of a woman, luminous, transparent, body rippling like a banner in the wind, congealed out of empty air to bar the way, and together, he and the avariel chopped and slashed it from existence.

They rushed on into the circle, then turned to stand with their friends against a horde of foes that, for a time, seemed endless.

Raryn swung his axe again and again, until it grew heavy in his hands, the breath rasped in his throat, and his heart hammered in his chest. He knew that Will, cutting with his hornblade; Taegan, fighting by turns on the ground and in the air; and even Dorn, despite the indefatigable strength of his iron parts; must have been growing just as weary. The spellcasters were undoubtedly running short of magic, too.

But at last they were visibly thinning the ranks of the enemy. They only needed to keep fighting a little while longer, then all the undead would be gone. It was going to be all right.

Or so he imagined. Until he noticed the long shape crouched on the crest of a hill.

He wasn't sure this was really the first time he'd caught a glimpse of it. Maybe it simply hadn't registered before, as, amid the frenzy of battle, he'd mistaken it for the fallen tree it resembled in the misty dark. But he realized the hulking shape hadn't been there when he'd first studied the ground ahead. It was something animate that had crept to its present position. Something powerful enough to command a horde of undead, which it had used simply to soften the searchers up for the kill.

A final ghoul sprang at Raryn, and he smashed its skull with the axe. Jivex crowed, "I win again!" Then the Hermit floated straight up into the air.

"Bright spirits of melody," Kara breathed. "It's a linnorn. A corpse tearer."

Will snatched the warsling from his belt. "That's a problem, isn't it?"

As he scrambled to ready his bow, Raryn was certain the halfling was correct. The reptile was colossal, maybe even bigger than Malazan, with patches of mold and lichen encrusting its dark, slimy scales. It had no wings, or hind legs either, and must move along the ground with a strange combination of striding and slithering. Still, it was plainly some sort of wyrm, ancient and accordingly wise and powerful.

Raryn struggled to draw what comfort he could from the fact that he had two—three, if you counted Jivex—dragons on his side. Then, without warning, Brimstone wheeled, lashed his wings, and sprang at Pavel with outstretched talons.

Flying several yards above the ground, Taegan caught a glimpse of sudden motion below. He looked down. As if the situation wasn't dire enough, Brimstone had evidently gone mad and decided to destroy the "sun priest" he so despised. Meanwhile, Pavel was gawking at the hovering linnorn like everybody else. He hadn't even noticed his death hurtling through the air.

Taegan dived.

He couldn't scoop up the human and fly away with him. His wings weren't strong enough. So he simply slammed into Pavel and knocked him to the side. Brimstone crashed down on the spot his prey had just occupied and wheeled to attack anew. His sweeping tail tore through brush and tossed rotting leaves into the air.

Pavel had fallen to his knees and was plainly still befuddled. It was up to Taegan to thwart the smoke drake once again. He touched down and whirled, interposing himself between Brimstone and the cleric. The vampire struck at him, and he sidestepped. As the huge fangs clashed shut, he drove Rilitar's sword into Brimstone's jaw.

Brimstone pivoted and raised a forefoot high to rake or trample. Taegan beat his pinions, trying to take to the air, but the wyrm shifted, spreading and interposing one of his own gigantic bat wings to cut him off. Taegan had no choice but to touch down once more.

Claws flashed at him. He dodged, tried to cut at the vampire's foot, and missed. Jaws gaping, Brimstone's head shot forward—

Red-gold light warmed the night and gilded the drifting tendrils of fog. Brimstone screeched and recoiled. Holding his glowing amulet high, limping slightly, lean, intelligent face resolute, Pavel advanced on the drake. Evidently he hadn't used up all his daily allotment of miracles fighting the ghouls and specters, and thanks be to Lady Firehair for that.

With Brimstone balked, at least for the moment, Taegan had the chance to glance around and see just how badly everything else was progressing. The Hermit hissed foul-sounding syllables, no doubt the opening words of an incantation in some devilish language. Wings pounding, Kara and Jivex soared toward the floating creature, even though its immensity dwarfed them both. Indeed, by comparison, the faerie dragon looked tiny as a gnat.

"Please!" Kara called. "There's no need to fight! We only want to talk to you!"

The corpse tearer continued its conjuring.

"Kill it!" Dorn bellowed, loosing an arrow. "Don't let it finish the spell!"

Kara managed another flare of bright, sizzling breath. Jivex optimistically spat his own glittering, euphoria-inducing exhalation at the Hermit's snout. Arrows pierced mossy scales as big as a man's hand. Will's skiprocks battered their mark, one after another.

The harassment didn't seem to bother the linnorn in the slightest. It certainly didn't hamper its recitation. It growled three final rhyming words, and a cloud of dark vapor billowed into existence around it. Caught inside the murk, Kara and Jivex floundered in flight, and their hides blistered. Jaws spreading wide, the Hermit lunged to seize the dragon bard in the moment of her incapacity.

Dorn drove an arrow straight into one of the black pits that were the corpse tearer's eyes. Even that didn't make the creature react as if it were truly experiencing any pain, but perhaps it annoyed it, for it left off rushing at Kara to glare at the half-golem and spew black, roiling fumes from its mouth.

Taegan caught a whiff of the nasty-smelling stuff, and for a moment, his muscles twitched and shuddered. The bulk of the Hermit's breath washed over Dorn, Will, and Raryn. All three staggered, but only the human and halfling caught their balance again as the fumes dissipated. Raryn collapsed and sprawled convulsing on the ground.

Meanwhile, Brimstone stopped retreating before Pavel's advance and Lathander's light. Eyes squinched nearly shut against the glow, he crouched, then charged forward into the aura of holy power like a man trying to smash down a door. Wings pounding, Taegan rushed to help his comrade stand against the drake.

Fighting Brimstone and keeping him away from the folk busy shooting and slinging at the Hermit left Taegan little opportunity to watch the rest of the battle unfold, but the few glimpses he caught suggested a catastrophe in the making. The linnorn possessed a seemingly inexhaustible store of spells, and no matter how everyone tried to hurt and hinder it, it cast them one after another.

A flying, rotating cylinder of blades shimmered into being in midair, shearing into Kara's flank before she spun clear.

Flame streaked down from the sky to engulf Dorn, burning his human half and igniting his clothing. He flung himself on the ground and rolled to extinguish the blaze.

Jivex summoned a gigantic owl to fight for him, but with a single snap of its jaws, the Hermit annihilated the bird before it even finished materializing. The faerie dragon next attempted to blind his foe by conjuring a whirl of colors before its eyes. The linnorn seemed simply to will the illusion away, and it vanished. The Hermit then lifted its prodigious talons, and would likely have ripped Jivex from existence just as easily if Kara, still singing despite the bloody gashes in her side, hadn't hurtled forward to distract it.

As he dodged a potentially bone-shattering flick of Brimstone's tail, Taegan struggled not to panic. He and his friends had stood against chromatic dragons, a dracolich, a sunwyrm, demons, and plenty of other formidable foes. Surely they could defeat the linnorn, too.

But no matter how he tried, he couldn't make himself believe it. Some other night, perhaps, but not then, when they were already spent and luck was running against them.

Unless . . .

He turned to Pavel and cried, "You have to hold Brimstone back by yourself!" He looked up at Jivex and Kara. "Flee! Get as far away as you can." He beat his wings and leaped closer to Dorn, Will, and Raryn, who, though still shaking, was struggling back to his feet. "Keep shooting! Hurt the thing!"

"What do you think we've been trying to do?" snapped Will, spinning his warsling. "Treat it to a sausage and a jack of ale?"

"Make the Hermit focus on you so Kara and Jivex can get clear," Taegan continued.

Dorn loosed an arrow. "What's the plan?"

"Just trust me." Taegan rattled off one of the few spells he hadn't already expended.

The world flickered and leaped around him and he was flying above and behind the Hermit's colossal head with its writhing hairlike cilia and encrustations of fungus. The reptile's neck was like a twisting highway beneath him.

Back on the ground, tiny with distance, Pavel, his mystical abilities apparently utterly exhausted, battled Brimstone with his mace alone. Hornblade drawn, Will scrambled to help him. Dorn and Raryn kept shooting at the Hermit and had likewise taken up Taegan's cry, bellowing for Kara and Jivex to get away.

The dragons were trying, but the corpse tearer wouldn't allow it. Ignoring the barrage of arrows, it pressed Jivex and Kara so hard they couldn't escape. Neither could turn tail without inviting a rear attack.

Taegan had hoped to put his own stratagem to the test before the Hermit even realized he was hovering nearby, but plainly, it wasn't possible. Kara and Jivex wouldn't break away unless he helped Dorn and Raryn distract the corpse tearer. He furled his wings and dived, hurtling at the linnorn's eye.

Up close, the Hermit smelled foul, not with the rotten stink of a dracolich, but a stale, musty reek suggestive of inconceivable age. From instant to instant, its eye looked like black emptiness or a plate of obsidian large as a tabletop, depending on how the moonlight struck it. A few arrows jutted from the dark surface, moisture seeping from around the tips. Taegan's sword made similar wounds, narrow punctures and cuts that only oozed fluid instead of gushing it.

Still, he succeeded in capturing the Hermit's attention. The dark, enormous head at the end of the flexible neck jerked away, then straight back at him, jaws spreading wide to engulf him. He lashed his wings and flung himself clear an instant before the stained fangs clashed together.

The Hermit struck at him again, and then a third time. He dodged, swerving, each time only narrowly avoiding the prodigious teeth. Occasionally he had a chance to strike back. Rilitar's slender blade pricked and sliced the reptile's snout and came away black with slime.

Gigantic claws slashed down, catching him by surprise and only missing by an inch. The Hermit's tail whipped around at him, and he swooped beneath it. In so doing, he caught a glimpse of Kara and Jivex past the linnorn's body. They'd fled as directed, but the faerie dragon was starting to wheel back around.

"Go!" Taegan shouted.

The Hermit lunged at him, cutting off his view, then pressing him so fiercely he had no opportunity for another look. He couldn't tell if his friend had heeded him or not.

The corpse tearer snarled an incantation, and Taegan felt a pang of ache and dullness shoot through him. His magical augmentations to his innate capacities disappeared, stripped away by the Hermit's counterspell. The reptile followed up by spewing a blast of its smoky breath, but with a beat of his pinions, Taegan jerked himself clear. The vapor's stink churned his guts and set him shuddering even so. The linnorn lifted its talons to shred him before he could recover, but then it faltered. Perhaps Dorn or Raryn had given it a particularly painful wound.

Regaining control of his limbs, Taegan thrust, dodged, and continued to evade. His heart hammered, and he panted.

Were Kara and Jivex far enough away? Since he didn't

see them and couldn't divert his attention from the Hermit to look about, he'd simply have to assume so, for Sune knew, he couldn't continue this way much longer.

He whispered an incantation, meanwhile continuing to defend with as much agility and vigor as before, for that was a bladesinger's art. His swordsman's magic was far more limited than the average wizard's store of charms, but he could conjure and fence simultaneously.

Talons lashed at him. He dived below the stroke and articulated the final word of his spell. Power prickled across his skin and momentarily turned the drifting fog a ghostly blue, but otherwise, nothing seemed to happen.

He hadn't known precisely what to expect, but he'd hoped for *something*. Perhaps the linnorn would hesitate, or leave itself vulnerable in some way. Instead, it simply kept on attacking, and, he suspected, there truly was no hope. For him, anyway. If he could keep the creature busy for a little longer, maybe one or two of his friends could escape.

He evaded raking talons, cut the Hermit's haunch, and the reptile growled words of power. Taegan's body stiffened into absolute rigidity. Unable to flap his wings, he plummeted.

He had little doubt the fall would kill him, but the Hermit evidently wanted to make sure. It plunged after him like a hawk swooping to catch a pigeon in its claws.

But it didn't use its talons to pierce him, nor its grip, painfully tight though it was, to crush him. Instead, leveling out of its descent, it recited another spell that gave him back the use of his body. Not that he could use it for much at the moment.

"What did you do to me?" the Hermit snarled, its voice a rasping, discordant rumble like a scrape of blades and distant thunder muddled together. It spoke Elvish with an accent Taegan had never heard before. "I feel it squirming in my mind!"

"Ah," Taegan wheezed. With the enormous digits clamping his torso, he could scarcely draw sufficient breath to speak. "That would be the Rage. Phourkyn One-Eye taught me a spell to crumble any wyrm's defenses instantaneously. I must compliment you. Most dragons, experiencing frenzy all of a sudden, go berserk. They certainly aren't capable of conducting a civilized conversation."

"I'm no dragon. My kind and theirs diverged eons ago."

"Apparently," said Taegan, "not quite far enough for comfort's sake."

"Lift the curse!"

"A wise request, for, left to fester, it will obliterate your reason. I haven't actually mastered the charm for dampening it, but fortunately, Lady Karasendrieth—the song dragon—has. Once you agree to conduct yourself in a more hospitable manner, I'm sure she'll be delighted to oblige you."

The Hermit glared. "I don't succumb to threats. I'll slaughter you all, raise you as my lifeless slaves, and command the song dragon to cleanse me of this taint."

"That would be ill-advised. Who can say with absolute certainty that an undead Kara would still recall the spell, or be able to cast it if she did? Even if it all worked out as you hoped, it wouldn't save you for long. The Rage is waxing ever stronger. It would swallow you eventually in any case. My friends and I are exploring all the dreariest corners of the northlands to prevent such a calamity from befalling dragons—and dragonkind—everywhere. Thus, it truly is in your best interests to welcome us as the benefactors we are. You could make a start by easing the pressure on my ribs."

The Hermit didn't release Taegan so much as toss him away like a piece of trash. Still, a couple wing beats turned his graceless tumble into directed flight, and he soared up in front of the linnorn's huge, dark mask, oily with slime and with its seething tendrils, sickening to behold.

"Shall we join the others?" the bladesinger asked.

Kara had no idea why Taegan, Dorn, and the others had exhorted her and Jivex to flee. Perhaps they simply hoped that if the seekers split up, someone could escape, and they thought the dragons, with their wings and magical abilities, had the best chance.

If so, that might be logical, but she couldn't abandon Dorn or any of her friends. It wasn't in her. But perhaps she'd succeeded in making the Hermit believe she was forsaking the field, and then had some slim hope of taking the creature from behind. Her wounds throbbing, chest aching with the effort to produce still more breath weapon, she wheeled. Jivex, his mirror-bright scales stained with a coating of his own blood, did the same.

When they turned, though, they saw things had changed.

Still floating dozens of feet above the ground, the Hermit clutched Taegan in its talons. It wasn't hurting him, though, nor was it casting any more spells or spitting additional blasts of its noxious breath. It seemed to be palavering with its captive.

That left Dorn, Pavel, Will, and Raryn free to deal with Brimstone, who, shrouded in sulphurous smoke, continued to attack. Bloody and reeling from the punishment they'd already taken, the hunters fended off the vampire as best they could.

"Brimstone's the greater threat now," Kara said. "We have to deal with him."

"Don't worry," Jivex said. "He's no match for me."

They dived. Jivex created blazes of dazzling light immediately in front of Brimstone's crimson eyes and blares of deafening noise by his ears. Pained, startled, the smoke drake thrashed, and failed to notice Kara's hurtling descent. Commencing a battle anthem at the last second, when it was too late for the reptile on the ground to dodge, she slammed down on top of him, dug her claws into his flanks and her fangs into his neck, wrapped her tail around him, and covered him with her wings, pinning him in place.

Weapons raised, the hunters rushed forward. But before anyone could strike a blow, Brimstone's body dissolved into smoke and embers. Kara fell through the cloud, which surged sideways as if a gale were blowing it. It coalesced back into solidity several yards away. Kara saw that Brimstone had a crooked leg and wing, and numerous rips in his mottled hide.

Still avid to make the kill, the others swarmed after him. "Wait!" Brimstone snarled. "When I attacked you, I was acting under coercion, but now the linnorn has released me from its control."

Dorn's only response was a sweep of his iron talons. Brimstone leaped backward, and the strike missed.

"The Hermit has been casting priestly magic," the smoke drake said, "and divines of a certain stripe can command the undead. You know it's so, Pavel Shemov! Tell your comrades!"

Pavel looked as if he would have liked nothing better than to ignore Brimstone's plea and keep attacking. Still, he said, "Wait! It's as he claims. The Hermit may well have forced him to turn against us. Though it's the fundamental corruption inside him that makes it possible."

"But we knew he was a vampire when we agreed to work with him," panted Will, "so I guess there's no point complaining about it now."

Scowling, Dorn lowered his blade. "I don't trust you," he said to Brimstone, "but I suppose I do trust the strength of your hatred of Sammaster."

The smoke drake sneered. "Like recognizes like."

"It's nice to see everyone getting along," Taegan said. "Guests should behave with decorum in front of their host."

Kara looked up. Black pinions half furled, the avariel came gliding down to earth with the gigantic, wingless linnorn drifting behind him.

With no spells left in his head, Pavel used his physician's skills to tend everyone's wounds as best he could, and they all drank their supply of healing elixirs dry. Otherwise, they would have been in no condition to attend to what the Hermit had to say.

At that, slumped around the crackling, smoky fire Dorn had built, they remained a weary and battered lot, each with his bruises, blisters, and swaths of bloody bandages on display. Only Brimstone, whose vampiric body shed wounds with unnatural speed, looked little the worse for the recent ordeal.

As if he'd discerned the tenor of Pavel's thoughts, Will whispered, "If the Hermit decides to break its promise to the maestro, I imagine we'll all wind up in its belly about a second and a half later."

"Should that occur," Pavel said, "I can only hope you'll sicken a corpse tearer as much as you've always nauseated me." Thanks to the sting of his burns and abrasions, he hadn't yet managed to get comfortable. He tried leaning back on his elbows, and it helped a little.

"I gave you time to drink your draughts and apply your ointments," the Hermit said. The greasy, lichen-spotted bulk of the creature loomed over everyone else, even Brimstone, and radiated not merely dislike but utter loathing, like an emperor forced to treat with beings made of dung. "Now ask your questions."

"As you wish," said Kara, in human form once more, "As we've already said, we seek a remedy for the Rage." She proceeded to explain with a succinct storyteller's clarity what plague Sammaster had unleashed on dragonkind, how they knew about it, and how they hoped to cure it. "So you see, you must aid us, if only for your own sake. Perhaps frenzy never touched you before, but it has now, and will never let you go, because Sammaster somehow altered the enchantment."

"We suspect," Pavel said, "he sought you out in the course of his explorations, though he may not have proffered his true name, or worn his true face, and you gave him information that advanced his schemes."

The Hermit crouched silent and motionless for what

seemed a long while, only the fine cilia spouting from its scales squirming sluggishly, like sated grubs in decaying meat.

At last it said, "A wizard did come, some years ago."

"Why would you help him?" asked Will. "Because he's a lich, and you're partial to the undead?"

A cup of brandy cradled in his hand, managing a certain elegance even when half sitting, half lying on the ground, Taegan grinned. "No. Ghouls and phantoms are the linnorn's slaves, not its friends. Sammaster had to compel cooperation, just as we did, and the shame of capitulation is the reason our new acquaintance is reluctant to discuss the incident. Isn't that right, Lord Hermit?"

The corpse tearer glared. "He persuaded me it would be more convenient to answer his questions than to destroy him, and did so without planting a seed of dementia in my mind. Do you find that amusing? Consider this, then: If I had difficulty, how will you mites fare when you come face to face with him?"

"We're hoping to duck that," said Will. "We just want to break the curse, not fight its master."

"But if we have to," said Dorn, his bastard sword naked and ready to hand in case the Hermit turned on them, "we have some of the most powerful dragons in Faerûn on our side. We'll kill whomever we need to kill. Now, tell us what you told Sammaster."

"Very well," said the linnorn. "As you surmised, he wanted to know all I could tell him of the age of the dragon kings, how they conquered, reigned, and finally fell."

"I gather," whispered Brimstone, "you know a good deal."

The Hermit sneered. "Of course. I was there, watching from the shadows, reveling in their downfall. For the insanity didn't touch me. Until tonight, I never dreamed it could."

Will cocked his head. "So you helped the elves fight your own kind? Why?"

"I help no one, and dragons are not my 'kind.'" The Hermit paused. "Once we might have claimed one another, but their race proved too greedy to share rulership of the world with us. The four-legs waged war against the linnorns, and at first we more than held our own. But their race was more fertile, more prolific, and over time, numbers told. They slaughtered the majority of us, and drove the rest into hiding."

Pavel suspected he'd just heard a singularly biased explanation of the cause of the conflict. Scholar though he was, he knew little about linnorns. He doubted anyone did. But every source that mentioned the species at all alluded to their boundless capacity for hatred, perversity, and destruction. Perhaps even the tyrannical wyrms of old had found them too abominable to tolerate.

But he supposed it would accomplish nothing to challenge the Hermit's account.

"When I lost my own realm," the creature continued, "the event was naturally an affront to my pride, though otherwise, I scarcely cared about it. I'd already come to see my subjects—tiny, scurrying, ephemeral vermin like you—for the contemptible things they were, and could take no more satisfaction in ruling them than one of you might take in lording it over an anthill. Indeed, all those with whom I shared this plane of existence so disappointed me that I might have lost my reason, or slain myself in revulsion and despair, had I not also managed to establish an intimacy with the only entities worth knowing and honoring in all this botched, sordid excuse for a cosmos. The four-legs could steal my throne, but they couldn't take that."

"What 'entities?'" Brimstone asked.

"The powers behind darkness and undeath," the Hermit said. "The forces that casually spawn your kind as a byproduct of their true business, the way a carpenter makes shavings when he planes a board."

Pavel felt a pang of disgust. "In other words, you became the priest of some evil deity."

"You aren't capable of comprehending what my words actually mean," the Hermit said. "Pray to your own little god that you never find out."

"I don't care about your faith," said Dorn. "Tell us about the coming of the Rage."

"All right. It was delightful. It was vengeance, if only vicariously, and to this day, I regret that, dwelling alone in the barrens, I missed the beginning of it. Soon enough, though, I sensed a change in the world, and started investigating. I discovered dragons everywhere running amok, laying waste to their own dominions, slaughtering their chattels and protectors, and in their wanton, reckless bloodlust, leaving themselves vulnerable to their foes. I picked off several myself, when I had the chance."

"You must," said Kara, "have wondered about the cause, and tried to find out what it was."

"Of course. I suspected the elves had unleashed some manner of curse, for of all the slave races, they possessed the most powerful magic. But if they were responsible, they'd covered their tracks well. Those I put to the question had no knowledge of it, and I couldn't approach the enchanters, diviners, and lords who might. They stood at the heads of mighty hosts assembled to assail the drakes, and would have made no distinction between a four-legged wyrm and myself."

"Still," said Will, "you're clever enough that you learned something, am I right?"

"Yes, halfling. In the end, I found out the elves had raised a secret citadel high in the Novularond Mountains."

Raryn sat up straighter. "In the midst of the Great Glacier."

"Not then," the Hermit said. "The ice formed thousands of years later. Still, it was a strange place for a fortress, remote from the rest of the *Tel-quessir's* holdings, and of no strategic importance. Thus, I surmised it might have something to do with the Rage. But I knew it would be imprudent to approach and investigate further, and as the millennia passed, other matters claimed my attention."

"Until Sammaster jogged your memory," said Will.

"Yes," the corpse tearer said. "If I'd realized why he wanted to know—"

"You wouldn't have told him," said Dorn. He turned to Raryn. "This has to be the place where the old mages and priests constructed their mythal. Can we scout the site and still be back in Thentia by the Feast of the Moon?"

The dwarf nodded. "The Great Glacier's dangerous traveling for any who weren't born there. But follow my lead and we'll be all right. It's funny. I always thought I might go home again someday, but not like this."

"You'll have no joy of it," the Hermit snarled, its eyes like pits of burning ink. "Venture on the ice, and you'll meet disaster."

The unexpected outburst shocked them all into silence. Then Taegan drawled, "I'm unclear, noble linnorn, whether you're speaking prophecy, laying a curse on us, or simply attempting to compromise our morale. In any case, perhaps you've lost sight of the fact that if we fail, you'll run mad as a pup in a hen house. Accordingly, more assistance and less menace might be in order."

"I've provided what you asked and more," the linnorn said. "Now I'll seek my own cure, with my own resources. Be gone from my lands by midday, and never seek me again, lest you find me." It wheeled and half stalked, half crawled away. Despite its immensity, it melted into the night almost instantly.

"Well," said Jivex, "that last part was cheery."

Brimstone spread his wings and departed shortly after the Hermit. Despite his own considerable store of arrogance, the vampire evidently took the corpse tearer's command to be gone by noon seriously. That meant he needed to leave forthwith, since he couldn't travel while the sun was in the sky.

With the night creature gone, Taegan grudgingly decided he ought to volunteer to take the first watch. Though he was every bit as weary as his companions, it was a fact of nature that elves required less rest than humans, and unlike either men or dragons, restored themselves by entering a dreamlike

Reverie. He couldn't lapse into that state involuntarily the way an exhausted sentry of another race might accidentally fall asleep.

He passed the time, and tried to distract himself from his aches and pains, by silently laboring to turn the expedition's most recent adventure into a diverting anecdote, with himself as chief protagonist, of course. He could use the tale to add luster to his reputation if he ever took up the thread of his old life back in Lyrabar.

He assumed he would, if he survived. He'd worked hard to achieve that existence, and relished it thereafter. Yet it was strange. He seldom missed it as much as he would have expected. His current life, its rigors and outright terrors notwithstanding, had its own satisfactions.

He didn't even mind trekking through places like windswept, empty Narfell and these dismal, haunted hills, and that truly was peculiar, given that conditions were no less rugged than those he'd escaped by forsaking his tribe. Perhaps the difference was that then, their primitive estate had been all he had, and all he was ever supposed to have or want. But since he'd carved out his place in civilization, and could return there whenever he—

He sensed a presence, and looked around. Dorn towered over him, the yellow firelight glinting on his iron arm and half-mask, the human side of his face in shadow.

"Can't you sleep?" Taegan asked, keeping his voice low so as not to wake the others. "Burns are unpleasant, as I discovered when my academy went up in flames. Fortunately, after Pavel prays for fresh spells at sunrise, he should be able to ease—"

"I have something to ask you," the human growled. "When you cast the magic to rouse the Rage, did you know how far Kara—and Jivex—needed to fly to be out of range?"

Hearing the anger in Dorn's harsh rumble of a voice, Taegan rose to his feet, but otherwise made sure his demeanor remained casual and relaxed. A stance that communicated his readiness to defend himself might further provoke his companion. "I could estimate, from seeing how the spell operated in the Gray Forest, when it overwhelmed the Queen's Bronzes but left the enemy wyrms untouched."

"All right. But were you sure our drakes were clear before you recited the incantation?"

Taegan sighed. "I confess it: No. It wasn't possible. The Hermit was blocking my view, and you saw how hard it was pressing me. Had I diverted my attention for even an instant, it would have killed me."

"That means you could easily have driven Kara and Jivex insane."

"Whereas the linnorn was about to rip them and the rest of us to shreds, which scarcely seemed preferable. I thought it time to take a chance."

"You should have told me—" The hunter stopped. "No. Never mind. You made the right move, it all worked out, and I'm babbling like a fool."

Taegan smiled. "Apology accepted. If I possessed a treasure like Kara, I'd be frightened of losing her as well. Though I must say, when I witness the burdens true love imposes on the smitten, I appreciate the advantages of pursuing romance as we rakes do in Lyrabar: Adore a lady for an hour or an evening, then saunter on to the next."

Dorn grunted. "What do you make of the Hermit's final words?"

"I wish I knew. Nexus or Firefingers might be able to take the measure of such an ancient and wicked being, but I'll own up to something I rarely admit: I'm out of my depth. I do know we must press on to the Novularonds, no matter how appalling the weather, and no matter who tries to warn us off."

"Right." Dorn flashed one of his exceedingly rare grins. "A few months ago, I kept trying to quit this craziness, but there's no escape, is there?" His usual scowl reasserted itself like a gate slamming shut. "I think I'll try again to sleep." He turned and limped toward Kara and their blankets.

THREE

14 Marpenoth, the Year of Rogue Dragons

As the five trotting kupuk pulled the sled toward the cluster of snow houses, the Novularond Mountains to the north and the plains and ridges of ice on every side began to blur into a blank, pale brightness. Joylin felt a pang of trepidation.

She hadn't been afraid to sneak away to explore the abandoned village some miles from their own, even if Papa had forbidden it as too dangerous. But she hadn't been expecting a whiteout to set in, rob her of her sense of direction, and cut her off from home.

She frowned away her misgivings. Whiteouts didn't last forever, and as long as she stayed put until this one lifted, or until night fell and put an end to it, she wouldn't have any trouble finding her way back. The only real problem was that it might delay her return long enough for her father to discover her absence. But there was nothing she could do about it, so she might as well concentrate on having fun, especially if she could expect to be punished for it later on.

She whistled the command to halt.

The kupuks were massive animals with canine bodies; hairless, leathery hides; tusks resembling those of walruses; and furry, prehensile tails carried coiled atop their hindquarters. Each was bigger and far stronger than an arctic dwarf child. But they were as obedient as they were powerful, and brought the sled with its greased bone runners to a smooth stop.

Joylin hopped off the back of the conveyance and moved down the line, giving each kupuk a word of praise, a rub about the head and ears, and a scrap of caribou jerky. She then took her harpoon in hand. She doubted the village was really dangerous. Grownups worried about a lot of silly things. But she knew better than to go anywhere beyond the borders of her own settlement without a weapon.

The team whined and yapped as she moved away. They wanted to accompany her. But she couldn't take all five lest they get in her way, and didn't want to play favorites. She told them to hush and stay, and they subsided.

The whiteout was growing worse. The nearest house, a pair of partially buried domes with connecting tunnels, the whole sculpted from pressed snow, was only a few yards away, and all but invisible even so. She groped her way to the low, arched entry and crawled inside.

As she moved from one dwelling to the next, she soon found reason to suspect her adventure wasn't going to prove as thrilling as she'd hoped. Other young explorers had come before her, carving their marks on the frozen walls, and pilfering all the good souvenirs. Which suggested she wasn't doing anything particularly daring or special after all.

Oh, well. It was still fun, and at least she was satisfying her curiosity. Maybe—

Outside, something clamored, the sound muffled and garbled by the thick walls around her. After an instant, the noise stopped as abruptly as it began.

Joylin's first thought was that it had been the kupuk. But if something had agitated them, they wouldn't just bark for a moment. They'd keep it up.

Unless something silenced them all just that quickly.

Her heart beating harder, she told herself that couldn't happen. Though docile and affectionate to their masters, kupuk were ferocious in the face of most any threat. Even the biggest, hungriest bear would avoid them and look for other prey.

Still, she had to check on them and make certain they were all right. Her father said the Inugaakalakurit owed the same loyalty to their kupuk that the animals gave to them.

She took a deep breath, then crawled back out of the house.

At once she felt a surge of disorientation severe enough to make her dizzy. The whiteout was so bad she could see no trace of the kupuk or the sled, and felt a stab of fear that she wouldn't be able to find them.

Then she noticed the tracks her bare feet had left in the snow drifts atop the perpetual ice. Obviously, she could follow those. She skulked forward.

"Tug!" she called. "Blue! Crooked!" None of the kupuk made a sound in response.

I did the wrong thing, Joylin thought. Something did happen to them, and I should have stayed inside.

But she was out in the open, and the part of her demanding to know what had happened was stronger than the inner voice screaming for her to run and hide. Holding her breath, she crept onward until shapes swam out of the whiteness.

The kupuk lay mangled and motionless in crimson pools of blood. A pair of tirichiks, each as long from its snout to the tip of its tail as a snow house, crouched over the slaughtered team devouring the remains. Tirichiks were like great serpents—or dragons—with sinuous bodies, eight stumpy legs, tiny horns, and fangs that protruded over their lips even when their jaws were closed. A pair of orifices opened midway up their snouts, and from one moment to the next, tentacles slithered forth from the pits to wave and flick about, or else wriggled back inside. The creatures were white as bone except for their pink eyes and the spatters of gore currently decorating their hides.

Joylin swallowed and backed away. Told herself the whiteout would hide her, too. A few steps, and there wouldn't be any chance of the tirichiks noticing her.

A bit of snow crunched under her heel. Terror jolted her, and she froze. But the tirichiks didn't look up from their kill.

She tiptoed two more steps, and already the creatures, huge though they were, were nearly lost to sight. Almost safe, she told herself, you're almost safe.

Then one tirichik's tentacles lashed madly about before extending in her direction. She recalled Papa telling her the members were some sort of sensory organs. They gave tirichiks a way of detecting prey which, on the glacier with its whiteouts, glare, and mirages, was often more reliable than sight.

The tirichik scrambled over the kupuk bodies and at her. Its companion surged after it. Joylin's father also said the creatures would kill and eat most anything, but preferred the flesh of dwarves and men.

She whirled, fled, and the tirichiks pursued, not hissing or snarling, silent as ghosts, though their charge sent tremors through the ice. She knew they could run faster than she could. Her only hope was that she had enough of a lead to reach the nearest snow house before they caught up to her.

For a second, she imagined she'd somehow lost track of where it was, even though she could still make out the footprints that ought to lead her there. Then its humped form appeared.

She dived through the entry and scrambled deeper into the dwelling. Just as she glanced back, a tirichik stuck its head in after her. Despite the close quarters, its long, sinuous neck shot its jaws at her with terrible speed. The spiked bony ridge on its spine scraped bits of compacted, hard-frozen snow from the ceiling.

The tirichik's fangs caught hold of her ankle and jerked her backward. Screaming, she jabbed her harpoon into its snout, and surely more startled than seriously hurt, it released her. She scuttled onward, leaving a trail of blood. Her foot throbbed.

The tirichik struck again, but fell short. It pulled its head and neck out of the house, and for a second, she hoped she was safe. Then the whole dwelling started to thump and shake as the creatures tore at it with the claws on their round, flat feet. Clumps of snow fell on top of her as it began to come apart.

She realized she was shaking and crying, and when she tried to stop, she couldn't. Still, somehow she found the grit to take a firmer grip on the harpoon. If she could manage it, she meant to get in one more stab before the end.

Then, beyond the walls, strange voices shouted, and the tirichiks stopped trying to hammer down the house. Apparently they had something else to occupy their attention.

At first, Will merely heard something bumping and thudding about. Thanks to this strange white light that masked instead of revealed, he had to skulk several paces farther before he spotted what was making the commotion. A pair of big white creatures—part wyrm and part centipede, as far as appearances went—were demolishing a snow house, no doubt to get at who- or whatever was inside.

How, he wondered, had Raryn detected the beasts? He suspected that under these conditions, even Kara, with her keen draconic senses, might have passed on by without noticing.

Well, however the dwarf had known, Will was glad he

had. With its relentless cold, ice that proved slippery, brittle, sharp, or treacherous in a dozen other unforeseen ways, and countless additional hazards, the Great Glacier had turned out to be every bit as dangerous and unpleasant as its reputation indicated. Worse, it had made him feel inept, for he knew he might not have lasted a day in this alien, unforgiving landscape without Raryn to shepherd him along.

But he'd been an expert hunter for some years, and a chance to demonstrate his own worth seemed likely to buck him up. He just hoped he could still jump, roll, and fight swaddled in his thick, layered fur and woolen garments, snow goggles, and heavy hobnailed boots.

"Now," said Dorn, loosing an arrow.

Raryn did the same. Pavel discharged a quarrel from his crossbow, and Will spun a skiprock from his sling. Despite the bewildering light, all the missiles found their marks.

Taegan and Jivex soared upward, positioning themselves to strike at the centipede-wyrms from above. Kara sang a spell, and with a boom of thunder, a bright forked blaze of lightning impaled both creatures. The reptiles convulsed.

But they appeared to possess something of a true wyrm's ability to withstand punishment, for neither went down. Rather, they charged, scuttling forward as noiselessly as the Hermit's pet wraiths.

They were fast, too. Will just had time to tuck his warsling away and snatch out his hornblade, then one of the beasts reared over him.

The crested tapering head with its thrashing tentacles plunged down. He sprang forward, evading the strike, and somersaulted. He'd been right, it was harder to play the acrobat dressed as he was, but he still managed to fetch up underneath the creature.

The centipede-wyrm's legs were short and bowed so that the space was cramped even for a halfling. He had room enough, though, to drive his sword into the reptile's pallid flesh.

The creature pivoted from side to side, trying to trample

him. He rolled clear and back onto his feet. Jaws gaping, it struck at him.

He skipped backward, and should have been out of range. But as it whipped forward, the reptile's neck stretched. Perceiving the danger at the last possible instant, Will frantically twisted aside. Stained with the gore of something it had killed previously, the beast's fangs clashed shut just a finger length from his flesh.

Its neck lifted and retracted a bit slowly, though, as if elongation had disjointed or unhinged something that would have to be hitched back into place. Will seized the opportunity to land three more deep cuts. His comrades attacked just as aggressively. Jivex swooped down and clawed at the creature's eyes, then dived away from a stabbing tentacle, which, the halfling observed, had a needle-like claw at the end. Gripping his sword in both hands, Dorn hacked at one flank, and Raryn whirled his ice-axe at the other. Kara's battle song soared through the air. Presumably she, Pavel, and Taegan were coping with the other beast.

The centipede-wyrm Will fought eventually froze, shuddered, flopped over onto its side, and lay still and quiet. Even death failed to wring a cry from its throat. Panting, he cast about and saw that the second beast was down, too.

"Is everyone all right?" Pavel asked, his steel buckler dented and a conjured mace of red-gold light floating in the air before him.

They all reported that they were.

"Then let's find out who the tirichiks were after," Raryn said. He strode to the collapsed snow house and heaved curved chunks of its frozen substance aside, digging for the person or persons beneath. "You can come out now. Everything's all right."

A figure considerably smaller even than Will crawled from the rubble. He realized she must be a little girl of Raryn's race. She had the same squat build, white hair, brilliant blue eyes, and ruddy skin, and her light clothing and lack of shoes displayed the same disregard for the chill.

Bloody-tipped harpoon in hand—she plainly had courage, if tiny as she was, she'd nonetheless managed to wound one of the tirichiks—she gawked at all her rescuers, but particularly at Taegan, Jivex, Dorn, and himself. He inferred that she'd seen humans before, but never an avariel, faerie dragon, half-golem, or halfling.

"Everything's all right," Raryn repeated. "We're all your friends." His eyes opened wide. "By the moon and stars! I believe you resemble somebody I know. May I take a better look?" He gently took hold of her chin, tilted her broad, flat-nosed little face upward, and studied it. "What's your name, young maiden?"

"Joylin Snowstealer."

Raryn smiled at his companions. "It appears I have a niece." Then Joylin dragged herself entirely clear of the shattered snow house, thus exposing her torn ankle, and his grin twisted into a frown. "Pavel! The child needs you."

Wurik Snowstealer had endured some hard times, particularly in recent months, but the past few hours had been especially difficult to bear. Once he determined that his daughter had been absent for the better part of the day, he'd naturally wanted to set forth immediately to look for her. By that time, however, the whiteout had set in. Even the Inugaakalakurit feared to travel under such conditions, nor would they have had any hope of finding Joylin if they did. All he could do was wait, until the blinding brightness gave way to night, and the crescent moon climbed into the sky to shed its glow on the ice.

He glanced around at the other members of the search party, and his heart sank. So few, to comb the ice in all directions for miles around! But it was not the time to brood over past misfortunes, or wonder if a wiser chief would have found a way to avert them.

"Let's go," he said, and they all whistled, clucked, or called to their teams. The kupuk sprang forward. The sleds lurched into motion and rapidly diverged.

Wurik headed for the forsaken settlement. Joylin had been curious about the place ever since first hearing about it, and he reproached himself for not taking her there himself. If he had, this might not be happening. But he'd been busy hunting, and had needed to be, if everyone was to eat.

Though eager to reach his destination, he dared not travel too fast, lest he rush right by sign indicating Joylin's whereabouts, or even the child herself, pinned beneath her overturned sled, fallen into a crevasse, or trapped in some other predicament. He held the kupuk to a deliberate pace even though his nerves fairly shrilled with the urge to make them run.

Then he spotted motion up ahead. Something—several somethings—tiny and indistinct with distance, sped in his direction. Three of the dots were on the ground, and were likely sleds. But two others were flying.

The prudent response would be to change course. But it would delay his reaching the abandoned village, and he'd done nothing to provoke the creatures so rapidly approaching. That ought to mean they wouldn't harm him, though in other circumstances, he certainly wouldn't have counted on it.

He kept his team aimed straight at them, and as they grew nearer, saw something marvelous. They weren't the creatures he'd imagined them to be, but rather as strange a company as he'd ever encountered. Not all strange, though. In the lead sled, a conveyance drawn, like the others, by huskies rather than kupuk, rode Joylin, and behind her, guiding the dogs, stood his long-lost younger brother Raryn.

They all brought their sleds to a halt. Joylin clambered out and hobbled on a bandaged ankle toward her father. He ran to meet her, and they flung their arms around each other.

"Are you all right?" Wurik asked.

"Yes. Except my foot hurts." She hesitated. "Tirichiks killed Tug and the rest of the kupuk. I'm sorry, Papa."

"Tirichiks!"

"Yes," Raryn said, "but at least this young hunter avenged her team. That's tirichik blood on the point of her lance. How are you, brother?"

"Well, now that I know this wayward child is safe, and crazy Raryn, whom I never thought to see again, stands before me." Wurik hugged Joylin for another moment, then released her to embrace Raryn.

"'Crazy?'" Raryn said. "Just because I wanted to see the world beyond the glacier? Would it change your mind to learn I've come home with enchanted weapons and a purse heavy with gold?"

"No," Wurik said, "because in all your years of roaming, did you ever spend a night with a female of your own kind?"

A lanky human armed with a mace and dented buckler laughed. "I like your brother, Raryn. He knows what's truly important."

The remark reminded Wurik of the strangers' presence and snapped him out of his euphoria at finding Joylin safe. This situation was far more complicated than that. Indeed, in most respects, it was little short of a nightmare.

The first thing to do was make sure his smile and hearty manner didn't waver. "Introduce me to your friends, Raryn, and then we'll go home and feast."

A fellow both shorter and slighter than a dwarf, with curling black locks framing his face, grinned. "The Hearth-keeper's blessing on you. We're sick to death of our own cooking."

"Do you eat bugs?" asked a silvery reptile with butterfly wings and a flicking tail. Wurik wondered if it could possibly be some sort of miniature dragon. Probably not, or it would be running mad or a servant like the rest of its kind.

In another minute, everyone was underway. Wurik periodically blew a signal on his bugle, an instrument carved from a rothé horn. Those who heard would know Joylin had been found, and relay the message to others.

What Wurik really wanted to do was talk to his daughter,

but it wasn't possible racing along on a sled. If they spoke loud enough to hear one another, Raryn and the strangers might overhear as well, and so it would have to wait.

At last they reached the village, at which point Wurik realized that too was a potential problem. Raryn was too observant not to notice there were fewer cook fires than formerly, and that some of the snow houses were vacant.

Sure enough, he took one look around and asked, "What's happened to the tribe?"

"Dragon attack," Wurik said. It was even true as far as it went, but it had only been the start of their troubles. "The wyrms surprised a big hunting party. We lost quite a few of our folk."

Raryn sighed and nodded. "It's happening everywhere."

The villagers came creeping forth. From their hesitancy and guarded expressions, Wurik realized they were feeling the same awkward tangle of emotions he was. Relief, of course, that Joylin was all right. Amazement at the strange appearances of Taegan, Jivex, Dorn, and Will. But underlying those emotions, stifling the excitement they might otherwise have sparked, fear and uncertainty.

But they needed to manufacture some enthusiasm. "Look!" Wurik shouted. "Joylin's all right, and my brother has returned, along with new friends. Come welcome them!"

To his relief, the other dwarves followed his lead and tramped forward, calling greetings and extending their hands. Perhaps some assumed from his demeanor that somehow, all really was well. The others realized they needed to pretend.

Wurik waited until a chattering cluster of old acquaintances surrounded Raryn. Then he said, "I'll leave you to catch up with these others. My disobedient daughter and I need to talk."

"Don't be too hard on her," his brother said. "It's too bad about the kupuk—from the looks of this place, you can ill afford to lose them—but Joylin did nothing we didn't do when we were small."

"I'll keep that in mind." Wurik picked up the lame child in his arms and carried her to the snow house where they'd dwelled alone since a fever ushered his dear wife down into the ice decades before her time.

As he set her down on a sealskin rug, Joylin said, "I am sorry, Papa, truly. I loved Blue and Tug."

He had, too, but he waved the memory of the poor slain animals away. "That doesn't matter now. I need to know what you told Raryn and his companions."

"What do you mean?"

He felt such a surge of impatience that, much as he adored her, for an instant he might almost have slapped her. "Did you say anything to them—anything at all—about the Ice Queen and those who serve her?"

Joylin blinked. "No, Papa. We only talked about my foot, and tirichiks, and how I look like you."

Wurik felt a bit of the tension seep out of his muscles. Joylin was a child, and the changes that had overtaken the Inugaakalakurit didn't loom as large in her awareness as they did in the minds of the adults. Thus, she hadn't spoken of them. It was all right.

Well, no, it was a long way from that. Ahead lay dread and shame. But he'd salvage something, no matter what the risk.

"Go on out," he said. "I'm not going to punish you. But you are *not* to talk to your uncle or the strangers about the queen or anything to do with her. Tell me you understand."

She stared up at him. Her eyes were troubled, but she said, "Yes, Papa, I understand."

Once she was gone, Wurik proceeded to the rearmost chamber of the house, untied and opened a leather trunk, rooted around in it, and from the bottom retrieved a small, intricately carved ivory box. Inside glittered a piece of ice faceted like some priceless diamond, and when he took it out, he winced.

Ordinarily, arctic dwarves were impervious to cold. They felt it to the extent of knowing if the temperature rose or fell, but it wasn't harmful or unpleasant. Whenever Wurik grasped the crystal, though, he experienced the same burning, numbing chill that would have afflicted a human.

He touched the ice to the center of his forehead.

When the village celebrated, it needed to do it in the open. None of the simple snow-block houses was anywhere near large enough to hold all the natives, let alone visitors twice as tall. Still, it wasn't so bad. Raryn's folk, aware that humans and their ilk required warmth, had given the outlanders the places closest to the leaping, crackling central bonfire. Though he could have done without the smell—the dwarves fueled the blaze with dried animal droppings and oily fish skins—Dorn was fairly comfortable.

The food was good, also. He sampled caribou, walrus, seal, fish, and the windblown, tumbling plant called snowflower prepared in four different ways. The entertainment was likewise as lavish as the village could provide. He applauded songs, stories, dances performed to the intricate thumping of three diversely shaped drums, and even a juggler.

And yet . . .

Dorn turned to Kara. "Maybe it's just me," he whispered. "I've always had trouble enjoying occasions like this. But it feels like they're trying too hard, without any real joy underneath."

"I agree," she said. "They're showing us hospitality, and I'm sure they don't begrudge it. But they've endured too much hardship for it to lift their own spirits." She glanced over at Raryn, seated with Wurik on one side, Joylin on the other, and a platter balanced on his lap. "Poor Raryn. I'm sure he hoped for a happier homecoming."

Dorn grunted. "Maybe you can do something to brighten things up."

She smiled. "Perhaps I can." When the juggler stopped flipping and catching his glistening icicles, and had acknowledged his applause, she rose, raised her hands for silence, and began to sing.

The song told of a young warrior wooing a haughty maiden who thought herself too good for him. She set him impossible tasks to perform, and by dint of boldness and cunning, he managed each in turn. As always, Kara made the story as compelling as the melody was sweet, her voice infused with the personality of each character as she spoke for him in turn.

Truly, it was a flawless performance. Until she went stiff, and a note caught in her throat.

She flashed a smile as if wryly amused by her slip, drew a deep breath, and took up the thread of the song. She managed three more lines, then stumbled once more.

"I'm sorry," she said, pain in her voice. "My stomach . . . I . . . must have eaten too much of this fine food . . . " Her knees buckled, dumping her onto the icy ground.

Dorn scrambled to her side. She tried to raise a trembling hand, but lacked the strength. Her complexion was always fair, but now it had turned ashen, and her lips, blue.

"Pavel!" he bellowed. "Something's wrong with her!" He looked around for the healer, and what he saw filled him with horror.

By the looks of it, all his friends had fallen ill, were all nearly paralyzed with cramps and weakness, while the villagers, for the most part, looked on stony-faced. Some babbled in dismay, or moved to help the afflicted, but their neighbors restrained them.

Everyone had taken his food from communal platters and the like. Still, by some legerdemain, the dwarves had plainly poisoned their guests.

Making a supreme effort, Pavel brandished his sun amulet and gritted out the opening words of a prayer presumably intended to counter the effects of the toxin. A dwarf bashed him over the head with a crank-handled, fire-blackened roasting spit, and he collapsed on his face. With a snarl, Will drew his hornblade and rounded on the attacker, but the weapon slipped from his fingers. The halfling fell retching beside his friend.

Pain stabbed through Dorn's guts, banishing the faint hope that somehow he'd avoided eating the tainted food. He looked back down at Kara. "Change form!" he begged her. In her dragon shape, maybe she could shake off the effect of the poison.

She simply lay still, not even shivering, and he discerned that, though her amethyst eyes were still open, she was no longer aware of him or anything else.

Furious, he reached for the nearest dwarf with his iron talons. But though his metal arm was impervious to poison, the brain guiding it wasn't, and he missed. The jabbing pain in his guts swelled into agony, and he couldn't manage a second try. He toppled onto his side.

From that position, he could see Wurik, Raryn, and tiny Joylin, her eyes wide with shock, watching everything unfold. Raryn tried to articulate the words of a charm. Wurik hesitated, then cocked back his fist and punched his brother in the jaw, spoiling the cadence.

"I'm sorry," said Wurik, "truly."

His ruddy, white-bearded face twisting, Raryn struggled to rise, but couldn't. He groped for Joylin and pulled her close. Dorn wondered if he hoped to use her for a hostage.

If so, it didn't matter. Her father grabbed her by the shoulders and yanked her away.

A surge of agony lifted Dorn and swept him into darkness.

Wurik looked about, counting up the stricken travelers, making sure none had escaped. No, they all lay unconscious where they'd dropped. The poison, brewed from a tirichik's vital organs, was potent stuff.

For the most part, his fellow villagers stood quiet, grim-faced, unable to look one another in the eye. Wurik felt the same shame they did. To betray guests was a despicable act.

"Are they dead?" Joylin asked.

"No," Wurik said. He'd measured out a dose that would incapacitate, not kill.

"They aren't just sick," she said. "You . . . you did this to them."

"We don't have time to talk about it now."

"Why?" Joylin wailed. "They saved me, and Uncle Raryn is our kin."

"Yes. Raryn's one of us, and we won't give him up." He bent down and lifted his brother in his arms. "The others, we must."

"But they're all my friends!"

"I said, we don't have time to talk about it." He turned to the other adults. "Tie up the prisoners. Half of them are so strange, we don't know how long the drug will make them sleep. Gather their possessions. The Ice Queen's servants will want those as well. I'll hide Raryn."

He turned and strode toward his snow house. Though it must have hurt her wounded ankle, Joylin scurried after him.

"Why do we have to do this?" she asked.

"Because Iyraclea ordered it, and she'll kill the hostages—the folk she took away—if we defy her. The lives of our own people have to come first. You'll understand when you're older. Maybe . . . maybe the queen will just question the strangers, then set them free."

"If you think that, why are you hiding Uncle Raryn?"

He glared at her. "Enough! No more arguing. Can't you see, this is hard enough already?"

She lowered her eyes. "Yes, Papa."

He hauled Raryn into the rear chamber of his dwelling, then hurried back to the bonfire. When they arrived, Iyraclea's agents would expect to find him waiting with the captives. Joylin hobbled along behind him.

As it turned out, they made it back with only minutes

to spare. Then the Ice Queen's warriors strode out of the night.

At the head of the procession stalked one of the spirits of the netherworld called an "Icy Claw of Iyraclea." Pale as ice and twice as tall as a human, it had a spiny-shelled, hunched, segmented body, and a long, heavy tail covered in blades. It carried a long white spear in one clawed hand.

Behind it tramped sneering frost giants, blue of skin with silvery or yellowish hair, even taller and more massive than their captain. Several human warriors, recruited or conscripted from elsewhere on the glacier, brought up the rear.

The dwarves cringed before the newcomers. Even then, after all that had happened to mar their pride, they weren't afraid of humans or frost giants, their principal foes for as long as anyone could remember. But the Icy Claw inspired a terror that even its hideous form and manifest ability to wreak havoc couldn't quite explain. Perhaps it somehow stank of boundless cruelty and malevolence. In any case, Wurik had never been able to look at one of the things without a spasm of dread trying to close his throat.

Still, as chief, it was his responsibility not just to look but to talk to it. He stepped forward. "The strangers are helpless and ready for you to take."

The Icy Claw stared back at him. With its antennae; bulging, faceted eyes; and mandibles, its buglike mask was utterly unlike the face of a dwarf or man, and thus impossible to read. At length it wheeled and prowled to the place where the outlanders lay bound and insensible. The villagers scrambled to clear a path for it.

It picked up Taegan for a closer look, then tossed him back onto the ground. Dorn, Jivex, and Kara likewise each received an extra moment or two of study. Then the spirit gazed back at Wurik.

"An odd group," it said, its voice a buzzing rasp. "Your orders were to detain them alive for questioning. I assume they'll wake in time. Otherwise, you'll be punished."

"They'll wake," Wurik said. "We were careful. Is there anything else you require?"

The Icy Claw turned to its subordinates. "Collect the prisoners and their gear."

Wurik's shoulders slumped in relief. They were leaving. In a little while, it would be over.

Then the towering, pallid devil oriented on the heap of the travelers' equipment. It bent down, peering, and plucked an ice-axe from the pile. Wurik realized it was Raryn's. In their haste, the villagers had simply thrown his gear in with everyone else's.

"The head of the axe is enchanted," said the Icy Claw. "You slaves make nothing comparable. But the haft is bone, and looks like an ice dwarf carved it. Even though none of the prisoners is of your kind."

Wurik did his best to project an air of nonchalance, as if he had no idea what the fuss was about. "The human with the iron limbs had the axe. An Inugaakalakurit must have traded it to him."

"I think it more likely that he and these others had an ice-dwarf guide. How else did they survive the journey across the glacier?"

"They're experienced travelers. They knew what they were doing."

The Icy Claw stared at Wurik, and he felt something alien to his experience, a psychic pressure on the surface of his mind. The devil was trying to look inside his head.

He had no idea how to resist such an intrusion. In lieu of any more sophisticated defense, he simply thought, I'm telling the truth, over and over again.

Eventually the feeling of pressure abated. He held his breath, wondering if by some miracle he'd succeeded in fooling the devil.

The Icy Claw pivoted toward its minions. "The thralls are playing games. Search the village."

The frost giants and human warriors obeyed. Since the snow houses were too low for them to enter easily, the former pounded and kicked the structures apart, and the latter sifted through the remains. The Inugaakalakurit watched in distress, or else looked to Wurik, silently imploring him to intervene.

"Wait!" he cried. "Please, stop! There . . . there was one more traveler, but he's one of our own folk. As you guessed, the outlanders met him on the rim of the glacier and hired him to guide them. But he isn't one of them. He doesn't know anything about their business."

"Produce him," said the Icy Claw.

"I'm telling you, it would be pointless for you to take him. He . . . he can't even answer questions. He's fallen ill."

The devil cocked its head. "Because you drugged him, too? Why do that if he's one of you? Why do it, then try to hide him from us?"

Because Raryn never would have allowed me to poison and surrender his comrades, Wurik thought. "Clearly, we wouldn't. It wouldn't make any sense. The guide is sick, that's all."

"Perhaps Iyraclea will see fit to cure him," said the Icy Claw. Some of the frost giants smirked at what they evidently took to be a joke. "We'll find out. Produce him."

"I promise," said Wurik, "to keep him here. If the Ice Queen wants him after she's questioned the others, you can take him then. But for now, please—"

The devil dropped the point of its long spear and jabbed. Wurik tried to jump aside, but was too slow. The weapon punched into his chest.

At first he felt no actual pain, just a sort of overwhelming shock. But tearing agony came when the Icy Claw lifted him into the air like a hunk of meat on a skewer. The devil raised him high enough to look him straight in the face.

"Slaves," the creature rasped, "should do as they're told, without arguing. Perhaps your example will help the others learn."

Joylin lunged forward, her fists balled. Wurik felt a pang of terror on her behalf, then gratitude when another dwarf grabbed her and pulled her back before any of the Ice Queen's minions noticed her defiance.

Wurik's pain faded to numbness, and his thoughts grew muddled. Sensation, awareness, and life itself flowed out of him with the red blood staining and dripping from the ivory shaft of the spear.

FOUR

17 Marpenoth, the Year of Rogue Dragons

Using her harpoon as a walking staff, Joylin limped across the ice. With her ankle still hurting, it would have been easier to move about on the back of a sled, but she'd doubted she could hitch up a team without somebody noticing and sending her back to bed. All the grownups were making a special effort to comfort her, attend to her needs, and supervise her as they deemed necessary.

Sometimes she hated them for it. What was the use of all their fussing, except to get in her way? Why hadn't they shown all this concern when it might have done some good? Why hadn't they risen up and attacked the Icy Claw before it speared her father? Better still, why hadn't they refused to surrender to the Ice Queen and do her shameful bidding in the first place?

The problem with such condemnation was that in large measure, it applied to her father, too. He was the leader who'd decided they must capitulate, just as he was the one most responsible for the treachery at the feast. Joylin, who loved and missed him with her whole heart, didn't know how to be so angry at him at the same time. It often felt like the contradictory emotions were tearing her apart.

But when she busied herself with the task she'd been given, things didn't hurt quite as badly. So she sneaked away from the village every night, to scan the starry sky and gleaming, moonlit ice, and listen for whatever other noises floated on the moaning of the wind.

Despite the resulting lack of sleep, she was vigilant, and possessed her people's ability to see in the dark. Yet when something finally happened, it still caught her by surprise.

She sensed a surge of motion overhead, and instinctively leaped backward. A huge reptilian form plunged down in front of her, the impact jolting and cracking the ice. The creature's scales were dark and mottled, with a jet-black ridge running down the spine. Its eyes glowed like embers, and it stank of acrid smoke. A ring of gems and pale metal gleamed at the base of its neck.

Just before Raryn had lost consciousness, he'd croaked, "A dragon follows us . . . jeweled collar . . . tell him."

Of course, the drakes native to the glacier were fearsome predators. But Joylin had assumed any wyrm affiliated with her uncle would be friendly, maybe even prankish and playful like Jivex.

But the dragon before her radiated a malignancy as terrifying as that of the Icy Claw. It had, moreover, just tried to kill her like an eagle diving to catch a hare in its claws. She screamed, knowing it was useless. Even if anyone heard, the village was too distant for help to arrive in time.

The drake sneered, and its eyes burned brighter. Joylin had a sudden sense that she ought to look away, but found she couldn't.

"Drop the lance," the reptile whispered, "and come to me."

Her fingers opened, and the harpoon clattered on the ice. She trudged forward.

The dragon sat back on its hindquarters, the better to pick her up with its right forefoot. It lifted her up to its jaws, and the smoky smell grew stronger. It inhaled deeply, taking her scent.

Joylin realized it was savoring her aroma, tantalizing itself with the promise of pleasure to come. In just another moment it would bite into her. The horror of it shattered her trance, or perhaps the wyrm released her from the spell. Either way, it came too late to matter. No matter how she thrashed and squirmed, she could no more break free of the drake's talons than she could have picked up a mountain and carried it on her back.

Then, however, the wyrm shifted her away from its mouth to regard her with its luminous eyes. "You have scents on you," it said. "Karasendrieth, Jivex, Taegan Nightwind, and the sun priest—where are they?"

Joylin took a deep breath. Even so, her voice shook. "They told me to find their dragon friend. Is that you?"

"I'm Brimstone," the reptile said. Seeing she didn't recognize the name, he added, "I am their ally. I've been seeking them for two nights. Where are they?"

"If you truly are their friend, put me down and promise not to hurt me. Then I'll tell you."

Brimstone bared his fangs, and Joylin realized how little inclined he was to release prey, or to bargain with the likes of her. Still, after a moment, he deposited her back on the ground.

"Assist me, and I swear to spare your life," said the dragon. "Now speak."

She did her best to explain what had happened. Telling the story made her feel a fresh pang of shame at her people's treachery, and renewed anguish at her father's death. She blinked, trying not to cry.

When she finished, the wyrm said, "I should have stayed with them, no matter how we grated on one another. I might have sensed your people's intentions. In any case, I would have had no desire to eat your tainted feast, and could have protected my helpers. Curse it, anyway! Where does Iyraclea live?"

"In a . . . " Joylin strained to remember the exotic word. "A *castle* made of ice."

"I haven't noticed such a thing hereabouts."

"Neither have I, nor anyone in my tribe. It's just what her servants told us. It's not anywhere nearby."

"Yet your father somehow summoned the Ice Queen's minions, and they arrived the same night?"

"Yes."

"That means they travel by aid of magic. Even if I was certain of besting a gelugon—"

"A what?"

"An ice devil. The baatezu you call an Icy Claw of Iyraclea. Even if I knew I could defeat it, giants, and human soldiers all at the same time, I have no hope of overtaking them on the march. They've reached the citadel already." He shook his enormous wedge-shaped head. "Why have I never heard of this Ice Queen? How is it that Raryn Snowstealer evidently knew nothing about her?"

"She wasn't always here. She came after Uncle Raryn left. Anyway, even though she's called herself queen for a long while, it's only this year that everybody started obeying her."

Brimstone's mouth twitched into a bitter grin. "Of course it is."

"What are you going to do?"

"Find a suitable patch of ice," Brimstone said, "and scry. Perhaps I can determine where the fortress stands, and what's become of the prisoners."

"Be careful," Joylin said. "They say the Ice Queen can feel things happening a long way off. That's part of the reason everyone follows her orders."

"Rest assured, child, I have my own tricks and powers." The crimson eyes burned brighter. "Now, what am I to do with you?"

She goggled at him. "You promised not to hurt me!"

"It wouldn't be the first oath I've broken, and your blood would be the sweetest I've tasted in a while. I know, I can smell it through that bandage." He glided forward.

It seemed that everyone practiced betrayal. Joylin felt a surge of disgust powerful enough to eclipse even her terror. She scuttled backward, snatched up her harpoon, assumed a fighting stance, and shrilled an ululating Inugaakalakurit battle cry.

Brimstone hesitated as if astonished that she hadn't run, frozen, or collapsed in fear. As he well might be, for she recognized that in relation to his hugeness and prodigious fangs and claws, she was like a rabbit striking combative poses in front of a bear.

He turned away from her. "Go home," he whispered.

She blinked, scarcely daring to believe it. "Really?"

"You're too small," Brimstone said, keeping his eyes averted. "Your blood would be tasty, but it takes more than a few drops to slake my thirst. Now flee, before I change my mind."

Pavel's eyes flew open. Above him danced something he'd never before beheld, though he'd read of it. Veils of green and purple light shimmered across the night sky.

For a second, he smiled at the miraculous sight, then recalled the ice dwarves and their poisoned feast. He bolted upright and cast about.

The situation in which he found himself was so strange and unexpected as to seem almost unreal. Someone had removed his clothing, all but the sun amulet, and lain him on a bier atop a tower. To all appearances, both the pedestal and spire were made of carved and polished ice. Yet despite his nudity, he felt warm. He experimented by removing the pendant, and at once cold pierced him and made him gasp. A spellcaster had plainly cast an enchantment on the pendant to protect him from the chill, and he hastily replaced it.

He moved to the parapet and looked around. The tower was only one portion of an enormous castle that had been hewn—or magically raised—from the glacier.

He couldn't see any way down from his perch, but a table, likewise shaped of sculpted ice, caught his eye. Atop it sat a pewter pitcher, goblet, and platter of food. The sight of the items gave him a pang in his stomach, and for a moment he feared he hadn't yet recovered from the poison. But it wasn't that. He was simply hungry, and thirsty too, his throat scratchy and dry.

He walked to the table and helped himself. The pitcher proved to contain a tart white wine. The pink bloody pieces of rothé meat on the tray were raw, but tenderized and seasoned in a way that rendered them palatable even so.

"Do you like your meal?" asked a dulcet soprano voice.

Startled, Pavel jerked around. Before him stood a slender, fair-skinned woman, not tall, but imposing even so, by virtue of a flawless beauty and an air of utter self-assurance. She wore only a light white gown with blue embroidered borders, evidence that she too was the beneficiary of some magical protection against the cold. At her back, a round hole pierced the roof. Evidently it had opened to grant her access.

Pavel had always had an eye for attractive women, and beholding such perfection, felt a stirring of desire despite the wholly inappropriate circumstances.

"The food is good, thank you," he said. "May I ask whom I have to thank for it?"

"My name is Iyraclea," she said, "and my palace holds many pleasures in addition to savory food. My retainers are free to enjoy them all."

"Why am I here?" Pavel asked.

"To enlighten me," Iyraclea said, sauntering closer.

"About what?" He wondered what would happen if he grabbed her by the throat. Could he force her to take him to Will and the rest of his friends, then set them all free? No, she surely wasn't as vulnerable as she appeared.

Besides, the thought of laying hands on her brought another pang of irrational excitement, as if he himself didn't truly know whether his intentions were aggressive or erotic.

Iyraclea smiled. Pavel had encountered some brutish folk and sordid circumstances during his travels, but rarely an expression so rich with lust yet devoid of any trace of warmth. He wouldn't have imagined a lovely woman's face could look like that, at least not with a sane mind behind the eyes.

It frightened him, but didn't dampen his steadily heightening desire. He realized he was trembling.

"You can touch me if you wish," she said. She took his hand, raised it to her lips, and kissed his palm. Her tongue caressed his skin.

Her mouth was cold as a corpse's. With any other woman, it would have been repellent, but instead it seemed delightful.

"Do you want to kiss me?" she asked.

Tell her no, he thought, or shove her away. You don't really want it. She's casting a spell on you.

"Yes," he said. He took her in his arms.

In another minute, he was fumbling at the fastenings of her gown. Over the years, he'd grown adroit at undressing women, but he needed her so fiercely it made him clumsy.

She laughed, assisted him, and the garment fell away. She was bare underneath, her silky alabaster skin painted with gray and white sigils.

He saw they were diamonds with snowflakes inside. Emblems of Auril, malevolent goddess of winter, ice, and cold. That too failed to extinguish his ardor.

He guided her to the bier, or perhaps she led him. They writhed atop it, tangled together, first kissing, then caressing, and finally joined.

Chill soaked into the core of him, but the sensation was pleasant, an aspect of the tide of passion lifting him high. The only unpleasant thing in his universe was the amulet brushing and bumping against his chest. It felt too hot, as if someone had dangled it over a flame. It almost made him want to toss it away.

His hands and arms altered, becoming a glassy blue-white, perhaps even translucent. It reminded him of the moment when Kara began her shift from human to song dragon, and he realized he too was undergoing a transformation. It frightened him, but the fear didn't matter. It was feeble compared to the urgency of his desire.

Something faded and frayed inside him. At first, he didn't know what it was. Then he realized his mystical bond with Lathander was attenuating.

Pavel's earliest memory was of gazing at a rose-and-gold sunrise above the steeply pitched roofs of Heliogabalus, and feeling as one with the power behind it. He'd adored his god his whole life long. Their communion anchored him and defined him. He could sacrifice his will, his very humanity, perhaps, but the thought of losing his priesthood was intolerable.

Iyraclea kissed him, twined around him, held him tight and close in every way a woman could embrace a man, and another surge of rapture threatened to drown his newfound desperation. He silently cried to the Morninglord for aid, and likewise groped for the sun amulet. Iyraclea reached to capture his hand, but not quite quickly enough. His fingers closed on the garnets and gold plating.

The pendant burned him like metal fresh from the forge, but denying the pain, he gripped it tightly. He sought for Lathander once again. This time, the deity's response was unmistakable. An inner light warmed Pavel's heart, driving out the chill.

He was still too drunk with passion to channel that infusion of strength into the precise articulations of a spell. But he could cast it forth in the same sort of raw blast sufficient to wither and repulse the undead. Maybe a servant of the Frostmaiden would find it similarly obnoxious.

He released the power, and the flash painted Iyraclea's ivory skin gold. She cried out. The spell of love she'd cast on him shattered, and she seemed but an enemy clutching at him to do him harm, and he only wanted to stop her. He pulled back his fist, preparing to strike.

Hands grabbed him and pulled him away. Their strength was prodigious, and he struggled helplessly in their grip, meanwhile looking about to see what had taken hold of him. Whatever it was, it was invisible, some infernal or elemental spirit. No doubt it had hovered protectively around Iyraclea the whole time.

It dangled him over the balustrade of ice. It would be a long fall to the snowy courtyard below. Standing, Iyraclea glared at him.

"If your lackey drops me," he said, "I'll no longer be able to 'enlighten' you."

"I have your companions to interrogate."

"Suit yourself. I understand the wrath of a spurned woman. Not that I've spurned many myself. I certainly could never have found it in my heart to say no to a lady as beautiful as you, if you'd been content to couple and let it go at that."

"Your faith is strong," she said. "In time, you could grow into a truly accomplished priest. Since my deity is at war with yours, that gives me all the more reason to kill you. But I suspect that you, with your learning, may understand things the other prisoners don't."

The spirit dumped Pavel back on the roof. He still couldn't see it, but he knew it was there, and he could feel the ogre-sized bulk of it floating in the air behind him.

"Tell me who you are and why you came to the glacier," Iyraclea continued, "and perhaps you'll survive the night."

"As you probably know," he said, "Raryn, one of my companions, was born in the village where the ice dwarves poisoned us. He simply wanted to visit his kin—"

The spirit gripped his forearms with all its strength. He gasped in pain.

"You have one last chance," Iyraclea said. "What do you know about Sammaster and his schemes?"

He studied her. "I'm surprised to hear you mention that name, and suddenly very curious to hear what *you* know."

"You're not here to question me!" She sighed in an exasperated way that, just for an instant, made her appear a hair less cruel and imperious. "But perhaps if I explain, it will show you it's pointless to lie."

FIVE

20 Eleasis-17 Marpenoth, the Year of Rogue Dragons

Iyraclea contemplated the wizard standing before her throne. His white face, composed as it was of living ice, was stiffer and less expressive than features made of flesh. Still, as he sensed the depth of her displeasure, his colorless eyes widened in dread.

He expected punishment, and well he might. Though she'd shackled his will, his mastery of magic and a measure of his intelligence remained intact. With the troops she'd placed at his disposal, he should have proved capable of defeating a tribe of frost giants. Yet the creatures had driven him away.

Perhaps if she had him whittled into a shape more painful and less convenient, it would incline him to try harder. She drew breath to order one of the Icy Claws to see to it, then felt mystical force pulsing through the air. The sunlight streaming through the round-arched windows dimmed.

The members of her court—a miscellany of human tribesmen, giants, devils, transformed magicians, and others—babbled in surprise. Iyraclea rose, strode to the nearest window, and peered upward.

A huge shadow in the shape of a dragon floated in the sky to dim the sunlight. It was already fraying at the edges, and she inferred it was simply a harmless, albeit impressive, illusion.

It still angered her, though. In light of recent problems, she took it for a taunt. She looked around, looking for the impudent wretch responsible.

She couldn't see him yet. Pale, icy spires and battlements were in the way. But she could hear the cries of gelugons buzzing from the direction of the castle's primary gate.

She wished herself there, and the fortress obeyed. The window dilated, and the patch of floor beneath her feet swelled and thrust itself forward, carrying her out into the open air. Still lengthening, arching and twisting as necessary, the extrusion hurtled across the fortress to fuse itself with the wall-walk above the barbican.

She stepped onto the platform atop the massive fore-gate. Then, confident her wards would protect her from any potential threat, she advanced to the battlements to view the scene below.

Staff in hand, hooded brown cloak and robe whipping in the frigid, howling wind, a man stood on the ice. Two of the Icy Claws were down there too, and had leveled their lances to spit him. Yet he hadn't assumed any sort of fighting stance. Something about his casual posture suggested he was simply talking to the devils, through Iyraclea couldn't catch the words at such a distance.

His nonchalance piqued her curiosity. Whatever he'd done to rouse the Claws' ire—it didn't take much—perhaps she ought to command them to hold off. But before she could give the order, the ice devils drove in.

The hooded man vanished and reappeared in a different spot a few paces farther from the fore-gate. The gelugons' spears stabbed through the empty space he'd just vacated.

The Icy Claws whirled, orienting on him anew. Iyraclea had the sense he was still talking to them, still trying to avoid taking aggressive action.

The hulking devils glared at him with their bulbous, faceted eyes. Fist-sized hailstones materialized in midair to hammer down on the stranger's head and shoulders. The barrage staggered him and his cowl slipped back, revealing withered skin. Whoever he was, he was undead. Probably a lich, a spellcaster who'd assumed his unnatural condition to cheat the grave.

The gelugons had their own power to translate themselves through space, and they used it to pounce at him. Probably they assumed the hailstones had hurt him, and meant to finish him off before he could shake off the shock.

The lich brandished his staff, and two bursts of bright yellow flame flared into being to engulf the devils. The spellcaster himself stood in the space where the explosions overlapped, but evidently had no fear of them.

Its pearly carapace blackened, one Claw collapsed. The other, though also bearing ghastly burns, managed to stay on its feet and ram its lance through the lich's torso.

The dead man stumbled and had to catch his balance, but otherwise the stroke scarcely seemed to affect him. He raised his staff and tapped the Icy Claw's brow. The gentle-looking contact smashed the pallid beetle head like a melon, and the baatezu dropped. The magician then ran a skeletal fingertip along the ivory lance impaling him, and the weapon crumbled into dust.

Iyraclea's fists clenched. The Icy Claws were valuable servants. Even more importantly, they were emblems of her power, and the Frostmaiden's. It was an affront for anyone to defeat even one of them, let alone two, especially with half the castle watching.

She looked up and down the battlements, at those who'd assembled to deal with the disturbance. "Destroy that thing!" she called.

Her barbarians flung spears and shot arrows, and frost giants hurled their own gigantic weapons. The lich planted the butt of his staff on the ice, stood still, and suffered them to do their worst. The missiles broke against, or rebounded from, some invisible barrier in the air.

But when the three ice wizards started conjuring, the lich swept one hand through a mystic pass. A high, chiming sound split the air, loud enough that folk made of flesh winced or covered their ears. The transformed mages cracked and shattered into pieces.

On the Great Glacier, the warlocks Iyraclea captured, altered, and enslaved were even harder to come by than gelugons. Truly furious, she chanted in a voice like a shrieking blizzard, then thrust out her hand.

A blue-white beam streaked from her fingertips to strike the lich in the breastbone. It should have frozen him solid, but he simply shrugged, as if to convey that it hadn't discomfited him in the slightest.

She howled words of power, sketched glowing sigils with slashes of her hands. A bright, ragged rift opened in midair and spewed an immense, streaming wave of snow, an artificial avalanche to crush and bury the cloaked, cadaverous figure in its path. But he raised his hand and the onrushing mass divided, rumbling past to either side but leaving him untouched.

Iyraclea silently spoke to the castle. The barbican heaved itself up, tearing away from the rest of the fortress and reshaping itself into a colossal and vaguely humanoid form. Most of the folk who'd been standing in their mistress's vicinity hunkered down and hung on desperately. A few slipped off and fell screaming.

Iyraclea sent the giant lumbering at the lich. The fused, oversized fists at the ends of its long arms swung up and smashed down, jolting and breaking the surface of the glacier, and surely annihilating the spindly figure of old brittle bone and decay caught in between.

Finally she bade the giant stop the attack, so she could

verify the results. But on first inspection, she couldn't see anyone lying amid the broken chunks of rime.

"I'm about to reveal myself," whispered a calm, oddly accented baritone voice. "When I do, have the construct pick me up."

Startled, Iyraclea cast about. No one had sidled up next to her, and it was plain from the oblivious attitudes of her retainers that they didn't hear the voice.

"I didn't want to fight," the whisperer continued, "but the gelugons insisted—vicious brutes, aren't they?—I was obliged to defend myself, and the situation deteriorated from there. I realize that at this point, with your vassals watching, the confrontation can't end unless you win it. Any other outcome might undermine your authority. So win it you will, but by capture, not slaughter, then we'll palaver. Agreed?"

She hesitated. His condescension rankled, but thus far, his confidence appeared justified, and as a practical matter, it might indeed be wise to bring this public spectacle to an expeditious conclusion. Besides, she was still curious about who he was and what he wanted.

Accordingly, she'd take him into the castle, which was likewise her temple, the sacred ground where she was strongest. Then, if she didn't care for what he had to say, she'd destroy him there.

"Show yourself," she whispered. She separated the giant's right fist into three fingers and a thumb.

The lich shimmered into view at the construct's feet. Iyraclea instructed the colossus to scoop him up.

"I yield," the dead man said. "I plead for mercy."

Iyraclea had him, and she felt tempted to tell the giant to squeeze and squash him in its grip. But she had the unpleasant feeling that might not incapacitate him, either, or else he likely wouldn't have risked such a betrayal.

"First we'll speak," she declared. "Once I take your measure, I'll deal with you as you deserve."

It took a little while to relieve the lich of his staff, conjure chains of ice to secure his wrists and ankles, turn the giant back into a barbican, and conduct the prisoner to the roof of the highest keep, where they could converse in private. The undead wizard endured it all patiently, but as soon as the guards withdrew, he gave his arms a little shake, and the frozen manacles shattered.

"This has all been more trouble than I anticipated," he said, "but I trust that when we're done, we'll both feel it was worth it. I'm told folk call you 'the Ice Queen,' so I assume I should address you as Your Majesty."

"And who are you?" she asked, trying to remain impassive. Up close, his shriveled, crumbling features and faint stink of dry rot were disgusting, even disquieting. She might serve one of the so-called powers of darkness, might even create undead herself when it suited her purposes, but she still shared the common human loathing for the things.

"Sammaster," he said, "First-Speaker of the Cult of the Dragon."

She hesitated. "Sammaster's been dead a long time."

Much of the flesh had rotted from his face, and what remained had dried to something akin to strips of thin, crumbling leather. It was essentially impossible for such a countenance to show a change of expression, but nonetheless, she had the feeling his stained grin stretched wider.

"Well, obviously," said the lich. "But if you recognize my name and are familiar with my history, you know death has never prevented me from resuming my sacred task."

Iyraclea realized she believed him, for if legend spoke true, Sammaster had indeed fallen only to rise once more, and certainly, the stranger's wizardry was formidable enough to lend credence to his claim. For an instant, she wondered if she'd made an error by agreeing to confer with him in private, with no guards at hand, then scowled away her misgivings. Her own magic and the favor of Auril would protect her against any menace, even this one.

"What's your business in my realm?" she asked.

"That will take a bit of explaining. Before, I alluded to my work. Do you understand its purpose?"

"According to the stories, you and your cult seek to create dracoliches, which will then conquer Faerûn and rule forevermore. A truly demented dream, which you've failed to realize time and again."

He glowered at her with his dry, sunken eyes. "I've seen the future, Majesty. It will take the shape I've predicted, and sooner rather than later. We stand on the very threshold."

"I understand why you think so," she said. "I have ways of gathering news from distant lands, and I know you and your followers have seized on the current Rage of Dragons as an opportunity. Hoping to produce dracoliches in unprecedented numbers, you're trying to convince chromatic wyrms to turn undead with the promise it will render them immune to frenzy. Some are heeding you, and you're laboring frantically to accomplish their transformations before they run amok and kill their own worshipers. Rest assured, the plan, like all your others, will come to nothing in the end. Somehow, the paladins, Harpers, gold dragons, and their ilk have learned of your efforts. One by one, they're finding and destroying your fellowship's hidden strongholds."

"Not all of them."

"Enough, I suspect, and in any case, the Rage must surely end soon. Then most of the chromatics will lose interest in becoming liches. I'm actually surprised they're interested now. In times past, they've embraced frenzy as a natural phase of their existence."

"Rest assured, Majesty, you don't truly comprehend the grand design transforming the world, nor am I free to enlighten you. But I am prepared to strike a bargain."

"What sort of bargain?"

"You've jeered at my defeats, but your own career has been less than completely successful. Oh, it started out auspiciously enough. A child in Halruaa—"

"How do you know that?"

"Like you, Majesty, I try to stay informed. A child in Halruaa discovers a love of the cold, even though, in those southerly climes, it virtually never is cold. She senses—and adores—the entity who lives behind frigid downpours and chill winds." Sammaster's voice took on a bitter edge, as if he was recalling some comparable epiphany from his own life, but one that ultimately led to misery. "She runs away to the mountains to dwell at the highest elevations, but even they aren't cold enough. So, heeding Auril's call, she treks north, from one end of Faerûn to the other. The journey takes considerably more than a lifetime, but the Frostmaiden's generosity preserves her youth like a frozen blossom. Obviously, the goddess has chosen her to accomplish some vital task.

"When the child—now a child no longer, but a woman three hundred years old, though still vital and fair in appearance—matures into a mighty priestess, Auril reveals the nature of this chore. Our heroine is to establish herself as the tyrant of the Great Glacier, and rule in her deity's name. In time, she's also supposed to extend her dominion, and the ice itself, to neighboring lands. To *every* land, ultimately, if she can manage it. Because that's Auril's 'truly demented dream,' isn't it? To me, raising up dracolich kings seems a modest scheme by comparison."

"Be warned: You mock the Frostmaiden at your peril."

The lich shrugged his narrow shoulders. "Auril is a small goddess in the scheme of things. I've spat at bigger ones in my time. But to continue the tale: You set out to conquer the people of the glacier, and enjoyed some initial success. You forced some of the human and frost giant tribes to bow to your authority. But other folk resisted you, and your campaign stalled well short of total victory."

Iyraclea scowled. "I've only been here a few years. I simply need more time."

"Perhaps, but I wonder if Auril is content with your progress. She invested centuries teaching you powerful magic, gave you gelugons to fight on your behalf, and still, it takes you more than a decade to seize control of a sparsely settled wasteland? In her place, I'd be waxing impatient."

"Auril loves me!"

"Interesting. I thought it an axiom of your faith that she doesn't truly love anyone."

Iyraclea had to clamp down on her anger to keep from lashing out at him. "If there's a point to this prattle, I suggest you make it quickly."

"Very well. I'm prepared to loan you a weapon that will bring all your defiant ice dwarves and what-have-you to heel: Dragons."

She made a spitting sound. "No, thank you. I already had a pair of wyrms in my service, until they went mad, killed and devoured a number of my finest warriors, and flew off to parts unknown."

"But I propose to lend you a whole company of wyrms, guaranteed impervious to frenzy, with a dracolich at their head. They'll serve you until the Feast of the Moon. Direct them intelligently and that should be plenty of time. In addition, I'll give you my word that in the Faerûn to come, the undead drakes will leave you and your dominions alone. They'll have the rest of the world for their empire. They can get along without this one dreary patch of ice."

"An interesting offer," Iyraclea said. "What do you ask in return?"

"One small service," said the lich. "Sometime over the course of the next several months, strangers may venture onto the Great Glacier."

"What sort of strangers?"

"I wish I knew. They could be metallic dragons, humans, or almost anything, really. But whatever they are, I need them found and killed."

"Why? What's it all about?"

"It's about dragons, Majesty. About you possessing the means to finally satisfy your ambitions and your goddess's requirements. Do you really need to know more?"

It only took her a moment to consider. Then: "No, I don't suppose I do."

Over the years, Iyraclea had learned to her cost that ice dwarves were a brave and stubborn folk. Thus, watching from the battlements, she rather relished the sight of the wyrms herding the small, squat, ruddy-skinned prisoners through the gate and into the courtyard. Some of the defeated Inugaakalakurit marched with heads high, clinging to pride even then. Many, however, overwhelmed by the terror wyrms inspired in lesser creatures, cowered and cringed. Likewise enjoying their fear, the whites with their beaked snouts and spiky dewlaps repeatedly executed short, sudden lunges or lifted their claws to make the captives jump.

But Iyraclea's amusement turned to anger when one of the wyrms snatched up a screaming dwarf in its jaws, chewed him, and swallowed him down.

"Stop that!" she shouted. At the same time, she commanded the castle, and a portion of the wall flowed into a moving ramp to deposit her on the ground.

The dragons loomed over her as they did everyone else, even the gelugons, and their dry, astringent odor pricked her nose. She glared up at Zethrindor.

If the whites were frightening, their dracolich commander was a stalking nightmare. He was larger than any of the others, and despite the hide hanging loosely in some spots and withered drumhead-tight in others, revealing his gauntness either way, and the slimy rot mottling the ivory, gray, and pale blue scales, his every move bespoke prodigious strength. His scent mingled the harsh smell of a living white with the carrion stink of decay, and his sunken silvery eyes glittered with a scalpel-sharp intelligence his subordinates generally lacked. Those eyes peered back at her with unconcealed dislike.

"Control your underlings," she said. "Unless the prisoners resist, they're not to be harmed."

Zethrindor sneered. "We've stuffed your castle full of hostages. What's one dwarf more or less? His kin back in his village won't know Ssalangan had him for a snack."

"You'll do it," Iyraclea said, "because I tell you to." She commanded the walls surrounding the courtyards, and they groaned and grated, shifting slightly, dropping pellets of rime, reminding Zethrindor of their ability to reconfigure themselves into any deadly shape required. Some of the younger whites glanced about uneasily.

Zethrindor tossed his immense shredded wings in the draconic equivalent of a shrug. "Have it your way, but only so long as my folk have enough to eat. Thus far, my minions have killed enough to fill their bellies in the course of subjugating the tribes and villages, but who now remains to terrorize? The Great Glacier is yours."

"Yes, it is. So I'm giving you a new task. To the east lies Sossal. I've tried for years to bring it under my sway and cover the land in Auril's sacred ice. But the druids there are powerful, they resisted me, and my rebellious subjects closer to home prevented me from bringing my full strength to bear. Now it's finally time, and you wyrms will fight in the vanguard."

"In the vanguard of what, precisely?" Zethrindor replied. "I've seen your troops. They're adequate to control the settlements now that we dragons have hammered the fight out of them, but too few to overrun a more populous land."

Iyraclea sneered, and the air grew colder. "Are you afraid to attack Sossal?"

"Of course not. Drakes are a match for any foe. But only a fool would rush to bear the brunt of an actual war for someone else's benefit. Besides which, I wonder how you can possibly hold the place once our term of service is complete."

"You needn't fret over any of that. You'll have a substantial force at your back, and they'll occupy the newly conquered territories after you depart. You see, all these hunters and warriors you've been rounding up are more than prisoners. They're conscripts."

Zethrindor cocked his crested, tapered head. "Do you really think they'll serve a queen they hate?"

She smiled. "What choice do they have? You dragons and the Icy Claws will command them, and they're too afraid of you—and me—not to obey. Even if they weren't, their kin here on the glacier stand hostage for their good behavior, just as the folk left in the villages grovel for fear of what we might otherwise do to those we marched away to an unknown fate. It's a clever arrangement, don't you think?"

The dracolich regarded her for a moment, then conceded, "It isn't bad. We'd better determine how soon we can march, as well as which wyrms will go, and which will stay."

"You're all going. Your work on the glacier is done, and I mean to make the most of you during the time remaining."

Zethrindor hesitated. "One or two of us might stay, to make sure the villages stay cowed."

"I've told you what I want, and Sammaster instructed you to do my bidding. Besides, I can't believe any of you would consent to stay behind. In Sossal, you'll find plenty of human flesh to eat, and an abundance of treasure to plunder."

As well as an outlet, she thought, for the urge to slaughter engendered by the Rage.

Sammaster had somehow dampened it, but he hadn't cured them of it. At odd moments, she felt it simmering inside the living whites, waiting to break free, and perhaps it was what made them hiss and roar in approval of the prospect she offered.

Zethrindor grimaced at his minions' bestial display. "So be it, priestess. Let's plan our campaign."

"I notice," said Pavel, when the story was through, "that you didn't keep your promise to kill outlanders. In fact, I suspect you sent every last dragon to Sossal partly so you could capture and interrogate wayfarers without the wyrms interfering."

"Of course," the Ice Queen said. During the course of her tale, she'd slipped her gown back on. "Because Sammaster's pledge is meaningless. If by some bizarre chance he does succeed in creating a horde of dracoliches, they'll seek to conquer all Faerûn, the Great Glacier included. His mad prophecies require it. Thus, I need to find out exactly what he's up to, so I can defend against it, and I think you and your companions know. It's part of the reason he wants you dead. Now stop stalling and tell me all about it, or I swear by the Icedawn that I'll fling you from the tower and seek my answers from one of your friends."

Pavel had little doubt that once Iyraclea understood Sammaster's designs, she'd want to thwart them. The problem was that in her own way, she was equally crazy and wicked, with her own poisonous dream of the future. He couldn't believe she'd be content simply to dismantle the mystical structure generating the Rage. She'd probably prove just as eager as the lich to twist the power to her own purposes.

Yet he truly had no option but to talk, and she was sufficiently shrewd that only something approximating the truth was likely to satisfy her. Accordingly, he spun his own essentially factual tale.

He withheld some key bits of information, though, including the fact that Kara was a song dragon. Thus far, her captors had presumably only seen her in human form, and he didn't want them to know what a formidable entity they'd brought into their midst.

When he finished, Iyraclea said, "I've always been curious about the ruined cities in the Novularonds, but I've never had the leisure to investigate them."

"Well, one of them is the heart of the Rage. We were sure of it before, and Sammaster's pact with you proves it. He knows—or at least fears—he has enemies looking for the place, so he found a pawn—"

Iyraclea stiffened. "A what?"

Pavel shrugged. "I apologize, Your Majesty, but the word fits. He found a pawn to guard his secrets for him. He attempted pretty much the same ploy in Damara. He's too busy calming frenzied dragons, and assisting with their transformations, to do all the guarding himself."

"Well, this time he tried to manipulate the wrong person, and I'll make certain he regrets it."

"You'll need our help."

"Don't be presumptuous. I *need* no one. I'm first among Auril's priestesses!"

"Congratulations. But my comrades and I have been investigating this matter for months. We explored the ancient sites, overcame the dangers, unearthed the lore, and conferred with the sages who interpreted it. Glories of the dawn, you wouldn't even understand what's happening if it wasn't for us. You'd be stupid to reject our aid if you can get it. And you can, so long as you treat us decently, because we share a common goal."

Iyraclea gave a grudging nod. "Perhaps so. I assume you want to see your companions and make certain they're all right."

"Yes, but before even that, I'd like my breeches back."

SIX

21-27 Marpenoth, the Year of Rogue Dragons

Like the tumbling snowflakes, Zethrindor floated on the wailing wind out of the west. Strangely, despite her avowed determination to conquer Sossal, Iyraclea had yet to take the field, but she had cursed the land with a fierce and premature winter. The assumption was that frigid temperatures and relentless blizzards would hinder and demoralize the defenders far more than it would the invaders from the Great Glacier, who faced such conditions every day of their lives.

Zethrindor was watching a huge white wolf lurking behind a stand of brush on a ridge. The beast scrutinized the string of poorly guarded ox-drawn supply carts slogging along the snow-choked trail below.

Sossal had turned out to be a country possessed of more than its fair share of skinchangers. The druids mastered the art in the course of their training, but apparently certain other folk were simply born with the knack. Zethrindor was reasonably certain the shaggy creature below was one such, a warrior wearing animal form to scout the convoy and evaluate whether his war band ought to attack.

The shapeshifter naturally wouldn't decide in the affirmative if he detected a dracolich gliding overhead, waiting to pounce when he and his comrades took the bait, but Zethrindor doubted that would be a problem. The night was dark, and just in case it wasn't black enough, he'd veiled himself in a spell of invisibility.

The wolf howled, and another answered. Then dozens of other lupines, some ghostly white like the scout, others gray, came slinking to join their comrade on the high ground.

In Zethrindor's estimation, humans in general were weak, stupid, contemptible creatures. Still he had to concede the cleverness of an elite company formed entirely of werewolves. No wonder these particular pests had proved so difficult to hunt down.

The wolves' bodies heaved and flowed, muzzles retracting, hind legs lengthening, paws melting into hands and feet, fur becoming woolen garments and scale and leather armor. A couple warriors grunted or gasped at the strain of transformation, but so softly even a wyrm's ears could barely catch it. The humans driving and guarding the carts certainly wouldn't.

As the warriors strung their bows and laid arrows on the strings, Zethrindor studied them, trying to pick their druid, his chief target, out from the others. Unfortunately, on first inspection, he failed to spot a telltale sickle, sprig of mistletoe, or the like.

Well, the conscripts with the carts were expendable. That was why Zethrindor had chosen them. So, for a moment or two, he'd permit the men of Sossal to attack without interference, in the hope that the druid would cast a spell and so reveal himself.

Arrows arced whistling through the air. Caught utterly by surprise, tribesmen dropped. The survivors clamored, cast wildly about, tried to ready their own weapons, but by then the attackers' next volley was already in flight. Half the conscripts fell before the rest could even begin to mount any semblance of a defense.

Zethrindor snarled in exasperation. The druid had yet to attempt a spell, and why should he? The assault was going so well, it only made sense to conserve his power.

But if Zethrindor attacked, that would surely elicit a magical response, and if not, he supposed he'd just have to slaughter the entire enemy force. That had always been his ultimate intent anyway.

He furled his wings and dived at the archers. Some, sensing a disturbance in the air, looked up just in time to take a blast of his pearl-white breath in their faces. Coated in rime, they dropped.

By attacking, he forfeited his invisibility, but that was all right. His appearance was a weapon in itself, one that made some of the bowmen drop their weapons and run screaming down the hill, where the men of the Great Glacier, organized at last and furious to take revenge for the devastating surprise attack, met them with flying javelins, stabbing spears, and hacking axes.

But a number of the skinchangers stood their ground and loosed arrows at Zethrindor. Most missed or glanced off. A couple lodged in his scales, but caused him no distress.

He flung himself to the ground, crushing a warrior beneath his bulk. He raked with his talons and ripped the heart, lungs, and splinters of rib from another man's chest. A snap of his jaws left a third in pieces, and a flick of a wing hurled a fourth off the hilltop.

Skinchangers scrambled to engage him. Some remained in human form to slash with swords or jab with lances. Others flowed back into lupine shape to bite with their fangs. It didn't much matter. Zethrindor found he could kill them just about as easily in either guise.

The combat was both exhilarating and useful, but where was the cursed druid? He wondered if he'd already killed the wretch and just didn't realize it. Then, in a burst of yellow glare and fierce heat, a salamander exploded into existence in front him. Shrouded in crackling flame, somewhat man-like from the waist up but scaly and serpentine below, the elemental spirit slithered forward, stabbing with its trident.

Zethrindor met it with a puff of his breath. The intense cold blew out its corona of flame like a candle, and it collapsed thrashing in agony. He ground it beneath his foot and looked around, trying to locate the human who'd conjured it.

There! Some ten yards away, a stocky human held a scimitar in a seemingly useless overhand grip, as if he could wield it like a dagger. The swordsmith had cast the silver pommel in the form of a unicorn's head, emblem of the goddess Mielikki. It was evidently a talisman a druid had flourished to cast the summoning spell.

Zethrindor snarled an incantation of his own, and a barrage of ice balls hurtled through the air, to hammer the priest and throw him to the ground. He struggled to rise again, but slowly.

Intent on finishing him off before he could recover, the dracolich charged, and the warriors of Sossal, those who were left, scrambled to bar his path. Blades and lupine fangs flashed at him, and he tore his assailants into fragments of gory meat and bone.

It only took a moment. But that was evidently time enough for the druid to collect himself, because, as Zethrindor killed the last of the soldiers, much of his dorsal surface, from his beaked snout to the tips of his ragged, decaying wings, burst into flame. The hot pain balked him for an instant, until his innate resistance to hostile magic extinguished the blaze.

By then, the druid had reached a gnarled, leafless, stunted tree and stretched out his hand to touch it. His body began to fade.

With a surge of frustration, Zethrindor realized what was happening. A spell was about to whisk the priest beyond his reach, and since his breath weapon hadn't yet renewed itself, he was probably too far away to do anything about it. He stared, trying to paralyze the human with his gaze, but the druid kept moving. His fingers clasped a branch, and his shape blurred into little more than shadow—

Crimson eyes glowing, a dark reptilian form, smaller than Zethrindor but dragon-sized nonetheless, pounced out of the darkness and caught the druid in his fangs. The newcomer wrenched the human away from the tree and shook him like a dog shaking a rat, likely breaking his neck. He then sucked and slurped at his victim, guzzling his blood before spitting the corpse out onto the ground.

Zethrindor had sensed the undead nature of the stranger as soon as he appeared, and wondered if he too might be a dracolich—but then recognized him for a vampire.

The blood-drinker glided forward. Before his transformation, he'd evidently been a smoke drake, albeit a remarkably large one, and still gave off a harsh smell of combustion. A choker of platinum, ruby, and diamond encircled his neck. Zethrindor wondered just how easy it would be to take the treasure, either through intimidation or combat, then set the notion aside for the moment, anyway. With the conquest of Sossal to complete, he had more important matters to concern him. Such as finding out about powerful new entities popping up unexpectedly in the middle of the disputed territory.

"Who are you?" he demanded.

"I'm called Brimstone," the smoke drake whispered. He glanced about, evidently making sure no potential dangers remained on the ridge. They didn't. Most of the skinchangers were dead. The others had either run away or lay shrieking and moaning in agony. "I hope I was of some assistance."

"I didn't need any," Zethrindor said. "In fact, I was looking forward to killing the druid myself. Still, I suppose your intentions were good."

"I'm glad to hear you say so," Brimstone said. "I've spent the past couple nights flying around Sossal, trying to locate you. It appears the war's progressing well. What a shame you and the other wyrms will reap such meager benefits from your victories."

We'll see about that, Zethrindor thought, when the time comes. "Why were you seeking me, vampire? What do you want?"

"To offer some genuine assistance, or, at the very least, information. First, I suppose I ought to provide some context. In my humble way, I'm like you: Sammaster turned me undead long ago, during the course of his early experiments. Unfortunately, after he moved on to making dracoliches, he ceased to pay me the deference which was my due. Our association ended badly."

Zethrindor snorted. "No true wyrm tolerates disrespect from any human, magicians included."

"Is that why you take orders from him, and how he could loan you to Iyraclea as if you were some sort of indentured servant?"

Anger brought Zethrindor's breath weapon welling up to chill his throat and the back of mouth, for all that it would be of minimal efficacy against another undead. "Have a care how you speak to me!"

Brimstone lowered his head. "Pardon me, High Lord. I meant no offense. I'm simply trying to explain why it is that for centuries, I've nursed a grudge against Sammaster, trying to wreck his schemes, and those of the cult he founded, whenever I could. Earlier this year, I learned he's become obsessed with an ancient shrine or mystic's stronghold—some sort of place of power at any rate—located somewhere in the northlands."

"Why?"

"That, I can't tell you. But haven't you suspected there's more to his schemes than he's letting on? Does it really make sense that he'd toil to change the face of the world, only to play a subordinate role in the Faerûn to come? Isn't it more likely he intends to set himself above you dracoliches and reign supreme, to continue controlling you as—if you'll forgive my bluntness—he's sought to manipulate you all along?"

"Sammaster is secretive, and naturally, I don't entirely trust him. But he has his uses."

"Obviously. Yet if his covert designs proceed unchecked, if they go too far for anyone to stop them . . . Let me continue my tale. I resolved to find and investigate the wizard's hidden lair. To that end, I reluctantly allied myself with the sort of folk you and I would normally destroy. A priest of Lathander. A song dragon. Wyrm hunters. Because they too had resolved to fight Sammaster, and guided by my hatred, I believed that was all that mattered."

A warrior with a shredded belly and legs gave a piercing scream. Irritated by the noise, Zethrindor pulped him with a ground-shaking lash of his tail. "You speak as if your attitude has changed."

"I loathe Sammaster," Brimstone said, "but events have reminded me he's not the only detestable thing in the world, nor is vengeance the only good. No matter how many times I helped them, my miserable allies, vermin unworthy even to speak my name, showed me only scorn. Now their own stupidity has ended their potential usefulness. Indeed, it has turned them into yet another difficulty.

"Meanwhile," the smoke drake continued, "dracoliches proliferate, even as the Rage spreads chaos and devastation, preparing the way for your eventual conquest. I realize now, I can't stop it. Nothing can. The best I can hope for is to be granted an important position in the Faerûn that will be."

Zethrindor tossed his wings in a shrug. "You're not a dracolich."

"And only they will reign. Except that's Sammaster's stipulation, not yours, and brings us back to the question of who will really make the decisions."

"Well, I suppose that if you proved exceptionally useful, you might find a role as a king's most trusted officer, or even the master of some small principality all your own." But not, Zethrindor thought, if he had anything to say about it.

Brimstone impressed him as far too wily and ambitious to trust in such a role. Still, why not feign willingness to consider such a concession, and find out what the vampire had to offer in return?

"Thank you, High Lord, that's all I desire. I mentioned that my worthless companions had come to grief. In fact, their current predicament came about as a direct result of Iyraclea's covenant with Sammaster. In exchange for your services, she promised to kill any strangers found wandering on the Great Glacier. It was the wizard's ploy to keep his enemies away from the ruin he'd discovered, a site somewhere in the Novularond Mountains."

Zethrindor cocked his head. "Sammaster underestimated Iyraclea if he imagined she'd keep such a pledge without trying to find out why it mattered to him."

"How true. But as you've surely noticed, he is deranged, and such folk, no matter how clever, inevitably make mistakes. At any rate, instead of killing my allies, Iyraclea captured them and put them to the question. Soon enough, they broke and divulged what they knew, with the result that the Ice Queen herself now seeks Sammaster's hidden lair in hopes of mastering the power there.

"As you can imagine, I don't want her to control it, either. Dragons must have it, to guarantee our supremacy in the days to come. But I know my limitations. I don't have the strength to confront Auril's high priestess, gelugons, and frost giants all by myself. But a dracolich leading a flight of whites could do it."

Zethrindor scowled, pondering.

He was far too wise to take everything Brimstone said at face value. The threat of a magic potent enough to grind all dracoliches into subservience seemed particularly farfetched. Yet aspects of the vampire's story dovetailed neatly with his own suspicions of Sammaster and Iyraclea. It explained why the dead man had urged him to serve the tyrant of an underpopulated wilderness, and why the Ice Queen had deemed it expedient to send every last wyrm off the glacier.

If some great power lay hidden in the Novularonds, Zethrindor wanted it, and not for the benefit of dragons in general, either, but to assure the ascendance of a single wyrm: himself.

The drawback was, his army would have to get along without its commander and the rest of the whites and ice drakes for a time, but their position was strong enough that they shouldn't get into any calamitous trouble. Since the tundra landwyrms couldn't fly, his troops would even have some dragons remaining to deter the enemy from attempting anything too ambitious.

"All right," said the dracolich, "we'll go. Rest assured, I'll reward you if the journey proves worthwhile, and destroy you otherwise."

"Fair enough. How soon can we depart? You understand, I can only travel by night."

Teeth clenched, body trembling, Raryn heaved the oblong boulder over his head, and onlookers cried out in triumph, or cursed and moaned in dismay, depending on how they'd bet. Taegan, who'd arrived too late to place a wager, simply marveled. One expected such feats from Dorn, with his hulking frame and oversized iron limbs, but it seemed miraculous that the squat little dwarf could be so strong.

Raryn tossed away the stone, and it thudded down on the icy ground. Victorious human barbarians and frost giants congratulated him, clasping his hand and pounding his massive shoulders, and collected their winnings, mostly in the form of amber beads and ivory scrimshaw, from the losers.

Farther up the trail, Iyraclea, clad in her gauzy white gown, gave the order to form up. Grumbling, folk clambered to their feet, shouldered their packs, and the column tramped on up the steep, slippery path.

Like Jivex, who, scales flashing rainbows, was flitting about gobbling the insects which apparently thrived in all climes, even those as inhospitable as the Novularonds, Taegan had no need to hike. Rather to his surprise, the Ice Queen had given him permission to use his wings, with the understanding that if he tried to flee, both he and his friends would suffer for it.

He spread his pinions, then noticed how Raryn's mask of hearty good fellowship had dropped away. The dwarf's ruddy, white-bearded face wore a somber frown.

Taegan suspected he knew what the problem was. He refolded his wings and tramped closer to the hunter, so they could have a private conversation as they climbed. In theory, the seekers were Iyraclea's "honored guests," but even so, at the start of their journey, their captors would have moved to break up any such exchange, for fear the outlanders were plotting mischief.

Accordingly, the prisoners had worked to ingratiate themselves with Iyraclea's minions and so defuse their suspicions. Kara regaled them with songs, jokes, and stories. Jivex created amusing illusions. Pavel used his prayers to conjure food and cure fevers. Dorn, Will, and Raryn helped scout, forage, and track game; or performed stunts for their fellow wayfarers to bet on.

None of it changed the attitude of the vicious gelugons, or the silent, emotionless ice wizards. But gradually, the human tribesmen and even the brutish giants relaxed their vigilance.

Though unfortunately, not enough to return the prisoners' weapons. Will had attempted to remedy the lack by pilfering items their captors were unlikely to miss. One of the frost giants, for example, had packed an extra head for his ponderous spear. Taegan carried the double-edged length of iron tucked in his boot to serve as a makeshift dagger.

"I know how you feel," he murmured.

"I'm all right," Raryn said.

"I understand what it is to be ashamed of one's own people."

"Well, it's new to me. I was proud to be Inugaakalakurit. Yet my own village—my own brother!—betrayed us."

"I confess, I wasn't entirely pleased about it, either. But I daresay they believed they had no choice. Consider the Icy Claws. You and I have overcome our share of perils, but I can't even look at the things without my bowels turning to water. Your people had to contend with the baatezu, dragons, and Iyraclea's magic and seizing of hostages. I'm not ready to pardon their treachery, but I do comprehend it."

Raryn sighed. "Maybe the one I should really hate is the Ice Queen, for oppressing them and breaking their spirit, and I do. But the person I'm most disgusted with is me. I promised to keep the rest of you safe, and instead I marched you straight into disaster."

"No one could have foreseen what happened."

"I should have. I should have sensed that the glacier had changed since my younger days. The signs were surely there, if only I'd had the wit to notice. A ranger knows, they're always there."

"Nonsense. The place was a desolate slab of ice when you left, and the same when you returned. Unless we'd happened upon a troop of gelugons playing hide-the-cherry, what could possibly have alerted you?"

Half hidden behind his shaggy moustache, Raryn's lips quirked upward. "Well . . . nothing, maybe. So I suppose I should stop rebuking myself and concentrate on the work that lies ahead."

"That's the Raryn we toast with brimming cups." Taegan grinned. "Of course, it would help to know exactly what form said work will take. Is it actually feasible to work with Iyraclea?"

"Maybe. She truly does seem to want to thwart Sammaster. But never trust her. Do you know, she tried to turn Pavel into one of her ice men, and unlike the wizards, he wouldn't even have been of any particular use to her afterwards. The transformation would have broken his bond to the Morninglord and cost him his magic. She attempted it out of simple cruelty, or just so her goddess could score a petty victory over the power who's her opposite."

"Believe it or not, I'd already discerned that she lacks a certain generosity of spirit. But if she shares our disinclination to see crazed dragons and dracoliches overrun the world...."

Taegan realized Raryn had stopped listening. Instead, the dwarf peered upward, his face intent. His nostrils flared as if he were a hound taking a scent.

"What is it?" Taegan asked

"The air's getting warmer," Raryn said, "and I can smell living plants."

"High above the glacier amid these freezing winds? That suggests some sort of enchantment is active hereabouts."

"I imagine so. Which means we'd better make up our minds about Iyraclea fast, because it looks like we've found the heart of the Rage."

The Ice Queen must have thought the same thing, because she exhorted her followers to hurry on toward the mountaintop. Before long, Taegan too could feel the slope growing warmer, until he had to start opening his heavy garments for comfort's sake. Snow, ice, and bare, frozen earth and rock gave way to moss, grass, and shrubs. The human tribesmen gazed at the greenery in wonder alloyed with mistrust. The huge frost giants, virtually born of cold and possessed of a total affinity with it, sneered and spat.

It seemed likely Iyraclea felt the same, but if so, her eagerness for discovery masked the underlying distaste. "What are you waiting for?" she cried. "Scout ahead!"

The Icy Claws vanished, transporting themselves through space, reappearing moments later to report to their mistress in their rasping, infernal tongue.

"Pardon me," Taegan said.

Eager to see what the ice devils had found, he lashed his pinions and leaped into the air. Silvery butterfly wings a blur, Jivex streaked upward to accompany him. They flew high to obtain a panoramic view of that which awaited them, and it made Taegan catch his breath. The mountaintop was hollow like a bowl, and inside gleamed a castle, or perhaps something more accurately described as a small walled town.

The avariel had only seen an elven city once before, in the dream Amra conjured in the Gray Forest, and the long-vanished inhabitants had shaped that glorious place from living trees. In contrast, the builders of the citadel below had worked in granite and marble, but their deceptively delicate-looking spires and battlements, simple and intricate by turns, embodied a similar aesthetic and achieved a comparable beauty. They'd shared the woodland elves' fondness for broad, straight boulevards and had evidently loved gardens as well. With no one to tend them, the lawns and flowerbeds had surrendered to tangled brush and weeds, but grown mighty with the passing ages, the weir trees had flourished. Autumn had begun stripping them of their foliage, and their leaves blew rustling through the vacant streets.

"Curse it," sighed Taegan, addressing the remark to all his fellow avariels, "see what splendor elves create. Everyone but us."

Jivex wheeled past him. "Come on!" the faerie dragon said. "What are you waiting for? Let's find the heart of the Rage and finish up."

As they all searched the crumbling citadel, forcing warped doors, prowling through dusty, echoing rooms, climbing spiraling stairs to the tops of watchtowers and groping their way down into lightless cellars, Dorn stuck close to Kara. Sammaster had left traps at key points along his trail of discovery, and it seemed likely he'd prepared something particularly nasty at the end.

Dorn wished the bard could shift to dragon form, for she was vulnerable as any other woman in her current shape. But he understood the wisdom of concealing her true nature from

Iyraclea and the priestess's retainers, including the paunchy, saggy-bosomed, blue-haired female frost giant tramping along behind them, ostensibly to assist in their efforts but most likely to keep an eye on them as well. Iyraclea had probably decided it did no harm to slacken the prisoners' reins while everyone stayed together, but more vigilance was required when the expedition split up.

Fortunately, the giantess's bulk kept her from squeezing through the smaller spaces, and it was there Dorn and Kara could confer in private, so long as they kept their voices down. Standing in the dark, empty bedroom at the rear of some long-dead dignitary's apartments, the bard shook her head.

"I don't understand," she said. "We've been searching for hours and haven't found anything."

Dorn shrugged. "It took days to search Northkeep."

"Then, there were only a few of us, and we were working underwater."

"Is it possible we don't recognize the . . . contrivance that makes the Rage when we see it?"

Kara brushed a stray strand of moon-blond hair away from her face. "It is possible, but I doubt it. In magic, appearance often supports reality. An enchanter puts on an impressive display to create a powerful effect. Thus, I'd expect the source of the Rage to be imposing, awe-inspiring, not some funny little knickknack in a drawer. There's another consideration as well."

"What?"

"You know that even with the proper ward in place, I still feel frenzy gnawing at my mind."

"Yes."

"Well, I expected that in close proximity to the source of the sickness, I'd suddenly find it harder to bear, but I haven't. It's as bad as before, but no worse."

"Then this is the wrong place?"

She shook her head. "I don't know what to think. The corpse tearer was right, elves did build it, far from their usual haunts. You can see their sensibilities reflected in every line. They surely had a reason. But—"

Muffled by the walls of the building, a trumpet blared. Other horns echoed the call.

"Out!" bellowed the giantess, her deep, heavily accented attempt at Common Tongue only barely intelligible. "Come out! Queen wants us!"

Dorn suspected it wasn't for anything good. He used his fingers of flesh and bone to take Kara's hand, then led her out under a blackening sky, where the first stars were already shining.

In the citadel, the largest thoroughfares radiated from a central hub. This nexus was a circular expanse paved with a dark green stone like malachite, each hexagonal flag inscribed with a character from an alphabet Dorn didn't recognize, and it was there Iyraclea had decided the expedition would rendezvous. By the time Dorn, Kara, and their lumbering, malodorous escort arrived, the last purple traces of sunset had vanished from the western sky. With all the ghost-pale gelugons, giants, and ice wizards prowling about in the gloom, the plaza resembled a scene from a nightmare, or a vision of one of the Hells.

Yet despite her flawless beauty, and her diminutive stature compared to many of her monstrous servants, the most frightening entity present was Iyraclea herself. Ensconced on an elevated throne she'd evidently shaped from conjured ice, she radiated power and displeasure.

"Well?" she demanded. "Has anyone found anything?"

"Not yet, Your Majesty," Kara said. "But we've been at it less than a day."

"I have Auril's sacred rituals to perform," the Ice Queen replied, "a realm to rule, and a war to oversee. My time is precious, and if it turns out you've wasted it, you and your friends will suffer."

"I told you the truth," said Pavel, standing between a barbarian warrior and Will. "About Sammaster, the Rage, and all the rest of it. What would have been the point of lying?"

"I don't know," Iyraclea said. "Why don't you tell me?"

"August and radiant queen," said Taegan, "the ancient elves enchanted this stronghold to keep the weather clement, and thousands of years later, the charm still holds the mountain's chill at bay. Wise as you are, surely you understand the builders wouldn't have lavished such powerful magic on the fortress unless the place was important. We may prove unable to unravel its secrets, but I know others who can, the learned sages who've pondered these mysteries for months. Please, allow me to fetch them."

"That's out of the question!" Iyraclea snapped. "Pavel said you and your friends possess the knowledge to solve the puzzle. That's the reason I dealt with you mercifully. Now you'd better hope your own wits are equal to the task."

Because, Dorn thought, the last thing she wanted was a band of magicians as powerful as the wizards of Thentia visiting the site. They quite possibly possessed the arcane strength to wrest control of the situation away from even the Frostmaiden's high priestess and her terrible servants.

Kara stiffened, and her fingers clamped tight on Dorn's. She turned to him, then, evidently recalling the hostile folk standing all around, quickly masked all traces of her excitement. Apparently she'd realized something important, and for whatever reason, had decided it was something she wouldn't divulge to the Ice Queen unless the tyrant left her no alternative.

Unfortunately, it seemed likely that was exactly what would happen. Distracted, Dorn had missed the last few words of the conversation, but he took up the thread:

". . . give you tonight and tomorrow," Iyraclea said. "But then, come midnight, and every midnight after, I'll offer one of you to the Cold Goddess. Starting with the halfling, I believe." She sneered. "I've taken your measure, Wilimac Turnstone, and I very much doubt you're scholar enough to contribute much to our efforts."

Kara gave Dorn's hand another squeeze, as if to reassure him that, one way or another, Iyraclea's threat would never come to pass. Will, meanwhile, offered the priestess a grin. "Now that's where you're wrong," he said. "I'm the clever one. The charlatan's the dolt. That's the pox for you. It rots the brain."

Iyraclea scowled. "All of you, resume the search!"

The gathering started to disperse. Intensely curious, Dorn looked forward to the moment when Kara could confide in him. Unfortunately, with the giantess once again slouching along in their wake, he supposed he'd have to wait a little while longer.

Enormous shadows swept across the ground, and something hissed and rustled overhead. Dorn looked up. Pale jagged shapes flapped and glided down from the heavens, as if the moon had shattered into pieces. Some of the white dragons and ice drakes—smaller than their companions but still big as a hay wagon and the team drawing it, with short, thick legs and wide, flat tails—lit on the ground. Others perched on battlements and rooftops. The reptiles' sharp, dry odor suffused the air.

"Your Majesty," one of the dragons rumbled, a sneer in its tone. Taegan glanced about, seeking the source of the salutation, and winced when he found it. Its pale hide mottled with rot and its sunken eyes glowing in the gloom, a dracolich crouched on the gable-and-valley roof of a once-splendid house.

Jivex snorted. "What's the matter, are you scared? We already killed one of those things."

"I remember," Taegan said. "I intend to dine out on the tale for the rest of my days. But as you may recall, Vorasaegha nearly tore it to pieces before we became involved, and even then, it was brisk work."

Still, that turn of events had one positive feature: To all appearances, the sudden advent of the dragons had startled and unsettled the rest of Iyraclea's minions. Even the Icy

Claws pivoted back and forth, keeping a wary eye on the gigantic reptiles looming on every side.

The gelugon that had been following Taegan and Jivex around was as distracted as the rest. The elf looked around, spotted Dorn, pressed a finger to his lips, and skulked in the half-golem's direction. He didn't know what was about to happen, but suspected he and his comrades would fare better united. Jivex flitted after him.

Meanwhile, Iyraclea emerged from the crowd to glare up at the dracolich. Unlike her followers, she appeared not a whit dismayed, and Taegan proffered a grudging admiration.

"Zethrindor," she said. "What are you doing here?"

"That's what I was about to ask you."

"Don't be insolent! I ordered you and the rest of these wyrms to Sossal."

"The war's going well," said Zethrindor." His tail switched, breaking loose clay tiles to clatter and spill off the roof. "It'll keep for a few days. But while we condescend to conquer a kingdom for the benefit of a human, you break your pact with Sammaster."

"What do you know about it?"

"In exchange for our help, you promised to kill strangers. Instead, you plotted with them to pry into the wizard's business."

Taegan and Jivex closed the distance to Dorn—and Kara, too, the bladesinger observed. Pavel, Raryn, and Will were likewise heading toward the same spot.

"What do you care?" Iyraclea said. "You're no true friend to Sammaster or anyone else. So why should it concern you if I play him false?"

"Because of the future he promises. I can't have you stealing or tampering with a magic that will help to bring it about."

Iyraclea curled her lip, and Taegan shivered as a sudden chill permeated the air. "But you'd steal it yourself in an instant, wouldn't you, to improve your own position."

"If it embodies the destiny of dragonkind, a drake should

look after it. That's obvious, and even if it isn't, I didn't come here to debate. Produce whatever it is you've discovered, and even though you broke your covenant with Sammaster, we'll keep faith with you. We'll finish the subjugation of Sossal, and leave you in peace thereafter."

"That's easily done. Behold." Iyraclea waved her dainty hand at an empty patch of dark, sigil-inscribed paving. "We found nothing, because there's nothing to discover."

"Truly? Well, in that case, you must be eager to return to your altars. Do so. Simply leave me your prisoners, as they're clearly of no use to you, and they and I will poke around this curious place a little longer."

"I think not. Go back to Sossal, complete your task, and content yourself with the plunder and feast of human flesh you win in the process. Otherwise, I'll destroy every last one of you."

The dracolich sneered. "A hollow threat, to say the least."

"Hardly," Iyraclea said. "Don't you whites and ice drakes understand your own natures? You're creatures born of cold. It infuses and sustains you, and the goddess who lends me her might is the source of it. With a mere thought, I can turn your own essences against you."

"If Auril herself were here," said Zethrindor, "perhaps I'd be afraid. Or maybe not. Sammaster proclaims the time of the gods is passing, and the age of the dracoliches is at hand."

Without the slightest preparatory shift to warn of his intentions, the wyrm sprang.

Iyraclea raised her hand, and defined by a whirl of fallen leaves, a twisting cyclone howled into existence between her and her plummeting attacker. The vortex hurled Zethrindor off course to smash down on the pavement. At the same time, the Ice Queen, gown lashing around her, lifted by another tame wind, perhaps, floated backward across the plaza, distancing herself from the white, cadaverous wyrm. She shouted words of power and swept her arms through sinuous passes. Suspended in midair like a curtain, rows of luminous blue blades appeared down the long axis of Zethrindor's body. Spinning like wheels, they hacked his rotting scales and withered muscle.

He roared, sprang clear of the effect, reared and cocked back his head, and spewed his breath weapon. Probably, like Taegan, Iyraclea expected frost, the substance whites usually expelled, and to which she was surely impervious, for this time she made no effort to defend. A plume of dark, billowing fumes washed over and made her flail in agony. Zethrindor had evidently cast a spell to change his breath into a green's corrosive, poisonous exhalation.

The dracolich lashed his pinions, took to the air, and hurtled toward her—and that was when mayhem exploded on every side, as everyone else decided to join the fight. Some excited whites largely wasted their first attacks spewing frigid vapors that froze human barbarians but had no effect on the rest of Iyraclea's retainers. The more clever whites, and the ice drakes, conjured blazes of magic, or sprang to engage their foes with fang and claw. Javelins and arrows flew to meet them. Spears stabbed and axes hacked. A gelugon materialized half a dozen lesser devils, crouching, snaky-bearded things armed with enormous saw-toothed polearms, to fight on its behalf. Ice wizards chanted incantations in their chiming, clashing, dispassionate voices.

Wings a silvery smear, Jivex hovered uncertainly. "Do we know what side we're on?"

"Neither," Taegan said. "We need to get out of the thick of it and under cover."

"Make for that keep," Raryn said, pointing a stubby finger. They all skulked forward, skirting lunging, wheeling, stamping combatants who, by virtue of their prodigious strength and size, could have trampled and killed them without even realizing they were there. They also had to dodge blasts of frost and lightning, flame and the distilled essences of death and disease, that dueling spellcasters hurled back and forth.

Grateful that he hadn't exhausted his store of spells in the fight with the tirichiks—his captors had confiscated his grimoire and so prevented him from preparing any new ones—Taegan augmented his natural agility and shielded himself in misty vagueness. His companions likewise enhanced their defenses. Like grouping together and slipping out of the midst of the fray, the tactic made sense, but didn't really answer the question of how to extricate themselves from their current predicament. It seemed wildly optimistic to hope that Iyraclea, Zethrindor, and their sundry followers would all exterminate one another.

Abruptly the air grew hazy. Taegan smelled smoke, and a floating spark stung his cheek. He smiled, and the vapor thickened, massing together and taking on definition. A pair of red eyes glowed from a tapered, coalescing head, and Brimstone crouched before them.

Will laughed. "I was starting to wonder if you'd abandoned us."

"The only way to rescue you," the vampire whispered, "was to fetch something capable of creating a considerable diversion. It took a little time." He turned to Kara. "Change form, singer. Together, we can fly Dorn, Raryn, Will, and Pavel out of here, and with Jivex's assistance, conjure illusions and the like to hinder pursuit."

"Sounds good," said Will. "All but the part about dragging the charlatan's useless arse along."

Kara's body swelled and heaved, and her smooth skin sprouted glittering scales. Brimstone murmured rhyming words. Then Raryn bellowed, "Watch out!"

Taegan looked around, spotted Icy Claws and frost giants glaring back, then felt an abrupt, excruciating chill. He cried out, and his muscles clenched. He struggled to get past the shock of it, while, their magic shifting them instantaneously through space, the gelugons appeared just in front of the would-be escapees. They lifted their lances high to thrust downward, and poised their massive bladed tails to bash and slice. Behind them, the giants scrambled forward. Their footfalls shook the ground.

A white spear leaped at Taegan. He jumped, beat his wings, rose above the stroke, and kept on climbing, veering repeatedly to throw off his opponent's aim. He'd avoided taking to the air before, lest it make him too conspicuous, but that was scarcely a consideration any longer.

He tried to ascend beyond the Icy Claw's reach, but despite its lack of wings, the devil too shot up off the ground. Sweet Lady Firehair, was there anything the towering, bug-faced fiends *couldn't* do?

Taegan dodged two more spear jabs, meanwhile conjuring images of himself, reflections created without the necessity of mirrors, to baffle his assailant. The gelugon rammed its spear into one of the phantoms, popping it. At the same instant, Taegan lashed his pinions, hurling himself at the creature's head, and aimed his makeshift dirk at one of the bulging, faceted eyes.

He hit the target. But instead of driving deep into the devil's skull and brain, the giant's spearhead simply scratched the surface of the eye and glanced off, as if it were made of polished stone. The baatezu lashed its tail at him as he hurtled past. Dismayed by his failure to incapacitate it, the giant nearly missed seeing the stroke in time to evade.

He realized he shouldn't be surprised, might even have anticipated what had happened if the irrational fear the devil inspired hadn't been gnawing at his mind. Some spirits were more or less invulnerable to weapons unless the blades bore magical enhancements. But the spearhead was the only weapon he had. All he could do was try to use it.

He drove home two more thrusts, but each merely chipped his adversary's pale, gleaming shell. Hoping to fly faster than the Icy Claw could pursue, he then rattled off an incantation to heighten his speed, but while that made it somewhat more difficult for the devil to target him, it didn't keep him out of its reach. It used its ability to blink through space to stay with him.

Struggling to stave off outright panic, Taegan insisted to himself that somehow, he could survive this confrontation. Then he glimpsed a flash of motion from the corner of his eye. He tilted his wings, dodging, and chunks of ice shot up from the ground to strike and destroy his last remaining illusory counterpart.

He saw that one of the ice wizards had conjured the attack. He assumed the transformed magician would keep right on throwing spells at him, but didn't know what he could do about it. The gelugon was the more dangerous threat. He started to shift his attention back to the devil, then realized what was hanging at the mage's hip.

It was Rilitar's sword! Taegan had previously observed that one of the ice wizards had taken possession of it, perhaps to study the enchantments used in its manufacture, and that was the sword.

Taegan faked a shift to the right, then furled his pinions and dived at the foe on the ground. He didn't know if he'd actually succeeded in buying himself a precious second, and didn't glance back at the gelugon to find out, lest it slow his plunging descent.

The mage slashed his hands through a mystic pass. More chunks of ice exploded in all directions from a central point in midair. Taegan shielded his face with his arm, and dodged. Some of the missiles battered him even so, but he refused to let the pain balk him.

He slammed into the wizard and knocked the thing backward onto the ground. Crouched on top of it, he stabbed at the milky, rigid, impassive features, breaking the ice that was the spellcaster's altered flesh and bone.

The magician stopped moving. Taegan jerked the sword from its scabbard, felt the surge of confidence and vitality that gripping the hilt always produced, leaped up, pivoted, and the gelugon was there, looming over him, ivory spear leaping at him.

He parried the thrust, beat his wings and rose back into the air, slashed at one of the devil's chitinous forearms. The elven sword bit deep, and the Icy Claw gave a buzzing cry.

Grinning, no longer frightened, Taegan cut it twice more before it could shift the lance to threaten him anew. He hovered before it, inviting an attack, and knocked it aside when it came. That enabled him to close the distance to the gelugon's barrel-shaped torso. The Icy Claw's tail swept at him, but he twisted out the way, thrust his sword into its chest, yanked it out, and followed up with a cut to the juncture of the baatezu's head and shoulders.

The gelugon floundered backward. It glared and shuddered as if it was straining to bring one of its supernatural abilities to bear. Then it collapsed.

Taegan couldn't tell if he'd actually killed it or not. He hoped so, but wasn't willing to invest any time making sure. The sooner he rejoined his friends, the better.

But perhaps he had time for one thing. He lit on the ground, kneeled beside the ice wizard, and rummaged through the creature's pockets and satchel. The transformed spellcasters naturally had no need of warmth, and stripped of their human emotions, cared nothing for modesty. But they needed the odd robe, haversack, and such to carry their talismans and other magical gear.

Taegan heaved a sigh of gratitude when he pulled a familiar blue-bound volume from the wizard's satchel. Of course, it made sense that the same mage who'd taken possession of his sword had likewise appropriated his book of spells.

The avariel also retrieved his scabbard, then lashed his wings and climbed high enough to oversee a significant portion of the frenzied, chaotic battlefield. His heart sank at what he found. The assault on his comrades and himself had thoroughly scattered their little band. On first inspection, he failed even to spot the majority of his friends.

But he did at least see Brimstone shrouded in a cloud of his smoky breath. The drake pivoted back and forth, ripping with fang and claw at the frost giants who hacked at him in turn with their pole-axes. Pinions sweeping up and down, Taegan rushed to help the vampire fend them off.

Kara charred a gelugon's white carapace black with a bright, crackling flare of her breath. The baatezu collapsed twitching, its body smoking. At the same instant, however, hailstones hammered down from the empty air to bruise and bloody her scales.

She pivoted and saw another ice devil glaring at her. Resuming her battle anthem, she beat her wings and leaped at the thing. It braced its spear to impale her as she plunged down at it, but she broke the lance with a swat, pierced and felled the Icy Claw with the talons on her other forefoot, and reached to grip its head in her jaws.

Chitin crunched between her fangs. The dense flesh inside was unpleasantly cold, and had a foul, bitter taste. She didn't let that deter her from biting the beetle-like head in two.

She spat out the vileness in her mouth and lifted her foot away from the mangled body beneath. No longer pinned, the Icy Claw's thick, bladed tail whipped up at her. By some dark miracle, the creature still lived.

The blow sliced the side of Kara's face, and a ghastly chill stabbed through her entire body. It couldn't quite keep her from stamping down and grinding the gelugon's mid-section to paste, but she shuddered through the process, and went right on shaking. The spasms made her slow and clumsy.

This will pass, she told herself. I just need a few seconds. Then frost blasted down on her, encrusting her dorsal surface with rime and turning her pain to utter anguish.

She hissed at the shock and looked up. One of the larger whites, old and powerful enough that a sprinkle of pale blue and gray scales showed among the ivory ones, was diving at her. She tried to spring out from underneath, but didn't make it. The chromatic's claws rammed deep into her back and slammed her to the ground.

The same giantess who'd guarded Dorn throughout the day chased him, sagging breasts and rolls of fat bouncing, driving him before her with sweeps of a long-handled, stone-headed warhammer. He backed and jumped away, looking for an opening to lunge inside her prodigious reach and make an attack of his own.

But she wouldn't give him the chance. Despite her bulk, she wielded her weapon adroitly, just as she advanced and when necessary, retreated with considerable agility. She always remained close enough to threaten her smaller foe, yet maintained enough distance to keep him from striking back.

In time she'd likely make an error, but Dorn wasn't willing to wait. He didn't know what had become of his comrades, and didn't dare look away from the giantess to find out. But his instincts yammered that he had to finish with her fast, so he could help the others. Otherwise, something terrible was going to happen.

The giantess feinted a backhand blow. Pretending the move had fooled him, he shifted in the direction she wanted him to go. She whirled her weapon over his head and struck from the other side. He lifted his iron arm to shield himself and twisted.

The hammer clanged against his metal parts. It couldn't break them, but it was likewise true that the iron couldn't stop the human half of his body from suffering a portion of the jolt. He cried out, and the blow flung him down on his side.

He lay still, pretending to be crippled. The giantess leered down at him, then swung the hammer over her head to administer the death blow. At last the weapon was out of his way, and she was standing still. He scrambled up and at her.

She struck, and the hammer crashed down on the cobbles at his back. She tried to skip backward, but not quickly enough. He lunged behind her and ripped at her hamstrings with his claws.

Blood gushed, her knee gave way, and she fell backward. At once she let go of the hammer, rolled, and reached for him with her bloated, filthy fingers. He swept his iron arm back and forth, slicing her hands, until she snatched them back. He jumped in to rip at the artery in the side of her neck.

More blood sprayed, spattering him from head to knees, the coppery smell mingling with the sour stink of the giantess's flesh. She flopped down on her face. He spat gore from his mouth, wiped it from his eyes, cast about, and faltered in horror.

Though the battle raged everywhere, it was at its most furious in the center of the plaza. Her gown burned away, her snowflake-and-diamond-painted skin raw and blistered, Iyraclea floated in the air at one end, while Zethrindor, his dead flesh ripped and hacked, crouched at the other. The two hurled blasts of blue and silver radiance, bolts of shadow, screaming winds, and pounding barrages of hail back and forth. The discharge of so much magic was nauseating to behold. An observer had a visceral sense the spells were beating at the substance of the world itself, and might conceivably break through.

Between and around the commanders, their minions battled like warring ants grappling under the feet of a pair of duelists. Some of Dorn's companions had gotten caught amid the fracas. Brimstone, Taegan, and Raryn were fighting three giants and an Icy Claw.

What appalled Dorn, however, was Kara's situation. She'd managed the shift to dragon form, but even so, a huge white held her pinned and was ripping gashes in her crystal-blue hide.

Dorn ran toward her, and several of Iyraclea's human warriors scrambled to intercept him.

He had no choice but to kill his way through them. The first to fall bore a kind of primitive sword, a length of bone studded with chips of flint. Once he snatched that up to wield in his hand of flesh, he could slaughter them a little faster, but still not fast enough.

As he clawed and hacked, parried and sidestepped, he caught glimpses of Kara. Flailing with her wings, she broke free of the white's coils and scrambled away. The chromatic, however, simply pounced after her and bore her down once more.

Curse Taegan, Brimstone, and even Raryn! Couldn't they see what was happening? Why didn't one of them break away from their own little skirmish and help her?

Dorn drove his knuckle-spikes into the last barbarian's heart. Ahead of him, the white roared and reared up from Kara's shredded, motionless body.

Dorn sprinted toward the two dragons. Kara couldn't be dead. She couldn't.

Iyraclea shouted, *"Auril!"*

The cry was deafening, like a shrill thunderclap. She thrust out her arm at Zethrindor and curled her fingers in a clutching motion. White vapor steamed from the dracolich's decaying flesh, and he bellowed. Dorn realized the Ice Queen was leeching forth the cold that was, as she'd warned him, a vital part of his nature.

But Zethrindor wasn't finished yet. He snarled words of power that cracked and crumbled the facades of buildings at the edges of the plaza. Dorn felt a pressure, a seething malignancy accumulating in the air.

All the countless characters graven on the cobbles shined like cats' eyes reflecting light. Brimstone, Taegan, and Raryn faded, their forms becoming vague and ghostly. Before they quite finished disappearing, though, Zethrindor screamed the final syllables of his incantation.

A towering mass of shadow appeared in front of the dracolich, then swept forward like a wave racing toward the shore. Giants and wyrms scrambled to get out of the way. Those who failed broke part into small fragments, which then crumbled to powder. The darkness likewise obliterated the paving stones in its path, and as soon as the first of them shattered, the symbols on all the others stopped gleaming.

The wave raced on amid swirling dust. It surged over Kara's body, and Raryn, Taegan, and Brimstone's misty forms, and they too disappeared. At the opposite end of the square, it engulfed its actual target and halted with a suddenness no mundane matter could have matched. It clasped Iyraclea's slender form like amber encasing an insect.

Fissures ran through her skin as if she were a clay figure on the verge of breaking. Yet she didn't perish immediately, as lesser beings had. She chanted the Frostmaiden's name, and her body glowed like ice refracting sunlight, the blaze piercing the surrounding murk. She grew taller, as though the Cold Goddess was lending her more strength than a human-sized frame could contain.

Then, however, Zethrindor roared another word, and the Ice Queen thrashed in agony. She was woman-sized again, her inner glow guttering out.

"Aur—" she croaked, and a jagged crack split her luscious mouth and perfect face in two. Her left foot dropped away from its ankle. Then the shadow devoured her completely.

Afterward, the magic dwindled and disappeared like water draining into the ground. Evidently exhausted, Zethrindor slumped down. Dorn looked around and saw nothing but drifts of dust and the broad new scar across the plaza. He hefted the gory bone-and-flint sword and marched toward the dracolich.

Will smiled at the fur-clad spearmen spreading out to flank him. "Wouldn't it make more sense to fight the dragons?" he asked. "They're the ones trying to kill your queen."

The barbarians kept coming.

"Have it your way, then." The halfling faked a lunge at one, then whirled and charged the other.

Startled, the second human nonetheless managed a spear thrust, but his aim was off, and Will didn't even have to dodge. He simply rushed on in, drove his pilfered skewer into his opponent's groin, and dodged around the stricken man as his knees started to give way. He was sure the other tribesman had run after him hoping to take him from behind, and he intended his maneuver to interpose the wounded barbarian between them.

Sure enough, when Will spun back around, his remaining opponent was right where he'd expected him to be, hovering as if he couldn't make up his mind whether to circle right or left. He was still thinking about it when a flying, glowing, red-gold mace bashed him in the back of the head. The tribesman pitched forward.

Will turned and felt relief at the sight of Pavel standing unwounded, a pilfered spear clutched in his hands. The half-ling tried to think of a fitting insult to greet his friend, then glimpsed what was happening at the center of the plaza. Shocked into silence, he pointed. Pavel pivoted in time to watch the heaving, rushing darkness consuming all in its path. Even Iyraclea failed to resist its power.

As the ravenous power ebbed away, Will spotted Dorn starting toward Zethrindor. Even in the dark, the big man's asymmetrical frame was as unmistakable as his intentions.

"Come on!" Will said. He ran toward Dorn, Pavel sprinted after him, and the flying mace brought up the rear.

It occurred to Will that this headlong dash was no way to skirt trouble. But maybe it would be all right. Some of the combatants on the battlefield were still busy fighting one another. Others, wounded or weary, needed time to regroup, and perhaps in the present circumstances, many of the towering gelugons, giants, and wyrms simply regarded a scurrying human and halfling as inconsequential.

One giant, an axe in either fist, his beard braided, did come stamping to intercept them. But Jivex swooped down out of the dark and puffed sparkling vapor in the behemoth's face. The giant tottered backward giggling like a happy drunk. The seekers raced on by.

Up ahead, Dorn halted and came on guard, iron arm extended, sword cocked back. Will felt a jolt of fear. The idiot was going to shout out a challenge, like a paladin in one of poor Kara's stories, and he was still just a little too far away to do anything about it.

Pavel snapped, "Silence!"

Though Will wasn't even the target, the magic imbuing the word made him feel something akin to a slap in the face.

Dorn froze.

That gave Jivex time to catch up to him, and the small dragon wheeled around the half-golem's head. "Don't be stupid!" he snarled.

"No," Pavel panted as he and Pavel stumbled to a halt, "don't. With Iyraclea dead, the drakes have won. They'll need some time to deal with the rest of her troops, and to collect themselves, but then they'll remember us. This is our last chance to slip away."

Painted and stinking with blood, Dorn spat. "I don't want to get away. I promised to keep Kara safe. I failed. But at least I'm going to avenge her."

"You can't beat Zethrindor," said Pavel, "certainly not with all these other wyrms ready to back him up."

"You go if you're going."

"Lathander teaches that suicide's a sin."

"Then bugger Lathander and you, too."

"We're all sad about Kara," said Will, "but she'd want us to go on, and wreck Sammaster's plans. The way I see it, he's the one who really killed her, and pissing in his tea kettle will be our true revenge."

"How are we supposed to do that?" Dorn retorted. "The search failed. We discovered nothing here. We just lost Kara—and Raryn, and the others."

"We did find something," Pavel said. "Unfortunately, Zethrindor destroyed it, but perhaps just hearing about it will help our friends in Thentia solve the puzzle. We need to return and tell them."

"You go," said Dorn. "You're the scholar, fit to help with mysteries and such. As I just proved, I'm useless."

"Damn it!" said Will. "With Raryn gone, you're the best hunter, forager, and pathfinder. Pavel and I don't have a rat's chance in a dog pit of getting off the glacier unless you help us. I know you loved Kara, but was she really the only one you ever cared about? Don't the rest of us mean anything?"

Dorn closed his eyes as if at a pang of headache. "We'll get off the ice if we can."

"Then what's our next move?" Pavel asked.

"We climb down the other side of the mountain. When the wyrms think to hunt us, they'll do it along the trail."

Pavel frowned. "Are you sure the climb is possible?"

"How could I be? We've never seen the ground. Now get rid of the shining mace. We can't have it floating along behind us like a firefly attracting attention."

<hr />

Zethrindor had imagined that once he became a dracolich, he'd never experience pain or weakness again. Iyraclea had disabused him of that notion. He felt sore from snout to tail, and it was an effort just to raise his head to regard his followers with the proper imperious demeanor.

He managed, though, despite the throb of his torn neck, and gave Ssalangan a glower. "Has anyone discovered anything of note?"

"No," said the living drake, "not yet, but everyone's still searching."

Zethrindor was aware of that. He could hear the crashes as dragons forced their way through openings and into spaces too small to accommodate them, and their gleeful cries as they made a game of the destruction. Their victory had left them in high spirits. Because, dunces that they were, they evidently didn't realize that by the foulest of luck, the prize they'd fought to win had slipped through their talons.

"Tell them to stop," Zethrindor said. "They won't find anything. The plaza itself was the secret. I started casting my spell of annihilation an instant before it became apparent, not that I could have avoided destroying it even if I'd known. I had to defeat Iyraclea. But the magic is lost. Curse it, anyway!"

"At least," Ssalangan said, "Iyraclea will never take possession of it. Sammaster's plans will move forward without her interference. We're all going to be dracoliches and the lords of Faerûn."

This cheery assessment so irked Zethrindor that for a moment, his aches and weariness notwithstanding, he considered rearing up and giving the lesser white a taste of his claws. Then, however, it struck him that, in his own witless way, Ssalangan might have stumbled within hailing distance of a valid point.

"It is true," the larger wyrm rumbled, "that I've freed us from the indignity of serving a human, and Sammaster won't even be able to reproach me for it." He leered. "For I killed to preserve his secrets, did I not?"

"Of course," Ssalangan said. "So what do we do next?"

"Complete the conquest of Sossal for our own benefit. I'll be the first of the new dragon kings, and you lesser wyrms, my barons. But before we fly east, bring me Iyraclea's prisoners, the ones who didn't disappear. I want to question them." He supposed he might as well make one last attempt to probe the hidden aspects of Sammaster's grand design before putting the matter behind him.

Ssalangan hesitated. "I don't think we have them."

"Did they die in the fighting?"

"It's certainly possible, but I haven't seen the bodies. To be honest, I don't think anyone's given them a lot of thought. They were just a pair of humans, a halfling, and some sort of winged lizard. Surely the song dragon was the important one, and we know what became of her."

Zethrindor glared, and Ssalangan cringed.

"Find the corpses," the dracolich growled. "If someone's already eaten the meat, identify the bones, and the cripple's iron parts. If you can't locate them, it likely means they've fled. Choose members of our company to hunt them down. Make it clear: The hunters can kill three of the four, but I want one alive to interrogate."

"By the silent dirk!" said Will, his voice shaking with the cold. The halfling was only a few feet above Pavel, but the darkness reduced him to a shadow. "If I hadn't already figured out you were a fake, pretty boy, this so-called ward you cast on me proves it. It isn't doing anything!"

"The spell I used on you," Pavel said, stammering in his turn, "protects the recipient from fire and such. I knew you wouldn't want to become overheated."

"Shut up!" snarled Dorn from farther down the slope. It was the first time he'd spoken in a long while. "Keep moving!"

Pavel obeyed. He groped with his foot for the next toehold, and the one after that, even though everything about the descent was hellish.

He was weary unto death, and felt as if he could scarcely suck in an adequate breath of the thin mountain air. The moaning wind shoved and tugged at him, trying to dislodge him from the steep, icy rock, and despite the protective enchantment he'd cast on himself, the cold soaked into his bones.

He didn't have any more such spells ready for the casting. If the ones currently in place failed before night's end, he, Will, and Dorn might well freeze to death.

Though not if Zethrindor's minions caught them first. Earlier, Pavel had heard a great rattle of leathery wings from the mountaintop. The wyrms roared and screeched to one another as they took flight. He'd cringed in fear that the entire horde was going to descend on the fugitives forthwith, but that hadn't happened. To the contrary, most of the drakes had evidently departed the vicinity. But he suspected at least one had remained to hunt for his friends and him.

If so, it had every had advantage at the moment, including the ability to see in the blackness. If not for Jivex flitting about scouting the steep slopes and sheer drops, his wingless companions would have had no hope of finding a way down.

Dorn's iron hand grated and clashed as he clawed handholds in the rock. Pavel suspected that he'd hear that rhythmic crunching in his nightmares, assuming he lived long enough to experience any more. He shoved his toe into another of the gouges the half-golem had torn in the mountainside.

Or at least he thought that was what it was, and perhaps that was why, in his misery and exhaustion, he forgot to test it before entrusting it with his weight. Rock crumbled beneath his foot, and he plummeted down the precipitous incline. He snatched, but found nothing to grab.

As they crept from the ancient stronghold, he and his friends had plundered the bodies of dead tribesmen, collecting all the gear they could. One of the barbarians had carried the sturdy braided leather line they'd used to rope themselves together. In theory, it might have enabled Will to arrest Pavel's fall. But when the line jerked taut, it tore him loose, and they both were sliding and spinning down the slope.

As he hurtled past Dorn, Pavel tried again to grab something solid. His fingers only closed on a lump of snow. A bulge in the stone bounced him into empty air, and he fell.

Something jabbed into his shoulder. For an instant, he didn't understand what, then glimpsed a blur of pale wings from the corner of his eye. Jivex had caught hold of him and fangs bared in a snarl of strain, was trying to hold him up. It was to no avail. The reptile was deceptively strong, but not strong enough to cope with so much weight.

Stone cracked, the rope jolted Pavel to a stop, and Dorn cried out. Will tumbled past the priest, and the line gave another painful jerk as he, too, abruptly stopped falling to dangle below his friend.

Pavel looked upward, at the spot where Dorn clung with his talons driven deep into the rock. The inhuman strength of his iron arm had served to anchor them all. Though, to judge by his contorted features, not without strain to the flesh-and-bone half of his body.

"Get off me!" Pavel gasped. "Your weight makes it that much harder for him."

Jivex spat. "Try to help and what thanks do you get?" He sprang clear.

Will swung himself against the slope and grabbed hold of it. Pavel stretched out his arms and accomplished the same thing, relieving Dorn of the last of his burden. Then the three of them simply clung to their perches for a time. Pavel shivered, and his heart hammered.

When he felt able to speak, he wheezed, "We have to rest for at least a little while. Otherwise, we'll make mistakes."

Will snorted. "Well, plainly, the imbecile among us will."

Jivex flew up from the well of darkness beneath them. "There's a ledge not too much farther down."

They climbed on down to the shelf, then collapsed there, shapeless, silent, shivering lumps in their layers of loose, thick clothing. Pavel looked to the east, through the vaguely discernible gap between two mountains, hoping to see a first hint of dawn lightening the sky. It wasn't there.

But the sun will rise, he insisted to himself. Lathander sheds his grace on the world every morning, without fail, and when he does, everything will be better. The air will grow warmer, we'll be able to see our way, and I can prepare new spells. We're going to survive.

Such being the case, they'd need to drink. He fumbled scoops of snow into a waterskin.

Perhaps his display of activity helped his companions shake off a bit of their own lethargy. Jivex, who'd been lying coiled and motionless, wings spread to cover him like a blanket, lifted his head and said, "Explain again about the paving stones."

"All right." Pavel resealed the waterskin and stuck it beneath his bearskin mantle and the garment beneath, where his body heat would thaw the contents. "My guess is, the elves built their true stronghold, the actual source of the Rage, somewhere even more remote than the Novularonds. Someplace they thought the dragon kings couldn't possibly find it, or march an army against it even if they did. But because that site was so far away from their own lands, they had to figure out a practical way to go back and forth themselves. To supply it with laborers, guards, building materials, provisions, and what have you. The outpost we discovered was their solution. The plaza was a kind of magical door. Open it, and people and goods could travel between the two citadels."

"What did open it?" asked Will, face shadowed by his hood with its white fur trim.

"I imagine," said Pavel, "Brimstone figured it out, and invoked the magic to whisk himself, Raryn, and Taegan away. Perhaps he thought it was their only hope of escaping the giants and Icy Claws of Iyraclea. Or else he realized Zethrindor was about to unleash a power that would obliterate everything in its path."

Jivex nodded. "So our friends did get away."

Pavel hesitated. "It's possible. I pray they did. But they were still visible, still in a state of transition, when Zethrindor's power sliced into the stones and disrupted the old enchantments. That means the sending could easily have gone wrong, and if it did. . . ." He spread his hands.

"Even if they did make it out the other side," said Will, "the gate's gone now. They can't come back through, and we can't follow. Curse it! Do you think Brimstone's enough of a sorcerer to quell the Rage by himself?"

Pavel shrugged. "Maybe, but we must also ask, are he, Raryn, and Taegan, by themselves, able to withstand whatever guardians and traps Sammaster left to protect the place? We wondered why we didn't encounter such things on the mountaintop. I'm reasonably certain they were waiting on the other side of the portal."

Jivex snorted. "Well, you warmbloods can whine and hang your heads, but I say, it's going to be all right. Taegan's not very clever—that's part of the reason he needs me, to do the thinking—but he's good at chopping things with a sword."

Pavel dredged up a smile. "Well said. We won't despair."

"What we had better do," said Will, "is give some hard thought to our own situation, and I have. Jivex, at first light, you need to strike out on your own."

The drake shook his head. "That's stupid."

"No," Pavel said. "It's likely the first sensible thing the simpleton's ever said. Flying, you can travel faster than we can. You can carry word to Thentia faster."

"Forget it," Jivex said. "We've lost some of our friends, and that's bad. If we split up again, things will be worse. Don't you understand, you people need me."

"We don't matter." Will grinned. "I can't believe I just said that. But maybe we don't, compared to stopping Sammaster."

"We'll stop him together," Jivex said.

"But—"

"No!" the faerie dragon snapped. "I've made up my mind."

With that, they all lapsed back into their cold, exhausted silence. Except, Pavel realized, for Dorn, who'd never emerged from it in the first place. Who, filthy with dried blood, simply slumped staring out at the night.

Once again, Pavel wondered what he could possibly do to comfort Dorn in his grief and despair. He was a priest of the Morninglord, and the big man's friend as well. He ought to be able to think of something. But he was still stymied some time later, when Jivex abruptly sprang to his feet. The little wyrm's head swiveled this way and that, and his nostrils flared.

"What is it?" Pavel whispered.

"I was right," Jivex said. "Zethrindor did leave somebody behind to hunt us, and he's not ranging along the trail, not anymore, anyway. He's on our side of the mountain. Don't move, or make any noise." The reptile faded into invisibility, then, with a telltale flutter of wings, took flight.

A moment later, the world dissolved into an incoherent jumble of twisting shadows and oozing smears of phosphorescence. Pavel gasped, then realized what had happened. Jivex had covered the ledge in an illusion to shield his companions from hostile eyes. The chaotic smear of light and dark was how the effect looked from the inside.

It was a good trick, and Pavel wished he could make it better still by shrouding the company in silence. But unfortunately, he only had a couple spells left in his head, and that wasn't one of them.

Nothing to do then, but crouch motionless, holding his breath, heart pounding. Until something on the slope above rasped, "Got you! You hid. Conjured . . . funny noises, led me wrong. But you couldn't . . . cover your scents. Now show yourselves!"

Pavel kept quiet, in the hope that the wyrm couldn't tell exactly where they were and was trying to get them to give their location away.

"Suit yourselves," said the guttural, halting voice. Something pounded, and the stone beneath Pavel shook. Then came a rumbling crescendo of a noise. He realized with a stab of terror what it must portend.

"Hang on to something!" he shouted, throwing himself flat and groping for handholds.

The streaming snow and chunks of stone the dragon had smashed loose from the mountainside swept over him a heartbeat later. With Jivex's magic bewildering his sight, he couldn't see the onrushing tide, but he could certainly feel it. Pebbles stung him. Ice particles sifted inside his garments to chill his skin. The wave shoved at him, striving to fling him out into space. He lost his grip, slid, his foot slipped over the edge . . . then the pressure abated.

"Is everyone all right?" he gasped.

"What's your idea of 'all right?'" Will replied.

"I'm still here," said Dorn.

"Show yourselves," called the wyrm, "or . . . I knock down more."

Pavel drew breath to explain the illusion wasn't under their control, but then it winked out of existence. Jivex, wherever he was, had evidently dissolved it.

With it gone, Pavel could see the enormous shape of the ice drake clinging to the sheer rock ten yards above his head. Head pointed downward, the creature had driven the claws at the ends of its stumpy legs and even the tip of its wide, flat tail into cracks in the stone to anchor itself, and had likewise spread its wings for balance. The black eyes in its bone-white mask glared downward.

Pavel lifted his spear with its long, broad flint point. It felt awkward and unfamiliar in his grip. The mace and crossbow were his weapons of choice, along with the magic he'd all but exhausted already.

Will and Dorn were in slightly better shape. The former had a sling, the latter, a bow, and both items had no doubt been crafted as skillfully as the barbarians knew how. But they were poor stuff compared to arms and armor infused with Thentian wizardry.

The three hunters aimed their weapons to threaten the ice drake, and it sneered back. "You throw sticks and rocks," the creature said, "and I throw . . . *real* avalanche."

"You could have done that already," said Will, "if you simply wanted to kill us. What do you want?"

"Zethrindor needs . . . prisoner to question," said the wyrm.

Will drew a long breath. "Then here's the bargain. Take me. I'm the lightest. You'll have an easy time carrying me. But my friends go free."

"No," Pavel whispered. "You can't trust it."

"As long as it's up there and we're all down here," Will replied from the corner of his mouth, keeping his voice just as low, "we're pretty much helpless. This is our best chance, so shut up!"

The ice drake hung, evidently pondering Will's offer. At last it said, "I agree. First, everyone, throw weapons off . . . the edge."

Will laughed. "Not likely."

"Then no deal."

"That means you'll have to fight us. Maybe we'll all die, and then what will Zethrindor say? Maybe Lady Luck will smile on us and we'll even manage to hurt you. Look, my friends can't throw away their weapons. They need them to hunt. But I'll disarm myself, and they'll set the bow and spear down. Then I'll climb up to you. How's that?"

The drake grunted. "Do it, then."

Pavel laid his lance on the ground, and Dorn put down the

bow. Will made a show of divesting himself of the weapons he'd collected, his sling, pouch of stones, two knives, and a hand-axe. Afterwards, he clambered upwards. Few observers would have recognized what an able climber he actually was. He faltered and fumbled, his skills evidently eroded by weariness, weakness, and the cold.

Pavel wondered what the wyrm would do once Will came within reach. Grip him and render him helpless, perhaps, then trigger an avalanche anyway. Or else summarily kill him and thus reduce the number of foes arrayed against it. It might adopt the latter course if it believed one of the humans was better able to answer Zethrindor's questions.

Will struggled nearly all the way up, then stopped. "Please," he whined, "I can't do this."

"We made . . . bargain," the reptile said. It yanked one set of foreclaws out of the rock and reached for the halfling.

Will cringed. He stretched out his right arm and leg, found something to grab and a place to set his foot, and shifted himself to the side, keeping just out of harm's way. The action made it clear he wasn't as spent and feeble as he'd pretended, and Pavel felt a flicker of hope.

"Stay still!" the ice drake snarled. "Still, or I hurt . . . you, kill everybody." It pulled the rest of its talons and the end of its tail from their moorings and crawled across the mountainside.

Will had a stone in his grasp. He hadn't divested himself of every last weapon after all, though his cunning hands had made it appear so. He flung the rock and hit the drake in its black, glistening eye. The creature shrieked and recoiled.

An instant later, dust puffed into being in the space surrounding the ice drake, clinging to its body and with luck, clogging its eyes, ears, and nostrils. The powder looked black in the darkness, but Pavel knew that in better light, it would gleam like gold. Jivex, whose talents included the ability to conjure the stuff, rippled back into view. He hurtled at the larger reptile, clawed its flank as he streaked by, and tilted his wings, wheeling for a second pass.

Dorn snatched up his bow and drove an arrow into the ice drake's belly. Pavel brandished his amulet and recited an invocation. The amulet glowed red and warmed his gloved but still half-frozen fingers. A shrill noise screamed through the air and split the ice drake's hide like a blade.

The immense creature lost its grip on the slope and tumbled toward the shelf, smashing loose chunks of stone, ice, and snow to plummet with it. Pavel supposed this was what they'd wanted, to knock the dragon from its perch, but he realized that in so doing, they'd more or less unleashed the very rattling, rumbling avalanche with which their foe had threatened them.

He scrambled to the side, trying to get out from under the wyrm itself, anyway. Falling pebbles pummeled him. One clipped him on the head. It dropped him to his knees, dazing him, but he forced himself up and onward. It occurred to him that he might be safest pressed up against the mountainside so he lunged in that direction, and something else came down on top of him. This time it was a great mass like a giant's hand, blinding, smothering, squashing him to the ground. An instant later, a tremendous impact jolted the ledge, and he pictured the whole thing breaking off and plunging into the valley far below.

That didn't happen, though, nor, evidently, was he dead. He thrashed and floundered clear of the snow that had buried him, to find himself almost within arm's reach of the ice drake.

The creature rolled to its feet and spread its wings. Dorn lunged at it, sunk his iron claws into the base of one pinion, and ripped out a handful of pale, bloody muscle.

The ice drake snarled, whirled, and, evidently discerning Dorn's location despite the dust encrusting its body, snapped at him with its fangs. He twisted out of the way and drove his knuckle-spikes into its snout. The reptile raked with its talons, and he blocked with his artificial arm. That kept the claws from piercing his flesh, but the force of the blow knocked him stumbling backward, toward the drop-off. The drake lunged after him.

Pavel poised his spear and charged, yelling to distract the wyrm. It stopped its advance and lashed its tail at him. He ducked beneath the horizontal blow, sprang back up, and thrust the lance into the reptile's hind leg.

It lifted the limb high, jerking his weapon from his grasp, and stamped down. He jumped back to avoid being crushed. The ice drake started again to scuttle toward Dorn. Jivex dived from overhead and bathed the white wyrm's head in a jet of his sweet-smelling, glittering breath. It didn't seem to have any effect. Will, who at some point had made it back down onto the shelf safely, scurried underneath the ice drake and drove a long knife into its belly.

The creature roared and stamped, trying to trample its tormentor. Will evaded the attacks and kept stabbing, only rolling clear when the drake smashed its entire underside onto the ground. By that time, Dorn was on its flank, punching, tearing, and hacking with his flint-and-bone sword whenever practical. For want of any better weapon, or any more attack spells, Pavel emulated Will and started throwing rocks.

A manifestation of Jivex's magic, bangs like thunderclaps exploded from the empty air around the ice drake's ears. Pavel felt a stab of fear that the noise would trigger another avalanche. But it was probably stupid to worry about that with a wyrm trying to rip them all to pieces.

He hurled another stone. Will scuttled under the ice drake, stabbed, and rolled clear. Dorn clawed gashes in its pallid hide. Jivex swooped, lit atop its brow, and ripped at its eyes.

Zethrindor's minion tossed its head, flinging Jivex clear, spread its jaws, and struck at him. Jivex beat his wings, narrowly avoiding the attack, and retreated. The ice drake lunged after him, and lurched off balance when the stone appeared to dissolve beneath its feet. Actually, Pavel realized, that bit of rock had never existed in the first place. Jivex had extended the ledge by dint of an illusion, then lured their foe into empty space. With the clinging dust and blasts of noise addling its usually keen senses, the larger reptile had failed to penetrate the deception.

It twisted as it started to fall and caught hold of the lip of the drop-off with the claws of one forefoot. Dorn sprang in and attacked the extremity with his sword. The wyrm struck at him. He blocked with his iron arm, then returned to tearing and cutting.

The ice drake lost its grip and tumbled down the mountainside, the constant banging receding with it, sounding in concert with duller thumps as it smacked against the rock. The wyrm got its feet underneath it, vaulted into empty space, and sought to spread its pinions. One unfurled, but the other, damaged by Dorn's claws, didn't. The reptile shrieked as it continued to fall.

Jivex wheeled. "I win!" he cried.

Will grinned. "That was neatly done," he panted. "Is anyone hurt? Dorn, you bore the brunt of it."

The half-golem grunted and sat back down to stare out into the dark.

All the world had become a dull, shapeless seething, rather like the murky stirrings a person sometimes saw upon closing his eyes. Somehow Kara could perceive it even though she no longer possessed eyes, nor any semblance of a body, just as she sensed Brimstone, Taegan, and Raryn suspended along with her. Just as she felt the void eating away at what was left of her, like fire or acid. The sensation wasn't painful, exactly, but it was terrifying and disorienting, so much so that it was difficult to think.

But she had to think, and remember. Had to understand what was happening. At first, nothing would come but images, moments charged with emotion but bereft of context. Dorn leaping back from a sweep of a giantess's warhammer. Brimstone whispering words of power. A prone, mangled gelugon slashing her face with its tail.

She pieced the scraps of recollection together like a mosaicist placing stones to make a picture until finally she understood.

The Icy Claw had hurt her, and a powerful white had attacked her immediately thereafter, borne her down and wounded her severely. It was going to kill her if she didn't get away from it.

She crooned a spell as she struggled, and manifested the charm when she tore free of her adversary's coils. A phantom Kara crouched before the white, while the real one retreated, shrouded in invisibility.

A master trickster like Chatulio might have conjured an illusion convincing enough to fool the white for a long while. Kara's effort would only flummox it for a heartbeat or two at best. Her wounds throbbing, she cast about for a source of help or refuge.

Nothing. Just the roaring frenzy of dragons, frost giants, gelugons, barbarians, and ice wizards struggling on every side, the titanic clash of Iyraclea and Zethrindor looming above every other battle. Brimstone, Taegan, and Raryn were nearby, fighting giants and a devil, but appeared to be in nearly as much trouble as she was. They certainly couldn't rush to her aid.

She could only think of one tactic that might serve to save her. She believed she understood the enchantment bound in the plaza, and even how to command it. She'd direct it to whisk her to the other side of the magical gateway, her and the hard-pressed vampire, avariel, and dwarf, too. She wished she could take Dorn, Jivex, Will, and Pavel, also, but she'd lost track of them amid the chaos.

As the white leaped onto her ghostly double, she sang an invocation under her breath, and the magic bound in the cobbles sprang to life. Obedient to her thought, it gathered her, Raryn, Taegan, and Brimstone into a cool, tingling embrace while leaving their foes untouched.

Then, however, Zethrindor created a towering wave of shadow. The rushing darkness crumbled stones to dust, damaging the pattern of forces the array had been designed to maintain and manipulate.

For that reason, the enchantment didn't shift the travelers all the way to the endpoint. Instead, the disruption stranded them inside the gate, in a timeless, somehow cancerous emptiness.

Their only chance was to force the damaged enchantment to function as originally intended, and maybe, just maybe, she could manage it. Of all dragonkind, song dragons were the greatest wanderers, with a natural affinity for magic facilitating travel. Unfortunately, she was relatively young, and had yet to grow into mastery of sending spells and the like. Still, perhaps she could exert influence over such an effect while already trapped inside.

She probed the weave of forces around her, trying to discern where it had broken and how to patch it. When she believed she knew, she started to sing. She had no lungs, mouth, or ears to hear, but the music sounded clear and precise in her imagination.

In response, disruption blazed through the bodiless essence of her, ripping, seeking to scramble her into something other than she was. She struggled to continue thinking, to cling to knowledge of her own identity, to insist on being herself and not some shattered unreasoning *thing*, and eventually, the threat of crippling metamorphosis abated.

In the aftermath, she thought she comprehended what had happened. Mired in the damaged enchantment, she was like a person buried beneath a tangle of fallen timbers. Her only hope of escape was to shift some of the massive lengths of wood, but in the process, she ran the risk of bringing the whole mass smashing down on top of her.

She wondered how many errors she could make, how many punishing jolts she could sustain, before they obliterated her.

But no, enough of that. She wouldn't dwell on the consequences of failure, nor even admit it was a possibility.

Seeking to determine why her first effort had gone wrong, she reexamined the mesh of the elves' enchantment, then tried a new song.

SEVEN

8 Uktar, the Year of Rogue Dragons

Dorn tried to move quietly, but wasn't unduly concerned when, even so, a fold of cloth flapped, or rubbed against another, or leather creaked. He was sure his companions were too exhausted to wake.

The days of climbing and hiking through freezing temperatures and bitter winds—the glare, sunburn, crevasses, and thin ice—had taken its toll on them all. Then there was the hunger and sickness, the wyrms, giants, tirichiks, colossal bears, and so many other predators indigenous to the Great Glacier. But they were weary most of all from the gnawing fear—a dread spoken by none but surely felt by all.

But they had survived. Drawing on all Raryn had taught them about coping with such hazards—and aided by Pavel's ability to conjure food from thin air, cure frostbite and other ills, and cloak a man in sunny warmth in the midst of a blizzard's chill—they'd made it off the eastern rim of the glacier into a land called Sossal, or so Dorn had heard.

On first inspection, its hills, lowlands, and patches of forest white with the snows of a premature winter, Sossal appeared little more hospitable than the wasteland they were leaving behind, but he knew the appearance was deceptive. The country was by no means warm or safe, but it was warm and safe enough. Will and Pavel would find adequate food and shelter as they trekked south then west into Damara, where Gareth Dragonsbane and his vassals would help them on their way.

Which meant they didn't need Dorn anymore. He'd kept his word and seen them safely off the ice, and he could depart.

As he took a last look at their grimy faces, thin with privation and fatigue, he feared that when they woke and found him gone, they'd think he'd truly never cherished their friendship, particularly since he'd never had the knack of showing it. He could only hope they understood him better than that.

He still prized them as highly as, for some inexplicable reason, they'd always valued him. In a way, that was why he was leaving. Because the worthless freak who'd let Kara die didn't deserve such friends. He deserved loneliness, and they deserved to be rid of him before he led them to their deaths as he had Raryn.

So he'd slip away and hike back onto the glacier. When his comrades woke, they'd fret, but in the end, they wouldn't follow, for they had to reach Thentia. Do their best to save the dragons from their craziness.

He realized he was having difficulty tearing his gaze away from them. Was he stalling? Hoping someone would wake and spoil his plan? The possibility generated another spasm of self-contempt, and somehow that enabled him to turn and skulk away.

He forbade himself to look back, and kept to his resolve until a first silvery gleam of Lathander's light brightened the eastern sky. Then, reaching a hilltop, he yielded to the temptation for one final glimpse of the hollow where he'd left them. It would hurt to look, and maybe that was why the urge proved irresistible.

He squinted, trying to make them out in the feeble gray light, then stiffened in dismay.

At last Stival Chergoba had found his way to a proper, natural autumn, with a bountiful harvest and exuberant harvest festival. The latter was a merry round of delights. He gorged on roast pig, fried trout, apple tarts, fresh-baked bread, and honey. Then he drank himself silly on ale and crowberry wine, and danced with all the prettiest maidens and widows.

The only problem was that one annoying lass behind him kept repeating his name. Intuition told him that it would be a mistake to acknowledge her, but eventually she became too irritating to ignore. He pivoted to tell her to hold her tongue, and sure enough, that simple action wrenched him all the way out of the dream and slumber itself. In the dim light—not dawn quite yet, but Lathander's anemic herald—he was just a hungry, weary ranger on patrol, his body stretched on cold, hard snowy ground.

It was Natali Dormetsk who'd roused him. Natali was a deadly quick and accurate archer with a natural ability to assume the form of an owl. Sometimes when she reverted to human, her trim body took its time shaking off every vestige of her avian shape. At the moment, her legs were too short, and her torso, too long. A few brown feathers grew on her cheeks and the backs of her hands, while her eyes were a round, glaring yellow.

"Why did you wake me?" Stival growled, tossing away his blanket and sitting up. "It had better be important." Actually, he was reasonably sure it would be. Natali was one of the ablest, most level-headed warriors in his command. It was hard to believe she'd never been a soldier until the invasion made a warrior out of most everyone capable of gripping a weapon.

"I saw a dragon," she said. Obviously, while scouting the countryside as he'd ordered.

"Damn it!" Divided into several companies, the Sossrim army was preparing to march south, and it was vital that the enemy not locate any portion of it prematurely. The commanders were exploiting every advantage of cover and terrain, while the druids and wizards did their best to shroud their comrades in spells of concealment, but even so, everyone conceded that if a dragon came too close, it was likely to notice them. "How far away?"

"Close," she said, "and on the ground." The feathers melted into weather-beaten skin, and the golden owl eyes dwindled into gray human ones, revealing a face that might have been fetching if she didn't always look so somber and severe. "But—"

Stival heaved himself to his feet. "We're lucky in that regard, anyhow, but I doubt we can kill a wyrm by ourselves. We're too few. We'll have to pray it stays put long enough for us to sneak back to camp . . . " He realized she was frowning. "I cut you off. What else did you want to say?"

"It's not the usual kind of wyrm. It's about as long as my arm from its snout to the tip of its tail."

"A very young one, then." A dragon they probably could kill. He picked up his coat of white dragon-scale armor and started pulling and buckling it on.

"I don't know. There's something funny about the shape of its wings, but even though it was asleep, I didn't feel like flying close enough to figure out exactly what."

"You were wise. A wyrm's senses are keen enough that you might have woken it, and then it might have been able to tell you weren't an ordinary owl."

"There's more you should know. It's got two companions sleeping alongside it, one a full-grown man, one that's either a child or a member of a small race."

"One of Iyraclea's dwarves."

She shrugged. "Could be. As I said, I kept my distance."

"Right. Eat something while I rouse the others."

The patrol consisted of highly competent warriors, their martial skills sharpened by the perils and hardships of the past two months. They only needed a short time to ready themselves for action. Stival explained the situation, and they moved out.

Everything was a little brighter once they exited the copse of oaks where they'd spent the night, but even then, it was hard to make out men just yards away. Their white garments blended with the snow, and they all stalked along with commendable stealth.

None more so than Natali, even though she was the one who'd gone without rest to scout by night. Stival gave her an admiring glance. If they both survived, if a day came when she was no longer a warrior under his command—but no. It was a stupid fancy. She was too sensible and prudish to lie with him simply for the pleasure of it, and too bereft of gold or land for a fellow with his aspirations to court in a serious way.

She led the patrol up a rise, and the two of them peeked over the top. In a depression on the other side lay the little dragon and its two companions, just as she'd described. The dwarf, if that was what he was, lay mostly concealed beneath the cloak he was using for a blanket. But from what Stival could make out, he seemed slighter of frame than the general run of arctic dwarves, while the hair on his head was black, not white.

"What do you think?" Natali whispered.

Stival didn't know. The little drake was no ordinary white, he was certain of that much. Even in the feeble light, its scales gleamed like silver, or a mirror. If the dwarf hailed from the Great Glacier, he was a member of a clan the Sossrim had never before encountered. Of the three, the human with his lanky frame and straw-colored hair was the least remarkable, but even in his case, his boots and other details of his filthy attire made him appear different from the common ice-dwelling barbarian.

It would be a foul deed to attack strangers if they meant no harm. If they weren't members of the Ice Queen's army. Yet what else could they be?

Stival decided that the wyrm at least must die while it lay vulnerable. Permit it to wake, and it might well strike at them with sorcery, or at least use magic to evade them. Then it could wing its way back to the dracolich and report where it had encountered Sossrim warriors.

So Stival and his comrades would pierce it full of arrows, but try to take the man and dwarf alive for questioning. If they turned out to be innocent travelers, he'd do his best to make amends.

He used hand signals to convey his orders. Silent and spectral in their white cloaks, his warriors rose, nocked arrows, and aimed them at the drake.

Taegan had neither glimpsed nor felt the attack that killed him, and as a result, it took him a while to realize he was dead. That he was a bodiless mote of awareness suspended alone in emptiness. A malignancy gnawed at him. In time it would extinguish him altogether, or at least drive him mad with the threat of it. Surely this was punishment for a life ill-spent, his own strange little oubliette tucked away in one of the hundreds of nightmare worlds comprising the Abyss.

Once the terror of that realization abated a little, he tried to comprehend what he'd done to deliver his soul into darkness. Certainly he'd committed an abundance of what one faith or another considered sins. He'd lusted after women and relished every sort of luxury and pleasure. He'd killed in anger, and when it wasn't strictly necessary. Perhaps he'd even been a trifle vain.

Yet if that had been sufficient to damn him, every rake in Lyrabar likewise stood condemned, and somehow, he couldn't believe that. His true offense lay elsewhere, and eventually he realized what it was.

Disloyalty. Coldness of heart. When he'd come to feel ashamed of his tribe, when he turned his back on those who loved him and his own nature, too, that was the moment he'd transgressed beyond hope of forgiveness.

But such a judgment wasn't fair! He'd been free to live life on his own terms, hadn't he? To choose an existence that fulfilled him?

No one and nothing responded to his protestations, or rather, nothing but his deeper self, and its answer was a paradox: He'd had every right to be selfish, and yet no right at all.

That bitter, irrational insight was as far as his wisdom could take him, and once he reached it, he had little to distract him from the endless aching misery of his condition. He wondered what would happen if he simply yielded to the power grinding away at his essential identity. How badly would extinction hurt? Was it remotely possible it would bring his punishment to an end, or would the unseen fiend overseeing it simply reconstitute his psyche and begin again?

He decided he had little to lose by attempting the experiment, but after a lifetime spent on the path of the sword, he found it difficult to drop his guard and surrender himself to extinction. Finally, though—after hours, days, years, centuries?—he mustered the courage, and heard Kara singing.

Or sensed it, rather, as he registered his own thoughts. Without ears, one couldn't hear anything. Yet he was certain the music was real, and equally sure he hadn't died and gone to perdition after all. It was plausible that a rascal like himself might land in the Abyss, but the dragon bard, never! No, they were alive but trapped in some peculiar predicament, and she was surely attempting to free them. Hoping she could perceive it as he could discern her song, he urged her on.

The shifting void blinked, giving way, for an instant, to a murky chamber or cavern paved with dark hexagonal stones, each inscribed with a glowing symbol. In that same moment, he had a body again, limbs, eyes, and lungs that tried to gasp in a breath before substance and a detailed, coherent world dissolved once more.

Kara sang more fiercely and insistently. The void and the chamber flickered back and forth, until abruptly, the transitions stopped, dumping Taegan finally and unambiguously into the realm of solid, stable matter. Across the floor, a number of the cobbles cracked and shattered, and all the runes stopped glowing, deepening the darkness. A trace of light still leaked in from somewhere, but even so, a human wouldn't have been able to see anything at all.

It felt wonderful to have flesh again, but unpleasant, too. The air was cold, and Taegan felt puny and brittle, as if just beginning his recovery from some disease. His magical imprisonment had taken a toll on him.

He stumbled a step, spread his wings to help him balance, and observed Raryn, Kara, and Brimstone gathered around him. They all looked dazed and ill, too, even the vampire.

"What happened to us?" Taegan croaked, addressing the question primarily to Kara. She seemed the person likeliest to know. "What is this place?"

She jumped away from him. "Stay back!" she said. "I can't—it's too strong here!"

"You mean the Rage?" he asked, and something dragon-shaped and dragon-huge lunged out of the gloom. It rattled and clinked, and its talons clicked on the floor.

⟡

Sprinting down the trail as fast as his mismatched legs could carry him, Dorn caught occasional glimpses of the white-clad men skulking toward Will, Pavel, and Jivex. For the most part, though, trees, brush, and higher ground cut off the view, leaving him to wonder just how close the strangers had gotten.

He'd assumed his friends would be all right slumbering unguarded for just a short while, then the imminence of sunrise would wake Pavel as it always did. But when he'd looked back from the top of the rise, and by the luckiest of chances spotted a dozen warriors emerging from a stand of trees, he'd realized just how stupid and negligent he'd been. It was clear from the way they moved and the direction they took that the men in white somehow knew about his comrades, and if they slaughtered them in their sleep, it would be his fault.

He reached the rim of the higher ground above the depression where he and his exhausted companions had flopped down to rest, and there he felt a jolt of horror. The warriors in white had arrived before him, and were aiming arrows down into the bowl. Their captain, a stocky fellow in a brigandine of ivory-colored dragon-hide, raised his hand to give the signal to shoot.

Dorn nocked a shaft of his own and drew the fletchings back to his ear. "Stop!" he bellowed to the captain. "If anybody shoots, I'll kill you!"

Startled, people spun around to look at him, sometimes goggling or screwing up their faces at his freakish appearance. Meanwhile, he observed that, judging by their more-or-less civilized attire, these moon-blond, fair-skinned folk were Sossrim, not glacier tribesmen bound to Zethrindor's service. That was good as far as it went. It meant they had no legitimate quarrel with the travelers, if only Dorn could convince them of it.

Down on the low ground, roused by Dorn's call, Pavel, Will, and Jivex jerked awake. The faerie dragon spread his wings. Will, realizing that if Jivex took to the air, it would precipitate a volley of arrows, shouted, "No!" The reptile froze.

The captain gave Dorn a level stare. "You have one arrow," the officer said. "We have many."

"True," said Dorn. "But if you people attack, my one is going straight into your chest."

"Why would you want to hurt us anyway?" Pavel asked. "You're Sossrim, aren't you, which means your enemies are our enemies. We just escaped from the same folk who've invaded your homeland. Look." Moving slowly, he fished his sun amulet out from under his grubby, twisted mantle and set it aglow with red-gold light. "I'm a priest of the Morninglord. Is it likely I've made common cause with people who offer to the Frostmaiden?"

The captain frowned. "Ordinarily, I'd say no. But you lie down and sleep beside a dragon. In Sossal, wyrms have always been a scourge, and never more so than this year."

Jivex sniffed. "I assume the only drakes living hereabouts are those brutish whites. But surely you can see I'm a more splendid sort of creature altogether." He raised his gleaming butterfly wings. Despite the still-dim light, rainbows rippled up and down his argent flanks. Dorn suspected he'd used his powers of illusion to heighten the effect. "I'm Jivex, lord of the Gray Forest, slayer of demons and dracoliches, and a friend to men, even when they're too dense to realize it."

The captain grunted. "Maybe so. But if you folk aren't part of the Ice Queen's army, what are you doing here? How did you even get here? Zethrindor's forces control the southern part of the realm."

"We came from the west," said Pavel, "off the glacier, with tidings that are sure to interest you. We'll be happy to explain, but the conversation will be more pleasant if no one's aiming an arrow at anybody else."

The man in the dragon-scale armor waved his hand. The warriors eased the tension on their bowstrings, and Dorn did the same.

Taegan froze at the recognition that the thing lunging out of the dark was skeletal. He could see the spindly angularity of it, the spaces between its ribs. It was a dracolich, and he and his companions were in no shape to contend with such a horror.

But when it struck at him, its vertebrae rasping and clinking together, reflex spurred him into motion, and he wrenched himself aside. Once his body was in motion, his mind likewise resumed its functioning, and he observed details that had eluded him before.

His huge assailant moved fast, but in a hitching, jerking sort of way, and with a rattle and scrape as its bare bones knocked together. It had no odor. Dracoliches moved fluidly, without any such racket, and reeked of corruption. This thing—Sammaster's watchdog, surely—was something more akin to the animated skeletons he'd left behind in Northkeep.

The discovery was reassuring, but only mildly so. Whatever the creature was, a single snap of its fangs or swipe of its talons would still suffice to tear Taegan to shreds.

Huge, curved claws leaped at him. He dodged onto the wyrm-thing's flank, and clattering, its fleshless tail swept around at him. With a beat of his wings, he sprang over the attack and continued in the air. Rather resembling the naked, forking branch of a tree in winter, a skeletal wing hammered down at him. He sped out from under and riposted.

Rilitar's sword splintered bone, but of course that one stroke didn't stop a colossus that, as best Taegan could judge, no longer even possessed anything analogous to vital organs. He might well need to break it into a number of pieces, and had no hope of accomplishing such a thing alone.

"Help me!" he cried.

The wyrm-thing spun to strike at him. He dodged high, swooped low, and chopped at its hind leg.

His flint axe lifted in a high guard, Raryn advanced on the skeleton. Glaring at the thing, ember eyes glowing, Brimstone whispered the opening words of an incantation. Kara, however, crouched by the wall, eyes closed, crooning a melody. It was almost certainly a spell, but Taegan suspected its purpose was to quell the madness seething in her mind, not to smite their current adversary.

Taegan whirled around the skeleton drake, and Raryn darted in and out, sometimes scrambling underneath it. Each fought defensively when their foe oriented on him, and struck hard when it focused on his comrade. The elven blade sheared through a rib, hacked loose a length of wing vane, cut deep into a vertebra midway down the serpentine neck. Even without the advantage of an enchanted weapon, Raryn's phenomenal strength and skill likewise inflicted a measure of harm. But none of the damage crippled the wyrm-thing or even slowed it down.

Taegan felt the stinging touch of power accumulating in the air. Patches of shadow swirled like water spinning down a drain. Brimstone's spell was nearing completion, and it occurred to him that, if the vampire deemed it expedient, he was entirely capable of creating a destructive effect that would engulf the skeletal dragon and his allies too.

"Get clear!" he cried, and, pinions lashing, distanced himself from the foe.

Raryn scrambled back. The wyrm-thing pivoted to pursue the dwarf, and a bright, booming blast of fire, expanding outward from a point in midair like a flower blooming, shrouded it. Taegan flinched at the searing heat.

The blaze, however, left the wyrm-thing intact, seemingly not even singed. The only effect was to make it orient on Brimstone. It pounced, caught the smoke drake's neck in its jaws, and wrenched him off his feet. It crouched on top of him, pinning him, biting and clawing.

Taegan expected Brimstone to escape by turning to a cloud of smoke and sparks, but he didn't. Perhaps his confinement in the void had left him too weak to invoke that particular ability.

Taegan flew at the enemy, and Raryn charged. They attacked, bone crunched, and chips of it flew, one striking Taegan just above the eye. The skeleton rounded on him, struck, lunged, drove him backward toward against a wall. He tried to dodge down his adversary's flank, and the wyrm spread its enormous wings, making a barrier to pen him in.

A battle anthem filled the air. Kara sprang onto the skeleton's back, bore it down, but failed to pin it. Coiled together, rolling back and forth, they tore at one another.

For the first time—everything was happening too cursed fast—Taegan noticed the song dragon's deep and gory wounds, sustained, evidently, during the battle back in the plaza. In her present condition, she wouldn't last long before the skeleton wyrm overwhelmed her.

He set down on the ground and cut at Sammaster's sentinel. Raryn dashed in and did the same. They were trying to draw the thing away from Kara. But the tactic wasn't working.

Taegan flew onto the wyrm-thing's lashing, heaving neck, spread his pinions to aid his balance, and cut repeatedly at the vertebra he'd already damaged. It was about as hazardous a perch as he could imagine. If Kara and her adversary rolled again, and he failed to spring into the air quickly enough, the prodigious tangled mass of them could flip over right on top of him. He tried not to think of that, or of anything but cutting at precisely the right spot.

With his target in furious motion, he missed as often as not. But he gradually enlarged the breach he'd made before, until finally the vertebra shattered into several pieces. With a crash and a clatter, the huge, wedge-shaped skull dropped away from the rest of the skeleton, and the thing stopped moving. Panting, Taegan offered a silent prayer of thanks to sweet Lady Firehair.

"Kara," he said, "are you all right?"

"Yes," she said, extricating herself from the clinking remains of her adversary. "I've stifled the frenzy for the moment, anyway."

"I rejoice to hear it, but I was referring to your wounds."

"Oh." She sounded surprised, as if she'd forgotten the punctures and gashes, though that scarcely seemed possible. "They'll be all right, I suppose."

"No doubt," whispered Brimstone, irony in his tone, "you'll all be delighted to learn that I'll survive as well." His wounds closing, but more sluggishly than usual, he turned his smoldering gaze onto the remains of their foe. "It was a sort of golem and thus more or less impervious to sorcery. With my mind still muddled from our imprisonment, I didn't realize that."

"So the only creatures your fire magic might have hurt," Taegan said, "were Raryn and me. Pray forgive my candor, but I've seen you make cleverer plays."

The vampire bared his fangs. "We were in desperate straits, and I trusted the two of you to scurry out of the way."

"As we did," Raryn said, "so let's not squabble about it. I'd rather hear what's happened to us, if anybody knows."

"I do," Kara said, and offered an explanation that was, Taegan supposed, no madder than all the other mad things they'd experienced. "Perhaps I panicked, but I was certain that if we didn't get away, we were going to die."

"Considering the magic Zethrindor unleashed at the end," Taegan said, "I daresay you were right. But I wish you could have brought the rest of our comrades along. Failing that, I wish we at least knew what happened to them."

"Perhaps I can scry for them," Brimstone said. "Or perhaps not. The same wards that keep anyone from finding this place by such methods may well prevent me from looking out. But in any case, we have more important matters to address. Didn't you understand what Karasendrieth told us? At last, we truly have reached the source of the Rage."

"I do understand," Taegan said, "and in some measure, I share your enthusiasm. I simply wish I didn't feel so frail and accordingly ill-equipped to contend with whatever additional surprises Sammaster emplaced to greet us."

"So do I," Raryn said, "but it doesn't matter if we're sick, or if we can't travel back the way we came. Somehow, we made it here, and we've got to go on with our work. Unless the heart of the magic is sitting right in front of us, and I just don't have the wit to see it, that means exploring."

"You're right." Kara dwindled back into the form of a woman, and Taegan suppressed a wince. It was even more troubling to see her cut and bloody in that slender, vulnerable shape. "Perhaps someone could help me with some bandages, and then we'll begin."

On further inspection, the chamber proved to be as wide as the plaza back in the Novularonds. But this place appeared to be a natural cavern, which the elves had shaped to suit their purposes.

A single tunnel led away, a passage broad and high enough that that the elves would have had little difficulty moving great quantities of material through it. At the end was a valley ringed by dark, snow-dappled peaks and domed by a black sky, and at the center rose a gigantic castle. Something about it reminded Taegan of the fortress the Cult of the Dragon had raised in the Gray Forest. It seemed sculpted from masses of living rock, not built of blocks of quarried stone. But where the madmen's stronghold had been a crude and graceless thing, the citadel before him, even though crumbling into ruin, battlements eroded and spires fallen, was as magnificent as the city Amra had shown him in their shared dream.

He realized he was gawking, and made haste to recover his composure. "It's a pity," he drawled, "that the gateway didn't deposit us in the castle itself. After all we've endured to come this far, the builders might have spared us a final hike over stone and ice."

"The separation," Kara breathed, "was yet another layer of defense, and they needed it." Her hand trembling, she pointed. "Look."

Taegan peered, then felt a fresh pang of amazement. At first glance, he'd failed to pick them out from among the snow drifts, rocks, and shadows, but bones littered the floor of the valley. Some were immense, and even broken and scattered by wind, freezing temperatures, and time, still bore a noticeable kinship to the wyrm-thing he and his companions had just defeated. Others were smaller, impossible to identify at a distance, but he didn't need to identify them to comprehend the essence of what had happened.

"The rebels," he said, "believed no dragon king would ever find their citadel, or bring an army against even if it did. But they were mistaken. At some point, their foes laid siege to the place."

Near the castle's massive barbican, a ragged blackness leaped upward like a tongue of flame from a bonfire. Pain stabbed through Taegan's temples, and he reflexively raised his sword.

"It's all right," Brimstone whispered, a sneer in his voice, "no one's attacking us. That was just a vestige."

"Thank you," Taegan said, "that's profoundly comforting. A vestige of what, precisely?"

"Of all the magic unleashed here in times past. Sometimes, when dragons fight and die in a place, the battlefield remembers, and such phantoms and echoes can be dangerous. Perhaps we would do well to fly to the castle. We might avoid some of the hazards, anyway."

"Or attract the notice of other guardians," Raryn said. "I'd rather walk and be careful."

Brimstone flipped his wings in a shrug. "So be it." He started out of the tunnel, and a dark, vast form, passing over the mountain at their backs, glided into view.

For a moment, Taegan thought it was a black dragon. The color was essentially right, but it had a stippled pattern of lighter scales running through the dark. Its wings were so torn and perforated it seemed unnatural that it could fly as well as it was manifestly capable. The entire body had a gaunt, shriveled look, not just the flesh on its head. The fangs and talons, moreover, were as black as obsidian.

Praying the reptile hadn't detected him, Taegan shrank back into the passage. His companions did the same.

With a lazy beat of its ragged pinions, the dark wyrm flew onward. It gave an eerie, screeching cry, and from other points around the valley, the voices of other drakes responded in kind.

Will reflected that, for a fellow who lacked any taste for soldiering, he was spending far too much of his time in the midst of armies. Though it was mildly interesting to note the differences. Gareth Dragonsbane's host had been the very definition of chivalry, with scores of knights, paladins, and men-at-arms encased in plate and mounted on towering destriers. By contrast, the Sossrim army, or at least the part of it encamped in this particular vale, had a more rustic, yeoman-ish feel to it. Virtually no one wore plate. A warrior was lucky if he had mail, or a nag bearing any resemblance to a genuine war-horse. Most people looked like the archers, scouts, and skirmishers who constituted an important but ancillary part of the Damaran military.

Still, they had an air of sober competence about them, especially the officers who'd crowded into the gray canvas tent to hear what the travelers had to say. Pavel did most of the talking, while Dorn withdrew into brooding silence.

When the priest finished a greatly abridged account of their adventures, Madislak, the bald, scrawny old druid who seemed to be in charge, shook his head. "Can the Ice Queen truly be dead?" he asked.

"Dead as a weasel's breakfast!" Jivex declared, clinging upside down to one of the poles supporting the tent.

"We saw her die," Pavel said.

"And of late," Stival said, "she hasn't cast her image into the sky to encourage her troops and demoralize us. I wondered why."

"Then why is it still so cold?" groused a warrior, fair of skin and silvery blond of hair like most of his folk, with a bronze hawk-shaped brooch securing his woolen cloak. He punctuated the question with a rattling sniffle.

Madislak shrugged. "Winter is nearly upon us. Even with Iyraclea's power broken, we're likely stuck with the snows till spring."

"What I want to know," said a burly man with a broken nose and a couple missing teeth, "is why, if the bitch is gone, Sossal's still overrun with giants and such."

"Sun and rain," the druid snapped, "use your head. Because Zethrindor and the lesser wyrms have decided to claim the realm for themselves."

"I'm certain you're right," Pavel said. "The chromatics expect to conquer all Faerûn in the months to come. Sammaster convinced them it's their destiny."

"Sammaster," Stival said. "I think I've heard one or two bogie stories about a necromancer of that name. But he disappeared a long time ago, didn't he, and never bothered folk in this part of the world even when he was around."

"Well," said Will, "he's bothering you now. He's found a way to bother everybody."

"Yes," said Pavel, "and if somebody doesn't foil his schemes, it may not even matter whether you Sossrim defeat Zethrindor or not. Your land, and all the world, could still go down in ruin. That's why you have to help us get back to Thentia."

The fellow with the runny nose snorted. "These wild stories . . . no offense, outlander, but we have our own problems, real problems, to concern us."

"When you can talk with the wind and the forests," Madislak said, "maybe your opinions on mystical matters will be worth hearing." He turned his gaze, fierce as an eagle's, on Pavel. "I believe you, son of the Morninglord, more or less. The signs corroborate your tale. But we Sossrim can't give you as much aid as you might like. We do indeed have a war to fight."

"We'll be grateful," said Pavel, "for any help you can provide."

"The early days of the invasion went against us," the old man said. "Zethrindor attacked in the south, where our principal settlements are, decimated our army, and put the survivors to flight. We separated into several companies, to make it easier to hide and forage, and started preparations for a counteroffensive. We're ready now. We'll march south, uniting as we go, and you can travel with us. When the time comes, I'll point you to hidden paths that, with luck, will enable you to sneak past Zethrindor's forces and westward into Damara. How's that?"

"It sounds good to me," said Will.

The meeting broke up shortly thereafter. Outside the tent, the air was cold, the day, gray and cheerless. Still, it came as a relief after the claustrophobic press inside, scented as it had been with the sour smell of humans in need of baths. Will's belly grumbled, and he looked around in hope of finding a cook fire and breakfast.

Dorn, however, turned without a word and stalked away through the dirty, much-trodden snow. It looked as if he was heading out of camp to avoid curious eyes, or to sulk in private. Frowning, limping slightly, Pavel hurried after him. Will sensed something was happening, and he too gave chase, running outright to match the longer strides of his friends. Platinum wings shimmering, Jivex brought up the rear.

Pavel reached out and gripped the shoulder on the half-golem's human side. "Hold on," he said.

Dorn turned and scowled. "What?"

"We need to talk," the priest replied. "Earlier this morning, when you woke us by shouting at Stival, you weren't in our campsite anymore. You were on higher ground some distance away."

"So?"

"You were about to desert us. If you hadn't spotted the patrol stealing up on us, we would never have seen you again."

"Nonsense!" said Will. "Charlatan, from the hour we met, you've been wrong about everything, wrong as a hog in a wedding dress, but this beats . . . " Then he noticed the way Dorn's mouth had twisted on the fleshy side of his face. "By the silent dirk! It's true? Why?"

"It won't happen again," said Dorn.

"My friend," Pavel said, "I know it's all but unbearable. Kara was wonderful. You yearned your whole life for a love like that, never dreaming you'd find it, then had it torn away from you. But Lathander teaches—"

Dorn slammed his human fist into Pavel's jaw. The punch flung the blond man backward and he landed on his rump in the snow.

"I said," the big man growled, "I won't sneak off again. You don't have to nag me about it." He turned and trudged away.

Brimstone regarded his companions, and took some slight solace in the fact that none of them appeared panicky or demoralized. They might be his inferiors, and an aggravation much of the time, but they had a toughness that made them useful pawns.

"The drakes are called Tarterian wyrms," he whispered, keeping his voice even lower than usual. He and his comrades had retreated a goodly distance back down the tunnel, but he assumed the creatures outside heard as well as dragons generally did. "They dwell in the Abyss and certain other parts of the dark worlds. Archdemons and the like employ them as jailers, sentinels, and coursing beasts."

Taegan arched an eyebrow. "I trust you aren't saying the elves built their stronghold in Baator or someplace similarly uncongenial, and we've landed there now."

"No," Raryn said. "We're in the far north of Faerûn, just as we expected. I only caught a glimpse of the sky and stars before we had to scurry for cover, but I could tell that much."

"Sammaster stationed the Tarterian dragons here," Brimstone said, "as he left a Styx dragon in Northkeep, and used shadow wyrms to mount a guard over King Gareth's soul. His primary concern was always the drakes of our own world, but he also had an interest in wyrms native to other levels of existence. He learned to command some varieties, and negotiated covenants with others."

"And here they are," sighed Karasendrieth, slumped, ashen, and generally haggard-looking, her makeshift bandages spotted and giving off the enticing scent of blood. The smell wore away at Brimstone's self-restraint. "I suppose the Tarterians were a better choice than chromatics, since he doesn't want the latter learning anything about the source of the Rage. But still, by all the stars and every melody they sing, how many barriers did he put in our way?"

"We've known from the start," Taegan said, "that he has a penchant for intricacy and elaboration. It was manifest in his cipher, so complex that even Firefingers and the other scholars couldn't unravel it. But we've outplayed him so far, and will again. Though I confess, I'm uncertain as to how."

Raryn scratched his silvery goatee. "I see two choices. We four can try to find and destroy the heart of the Rage without running afoul of the Tarterian dragons and whatever other dangers are lurking about. Or, someone can go for reinforcements."

"The latter," Brimstone said, "is the wiser course, and I'm best equipped to do it. I can fly, I command the most potent magic, and I emerged from our recent battles relatively unscathed. I am, moreover, impervious to the cold. I believe a fading enchantment like the one protecting the site in the Novularonds still warms the valley to some degree, but none of you could bear the chill that prevails beyond the mountains."

Raryn smiled. "I could, but I don't see how I'd manage if I was riding you and you had to turn into smoke. Anyway, I'd rather bide here, because I think we should try both plans. You go for help, and the three of us will try to sneak into the castle."

Taegan nodded. "With time slipping through our fingers— or talons as the case may be—I agree."

"So be it." Brimstone rose and stretched. Twinges shot through his body as if he were a mortal creature. "You'll want to find a different hiding place, and keep your heads down for a while. If the Tarterians spot me, they may think to search for other intruders, and a tunnel leading to a magical gate is the first place they'll check."

Kara said, "You could rest before you venture forth."

Brimstone sneered. "I've already recovered about as much of my vigor as can be expected until I slake my thirst. So, unless one of you is volunteering his or her blood, I see no use in delaying."

He turned and crept down the tunnel to the exit. Then he invoked his gift for transformation. For a moment, nothing happened, or rather, nothing but a fresh stab of pain, but then his body dissolved into smoke and embers.

Though a sentient cloud, he could see and hear as clearly as before. Crouching in the mouth of the passageway, he peered about. As far as he could tell, none of the Tarterians was in the immediate vicinity, so he skulked out and up, hugging the rocky, snowy slopes as he drifted, snaking through fissures in the stone whenever available, making himself as inconspicuous as possible.

Twice, he froze and waited while one of the dark, gaunt Tarterians glided overhead. But he ascended to the gap between two peaks without Sammaster's sentinels detecting him, and from there, he could survey the country beyond.

It was endless desolation, mile after mile of ice and stone, where nothing stirred but the moaning wind, and here on the threshold of it, where the ancient wizards' enchantment of warmth began to fail, the temperature plummeted. It caused Brimstone no distress, but it was cold enough to stop Taegan's heart in a matter of moments. He doubted even Karasendrieth could endure it for any length of time, certainly not in her current injured and debilitated state.

That might have its positive side, if it meant that even the Tarterians were averse to venturing far beyond the zone of relative warmth. If such was the case, once he put some distance between himself and the mountains, he'd be safe.

Encouraged, he flowed onward, until, without warning, the world whirled and tumbled. Silvery light flashed and glimmered around him. Then, when the vertiginous spinning stopped, he found himself hovering in a corridor of milky translucent crystal, or possibly curdled light. The passage forked ahead of him, and doglegged out of sight behind.

Taegan, Raryn, and Kara crept through the scree and litter of bones at the base of the mountains, looking for hollows in the rock. According to the dwarf, since there was one cave, there were almost certainly more.

He, naturally, led the procession, and Taegan served as rearguard, leaving the middle position, the safest spot, to Kara. The bladesinger supposed the arrangement was paradoxical, considering that she was the most formidable. But primarily in dragon shape, and that close to the heart of the Rage, it was more important than ever that she keep to her womanly form as much as possible.

It was a nerve-wracking trek. Periodically, one of the Tarterian wyrms screeched or glided near, and the seekers ducked undercover until it passed. They also spotted the vague, semitransparent semblance of a dragon stalking along the ground. For a moment, Taegan wondered if it was Brimstone, back already and congealing from vapor. Then he realized it was a ghost, still haunting the battleground where the ancient elves had killed it.

Such obvious menaces were alarming, but in essence, they were the same sort of horror he'd been fighting for the better part of a year, and perhaps for that reason, they didn't daunt him quite as much as they would another. It was actually the bizarre manifestations of enchantment gone to rot that he found most disquieting, even though the majority didn't appear particularly dangerous. A stone spoke to him in a language he didn't recognize. His mother's face formed and dissolved in a trickle of water pattering down the escarpment. Fragrant black lilies sprouted from the frozen earth, rubbed and twined together in an exploratory kind of way, then exploded into furious motion, tearing at one another with barbs concealed among their petals.

With such wonders to distract him, it was a while before he actually registered what he was picking his way through.

What he even trod on and crushed occasionally. But when he finally did notice, he froze.

Perhaps he made a sound as well, for Kara and Raryn turned around. "What is it?" whispered the bard.

"The bones," he breathed.

Raryn stooped to examine one of the skeletons. Took hold of a bone and lifted it up. For a heartbeat, the armature of a bird-like wing hung revealed, then the structure crumbled.

"I've never actually seen the skeleton of an avariel before," the white-haired hunter said, "but I assume this is one."

Taegan swallowed. "And there's another, and over there, another. Sune's ruby comb, they're all around us, everywhere!" He paused, studying their faces. "Do you see what it means?"

"Keep your voice down!" Raryn said.

"Yes, my friend," Kara said. She took Taegan's hand. "I do understand."

"It could have been any breed of elf wizards who created the Rage," he said. "But it was avariels who defended this place. Who died by the hundreds, perhaps the thousands, protecting it when the wyrm lords and their minions attacked."

"Interesting," Raryn said, "but now's not the time to stand and chat about it."

Taegan struggled to regain his composure. "Yes, of course. Pray, pardon my foolishness."

As they skulked on, he did his best to keep watching for trouble, but found it considerably more difficult. He couldn't wrench his thoughts away from his discovery.

The avariel race, his own race, whom he'd spent his life disdaining, had been instrumental in overthrowing the dragon kings. His ancestors had fought and died so Faerûn could be free. They hadn't been cowards then, nor later, he was certain, when they'd withdrawn into the wilderness. With so many of their kindred slain, and probably, vengeful drakes intent on slaughtering the rest, reclusion had been their only hope of survival.

Taegan started to cry.

Brimstone resumed solid form. If he couldn't escape the snare that had caught him, he'd likely find himself facing one or more of the Tarterians in the very near future, and they probably commanded magic capable of hurting him even in his guise of sulphurous vapor. Better, then, to wear a shape that would allow him to strike back.

He supposed that Sammaster, aided by the Tarterians, who reportedly favored magical traps such as that, had laid the enchantments throughout the ring of mountains. Though the labor involved in such an endeavor must have been considerable, particularly in light of the fact that the only conceivable purpose was to catch folk who somehow learned of the ruined castle's location, traversed a trackless, frigid wilderness to reach it, then tried to climb over the peaks.

Only mad, brilliant Sammaster, endlessly obsessive and wary of Mystra, the Chosen, and the other foes who'd foiled his previous schemes, would have bothered. Brimstone had never hated the lich more than he did at that moment.

But hating wouldn't help him . He had to think. He lacked the power to cast enchantments like that, but had learned of them in the course of his studies. None of his counter-spells would set him free, but supposedly, an exit existed somewhere, just as if the extradimensional prison were an ordinary maze.

So he scuttled along, seeking it, the edges of his wings brushing along the pearly, featureless walls and ceiling. He took one turn, another, reached a dead end and doubled back, meanwhile striving to construct a map of the labyrinth in his mind.

Still, before long, he was all but certain he'd blundered down a blind alley he'd explored before. With every surface flat and blank, the maze was more like an abstract exercise in geometry than an actual place, and that made it easy to become confused.

But he had to get out, and quickly. It wouldn't help him to

escape back into the mundane world if he found every Tarterian in the valley already waiting to pounce on him when he did.

If, somewhere, an opening connected the maze to normal space, then perhaps air was flowing. In or out, it didn't matter, he could still use the breeze to orient himself. He tried to feel a draft, but couldn't.

He spewed a cloud of his hot, smoky breath, then studied the billowing fumes. They hung in the air for what felt like a long while, then started to waft in one direction.

Or at least he hoped they had. The drift was so subtle, it was impossible to be sure. No creature with vision less acute than a dragon's could have observed it, and it was possible that even he was only imagining it.

Instinct prompted him to dash against the current instead of with it. When he reached a choice point, he spewed more smoke. At that rate, he'd have no breath weapon left for fighting when he emerged onto the mountainside, but he'd just have to manage without it.

Soon his chest started to ache with the effort of generating so much vapor, and only a thin haze emerged when he expelled it. He lost track of how many turns he'd taken, and started to fear that, somehow, his plan was flawed, or else no egress existed. Then a rectangle of dark sky and stony earth appeared in the whiteness ahead.

He was so relieved to see it, he nearly flung himself heedlessly through, but remembered caution just in time. He stuck his head out, twisted his neck, peered, and spotted the Tarterian wheeling overhead.

He scrambled through the doorway, and with a magician's heightened awareness, felt the maze, deprived of its prisoner, wither from existence. He focused his attention, however, on the enemy above. He couldn't look up, because he didn't want it to know he'd sighted it, but trusted his hearing to tell him what it was doing.

Hide rattled and creaked as it furled its wings and dived. Brimstone waited until it was plummeting too fast to change course easily, then sprang. The Tarterian slammed down into the space he'd just vacated. Brimstone lashed his pinions and took to the air.

For the moment, he possessed the advantage of height, but it wasn't enough. Across the valley, other Tarterians shrieked and hissed as they raced in his direction. He had to end the confrontation quickly and get away.

Eyes burning like green fire, his foe glared at him, and power whined through the air. Brimstone tilted his wings and spun himself to the side. A bubble of shadow shimmered into existence where he'd been a split second before.

He riposted by conjuring darts of flame, which streaked at the Tarterian, splashed against its dorsal surface, but didn't seem to cause it any pain. It cocked back its head, opened its jaws, and spewed expanding ripples of something akin to pure force. Brimstone tried to dodge, but the breath weapon still clipped him, snapping the end of one pinion. He plummeted and smashed down hard.

The Tarterian sprang on top of him and pressed him against the cold, rocky ground. Its talons punctured his scales, and its jaws sought his neck.

All but immobilized, Brimstone frantically twisted his head into position to gaze into his adversary's luminous emerald eyes. Stop, he thought, stop fighting me. I'm your master, and you're my slave.

For a moment, it didn't seem as though it was going to work, and small wonder if it hadn't. The Tarterian had a dragon's strength of mind. But then it stopped tearing at him and cringed. Brimstone plunged his fangs into its throat. The Tarterian writhed for a moment, then went limp.

Yet Brimstone too found his will constrained, by need and greed. He was parched, weak, and the Tarterian's blood, though laced with bitterness, was an intoxicating fountain of vitality. He guzzled in a frenzy as fierce as the Rage.

But he had to stop. Had to, or his prey's kindred would overwhelm him, and Sammaster would win. Finally he managed to wrench his mouth away from the gushing wounds.

At once he discerned that he might have waited too long. Ragged shadows against the stars, the other wyrms were nearly upon him.

He couldn't retreat directly away from them, farther into the mountains. It was too likely he'd blunder into another snare. He'd have to flee at a right angle to their approach and swing back into the valley, even though it meant letting them get even closer than they were already.

At least his drink of blood had mended his broken wing. He sprang into the air and flew, meanwhile whispering a charm to augment his speed.

He beat high, swooped low, and zigzagged from side to side to throw off his pursuers' aims. Even so, some attacks found him. Another blast of breath weapon bashed him, shadowy, disembodied hands clawed him, and a mesh of gummy cable materialized on his wings, binding them until, with a flap, he tore the web apart. It was only a matter of time until one assault or another would kill him, cripple him, or at least slow him down enough for the Tarterians to catch up.

Peering about for anything that could help him, he spotted the entrance to the portal up ahead. He took stock and realized that his breath had renewed itself at least to a degree. He dived to earth in front of the cave, spewed smoke and embers, then scrambled inside.

As soon as he was out of his pursuers' view, he dissolved himself into vapor and sparks, identical, or so he hoped, with the haze he'd created a moment before.

The Tarterians thudded onto the ground and charged through the two overlapping clouds without perceiving any difference between them, then hurtled on down the passage.

Brimstone waited while his enemies vanished in the dark. Then he flowed through the smoke that was not himself, out into the open air, and onward, until he found a hiding place amid big, jumbled stones which, on closer inspection, turned out to the broken remains of a huge golem or earth elemental. Despite the erosion that had blurred its features, he could still make out eyes, an ear, and the contours of a three-fingered hand.

From that vantage point, he watched the Tarterians emerge, hissing and snarling to one another, presumably marveling at the abilities of the quarry who'd managed both to escape through the gate and to destroy it in the process.

He waited for some time after they dispersed, then skulked onward in search of his comrades. Eventually, he found Raryn scraping lichen from a rock. Alert as ever, the dwarf sensed his approach, pivoted in his direction, and raised his axe.

Brimstone congealed from smoke into solid form and said, "Don't be alarmed. It's me."

"I take it," Raryn said, "something kept you from stealing away."

"Magical snares seeded through the mountains."

The burly, white-bearded scout returned his attention to the lichen. His knife scritched against the stone. "Then it's good there's at least a little something to eat. I spotted bistort and coltsfoot, too."

Such provender may sustain you and the others for a time, Brimstone thought. *But when my thirst becomes too keen to bear, the only things I'll have to eat are you.*

EIGHT

13-16 Uktar, the Year of Rogue Dragons

In Sossal, corpses weren't hard to find. The slain lay where they'd fallen, buried only by the premature snows. But even so, Zethrindor's instincts led him to seek out an old cemetery, where sunken graves crumbled in on themselves, and weathered markers listed, a place given over by ritual and custom to the dominion of death.

He waited for the moon to set, then, hissing and murmuring incantations, used a talon to inscribe pentacles and sigils, some in the frozen earth, others on granite headstones and the facades of mausoleums. Several of the monuments, hallowed in the name of one beneficent power or another, couldn't bear the desecration without cracking or crumbling.

Gradually the night grew even colder, though, paradoxically, the graves began to smell more strongly of decay. Neither manifestation bothered him.

He snarled a final invocation, and something—the underlying structure of the world, perhaps, on which seas, plains, and mountains lay like paint on a canvas—moaned in protest. The patch of ground before him spun and churned like a whirlpool. A hollow formed at the center, and a horror oozed and clambered out of it into the open air. Essentially, it was shapeless, though Zethrindor could make out forms within the squirming central mass: a femur, skulls, a tarnished brass coffin handle, worms, and a length of stained and filthy winding sheet.

The thing peered back at him with several rudimentary eyes made of earth, mold, and scraps of rotten wood. "I wondered," it said, in a slow, slurred voice, "when you would next summon me."

"I name you G'holoq," Zethrindor said, "and I bind you by the staff, the crown, and the hexagon."

G'holoq laughed a muddy laugh, intensifying the ambient stench of rot, and a marker sculpted in the shape of the Earthmother, crowned with roses and holding a sheaf of grain, flowed and deformed like a melting candle. "Such caution between old friends! When did I ever attempt to deny you?"

"Never," Zethrindor said, "because I always constrained you properly."

"Ah, but then you were a mere wyrm. Now you're an omnipotent dracolich, predestined lord of a goodly portion of Faerûn. How, then, would a humble spirit like me dare to defy you, whether you performed the ceremony properly or not?"

Zethrindor bared his fangs. "Continue to mock me and I'll show you how powerful I've become."

"No need. I watched your final spat with Iyraclea. Very impressive. Have you wondered, though, what the Frostmaiden thinks of you, now that you've killed her special servant?"

"I don't care. The time of the gods is over."

"Is it, indeed? I can't image why you bother fishing oracles out of graveyards when you're already privy to such extraordinary secrets."

"With the staff," Zethrindor said, "I strike you."

G'holoq's amorphous body burst into blue flame. The demon writhed and howled until the dragon willed the blaze to go out.

"I warned you," Zethrindor said. "I'm not in the mood for your japes."

"So I see," G'holoq croaked. "Ask your three questions, then, and we'll be free of the annoyance of one another's company."

"The portal in the Novularonds. Where did it lead?"

"I don't know."

"By the crown, I rule you."

The blue flame burned brighter, and didn't just sear G'holoq's surface. It devoured portions of the demon's body entirely. When Zethrindor extinguished it, G'holoq lay in several chunks, which sluggishly extended feelers toward one another and seeped back into a single mass.

"I've already invoked the staff and the crown," the dragon said. "If we proceed to the hexagon, you'll burn until my own existence comes to an end, and that, I assure you, means forever."

"I can't answer if I don't know the answer! A wizard as powerful as Sammaster can conceal his designs even from entities like me."

"Then we'll turn to matters of more immediate concern. I'm having difficulty locating what remains of the Sossrim army."

"Despite all your sorcery, and all your flying scouts flapping hither and yon? It's all but impossible to imagine."

That, too, sounded like mockery, and Zethrindor felt tempted to punish G'holoq yet again. Unfortunately, though, he had, in his impatience, already run through the lesser, finite chastisements. Satisfaction would come at the cost of terminating the interview, and deprive him of the opportunity to make use of the demon in times to come.

"The surviving druids are powerful," he gritted, "and this is their country. They know every inch of it, and have a special bond with it."

"Also," G'holoq said, "the snows Auril sent to help the Ice Queen are, understandably, no friends to Iyraclea's slayer. They baffle the eyes of your observers, and likewise hinder your divinations."

"Well, for your sake, let's hope they won't hinder you. Where are the Sossrim forces?"

"I'll show you." The patch of ground in front of G'holoq heaved and twisted, configuring itself into a three-dimensional map of Sossal. Several squares of green phosphorescence appeared on hills and in valleys. Presumably, the larger the luminous rectangle, the bigger the band of soldiers.

"Good," Zethrindor said. "Now, where are they heading, or, if they aren't moving yet, where do they intend to go?"

The fiend responded by willing glowing bluish trails into being. They all converged on a single point. The Sossrim were on the verge of uniting into one force.

But they hadn't done it yet. At the moment, each of the companies was vulnerable. Zethrindor poised a claw above the representation of the largest. "I'll wager Madislak Pemsk is traveling with this force."

"I've already answered three questions."

The white spat a puff of frost. "And need answer no more. My course is obvious. If my army marches immediately, I can intercept the biggest Sossrim company here, before it links up with the others. With luck, I'll take it by surprise; I'll overwhelm it with superior numbers in any case. Then it will be easy to pick off the rest."

He wouldn't even need his fellow wyrms anymore, and that was just as well. They were growing restless, eager to abandon the war and undergo their own transformations into dracoliches before madness overtook them. Well, after they helped him win a final, decisive victory, they were welcome to depart. It would mean that much more plunder for their chieftain.

"It should work," G'holoq said. "I see no reason why it wouldn't. Milord . . . if you do become one of the kings of Faerûn, remember me kindly. If I've ever spoken to you scornfully, it's only because it's my nature. In the end, I've always served you well."

Zethrindor sneered. "If you were prudent, you'd be hoping I'll forget you." He turned, unfurled his pinions, and leaped into the air.

The smoke stung Taegan's eyes, and considering what a niggardly little fire Raryn had built—fuel was all but nonexistent, and they didn't dare produce an excess of light in any case, for fear of attracting the Tarterians' attention—that hardly seemed fair. How could a blaze that scarcely warmed a person even when he was sitting right beside it foul the air throughout the entire cave?

Brimstone crouched peering into the flames and whispering. Kara and Raryn watched intently, even though Taegan assumed that, like himself, they'd pretty much abandoned hope of the smoke drake's trick ever working. Brimstone had attempted it several times already, and sure enough, eventually he scowled and shifted his smoldering gaze away from the fire.

Kara sighed. Despite meager food and the constant chill, her cuts were healing quickly, thanks to her draconic vitality and Raryn's healing charms. But she seemed strained and dispirited even so.

"I don't understand," she said. "You spoke to me when we were hundreds of miles apart. Firefingers surely has a flame burning somewhere close at hand—"

"Our current location is warded," Brimstone whispered. "You know that perfectly well, so why are you prattling?"

"I—" For an instant, anger blazed in her amethyst eyes, and a blue tinge washed across her skin, but then she mastered herself. "You're right. I didn't mean to criticize. I'm simply frustrated."

Raryn, who'd set his broad, ruddy hand on his axe when the two dragons began to quarrel, casually moved it away again. "As are we all. But even if we managed to contact Thentia, who's to say it would do any good? We couldn't tell the mages where we are, because we don't know ourselves."

Taegan grinned. "If that's your idea of providing solace, your technique needs work."

Kara stood up and adjusted the folds of her mantle. "It's time to go."

"I don't know about that," Raryn said. "My hunch is that the Tarterians are still stirred up from their brush with Brimstone. We could give them another day to settle down. The less active and alert they are, the safer we'll be wandering around in the open."

The bard smiled a twisted smile. "Trust me, my friend, you don't want to spend two more days just sitting cooped up in a hole with me. Not . . . not in my present humor."

Raryn shrugged his massive shoulders. "I trust you, singer, now and tomorrow, in a cave or anyplace else. But for that same reason, I'll follow your lead."

"Whereas I," said Taegan, "have always followed where beauty led, and never regretted it yet. Well, give or take a few disgruntled husbands."

"It's time to be quiet," Brimstone said. He led his companions to the mouth of the cave.

Outside, it was night. As Taegan had discovered, the far north, at the time of year, the nights were absurdly long and the days, ridiculously short. It was one of the many unpleasant peculiarities of the place, albeit one for which eldritch sorcery bore no responsibility.

At least it made it marginally safer to sneak around. Dragons could see well in the dark, but not as far as they could by day. Or at least that was the way it worked with earthly drakes. It hadn't bolstered Taegan's morale to learn that Brimstone and Kara weren't entirely certain the same was true of wyrms hailing from the netherworld.

Raryn took the lead, prowling several yards ahead of his companions. In theory, he'd spot any danger first. But after a while, Kara, in a low but urgent voice, called to him to stop and back up. The hunter retreated a few steps, and a reddish shimmer danced through the air as another vestige of ancient magic manifested. It nauseated Taegan to look at it, and though it didn't throw off any perceptible heat, stones on the ground beneath it cracked apart, or melted and bubbled into liquid.

The display ended after a few heartbeats, but the seekers still swung wide around that particular spot. Then they crept onward, while disembodied voices whispered, and the landscape periodically seemed to alter, though afterward, Taegan could never say exactly how it had changed. He picked his way through bones—avariel bones, as often as not—and the cold wind moaned and plucked at his garments. Those things, at least, didn't change.

Something vast—vague as mist, but projecting a terrifying sense of power and malice nonetheless—floated upward from the ground on the procession's right flank. As it spread its bat-like wings and opened its reptilian jaws, Taegan realized it had actually oozed through and risen out of the earth. It was a ghost dragon they'd seen before, taking advantage of its insubstantial nature to sneak up on them.

Until then, the seekers had only observed the wraith stalking around one particular area in the northern part of the valley, a spot well removed from their present course. They hadn't expected to encounter it here, and it looked as if that miscalculation might cost them dearly.

Taegan raised Rilitar's blade, unfurled his pinions, and rattled off the first line of a defensive charm. Swelling from woman into drake, Kara started singing a spell of her own. Raryn lifted his axe.

"No!" Brimstone snarled. "Don't attack it!" With a bound and a snap of his charcoal-colored wings, he interposed himself between his companions and the ghost.

For what seemed a long while, he and the specter simply stared into one another's eyes. Then the ghost turned and crawled away.

"Nicely done," Raryn said. "I take it that one undead recognizes another."

"Tonight it did," Brimstone whispered. "Its mind is faded and broken, and I can't vouch for what it might do in the future. Let's hope we can avoid it from now on."

Kara dwindled back into human form.

They wanted to get inside the castle as quickly as possible, to make sure the Tarterians wouldn't spot them. Still, as they drew near, Taegan had to pause for a heartbeat or two to marvel at the place. Towering and massive as it was, the stronghold simultaneously, paradoxically, gave an impression of exquisite grace surpassing the loveliest temple in Lyrabar. He supposed the builders' mastery of proportion was responsible.

"The ancient wizards raised this place for a fell purpose," he said, "in desperate times, in the most remote, inhospitable place they could reach. Yet it's beautiful."

Kara smiled. "Your people," she said, "rarely build anything that isn't."

Brimstone spoke a word of power. The immense gates at the end of the barbican groaned open, and behind them, a rattling portcullis rose. The tunnel-like passageway into the castle lay open before them. The vampire stalked to the threshold, took a look around, then stepped inside.

He vanished.

Taegan rounded on Kara. "What just happened?" he asked. "Did he blunder into another maze trap?"

"I don't think so," she said. "Not exactly."

"Then what did happen?"

"I'll try to find out." She crooned spells, and power tingled over Taegan's skin. He and Raryn looked around, watching for Tarterians and other menaces.

A dark, winged shape wheeled and set down in front of them. Taegan felt a jolt of alarm, then perceived that the wyrm's eyes shined crimson, not green, and that it smelled of burning.

He lowered his sword. "I trust that wasn't your idea of a jest," he said. "Otherwise, your timing is exceptionally poor."

Brimstone showed his misshapen fangs. "I ran afoul of another ward. Fortunately, not a lethal one. A single stride carried me beyond the far wall of the citadel, as if it, and the ground it sits on, don't truly exist."

"Someone twisted space," Kara said.

"Who," Taegan asked, "the builders, or Sammaster? I ask because it occurs to me that a barrier erected by elves might not keep out an avariel."

"A reasonable conjecture," Brimstone whispered. "But I suspect it was Sammaster. I recognize the taste of his power."

"Whoever did it," Raryn said, still watching their surroundings instead of his companions, "maybe he only put the enchantment on the doors. The three of you can fly over walls."

Taegan grinned. "Astutely reasoned. I'll find out." He lashed his wings and took to the air.

As he rose toward the pale, crumbling battlements, he felt horribly exposed, but exhilarated, too. It felt good to fly after days spent creeping on the ground. It would have felt even better with Jivex for company, and he wondered if the faerie dragon was still alive.

He climbed high enough to look over the ramparts, at towers and keeps, some collapsing, others not, and the bones of those who'd perished inside the fortress. He raced forward—

Nothing lay before him but desolate snowy ground and the mountains beyond. He had to turn around to see the castle. It didn't have any major entrances on that side, just a sally-port or two.

He recited his spell of translocation. The magic discharged itself over his body in a stinging, sparking crackle, but failed to shift him inside the fortress as he'd commanded.

He cursed and flew over the merlons on that side. An instant later, the long, protruding structure that was the barbican lay beneath him.

As he descended, Brimstone, then dissolved into billowing smoke, flowed into the mouth of the gateway. From his vantage point, Taegan couldn't see what happened, but from Kara and Raryn's subsequent failure to exhibit any excitement, he was able to surmise. The vampire hadn't been able to enter the citadel in cloud form, either.

At least, like Taegan, he'd realized he could use the ward to return to his starting point quickly. Solid flesh and bone once more, he reappeared just moments later.

"It looks to me," Raryn said, "as if there's only one way we're getting in. You sorcerers will have to use your own magic to knock down the ward."

Brimstone spat sulfurous smoke. "Pit our power against Sammaster's."

The dwarf shrugged. "It's two of you against one of him."

"The notion," Taegan said, "also appears to be the only arrow left in the bag."

"They're right," Kara said. "We have to try."

"Of course," Brimstone growled. "But no ordinary counterspell will do the job. We'll need to prepare the ground . . ."

The two drakes embarked on a technical discussion that Taegan simply couldn't follow. He put himself back on watch, but it was Raryn who abruptly whispered, "Everyone, be quiet! Get under cover!"

Taegan, the dwarf, and Kara scurried into the shadow of a mound of rocks. Brimstone was too large to conceal himself there or anyplace else close at hand, but he scrambled back inside the barbican and disappeared.

A Tarterian screeched its mournful screech as it glided overhead, and along with the usual dread, Taegan felt a surge of frustration and futility. Because he and his companions were fools. Kara and Brimstone were discussing a ritual that sounded as if it would take a long while, and the Tarterians were bound to come and check on the fortress before the ceremony could reach a successful conclusion.

The scalp on the human side of Dorn's head itched, and he scowled, pushed back his hood for a moment, and scratched. Maybe he should have washed, trimmed his hair, and shaved when it would have been convenient. But he hadn't felt like bothering, nor did he truly regret it even then. It suited him to be filthy and uncomfortable.

At his back, Will cursed. Dorn glanced around. The half-ling was all right, simply floundering through a particularly deep snow drift that lay across the steep, narrow mountain trail.

" 'Hidden paths,' my freckled arse," said Will. "This is supposed to be a path? Well, maybe if I could turn into a wolf or a hare like half these Sossrim can."

"I'd be thrilled," Pavel drawled, "if you could turn into one of those beasts. Or any creature more intelligent than is your natural state. It would be a blessing." He had a new mace dangling from his belt, and carried a new arbalest in his hands. The Sossrim had given him and his fellow travelers some of their surplus gear.

"Since when do you know anything about blessings?" Will replied. "Such matters are the province of genuine priests."

They bickered on, trading gibes, while anger clenched in Dorn's guts and swelled inside his chest. Finally, he had to let it out. "Enough!" he snapped, and only realized he'd yelled when the sound rebounded from another mountainside. Startled, his comrades gawked at him.

"We need to be quiet," he said awkwardly.

Will waved a gloved hand at their snowy surroundings. At the moment, they could see for a considerable distance in every direction. "Nobody's around. Anyway, the charlatan and I were talking quietly. The fool making the most noise was you."

Pavel set his hand on the halfling's shoulder. "No, Dorn's right," he said. "It's better to be safe."

Dorn could tell the priest was simply humoring him and trying to avert a full-blown quarrel. That, and the pity in Pavel's brown eyes, triggered another spasm of ire. But he didn't want to fight either, so he clamped down on the emotion, pivoted, and trudged on up the trail. His friends tramped—and Jivex flew—after him in silence.

They reached the top of one peak, descended a bit, crossed a saddle to another mountain, and climbed once more. Scales rippling with rainbows, Jivex streaked ahead of Dorn, reached the next summit, then hissed. Dorn scrambled the last few paces to find out what had surprised the little drake.

An army marched in the vale below them. Like the Sossrim host with their fair skin, moon-blond hair, and snow-colored cloaks, on first inspection, Zethrindor's force seemed ghostly white. The towering frost giants were pale as marble, the dwarves had silvery hair and wore the fur of polar bears and arctic wolves, and the dragons, ice drakes, and tundra landwyrms were like gleaming ivory gargoyles brought to life.

Hide mottled with patches of rot, sunken eyes gleaming, Zethrindor strode along in the midst of his warriors. Here was the abomination whose magic had killed Kara, and rigid with hate, Dorn stared at him.

Pavel hurried up behind him, took in the vista below, and said, "Get down!"

Dorn knew his friend was talking sense, but it didn't matter. At the moment, he couldn't do as he'd been bidden, and wasn't even sure he wanted to.

At some point during the last couple heartbeats, Jivex had become invisible. Dorn felt a gust of displaced air and caught the rustle of beating wings as the faerie dragon flew close to his head. Then pain, abrupt and unexpected, stung his ear lobe. The reptile had either nipped him or pinched him with his talons.

"Now," Jivex snarled, "is not the time to go all strange and stupid. Get down!"

Dorn crouched down in the snow, as did his friends. Perhaps not a moment too soon, for he spotted a couple of wyrms—lookouts, plainly—gliding high above the host on the ground.

"Well," said Will after a time, "there are a lot of them, but I imagine we can sneak by if we're careful. Or, we could stay put and hide until they pass us."

"Unfortunately," said Pavel, "it's not that simple. It's obvious from the direction they're headed that Zethrindor somehow knows the location of Madislak's company. He means to come up on their flank, attack by surprise, and slaughter them before they can link up with the rest of the Sossrim."

Will sighed. "You're saying somebody needs to warn them."

"They're on the right side of this war, and if that's not enough for you, they helped us."

Jivex sniffed. "At first they were going to shoot me full of arrows in my sleep. But then, they are just warmbloods. I suppose I have to make allowances."

"I sympathize with them," said Will, "I swear by the silent dirk I do, but if we turn back now, it won't be easy to reach these paths a second time. Zethrindor's army will be in the way, and we have our own business to attend to. You and I, charlatan, diverted from it once already to help drive the Vaasans out of Damara, but I figured that was because Damara's your homeland. Do you really want to push our luck again?"

"No," Pavel said. "But we can't simply turn our backs on folk in need, no matter what other matters weigh on us. It would be a sin."

"You three press on to Thentia," said Dorn, his torn ear smarting and dripping blood. "I'll go back and warn the Sossrim."

Will and Pavel regarded him in silence. Then the priest said, "No. It's as Jivex said, back in the Novularonds. We four should stick together."

"Right," Will said. "If Lady Luck smiles on us, maybe we'll still make Thentia in time for the conclave. If not, well, what did we truly have to contribute anyway? News of a magical doorway that doesn't open anymore. How's that going to help?"

As he looked at their faces, Dorn realized why they wouldn't let him go alone. They believed he meant to use the Sossrim's war as a means of engineering his own death.

He wasn't even sure whether their fears were justified, but he did know he resented their solicitude. For a moment, he felt as if he was going to curse them for it. But in the end, he simply growled, "We should get moving, then. We can travel faster than an army, but we still need to hurry if we're going to arrive far enough ahead of them for it to matter."

Taegan gave Kara a rake's grin, full of bravado. "I'm flattered beyond words," he said, "by your concern. I daresay Raryn feels the same. But we'll be fine. There are only six Tarterians in the valley, and I imagine one is still feeble from Brimstone's bite. We should have little difficulty flummoxing such a paltry force."

"It comes down to this," said the dwarf, sitting cross-legged on the floor of the cave and scraping away at the flint head of his axe with another stone. "Brimstone discovered that if something creates a disturbance, all the dark wyrms come rushing to investigate. Scouting, I've learned more about their habits. Now we need to put the knowledge to use. It's the only edge we've got."

"I know," said Kara. "But perhaps if we studied the situation a while longer, we'd hit on a better idea."

"Or else we wouldn't," said the dwarf. "We'd just grow hungrier, weaker, and—forgive me—less clear-headed, less able to work magic, with the passing time."

"Raryn Snowstealer is right," whispered Brimstone. He crouched deeper in the cave—Taegan suspected he was keeping his distance from his companions to help rein in his blood-thirst—and the gloom reduced him to an enormous shadow with burning scarlet eyes.

"Perhaps," Kara said, peering at Raryn and Taegan, "but at least promise me you'll be careful. Look in your hearts, and make sure you aren't doing this for the wrong reasons."

Raryn smiled. "You mean, because I blundered on the glacier, led us all into disaster, and now feel a need to atone? Or because I'm suddenly ashamed of my people and their treachery? Don't worry, singer. I'm not happy about any of that, but I'm not giving it a lot of thought, either. I'm concentrating of the job that needs doing here and now."

"Nor am I," Taegan drawled, "ashamed of holding my own race in less esteem than is its due." Actually, he was, but it wasn't his habit to admit his blunders. "I have, however, discovered I possess a noble heritage, and arguably ought to make some effort to live up to it. My ancestors gave their lives to liberate Faerûn from the tyranny of evil dragons, and it would be poor form for me to let Sammaster undo their achievement."

Brimstone spat, suffusing the cold air with the stink of acrid smoke and rotten eggs. "It doesn't matter why they'll do it, Karasendrieth, only that they're willing. You must know that, even with frenzy gnawing at your mind."

Kara sighed. "Yes, of course. Let's lay our plans."

Pavel had learned that druids dominated the religious life of Sossal. Priests of his sort were a rarity. Still, like most decent folk, the Sossrim honored the Morninglord, and the warriors welcomed whatever aid and solace one of his servants could give them. Accordingly, when the company made one of its brief stops, he had less opportunity to rest than his companions, even though, after the frantic trek to warn them of Zethrindor's approach, he probably needed it more.

His sun amulet clasped in his hand, he prayed for Lathander's blessing, invoking bursts of dawnlight that lifted the spirit and temporarily banished fatigue from weary muscles. He used magic and his physician's skills to help men afflicted with blisters, fevers, and coughs.

Then the army rushed on once more, and he rushed with it, his bad leg aching. He struggled against the temptation to ease his own pain with a spell. He was running through his store of magic quickly, and didn't want to waste power he might truly need later on.

Stival fell into step beside him. "You're limping," the stocky ranger said. "Are you all right?"

"Fine," Pavel gasped. "I've had this for a while."

"The river's not much farther," Stival said. "Once we're across, I imagine Madislak will let us camp."

Upon learning of Zethrindor's intentions, the old druid had turned his army east, toward a river that had supposedly frozen solid enough for them to cross. When they reached the other side, Madislak, aided by his fellow spellcasters, planned to melt the ice, thus balking their foes. Only winged creatures like the dracolich, the white wyrms, and the ice drakes would be able to continue the pursuit, and Stival and his fellow captains doubted the reptiles, mighty though they were, would opt to attack without the support of their underlings.

Pavel's steaming breath glowed in Selûne's silvery light. The army advanced with a muted crunching as hundreds of footsteps broke through the crusted snow. The world repeatedly lurched and shifted, and he realized he was dozing off and jerking awake again. It didn't seem to stop him from walking, so perhaps he should be grateful not to experience every miserable instant of the march.

"I keep thinking," Stival murmured after a time, "I could have been in Damara by now, serving this Dragonsbane you talk about, or one of his barons."

Pavel snorted. "You wouldn't abandon your own country in its time of need."

"Apparently not, but I did consider it," Stival said. Evidently, cold as it was, the march was making him too warm, for he pulled open the front of his bearskin mantle. "My idea of soldiering is, you chase bandits and goblins. Enemies trained warriors can handle without a lot of trouble. Or, if you have to fight something awful, like a dragon, you make sure it's only one, you bring overwhelming force against it, and you make sure you get the bulk of the credit for killing it. That's the way to build a reputation and still keep all your limbs attached to your trunk. This craziness . . . " He shook his head. "A man could get hurt in the middle of this. Yet here I am."

"Perhaps you just couldn't bear to leave Natali behind. I've seen how you look at her when her back is turned."

"You must have bad eyes to go with the gimpy leg. She's a good lass, but a rich widow's what I want. A woman with the experience and gold to take care of me in and out of bed."

"Then you won't mind if I whisper in Natali's ear?"

Stival made a sour face. "Go ahead and try. She won't—" He looked up at the black and starry sky. "Curse it!"

Pavel peered upward, too, and after a few moments, spotted pallid wings lashing high overhead. A clamor of dismay swelled among the company as other men caught sight of the creature.

For another heartbeat or so, Pavel dared to hope that the situation wasn't so bad. If the white was simply a lone scout, flying well in advance of the rest of Zethrindor's army—

But no. Other serpentine shapes winged their way across the sky, over the Sossrim and into the east. Pavel was no master strategist like Dragonsbane, but it was easy enough to understand what was happening. The drakes would block the way to the river, and could almost certainly hold there long enough for the rest of Zethrindor's host to catch up with their foes. Then Madislak's company would find itself trapped with enemies in front and behind.

The procession stumbled to a ragged halt. Some men milled around. Others, like Pavel, flopped down in the snow until new orders made the rounds. It seemed that the company was marching north.

Wherever they were headed, Madislak meant to get their quickly. He must have inferred from the dragons' maneuvering that the rest of Zethrindor's force had nearly caught up with them. Stival and other officers ranged among the common soldiers, encouraging them and bellowing threats by turns, exhorting them to greater speed.

Finally Pavel had no choice but to use a healing prayer on his leg, in his exhaustion nearly fumbling over the proper cadence. Even magic didn't produce the surge of strength or exuberant sense of health it sometimes did, but at least it numbed the pain.

Sometime after that, he realized with dull surprise that Dorn had put his arm around him and was half-carrying him along. He thanked him, and the big man responded with a grunt.

The ground rose, and the edge of a sizable forest loomed up on the right, where it could guard an army's flank. As the sky brightened behind the trees, the Sossrim clambered up onto a tableland, and the officers herded the various squads to one position or another, establishing a formation. Obviously, that was where Madislak wanted to make his stand.

As soon as their superiors gave them leave, warriors collapsed wherever they happened to be standing. Pavel wanted to do the same, but had to attend to his observances first. He disentangled himself from Dorn's arm, faced the dawn, and somewhat groggily started to pray.

Soon he felt Lathander's bright and loving presence hovering near. The communion didn't purge the exhaustion from his body, but it cleared his mind and refreshed his spirit, dampening fear and the urge to despair.

He asked for the spells he'd need to see him through the battle to come, and with flares of bracing light and warmth that only he could perceive, the god emplaced them in his mind like arrows in a quiver.

When the process was done, he lay down wrapped in his cloak and bedroll, to sleep as long as Zethrindor would permit.

NINE

17 Uktar, the Year of Rogue Dragons

Kneeling, gripping Rilitar's sword partway down the blade, Taegan scratched away with it as if it were a stylus, and the point inscribed lines and curves in the slope. He disliked treating the superb weapon in such a churlish way, but it cut the frozen earth far more easily than a chunk of rock would have done, and it was an aspect of its excellence that even such rough usage wouldn't dull it.

When he finished, he worked the incipient soreness out of his fingers—it had been awkward to grip the blade in a way that ensured he wouldn't cut himself—and inspected his handiwork, a crude but recognizable copy of the flame, eyes, and claws emblem of the Cult of the Dragon. Presumably the Tarterians, being Sammaster's allies or servants, knew what that particular device signified. Even if not, it would still give them something to puzzle over.

It was time for the difficult part. Taegan contemplated what was to come, and despite all that he'd already experienced and survived, felt a pang of dread.

He currently possessed every advantage his magic, and that of his comrades, could provide, layered enchantments to make him as elusive as possible. Bladesong rendered him stronger, more nimble, and could provide other benefits when he found himself hard-pressed. Kara had shrouded him in invisibility. Raryn had heightened his endurance, granted him the ability to see in utter darkness, deadened his scent, and insured his feet would leave no tracks. Brimstone claimed to have sharpened his wits—though Taegan preferred to believe that was scarcely possible—and to have supplied a protection that might enable him to go where even Tarterians wouldn't follow.

Yet against half a dozen wyrms, creatures Sammaster had conjured from the foulest reaches of the netherworld, could such tricks possibly prevail?

Well, Taegan told himself, pushing trepidation aside, they'd have to, wouldn't they? Because, while he and his friends could die—indeed, expected to, in one way or another, for all that they forbore to say it outright—they couldn't fail. The stakes were too high.

He breathed a prayer to sweet Lady Firehair, then, on impulse, petitioned Aerdrie Faenya, principal goddess of the avariels, as well. Since he hadn't acknowledged the Winged Mother since forsaking his tribe, it seemed unlikely she'd listen with any particular sympathy, but perhaps she'd help him in order to preserve the legacy of his ancestors.

He drew a deep breath, then shouted across the valley: "Sammaster is here! Attend me!"

Then he fled, flying fast along the inner slopes, skimming low over scree, snowdrifts, and the gouged places where the Tarterians, who could apparently subsist on most anything, had made a meal of earth and rock.

He kept on for as long as he dared, while, hissing and screeching to one another, the Tarterians winged their way closer. Finally he lit in the shadow of a boulder. He was trying his best to be stealthy, but still worried that, once the drakes drew near enough, their keen ears would catch the snap and rustle of his pinions.

He waited tensely until it became clear that the gigantic reptiles' attention was centered on the approximate point from which he'd called, not his current hiding place. They hadn't perceived him moving from one spot to the other. That was reassuring, albeit, not profoundly so, not when they were casting their net widely enough that, on two occasions, a vast winged shadow swept right over him.

It only took a few moments for one of the reptiles to notice the mark he'd left behind. It cried to the others, and tilting and furling their wings, they all came wheeling and thudding down to earth to inspect the sigil more closely, peer about, and hiss and snarl.

Taegan couldn't speak their language and had no idea what they were saying to one another, but he thought they had an air of perplexity that might have been comical in other circumstances. To say the least, it seemed unlikely they actually believed that Sammaster had returned to the valley to play childish games with them, but they couldn't figure out the point of what really was happening.

The answer was simple mystification. Anything to befuddle them and keep them on that end of the vale while Kara and Brimstone labored to penetrate the citadel.

Three of the Tarterians bounded back into the air and resumed their wheeling scrutiny of the slopes. Their fellows stalked around on foot, forked tongues flickering, sniffing the air and ground like enormous hounds. Taegan held his breath whenever one prowled too close, but feared the reptile might still hear the pounding of his heart. He could certainly feel it, beating in the arteries in his neck.

They didn't find him, though. His father had taught him how to conceal himself, his comrades were able spellcasters, and perhaps the fact that the Tarterians were probably looking for Brimstone again, not a considerably smaller creature, aided him as well.

So it was all right. Until the great dark creatures with their mottling of lighter scales and lambent green eyes shrieked to one another, and the trio on the ground beat their ragged wings. Then all six flew out over the ancient battlefield with its carpet of tangled bones.

Which was to say, they were moving their hunt elsewhere, and Taegan couldn't allow that. He picked up a stone and threw it as far as he could, to crack down on the slope and start other rocks tumbling and rattling.

The Tarterians wheeled, orienting on the noise. Taegan flew in the opposite direction, toward a shadowy depression that ought to serve for a second hiding place.

Will found Pavel still asleep, and taking care not to bump the gimpy leg, or do any other actual harm, kicked him in the side until his eyes fluttered open.

"You poxy dung beetle," the human croaked.

Will grinned and proffered a steaming tin cup. "Lentils and beef stock. Not too vile, for army food. Drink it while you have the chance."

Pavel tossed off his blankets and stood up. Will was relieved to see that his leg didn't appear to be giving him any more trouble. He sipped the soup, then asked, "How long did I sleep?"

"Most of the day, sluggard. Once we won the race to get here, Zethrindor and his crew apparently slowed down. So they could march up in good order, maybe, with all sorts of obnoxious enchantments in place. But they're coming now." He pointed.

Some distance beyond the foot of the tableland, the snow appeared to stir like the rippling, heaving surface of the sea. Then the eye picked out individual shapes from the all-encompassing white: Striding giants, barbarians, and dwarves; and crawling wyrms. Other drakes wheeled and darted against a leaden sky.

Pavel studied the oncoming horde, then gulped the rest of his meal, stooped, and collected his weapons. "Let's find Dorn."

"He's with Stival and his troop. Madislak shuffled the squads around and put them—us—over this way."

They wended their way through a host making its final preparations for battle. Warriors honed blades and arrowheads, reinforced ramparts built of branches and packed snow, or kneeled to accept the blessings of one or another of the lesser druids. The greater ones were busy at the center of the company, swaying and murmuring in front of fires that leaped and changed color in response to their incantations, or declaiming words of power that made the cold air gust and the ground tremble and grumble. Wolverines, badgers, stags, and even a shaggy, hulking bear prowled among Mielikki's servants as though awaiting instructions.

A bowman bustled into the midst of the ritual preparations and jabbered a question, interrupting Madislak in the midst of a prayer. The stooped, scrawny old man with his bald, brown-spotted crown spun around glaring.

"You officers know the strategy!" he snarled. "Is it too much to ask you to manage the tactics by yourselves? It is supposed to be your area of competence, isn't it? Then go away and let me work!"

Stival's troop stood on the western side of the ridge, not too far from the point where the ground fell away so precipitously that it would be difficult for any of the Sossrim's foes to flank them on that side. Well, any but the white dragons and ice drakes, who could probably fly wherever they cared to go. Dorn was there, filthy and sullen, iron fingers repeatedly clenching on his longbow. Wings flickering, snapping the occasional bug from the air, Jivex darted hither and yon. The bands of color streaming down his flanks seemed almost dazzling on an afternoon when everything else was white and gray.

For the moment, at least. Will reflected that he'd likely start seeing plenty of red in just a little while.

"Hello," Stival said. "You look like you feel better, Master Shemov."

"I do," Pavel replied.

"Then may we have your blessing?"

"Of course."

The Damaran brandished his amulet, invoking a golden glow. Will felt a bracing surge of resolution and vitality. Other folk smiled, or sighed and closed their eyes, as Lathander's grace buoyed their spirits. Dorn, however, scowled and turned away from the light, spurning the god's gift as, since Kara's death, he'd rejected all efforts at comfort.

"Now, then," Pavel said, "what's our specific role in Madislak's strategy? Knowing will help me determine how best to employ the rest of my spells."

"Well," Stival said, "naturally, it's everybody's job to hold the ridge. But beyond that, you have experience fighting dragons, so do I, and so do the rest of these fellows. So, if somebody has to get in close and meet one of the beasts blade to claw, it's likely to be us."

Jivex hissed. "Dragons aren't 'beasts.' Not even the dull-witted runts out there."

Some of the warriors grinned at the little drake's display of indignation, or maybe, at his calling wyrms a hundred times larger than himself 'runts.' Trying to suppress his own smile, Stival began to offer an apology. But before he could finish, the enemy attacked.

Enormous hailstones hammered down on portions of the Sossrim line, breaking heads and limbs despite the protection of helms and armor. Flares of pure cold froze men into rime-encrusted statues. Bursts of shadow, rushing in like breaking waves or leaping up from the ground like geysers, rotted flesh, or sent folk reeling in shrieking terror.

Behind the cover of that sudden barrage of magic, Zethrindor's army charged. The warriors on the ground roared their battle cries and sprinted forward. The drakes in the air lashed their wings and hurtled at the top of the hill.

Unfortunately for them, however, their initial ploy didn't work as well as Zethrindor had no doubt hoped. Sorcery had torn chinks in the Sossrim line, but hadn't thrown it into disarray. The wards and blessings cast beforehand, and the protection afforded by the improvised fortifications, had saved most of the defenders, and they drew their bowstrings back to their ears. The whole ridge seemed to creak with the sound of flexing wood.

"Shoot!" Stival shouted. Other captains yelled it, too.

The volley clattered and thrummed. Pavel's crossbow, the only such weapon in the immediate vicinity, gave a distinctive snap amid the ambient drone.

At the same time, the Sossrim druids and wizards struck at the dragons on the wing. Explosions of flame engulfed them, twisting, crackling thunderbolts speared them, and howling whirlwinds, visible thanks to the snow spinning inside, leaped at them. Clouds of stinging flies materialized to swarm on them.

The magical harassment flung the flying dragons backward, while the hurtling arrows balked the attackers on the ground. Many toppled, pierced. Some tried to shoot back, but the bows of the Great Glacier were inferior to those of Sossal, where the proper sort of trees for bow-making grew, coaxed by druids to provide wood perfectly suited to the purpose, and most of the shafts fell short.

Though the frost giants could cope with the range and the disadvantage of lower ground. Their strength compensated for the inferior quality of their gear. An arrow the size of a human longspear drove into the torso of a warrior near Will and slammed him back into the soldiers standing behind him.

When the first exchange concluded, Will couldn't tell who, if anyone, had gotten the better of it. The Sossrim had kept the flying dragons from descending on them, and their defensive line remained intact. But they'd also, in just a few heartbeats, sustained casualties that no army, facing superior numbers, could easily afford.

At the foot of the hill, Zethrindor snarled orders. Will couldn't catch the words, but the meaning became clear enough when some of the attacking force split off and headed into the forest. They meant to use the trees to shield them from further volleys of arrows while they advanced on the Sossrims's eastern flank.

Will hoped some defensive measure was in place to counter such a move, but he didn't know what it was. That was one of the many things he hated about war: the feeling that most of the time, he didn't fully understand what was happening and certainly had no hope of controlling it.

Arrows flew back and forth. Magic filled the air with strange smells and pulses of warmth and chill as the spellcasters chanted it into being. The white dragons tried again to fly at the ridge, and as before, the Sossrim druids and wizards created bursts of flame, and conjured warriors of living fire and wind, to bar the way. The wyrms fell back.

Their quivers nearly empty already, archers cried for more arrows, or yanked shafts from the ground, the ramparts of snow and sticks, and the bodies of fallen comrades. A man near Will caught a shaft in the chest, smiled as if delighted to discover the wound hadn't inconvenienced him in the slightest, then collapsed.

Stival chaffed Pavel on how long it took to cock an arbalest. The human side of his mouth sneering, Dorn shot methodically at whatever target presented itself. No doubt he would have preferred to attack Zethrindor, but the undead white hadn't yet ventured into range. Thus far, the dracolich was directing his army more or less from the rear, evidently holding his own terrible prowess in reserve for later.

Meanwhile, Will simply stood and watched. The sling the Sossrim had given him was a decent weapon, but it couldn't throw a missile as far as a bow, and at that point, the enemy was simply too distant.

Or so he imagined. But then, closer to the center of the battle line, earth and snow heaved, a section of the ramparts collapsed, and a gigantic, wingless dirty-white wyrm burst up out of the ground. Pale blue eyes blazing, it snagged an archer with its stubby foreclaws, conveyed him to its jaws, plunged its fangs into him, and sucked at him in a way that reminded Will of Brimstone. The white drake only guzzled for an instant, though, before spitting out its first victim and reaching for another.

The blood-drinker was a tundra landwyrm. Will had never encountered one before, but recognized it from Stival's stories. It shouldn't have been able to tunnel all the way up through the hill so quickly, but presumably, magic had augmented its natural capabilities.

As well as those of its kin, for, farther down the ridge, two more landwyrms exploded up out of the earth. The trio slaughtered at least twenty men in just a couple moments. Other soldiers, overcome by fear, scrambled away from the drakes. Madislak's entire formation was in danger of disintegrating.

Zethrindor knew it, too, and flung his troops into another charge at the hilltop. Men, dwarves, and giants ran. Dragons beat their way through the air.

Nearly knocked down and trampled by fleeing Sossrim, Will felt an uncharacteristic panic welling up inside. For a moment, he too nearly bolted. Then he glimpsed Dorn shoving his way toward the nearest landwyrm, and the sight steadied him. Maybe it was because he and Pavel felt responsible for their friend, or perhaps it was simply that he was used to following where Dorn led. In any case, he scurried in his wake, meanwhile switching out the sling for his new short sword.

Dorn sprang at the reptile's flank, ripped its scaly hide with his iron claws, then slashed it with his hand-and-a-half sword. The landwyrm screeched and whirled, and he leaped backward, evading a snap of its jaws.

It was at that point that Will squirmed his way out of the press of humans fleeing in the opposite direction and got his first good look at the fight as a whole. To his relief, he and Dorn were by no means battling alone. Pavel had conjured a glowing, flying mace to hammer at the landwyrm, and it bloodied the wyrm's shoulder with a shrill whine of concentrated noise. Wheeling around the reptile, Jivex evoked a hood of glittering golden dust, which unfortunately fell away without sticking to the larger creature's head. Stival, Natali, and other members of their troop assailed the foe with swords and spears.

Though it was difficult to imagine what good it could possibly do. Even if they managed to kill the landwyrm, other drakes, giants, dwarves, and barbarians were already rushing to overrun the ridge.

Will shoved such reflections out of his head. The task at hand was to slaughter that particular dragon. He'd worry about other perils later.

He waited until the landwyrm's head was pointed away from him, then, wary of its stamping feet and lashing tail, darted underneath it. He plunged his short sword into its guts.

He stabbed four times before the landwyrm's flesh shuddered in response to what might have been a particularly telling stroke. The drake would try to retaliate. Will scurried to get out from under it, and his boot slipped in the snow, costing him his balance and forward momentum.

The shadow of a huge foot fell over him. He struggled to regain his equilibrium and realized it wasn't going to happen quickly enough. Then Pavel lunged forward, grabbed him, and yanked him out of harm's way. The wyrm's foot slammed down, jolting the frozen earth.

They were both off balance, and the landwyrm twisted its head perpendicular to its usual attitude and spread its gray-white jaws to strike at them. Stival scurried to interpose himself between the reptile and its intended prey and cut with his broadsword. The straight, heavy blade sheared so deep into the underside of the drake's jaw that bone crunched, and blood gushed in bright, rhythmic arterial spurts. The landwyrm screamed and whipped its head away.

Dorn gripped his bastard sword with both hands and hacked at the base of the reptile's neck. Jivex lit midway down its back, beside the heavy, jagged, segmented dorsal ridge, and ripped at its flesh with fang and claw. Natali and her comrades slashed and stabbed.

The landwyrm froze. Shuddered. Flopped over onto its side to roll and thrash. A couple warriors were too slow scurrying out of the way, and the reptile crushed them.

As its death throes subsided, Will, panting, turned to find the next threat.

Rather to his surprise, all three tundra landwyrms were dead. Better still, it seemed the panic the creatures had inspired had been less universal than his initial impression of it, because folk who hadn't engaged the burrowing drakes had resumed the task of holding back the rest of the enemy. The giants, dwarves, and barbarians had gained some ground, but their advance had bogged down short of the top of the rise. Nor had the flying dragons penetrated the mystical barriers the Sossrim spellcasters kept placing in their way.

Will spotted movement in the forest. Limbs slashed up and down, shaking snow and icicles loose. Was it possible the trees themselves were walking and striking at creatures on the ground?

Dwarves and barbarians reeled out into the open with bears, wolves, and hawks in pursuit. A frost giant likewise tried to flee, but something even bigger than itself grabbed its head in gnarled brown hands and gave it a neck-breaking twist. The killer was a treant, a creature like a tree with a face, and a divided trunk that served for legs. Bare bark from its root-like feet to its highest branches, denuded of leaves by the advent of winter, it turned and strode back into the forest, presumably in search of other intruders.

It didn't seem as if the invaders could flank Madislak's army by looping around to the east. In fact, for a moment, Will found the entire situation encouraging, and grinning, was about to say so. Then he noticed how many more Sossrim the landwyrms had left smashed, torn, and lifeless in crimson pools on the ground.

Does it truly all just come down to numbers? he wondered. No matter how well we fight, Zethrindor and his flunkies just grind us away in the end?

No. He refused to believe it. Though if it did happen, then sometime before the finish, he'd make a point of reminding Pavel he'd predicted it would turn out to be a bad idea to backtrack.

Dragons flew high, then circled, plainly intending to attack from multiple directions at once. Stival herded his surviving warriors back to what remained of the ramparts. Will grabbed the edge of a dead archer's tabard, wiped the blood from his short sword, replaced it in its scabbard, and pulled the sling from his belt.

Taegan remained absolutely still. Breathed as softly as possible. Did his utmost to remain calm, lest the pounding of an agitated heart, or the smell of fear, somehow leaking through Raryn's enchantment, betray him. Meanwhile, the huge Tarterian, with its luminous green eyes, tattered wings, and black teeth and talons, stalked closer, while its fellows prowled higher up the mountain, or wheeled against the stars.

Taegan supposed that, incongruous as it seemed to posit such a thing about such a precarious situation, his daft scheme was going relatively well. The dark wyrms hadn't located him yet, which meant that, if Tymora smiled, Kara and Brimstone might actually have sufficient time to penetrate the ruined castle.

Had Taegan been directing the Tarterians, such would not have been the case. If he'd recognized that odd things were occurring on one side of the valley, he would have dispatched some of the wyrms to make sure all was well on the other. But these particular dragons evidently didn't think that way. According to Brimstone, their one great ruling instinct was to hunt, catch, torment, and slaughter prey. If so, perhaps none of them could bear to abandon the search for the trickster lurking close at hand.

Black, wedge-shaped, withered-looking head swinging back and forth, the nearest Tarterian glided a step closer. Taegan felt a sudden stab of alarm.

Had the wyrm spotted him? His instincts screamed yes, but he didn't know why. Had he observed something without quite realizing what, or was that prolonged game of hide-and-seek simply wearing on his nerves?

He studied the Tarterian. To superficial appearances, it was searching for him in the same manner as before. It peered this way and that. Sniffed the snowy ground and the frigid breeze. Cocked its ragged-edged ears to listen.

Yet it seemed to him that it might be crawling a trifle faster as it made its way in his general direction, as though it had already spotted its quarry, and all the subsequent casting about was just a show to conceal the fact. He likewise had the impression that, as its head pivoted at the end of its serpentine neck, it spent just a little more time gazing in his direction than it did looking elsewhere.

He realized he was certain. It knew where he was, and he had to start moving before it eased into striking distance. He spread his pinions, sprang into the air, and flew away from the boulder he'd been using for cover. The dragon immediately turned, tracking the motion just as if it could see invisible people, and charged, unfurling its own ragged, leathery wings as it bounded along.

He kept ahead of the creature, gained some altitude on it before it too took to the air, but the other Tarterians were orienting on him. Screeching and hissing, wings lashing, they wheeled, swooped and leaped in his direction.

Racing out over the valley, he rattled off an incantation and flourished the innocuous-looking scrap of licorice root that—praise Sune—none of his former captors had bothered to take from him. Power jolted through his limbs, accelerating his reactions. When he glanced back at the Tarterians, they appeared to be moving slower than before.

But they could still fly faster than he could. His advantages, to the extent that he could be said to possess any, were that they couldn't actually see him, and that he could maneuver more nimbly. He veered and turned, trying to shake them off his trail, or, failing that, at least keep them from catching up with him.

Snarling, they compensated by spreading out, so a turn away from one was likely to carry him closer to another. They also started spewing their breath weapons and employing their mystical abilities, and he had to trust his veil of invisibility and zigzagging mode of flight to spoil their aim.

It soon became apparent they wouldn't spoil it by much. A blaze of force missed him, but blasted close enough to agitate the air around him and make him flounder. He sensed a raw ache in the fabric of existence, a flaw that engendered a sympathetic throb in his own head, manifesting just in front of him. He dived, and a floating bubble of shadow seethed into existence above him. A rippling hole in empty space opened to his left and sucked at him as if he were bath water in peril of swirling down a drain. Inside it, he glimpsed a maze of pearly, featureless corridors like the one Brimstone had described. He lashed his pinions and broke the magic's grip on him. Balked of its prey, the hole melted from existence.

Rather to his own amazement, he was unscathed and uncaught so far, but he was rapidly approaching the wall of dark, snow-dappled peaks on the other side of the valley. He couldn't fly very far into them, lest he blunder into one of the maze traps. He had to turn, but a simple change of course was no longer possible. The Tarterians were too close, and would catch him if he tried.

He felt tempted to use his final trick. Certainly, it offered his best hope of survival. but even assuming it succeeded, it would bring the chase to an early end, and he'd promised himself he'd buy Kara and Brimstone as much time as possible.

To Baator with it, then. He'd play the game as he'd originally intended. He veered right and swooped low, into the area where he and his comrades had most often observed the largest of the several ghost dragons.

Though sometimes the spirit wandered elsewhere, or simply vanished altogether, and such appeared to be the case at the moment. When Taegan glanced back, he discerned that the Tarterians had nonetheless hesitated before entering its domain, but they cried to one another and drove forward.

That meant his ploy hadn't done him any good. Indeed, by requiring him to swoop lower, ceding the Tarterians the advantage of height, it had worsened his chances.

Prompted, presumably, by magic gone senile, strange, crumbling skulls laughed as he hurtled by. Rocks rolled and hitched themselves into a curving line which, for a moment, became a pale, slithering serpent. Then an enormous shadow fell over him. He looked up. A Tarterian hung directly overhead, its jaws spreading and its head cocking back to spit its breath.

It was going to kill him if he didn't get away. Probably he'd waited too long already, because he was supposed to shout first, that was his idiot plan, and he doubted he had time for that and an incantation, too. Still, he sucked in a breath to try, then the dark wyrm lashed its wings and veered off. At the same instant, he sensed something cold and terrible on his right.

He turned, and misty and insubstantial yet somehow, paradoxically, seeming the realest thing in the world, the ghost drake was right beside him, had only to stretch out its neck to seize him in its jaws. The sight of it paralyzed him, and he fell to the ground. Cocking its head, it peered down at him. Plainly, perhaps because of its own phantasmal nature, it had no difficulty discerning the invisible. Though the rest of it remained blurry, as it stared, its eyes resolved themselves into cavities as sharply defined and full of darkness as the orbits of a skull.

Taegan yearned to draw Rilitar's sword. Instead, he forced himself to lie still and return the colossal specter's regard.

After a moment, the thing lifted its head to glare and snarl at the Tarterians gliding overhead. Brimstone's enchantment had worked, fooling it into believing Taegan was an undead entity like itself, and thus it evidently felt no inclination to molest him.

Whereas the Tarterians, their infernal origin notwithstanding, were living creatures encroaching on its territory. They turned off to avoid a confrontation.

For a heartbeat, Taegan considered staying put, where Sammaster's watchdogs couldn't reach him. But he had no idea how long the spell of disguise would continue to deceive the wraith, and in any case, he simply couldn't bear to linger near it. Somehow, its mere presence was fouler and more horrific than even that of a dracolich, and he flew on toward the far side of its barren patch of ground.

That increased his lead. Enough for the Tarterians, flying high over the edges of the ghost dragon's territory, to lose track of him? No. When he veered, they adjusted.

One of them snarled rhyming words of power. A stinging heat danced over his body, and his wings flailed spastically, abruptly unable to beat as quickly as before. A counterspell had stripped away his charm of heightened speed, and most likely, his veil of invisibility as well.

He could quicken himself a second time, but a spell of invisibility was beyond his powers. He made do with lesser sleights, sheathing himself in murky vagueness and conjuring illusory twins to fly alongside him. It wasn't good enough. The Tarterians' attacks struck closer and closer, obliterating the phantom Taegans one at a time. Then a burst of draconic breath slammed into him like a battering ram.

He tumbled. Fell. Forced himself to shake off the shock of the blow and lash his wings. They still worked, and pulled him out of his plummeting descent, but every stroke stabbed pain through his shoulders. He turned and raced for a space where the night was ever so slightly darker, like the ghost of a black tower rising against the sky. According to Kara, it was both the largest and the most virulent pocket of old, decaying enchantment left in the vale, and the Tarterians kept clear of it just as they avoided the wraith dragons.

The dark wyrms roared, screeched, and flew their fastest to keep him from entering the murk and evading them as he had before. A flare of breath weapon missed him by a finger length. Then he plunged into the looming shadow.

He was simultaneously hot and cold, elated and despondent, weak with sickness and bursting with health, calm and enraged, blind and cursed with an acuity of vision that made every sight pierce him like a poniard, and famished and sated until his guts were sore with gluttony. He couldn't resolve nor even contain the contradictions. He could feel his mind breaking under the strain.

So don't think about them! Or anything but flying out the other side of the magic.

He struggled to empty his mind, and it made the chaotic sensations slightly more bearable. After a few more breaths, they ceased, as if the magic, unable to score with its first attack, had given up.

He doubted that, however. He suspected it would strike again before he managed to get clear. But since he had no idea what form the assault would take, all he could do was—

All he could do was hang his head as his mother scolded him. She hated it when he climbed trees, or the ivy-covered walls of their manor house in the country. She was sure he was going to fall, and couldn't understand why he loved to be up high. Nor could he explain, for he didn't comprehend it, either.

It wasn't that he lacked for other diversions. As the scion of one of Lyrabar's wealthiest families, he could fence, ride, hunt, hawk, and play at lanceboard whenever he felt so inclined. As he grew older, he added dancing, wenching, drinking, and gambling to his amusements. It all made for as pleasant a life as any young man could desire.

Yet he never stopped climbing, even when it made his shoulders tingle and itch in a peculiar, disquieting way. Even when, upon reaching the top of one spire or another, he experienced a sudden urge to jump. Not because he wanted to kill himself, but for some other reason he couldn't articulate.

His parents indulged him when he squandered coin on clothes, cards, and dice, impregnated serving maids, and even when he dueled. Yet they continued to rebuke him when he climbed. They swore it would be the death of him, and threatened to cut off his allowance if he persisted.

They were so upset, he feared they might be serious, and he did stop for a while. Ultimately, though, the impulse to scale the heights became too powerful to deny. One night, he crept outside the family mansion in Lyrabar, and not even caring that the stonework was slick with rain, clambered up the intricately carved facade of the structure to the conical slate roof of the tallest tower.

Perhaps it was because he'd denied his forbidden desires for so long that his back burned worse than ever, and the edge of the roof called to him as never before. Terrified and exhilarated, he realized that he really was going to jump. He moved forward.

"Stop!" his mother cried.

Startled, he glanced back, and there she was, perched behind him. But he'd been alone an instant before, and it was inconceivable that she could have climbed up after him in any case. Assailed by such irrationality, the confusion in his mind unraveled.

"You're not my mother," he said, "and this is only a dream."

"Whatever else it is," she said, "it's everything you've always wanted. You're human and thus a part of your beloved Impiltur as never before. You have all the coin you ever craved, and don't even have to work for it. Your father earned it, and you can spend your days enjoying it."

"While lost in a delirium."

"No. Have you never heard, there are many Torils, many worlds, lying side by side like pearls on a string. In the one you currently inhabit, Sammaster never lived, Taegan was born into one of Lyrabar's richest families, and the Rage never happened. It's better than your previous existence, isn't it? There, the Tarterians will soon tear you apart. Or Kara will, or Brimstone, as their respective curses overwhelm them. Or you'll eke out the brief remainder of your life in fear, misery, and the knowledge of futility and defeat, until the food in the valley runs out. Wouldn't you rather stay here?"

He grinned. "You make a compelling case, but alas, my preferences aren't the point." He turned back toward the drop-off.

"Please," his companion—Sune only knew what it truly was—wailed in a convincing imitation of maternal anxiety. "Don't you understand, you're human here. You don't have any wings!"

"We'll see." He took a deep breath, then leaped into space.

Lyrabar melted, and he found himself back in the valley, and back in his proper body. Thus, he did have wings, but it seemed he'd stopped flapping them when the dream possessed him. He was falling, and the ground was rushing up fast.

Heedless of the pains that had reasserted themselves along with the remainder of reality, he beat his pinions as hard and fast as he could, fighting to level off. He managed it with scant inches to spare, the tips of his pinions actually rattling against the ground.

He drove onward. Felt rather than truly heard the magic howl with frustration as he burst out of the shaft of gloom. He smiled at its vexation, then sighted the Tarterians hovering before and above him. They'd sped around the column of shade to cut him off, and unless he was willing to retreat back into the dark—suicide, he suspected, since he'd roused the forces lurking there—he had nowhere left to go. Nowhere his wings could carry him, anyway.

"All right!" he cried, loud as he could. Loud enough, he prayed, for Raryn, Kara, and Brimstone to hear. "Come take me if you can, you dull-witted lizards!"

They obliged. One flew directly at him, black talons poised to seize and rend. The others maneuvered left and right, up and down, boxing him in even more thoroughly than before.

Rattling them off as quickly as he dared, he whispered words of power. A drake to his left realized he was attempting magic, and spewed a flare of its breath. He lashed his wings, flung himself out of the way, and the world spun, broke apart, and reassembled itself. Unexpectedly, he was standing behind a stone on one of the mountainsides. Clumsy with the jarring, instantaneous transition from flight to a stationary position on the ground, he hastily folded his wings and crouched.

At the same instant, Raryn, his timing impeccable, shoved the stones he'd piled up for the purpose banging and bumping down a slope near the entrance to the ruined portal. The purpose was to convince the Tarterian that their quarry had shifted himself to that distant point, and peering out from his hiding place, Taegan saw the ruse was working. Screeching, the dragons beat their way toward the gate. They were flying fast, but Raryn should still have sufficient time to scurry away from the rock fall and conceal himself as ably as a skilled ranger could.

Presumably, after the Tarterians failed to find anyone lurking outside the tunnel, they'd revisit the portal chamber itself, where Raryn had cast a petty charm of one sort or another. If they sensed the residue of magic lingering in the air, it might well persuade them that, even though the magical cobbles were damaged, Taegan had still managed to employ them to transport himself out of the vale.

Meanwhile, with their keen ears, Kara and Brimstone had surely heard him yell, the stones tumble, or both. If they'd penetrated the citadel, that was their signal to make sure they were indoors, out of sight. If not, it was a warning they were out of time and needed to get away.

Taegan waited a while, catching his breath, then, his bruised and battered body throbbing, started creeping along the slopes. When they departed the vicinity of the gate, the Tarterians split up and glided back and forth across the battlefield, and he crouched motionless whenever one ventured near. It slowed his progress, and he wondered if Kara and Brimstone might destroy the heart of the Rage before he even had a chance to see it. If so, it would be all to the good, but still, a bit of a disappointment.

Eventually, white wyrms and ice drakes lit on the tableland behind the Sossrim force. Will supposed it had been inevitable. All the reptiles had needed to do was invest the time to fly in a wide arc around the battlefield, a course that took them beyond the range of the spells the druids and wizards could cast to deter them.

The maneuver placed the Sossrim between two contingents of their foes, and Stival rushed Will and the rest of his troop—designated dragon killers, the Defender help them—to the rear. There, aided by many of the spellcasters, they gave the whites a difficult time of it.

Violent winds howled overhead to keep the reptiles on the ground. Frozen earth melted into sucking quicksand beneath their feet. Walls of crackling flame, and light curdled hard as steel, sprang up before them to block their frosty breath and prevent them from closing with their foes. Meanwhile, dazzling thunderbolts, explosions of fire, arrows, and all the stones that Will could sling assailed them.

With its steadfast valor and tactical brilliance, the defense was awe-inspiring—and insufficient. On average, whites didn't command sorcery as potent as that of other chromatics, but they knew their share, and conjured darts of ice and bursts of hail to batter their foes. Often enough, they slipped a blast of milky breath through the wards to freeze archers and spearmen where they stood. Sometimes they even managed to rush in close enough to rend with fang and claw.

In consequence, people died. Will had little leisure to keep track of what was going on behind him, but the occasional glance revealed that the situation was equally dire in the front of the Sossrim formation. At least twice already, Zethrindor's other minions had reached the crest of the ridge. Thus far, Madislak's warriors had flung them back, but with their ranks thinning, it was difficult to imagine they could repel many more such assaults.

A crimson sun was sinking in the west, and all things considered, Will wondered if he and his friends would hold out long enough for one last look at the stars.

"On the left!" Pavel shouted.

Will jerked around to see a stubby-legged ice drake, its ivory scales tinged with blue, charging straight at them. He spun his sling, and his companions loosed their arrows. Some of the shafts lodged in the creature's hide, but didn't stop it.

Hovering, Jivex stared and shrouded the larger reptile's head in an illusory mass of flame. That didn't balk it, either.

Madislak scrambled up behind the warriors, brandished a bronze sickle, and growled a word of power. Sprouting in an instant, brambles thick as a warrior's arm, with thorns as long as daggers, erupted from the ground and twined around the ice drake. The wyrm roared and bounded onward, breaking its bonds apart as if they were no more substantial than cobwebs.

"Steady!" Stival called. "Steady! Flank it if you can."

Head still burning, or at least appearing to, though its body radiated a chill that made Will's body clench, the drake leaped into their midst. Two Sossrim fell, crushed and torn beneath its claws. Its broad, flat tail flicked and smashed the skull of a warrior seeking to scramble around behind it.

Will scurried underneath it, stabbed twice with his short sword, and dodged clear. That put him near Pavel, bashing away with his mace, and Natali, hacking with her blade. Though she remained human in other respects, the excitement of combat had given her round golden owl eyes.

A blue-white wing hammered down at them, and they jumped out of the way. The drake wheeled toward them, jaws opening wide. Dorn lunged from somewhere and ripped at the base of its neck with his talons.

Then Madislak stepped in front of it. "Look at me," he rapped, and the wyrm did.

A grayness washed through its scales, and it screeched. It strained to reach for the old man with its jaws, but its body was already stiffening and slowing into immobility. Its tail twitched a final time, then it froze into a figure of lifeless granite.

Will grinned at Madislak. "Nice trick."

"Point me at another wyrm," said Madislak, his eyes closed. "I need to make the most of this magic before it runs its—"

He took a lurching step forward, then buckled at the knees and waist. Stival caught him just before he could collapse entirely, then Will saw the arrow jutting from his back.

The halfling looked around and discovered onrushing tribesmen and frost giants. Either they'd fought their way through the treants and animals guarding the forest, or else Zethrindor had translated them onto the ridge with his sorcery. Will suspected the latter, not that it mattered. They were here, attacking by surprise, and the dragons, inspired by the appearance of reinforcements, redoubled their efforts to wreak havoc.

Will started to switch out his sword for his sling, then realized some of the charging barbarians were only a stride or two away. In the mad, screaming confusion of the moment, he hadn't noticed until then. He dodged a chop from an axe, darted behind his attacker, and sliced his hamstring. Sensed a threat behind him, he whirled, parried a spear thrust, and lunged to bury his sword in his second attacker's guts. Hesitated, momentarily uncertain what to do next, with combatants twice as tall as himself lunging, stamping, and reeling all around him.

Surrounded as he was, he could no longer see the dragons,

but he could hear them roaring and snarling close at hand, and people shrieking. He was sure the reptiles were overrunning the formation, but when the final barbarian crumpled with Dorn's talons buried in his chest, and the wall of human bodies broke apart, he saw it hadn't happened. Despite the distraction of new opponents leaping out of nowhere, the Sossrim line had held.

But at a ghastly cost. Dozens of warriors had fallen. So had Madislak and several of his fellow spellcasters, and the defenders could afford those casualties even less. This pretty much answers my question, Will thought. I won't get a chance to bid farewell to the stars.

But there was no point regretting it, or thinking about anything but fighting as well as he could. He'd just about exhausted his supply of sling stones, and accordingly inspected the bodies—some inert, some screaming, moaning, or twitching—littering the gory, trodden snow.

He spotted a dead barbarian who'd been a slinger, and as he stooped to untie the fringed leather pouch of rocks from his belt, noticed his attire. Evidently he'd served Iyraclea for a while, for, unlike the recent conscripts, he wore a tunic crudely dyed with the Frostmaiden's emblem, the white snowflake in the gray diamond.

For some reason, the badge tugged at Will's attention. Frowning, he struggled to figure out why, then cursed at himself. "I'm an imbecile!"

"Finally," panted Pavel, laying a quarrel in the groove atop his arbalest, "a moment of clarity."

"Don't be snotty," Will replied, "you're one, too. We all are, not to understand what's right in front of us. And I need a real spellcaster, not a charlatan!"

He turned, casting about for a wizard or druid. Those who yet survived were conjuring frantically. Would any of them pause long enough to listen to him? Would the defense crumble if one of them did?

Jivex flitted around to hover in front of his face. "What are you looking for?" the faerie dragon asked.

"You. I need to go down the hill to the other part of Zethrindor's army. You need to fix it so nobody kills me on the way. Can you do it?"

The little dragon sniffed. "Of course! Am I not Jivex?"

"Then let's go."

They worked their way through the Sossrim formation—or what was left of it—to the top of the ridge. Jivex faded from sight, and a moment later, magic seethed and tickled across Will's skin.

"We're ready," said the drake.

Will took a breath, steadying himself, then stepped over a corpse and through a broken place in the rampart of branches and snow. A warrior exclaimed in surprise and reached to haul him back. But the human was too slow, and too wary of the enemy host spread out below, to come out from behind the barrier to save a lone outlander from the consequences of his folly. Will hurried on downhill, wading and slipping in the cold, deep snow, past the bodies of those who'd fallen trying to take the summit.

"Not so fast," Jivex said, his voice seemingly sounding from empty air. "To the bad people, you look like a wounded dwarf struggling to rejoin his comrades. If you want the trick to be convincing, you have to creep and stagger, not sprint like you're trying to win a race."

"We are trying to win a race," Will said. But he slowed down as much as he could bear.

A few breaths later, a mixed band of frost giants and barbarians charged the top of the ridge. Will cringed as they pounded nearer, but most of them ran by without paying him any mind. One huge warrior in the rear of the pack, however, its eyes and matted beard both piss-yellow, broke stride to peer at him.

"It's nothing," crooned Jivex's disembodied voice, "just a dying dwarf. Keep running. You don't want the other giants to have all the fun."

The creature thundered on. Jivex had evidently tampered with its thoughts.

Will surveyed the troops ahead, most of whom appeared to be preparing for another advance. A company of arctic dwarves caught his eye. The treachery he'd experienced at such folk's hands scarcely served to inspire confidence in their kind, but his long friendship with Raryn did. He tramped in their direction, through other warriors who gave him no more than a glance.

"All right," he said, "I need to look like myself again."

"That sounds dangerous," Jivex answered. "But suit yourself."

Will couldn't feel his mask of illusion dissolve, but it was obvious when it did. The nearest dwarves—a glum, bedraggled, hungry-looking lot, who, judging from the wounded lying on the ground at the rear of the troop, had been up the hill at least once already—goggled at him. One fellow leveled his spear and charged.

"Wait!" said Will, retreating a step. "I'm not here to fight!"

His assailant didn't heed him. But Jivex shimmered into view and puffed sparkling vapor into his face. Giggling, the dwarf stumbled to a halt and allowed the broad flint point of his weapon to droop to the ground.

"We're not here to fight!" Will insisted. "Would the two of us sneak into the midst of your army to do battle all by ourselves? We want a parley."

A dwarf even more massively built than his fellows, with white, braided mustachios that dangled far longer than his tuft of beard, stepped forth. He carried a warhammer with a steel head and wore a coat of mail, marks, most likely, of authority, but looked just as haggard and morose as the common warriors in his charge. He gave the newcomers an appraising look, then shook his head as if unable to decide what to make of them.

"If you're here bearing the Sossrim's offer of surrender," he said at length, "I'll take you on to Zethrindor."

"We didn't come to see him," said Will. "We came to talk to you, and all the ordinary folk compelled to follow him. You need to know: The Ice Queen is dead."

The dwarf snorted. "What?"

"Iyraclea's dead. Jivex and I saw her die ourselves."

Another dwarf spat. "This is a trick."

"Obviously," said the captain, "and a daft one at that. Fools, surrender yourselves or die." His warriors lifted their weapons.

"Please," said Will, "listen to what we have to say, then judge."

"Perhaps you noticed," the leader said, "we're in the midst of battle. My comrades and I have no time for idiotic lies."

The other dwarves spread out to flank the newcomers, and Will felt a pang of fear and frustration. By the silent steps of Brandobaris, why had he ever imagined that ploy could work? He hesitated, uncertain whether to surrender or fight—neither option seemed likely to extend his life for very long—then Jivex swooped to position himself directly in front of the captain.

The faerie dragon crooned, "We're your friends, come to help you. You *have* to listen."

The dwarf's bright blue eyes blinked as if in momentary confusion, and Will realized Jivex had attempted to color his thoughts and feelings with magic. It was a risky tactic, for if the captain or any of his command comprehended what had happened, they'd surely respond violently.

But no one threw a spear or axe, and after another heartbeat, the officer said, "I . . . speak your piece then. Quickly."

"All right," said Will. "As I told you, the Ice Queen's dead, I swear by the Hand of Fellowship, she is, and if my oath's not enough for you, consider this: Didn't she used to appear to you, glowing and taller than a mountain in the western sky? Has she done it lately?"

The captain frowned. The warriors murmured.

"No, she hasn't," Will persisted. "Because she can't. She's gone!"

A towering, azure-haired frost giant came striding up, sword in hand, a bloody strip of linen knotted about his brow, and an empty quiver flopping on his hip. He was slimmer and not as coarse-featured as the majority of his race, with an air of youthful energy that the hardships of the campaign had yet to smother. On the Great Glacier, giants and dwarves were bitter foes, but perhaps their enforced servitude in the same host had stifled the traditional animosity, for his manner was brisk and matter-of-fact.

"We're about to move," he rumbled, his voice deeper than most any human's and certainly any halfling's. Then he caught sight of Will and Jivex, and stared in amazement.

"They claim," said the dwarf with the plaited mustachios, hope and doubt mingled in his voice, "that the Ice Queen is dead."

"She is," said Will, "and what's more, all the white dragons and landwyrms and such are here. Every hissing, slithering one of them! Do you understand what that means? Nobody's ruling over the Great Glacier anymore. Nobody's holding the kin you left behind hostage to coerce your obedience. You aren't obliged to fight this pointless war. You can go home."

The giant studied him for a time, then sighed and shook his head. "I think I could almost believe you, small one. Maybe because it seems unlikely anyone would have the nerve to peddle such a bold lie. But what does it matter? Whatever's happening back on the ice, the dragons rule us here."

"To the Abyss with the dragons!" cried Will. "They can't stand against all of you and all the Sossrim, too. We'll kill them together, and afterwards, you can depart in peace. All we have to do is find a way to stall the next attack while we pass the word from one company to—"

A horn blared, and others answered. The invading army lurched into motion, feet crunching in the snow. A few warriors shouted battle cries. Most just trudged with taut, grim, weary faces, their reluctance manifest. But everyone marched. As the sun touched the western horizon, Zethrindor was hurling every iota of his strength at the folk on top of the ridge.

Will cursed. Thanks to Jivex, the dracolich's captive warriors had actually listened to him, actually seemed as if they might believe him. But he was out of time.

Jivex narrowed his eyes and gritted his teeth in a grimace of concentration. A dozen high-pitched, slightly sibilant disembodied voices, each sounding like his own but considerably louder, cried out at various points above the ragged ranks of striding warriors: "The Ice Queen is dead!"

"The Ice Queen is dead!"

"The Ice Queen is dead!"

Startled, bewildered, people stopped to peer around. The advance ground to a halt.

Unfortunately, the phantom voices also brought Zethrindor leaping up from the center of the host. Vast, leprous wings beating, the undead white soared above his warriors, many of whom crouched and cowered despite the months they'd had to grow accustomed to him. Plainly, he was seeking the source of the disturbance.

We could hide, Will thought. Or Jivex could cloak me in another illusion, and turn himself invisible. But he doubted such measures would serve, and in any case, his instincts told him that if he showed fear, his attempt to sway the folk of the glacier would come to nothing. He needed to stand his ground and brazen the situation out.

"Hey, stinky!" he yelled, waving his hand. "If you're looking for us, we're over here!"

Zethrindor wheeled. Luminous in the gray, failing light, his sunken, silvery eyes glared. Will took care not to look at them straight on, lest they paralyze him, but tried his best not to appear to flinch, also. To look brave and confident as the gigantic, festering horror, his pallid scales slimy with pockets of rot, plummeted down at him.

"Don't worry," Jivex said, "this puny thing's not even as big as the dracolich I killed in the Gray Forest."

Will surprised himself by laughing. Because he'd been holding his breath without realizing it, the sound came out in a stuttering, strangled sort of way. "Thank you for that piece of information. It's very reassuring."

Folk babbled in alarm and scurried out from under Zethrindor's swelling shadow. One dwarf wasn't quick enough, and the white's hind foot pulverized him as he slammed down on the ground. The jolt made Will stagger a step.

"I thought I spotted you and your friends," Zethrindor growled, "fighting among the Sossrim."

"Your ice drake said you want to talk to us," said Will. Maybe it was the only reason the dracolich hadn't slaughtered Jivex and him on sight. "Right before we killed it. Well, here we are, and we'll be happy to chat, but I have some business to finish first. I thought your troops would enjoy hearing tidings from home."

He looked around. Dwarves, barbarians, and giants had all gathered round in a circle to witness the confrontation. In essence, he had the attention of the entire army.

"Iyraclea truly is dead!" he called. "I swear it by the Blessed One. She can't threaten you or your kin anymore."

Zethrindor sneered. "Is this ploy the best that doddering old druid could conceive?"

Trembling slightly, as though susceptible to the cold for the first time in his life, the youthful giant stepped forth from the crowd. "My lord," he said, his voice breaking, albeit, octaves lower than if a smaller creature were speaking.

Zethrindor's withered head jerked around to glower at him. "What?"

The giant swallowed. "Is Iyraclea dead? You have yet to deny it outright, and we've all noticed she doesn't appear to us anymore. Nor do her Icy Claws come bringing us her orders."

"Because," Will said, "the gelugons were her familiar spirits, and now that she's dead, they've gone home to whichever hell she whistled them out of. Come on, Zethrindor, tell your faithful followers the truth! You know better than anyone that the Ice Queen's dead, because you killed her, when you absented yourself from your army some tendays back!"

Though Will found it difficult to conceive, it was possible that some of Iyraclea's vassals—the frost giants, perhaps, whose fundamental natures partook of ice and cold—had served her out of honest devotion rather than fear. If so, he hoped this particular revelation would rouse a thirst for vengeance.

Zethrindor laughed, a nasty sound like stones grinding together. "All right, halfling, have it your way. I admit it. I killed her, for the crime of imagining she could dictate to a superior being, and that's why this witless little plan of yours will come to nothing. These folk understand that if I could destroy the Ice Queen, favored of Auril, the tyrant and supreme terror of the Great Glacier, then I can annihilate them just as easily. Any one of them, or all of them together. Their only hope of survival is to please me."

"If you were all that mighty," Jivex piped, "you wouldn't hang back and let them do all the fighting."

"It's proper," said Zethrindor, "for thralls to fight and die for their king, just as it's proper for those who insult him to suffer for their impertinence."

Swift as an arrow launched from a bow, he lunged.

TEN

17 Uktar, the Year of Rogue Dragons

Will had plainly hit on some sort of scheme, probably a risky one, and Pavel was disinclined to let
him and Jivex attempt it by themselves. He started
after them, but at that moment, cold, swirling, milky
fog billowed into existence around him, a magical
effect surely intended to blind him and everyone
else in the immediate vicinity. Hunter's instinct, or
perhaps the Morninglord himself, warned him what
was coming next.

"Get down!" he shouted, and flung himself to
the ground. Some of the warriors around him did
the same. Others failed to heed him, or moved too
slowly.

A different sort of vapor blasted through what
had formed previously. Lying on his belly, Pavel
was underneath it, but its mere proximity chilled
him. Those who were still upright and so suffered

its touch screamed and staggered in pain, or toppled, frozen, hearts stilled by the shock of unbearable cold.

The air was still misty, though the jet of dragon breath had somewhat dispersed the fog. Pavel rose, then pivoted, squinting, trying to pinpoint the attacker's location. By the time he spotted it, it was charging.

"There!" he screamed, pointing with his crossbow. "It's coming."

He loosed a bolt and managed to pierce its mask. Warriors loosed their arrows. He swapped out the arbalest for his mace, then the dragon crashed into their ranks.

It struck, and a spearman tumbled in pieces from its jaws. A lash of its tail hurled a soldier through the air, and the slap of a wing smashed another to the ground. Other Sossrim stabbed and hammered at its flanks, but the strokes failed to penetrate the alabaster scales.

Pavel conjured a whine of concentrated sound, and the magic punched a bloody rent in its snout. He edged forward, waiting for the drake to pivot away, for a chance to spring in and strike with his mace.

Dorn planted himself in front of the reptile, and it swiped at him with its claws. He tried to dodge, failed, and caught the blow on the iron side of his body. The clanging impact hurled him back and dumped him on the ground.

The white flexed its legs to pounce after him, and other adversaries, Pavel, Stival, and Natali among them, rushed in to cut, thrust, and pound at it. Pavel's mace failed even to scratch the pale, gleaming beauty of its hide, and though he scarcely dared look away from the drake to make a proper assessment, it was his impression that none of his comrades was faring any better.

But perhaps the dragon disliked being surrounded, having too many men assailing it all at once, for it snarled and whirled. The maneuver wasn't even a deliberate attack, but the reptile's size and speed, its stamping feet and sweeping tail, made it a hazard even so. It left another warrior sprawled bloody, smashed, and lifeless in the snow.

The white bounded away, distancing itself from the Soss-rim, no doubt to resume attacking at range. Perhaps its breath weapon had renewed itself. To all appearances, the sword strokes, axe cuts, and spear thrusts it had just endured had scarcely even bloodied it.

But at least it was no longer ripping its way into the formation. Pavel could return to the matter of Will and Jivex. Or so he imagined until a fallen warrior, a gangly, half-grown adolescent boy with acne spotting his brow, moaned and gestured feebly from the ground. Rime, the residue of the white's breath, encrusted much of his body, and patches of his exposed skin displayed the dead-white pallor of frostbite.

Pavel couldn't ignore his plea for succor. He stooped down, murmured a prayer, grasped his amulet with one hand and laid the other on the stricken boy's chest. Lathander's warmth flowered inside him and streamed into his patient, thawing frozen tissue, mending damage, restoring ruined arteries and veins and thus enabling fresh blood to pump to points it hadn't reached before.

The lad smiled and closed his eyes. Pavel squeezed his shoulder, then jumped up to hurry on his way.

By that time, though, Stival had discerned his intent, and came striding up to accost him. "Where are you going?" the stocky captain asked. "We need you!"

"I'm following Will and Jivex," Pavel said. "They've got some sort of idea, and it might be our only hope. I thought I'd try to help."

Stival's brow creased as he thought it over. Then he turned, spotted one of the seasoned veterans under his command, and called, "Gant! You're in charge!" He looked back at Pavel. "Let's go."

They hurried deeper into the formation, away from the roars of attacking wyrms, the booming, hissing blasts of their breath, the drone of arrows in flight, the shouts and screams. Natali and Dorn fell in behind them.

At first Pavel feared Will and Jivex had too much of a lead, that he and his companions wouldn't be able to find them amid the scurrying confusion of the embattled Sossrim host. Then, however, he observed that while people were still fighting desperately in the rear, where the drakes were attacking, it was strangely quiet in front. There, people were no longer shooting arrows or jabbing with lances, just staring down the hill. He hurried up to the ramparts to find out what everyone was looking at.

"They were all coming up the rise," said a warrior with the loose skin of someone who'd been fat before the privations of campaigning put him on short rations. He'd taken advantage of the lull in the hostilities to dig out a hunk of venison jerky, and gnawing and drooling, spoke through a mouthful of the leathery stuff. "Every stinking one of them. Then there was a funny kind of yelling—I couldn't make out the words—and they just stopped."

Not all of them, Pavel observed. Zethrindor was flying above his minions, and even at such a distance, the sight made the priest's muscles clench in revulsion. Ignoring the feeling as best he could, he peered intently, trying to locate his missing friends, but it was Natali, with her glaring inhuman eyes, who pointed and said, "There."

Natali having indicated the proper direction, he made out a hovering, glittering mote that might well be Jivex, and a spot on the ground that could be Will, toward the front of the enemy army. Somehow they'd made their way down there without getting shot full of arrows in transit, or cut to pieces immediately on arrival.

But it seemed Lady Luck had stopped smiling, for Zethrindor furled his ragged, decaying wings and plummeted at them. Pavel cried out in the anguished certainty that the reptile was about to kill them. But the huge white didn't smash down on top of them, instead alighting a short distance away. Resembling a swarm of ivory-colored ants, his army started to form a circle. To listen as he, Will, and Jivex palavered?

Pavel wheeled to face Dorn, Stival, and Natali. "I don't know what's happening," he said, "but it can't last. Whatever that idiot halfling has to say, Zethrindor won't tolerate his insolence for long. We need to get down there immediately."

"We'll never make it in time," Dorn growled, "not running, even if they don't start shooting as we charge down the slope. We need magic to shift us there."

Pavel cast about, and failed to see a druid or warlock anywhere nearby. Naturally. The invaders had left off assaulting the front of the formation, and all such folk were in the rear, fighting dragons. He took a stride in that direction, and someone wheezed, "No. Gather round me."

He turned to find Madislak Pemsk leaning on a spear, and looking as though he'd topple should someone deprive him of the makeshift crutch. His skin was ashen, much of his ratty brown robe, dark and sodden with blood, and more of it bubbled on his lips.

"Master," Stival said, "you're badly hurt."

The old man closed his fierce gray eyes. "Why," he rasped, "is everyone stupid but me? Didn't you hear Lathander's priest say we're out of time? Gather close! Even wounded, I think I can manage the five of us."

They grouped in around him. Arm shaking with strain, he swept a bronze sickle through a mystic figure and whispered words of power.

Magic burned through Pavel's body. The wind howled, picked him and his companions up, and swept them down the hill. Or perhaps they had themselves become the wind, for their bodies had altered into something as light and translucent as mist.

Dorn felt as if it was sheer yammering hatred as much as Madislak's magic that was sweeping him along. With Kara slain, the chance to fight her killer was the only thing left to desire in all the world, and after tendays of frustration, it had come to him at last.

But his fury yielded to a pang of dread as the wind carried them over the rings of spectators, and Zethrindor sprang at

Will and Jivex. Dorn was still flying yards above the ground, still a phantom made of vapor. His friends were about to die, and he couldn't do anything about it.

Then Madislak's will jerked the newcomers to earth so violently that Dorn felt his misty body stretch taller, like dough in a baker's hands, and retract back into shape. The sudden drop served to interpose the travelers between Zethrindor and his prey.

At the moment, they were still intangible. The dracolich could plunge right through them if he chose. But evidently the abrupt appearance of their ghostly forms made him wary, for, with an agility almost inconceivable in something so huge, so slimy, shriveled, and stinking with the ravages of death, he stopped short.

Dorn felt his form congeal into solidity. For an instant, his returning weight seemed too heavy to bear. Then his perceptions adjusted, and he was simply his normal self again.

He took a stride toward Zethrindor, looming like a whitewashed plague house in front of him, and Pavel grabbed him by his human arm. "Not yet!" the blond man snapped.

Dorn tried to pull free. Even on his right side, he was stronger than Pavel, but somehow his friend managed to hang on anyway.

"Damn it!" said the priest. "If I can bear to be this close without lashing out at the thing, so can you. Something's happening here. Don't muck it up!"

Dorn took a deep breath. "Get off me," he said. "I'm all right."

Pavel studied his face, then, somewhat gingerly, released his grip.

Meanwhile Zethrindor, his pale eyes gleaming, took stock of the new arrivals. "This," he said, "is an unexpected bounty. Everyone I ever sought in vain to capture, now standing at my feet." His head whipped around to peer directly at Madislak. "Though you, old man, don't look as if you'll be standing much longer. Humans are so fragile. One little poke with an arrow or knife, and you're done."

"Yes." Madislak coughed blood. "Here we are, and if you want a parley, you'll have to do it properly. Order the dragons up on the high ground to leave off attacking. Otherwise, I can whisk us all away from here as easily as I brought us."

Zethrindor sneered. "I doubt it. It takes time to melt flesh and bone into wind. Even if I can't cast that particular spell myself, I understand how it works. Still, I suppose I'm willing to indulge you. Your fools are behaving so strangely, you've piqued my curiosity."

He hissed and snarled words in the draconic tongue, and power seethed and shimmered in the air. Over the course of the next few moments, the commotion on top of the ridge—what Dorn could make out of it, anyway—quieted. Apparently the other wyrms had heard their chieftain's order and fallen back.

"Now, druid," said the dracolich, "what is it you want? To surrender? I might be willing to spare your lives. My fellow wyrms have already slaughtered enough of your men to fill their bellies for a while."

Will laughed. "Not likely. They came to vouch for what I already told your soldiers. The Ice Queen's dead. The glacier folk don't have to fight anymore."

Zethrindor spat, further chilling the air and deepening the ambient smell of carrion. "I told you, vermin, your revelation changes nothing, except that my slaves now realize they have the privilege of fighting to win a crown for me."

"I think they'd rather go home," said Will. "I also think you won't be able to stop them."

"Certainly not after your duel with Iyraclea," Pavel said. "You were lucky and defeated her in the end, but she hurt you first. She leeched a goodly portion of your strength right out of you. Since then, I daresay you're only a feeble shadow of what a dracolich is meant to be."

"Which is why he doesn't fight," Jivex cried. Wings shimmering, he wheeled to regard a troop of arctic dwarves. "It's like I told you."

A whispering ran through the ranks of Zethrindor's army. He roared, and the soldiers fell silent, everyone's eyes, even those of the giants, wide with dread.

"I am your god!" the dead creature bellowed. "Be thankful I don't slaughter each and every one of you for giving even the slightest credence to such lies."

"If they're lies," said Dorn, "prove it. Fight us. Just you against my friends and me. That's not too big a challenge for a dracolich, is it?" He hadn't know he was going to say such a thing until he did, then he remembered he had no authority to speak for anyone but himself.

But Madislak nodded as if they'd planned it all beforehand. "Yes, Zethrindor. Defeat us and my company will surrender. I swear it by the oak and the unicorn's horn. But if we kill you, your host goes home, and the war's over."

Zethrindor eyed them like a skeptical shopper in a marketplace, who deems a vendor's offer too generous to be true. "Your army is doomed anyway."

"Of course it is." Hand shaking, Madislak wiped at the blood on his lips and chin. "That's why I'm making the offer. But if you can kill us, it still works out to your benefit. Otherwise, my company will fight to the last man. You'll lose troops slaughtering them, strength you could otherwise use to conquer the rest of Sossal."

"Not only that," Will said, "but if you refuse the dare, you'll show your men you really are weak and afraid to fight. I'm not saying they'll all rise up against you—or saying they won't, either—but I guarantee they'll start deserting whenever they get the chance."

Zethrindor hesitated. Maybe he was wondering how a few taunts and unproven assertions had so tarnished his image of invincibility that, if he wished to maintain his absolute authority over his warriors, he needed to prove himself. But it seemed more likely he was simply marveling at the folly of the puny mites who imagined they had any hope at all of standing against him.

Either way, after a moment, he said, "You, old man, must

advise your company of the bargain, so they'll know they are to lay down their arms after I kill you and these others."

Madislak waved his free hand, the one that wasn't clutching the spear for support. The scent of fresh greenery suffused the air, briefly masking the stench of Zethrindor's corruption. "Done. My fellow druids understand."

Zethrindor's head cocked back, and his throat swelled. He was about to spit his breath weapon, and Dorn knew that single attack might well kill each and every one of them. He scrambled, hoping to at least dodge the central, coldest part of the fan-shaped blast of frost, and his comrades did the same.

All but Madislak, who, Dorn belatedly remembered, was likely incapable of such physical exertion with the arrow wound in his back. The stooped old man simply placed his hand on his sternum—possibly clutching a talisman concealed beneath his robes—and a barrier of yellow flame, long enough to shield him and his comrades too, and tall as any of the watching giants, leaped up from the ground. Zethrindor's frigid spew extinguished the flames, but exhausted itself in the doing. It failed to reach its actual targets.

The dracolich snarled and crouched to spring at Madislak. Hurtling through the air, Jivex conjured an illusory swarm of scorpions onto Zethrindor's head, but the phantoms melted away on contact. The faerie dragon then dived at the undead white, clawed, and streaked on by. Scattering so Zethrindor couldn't target them all at once, the fighters on the ground scurried to position themselves on their adversary's flanks. Dorn, Stival, and Natali loosed arrows, Will slung stones, and Pavel evoked a flare of hot golden light that charred and blackened a section of the colossal reptile's scales.

Zethrindor pivoted and half clawed, half stamped at Pavel. The lanky blond priest dodged, and the dragon's foot, when it slammed down, jolted the ground. The reptile surged forward, reaching for Pavel with his jaws.

Bellowing, Dorn dashed a few more strides, shot, and managed to drive an arrow into the undead's silvery eye.

Screaming also, Will, Natali, and Stival assailed the dracolich with their own missiles. Wheeling above Zethrindor, flickering in and out of view as the use of other abilities interfered with his invisibility, Jivex created a whine loud and shrill enough to make any hearer wince. Dorn assumed he'd placed the source of the noise inside one of Zethrindor's ears. With luck, the dracolich would find the torment excruciating, or at least distracting.

Acting in concert, Dorn and the other attackers managed to divert Zethrindor, and he left off chasing Pavel. Unfortunately, he also flexed his legs and spread his ragged, rotting wings to take flight.

Dangerous as Zethrindor was on the ground, he'd pose an even greater threat in the air. An unbeatable one, most likely. Dorn loosed another shaft. It pierced Zethrindor's serpentine neck, but didn't stop the white from lifting his gigantic leathery pinions.

Then, however, instead of sweeping vigorously downward and lifting him into the air, Zethrindor's wings clenched and twitched in useless spasms. Dorn glanced around and saw Madislak still gripping the object under his clothing. Apparently it held a number of spells useful for fighting wyrms, which the druid had hoarded in anticipation of the hour when he and Zethrindor would meet in battle.

Zethrindor started snarling a charm of his own. The words of power chilled the air and sent cracks snaking and forking through the ground. Dorn had no idea what the magic was meant to accomplish, but knew he didn't want to let the creature complete it.

Nor did he want to stand back and shoot arrows any longer. Reckless though it was, he yearned to tear and cut Kara's killer at close range. Infused with enchantment, his iron talons might do more damage anyway. He dropped his longbow, drew his sword, and charged.

He hoped to land at least one attack before Zethrindor sensed him, because he was rushing in on the side where his arrow had pierced the reptile's pale, sunken eye. But when the white's head twisted, orienting on him, he realized the optic could still see. Just as it would still see when the process of decay advanced, and the soft tissue inside the bony orbit eroded away entirely.

The luminous eye also still possessed its power to freeze a foe in his tracks. Dorn's muscles locked, and he lurched off balance. No, he insisted, no, I won't fall down at this foul thing's feet, and the crippling power lost its hold on him.

He gripped the hilt of his sword in both hands and cut at a hollow between Zethrindor's ribs. The blade sheared through ivory scales, releasing a stomach-churning stink and a thick black ooze. The dracolich lashed his tail around, and Dorn flung himself to the ground, underneath the stroke. Zethrindor kept on declaiming his spell, the precise cadence and articulation unspoiled. Arrows and stones flew at his hide, some piercing, many glancing harmlessly away. Jivex bathed the dracolich's dorsal surface in what appeared to be a bright jet of flame. None of that disrupted the incantation, either.

Zethrindor's tail whipped back around and straight down at the still-prone Dorn. Unable to roll out of the way in time, Dorn twisted and caught the blow on his iron arm and the rest of his golem side. The move saved his life, but the impact still bashed him flat against the earth, knocking the wind out of him.

As he struggled to shake off the shock and scramble back to his feet, he saw Will dart under Zethrindor's belly and stab twice before scurrying back into the clear. Still, the white snarled on, chanting his magic into being. The gray clouds overhead spun and churned like whirlpools.

Then Pavel, wherever he was, shouted, "Lathander!"

Warm, red-gold light pulsed through the air and gilded the trampled snow. Zethrindor jerked, and at last must have bungled his spellcasting, for the clouds stopped spinning, and the feeling of power massing abated.

Zethrindor snarled and took a stride away from Dorn.

Charging Pavel, evidently. Intent on distracting him from the priest, Dorn rushed after the dracolich, and sensed some or all of his other comrades racing after him.

Zethrindor leaped, widening the distance between himself and his pursuers, then, to Dorn's surprise, whirled to face them. Pavel wasn't his current target after all. They were, and by tricking them into chasing him, the white had induced them to bunch up.

He whipped his head back, and his neck expanded. A hint of pearly vapor steamed from his nostrils and mouth. Dorn realized that he and his companions had little hope of dodging the worst of the breath weapon this time. The distance was wrong.

"Behind me!" he bellowed. Raising his arm to shield his face, he turned his iron half toward Zethrindor.

The sheer force of the blast staggered him, as if he were attempting to stand before the sort of gale that flattened trees and houses. But the bad part was the terrible chill that pierced him to the core, that made his entire body clench as if he'd literally frozen solid.

Thanks, no doubt, to the protection of his inhuman side, and the blessings and spells of warding that Pavel, Madislak, and their ilk had cast on him earlier that day, he survived the attack. Maybe the people behind him had, too. But what did it matter? Hurt as they were, they couldn't endure what would happen next. Zethrindor sneered, crouched to spring, and it was all Dorn could do to come back on guard. He was shaking as through crippled with palsy, and couldn't even feel the sword hilt clasped in his numbed human fingers.

Then a shadow fell over him and Zethrindor, too. Startled, the white looked up, just as a shaft of brilliant light blazed down to cut his dorsal surface like a blade. The radiance, Dorn perceived, was the breath weapon of another dragon, a pale, glittering, almost translucent wyrm that looked as if it had been carved from diamond or crystal. It plummeted at Zethrindor and plunged its claws into him.

Grappling, ripping and biting, twisting around one another, the two reptiles rolled around the ground. Dorn stumbled backward to avoid being crushed. In the process, he nearly fell over Will, who, like Stival and Natali, was trying to exert sufficient control over his shuddering, frostbitten body to distance himself from the duel. It was a mercy the three of them were still alive, but likewise obvious they were no more fit to resume fighting than Dorn himself.

Jivex, who'd evidently avoided Zethrindor's breath, was still unharmed, and still gamely attempting to influence the outcome of the battle. He swooped and wheeled above the other, vastly larger reptiles, trying to blind Zethrindor with illusions, close-fitting constructs of pure glare, gigantic, swarming ants, and thick, tangled briars meant to hood him like a falcon. Unfortunately, the masks all dissolved as soon as the faerie dragon created them.

But maybe, thought Dorn, it wouldn't matter. The crystal dragon was even bigger than Zethrindor. Maybe it could destroy the dracolich all by itself.

Or so he hoped until he spied the raw, gaping rent between the gem wyrm's wings. The ichor streaming from the wound was clear as water, not red anymore. A shapeshifting spell altered the caster's blood along with the rest of his body. But even so, it was apparent that the crystal dragon was Madislak, and that, even transformed into such a mighty creature, he still bore his debilitating wound. Such being the case, it was impossible to imagine he could win.

The dracolich wrenched his neck free of Madislak's grasping talons, pointed his head at the druid's, and vomited frost. The crystal wyrm convulsed at the touch of the freezing jet. Zethrindor took advantage of the other dragon's momentary incapacity to rake away masses of glassy flesh.

Dorn took a shuffling step toward the confrontation. He knew it was ridiculous. He couldn't fight as he was. But he had to try.

Then, his limp again apparent in his gait, Pavel came dashing up. "Wait," panted the priest, "all of you, wait." Rattling off prayers, conjuring ruddy light from his amulet, he infused his touch with warmth and restorative power.

The magic replaced the numb, shuddering weakness in Dorn's human half with a kind of burning ache, but that was all right. It wouldn't stop him from fighting, and evidently Will, Natali, and Stival felt the same. They drew themselves up straighter and grasped their weapons firmly.

"That's it," Pavel said. "I'm out of spells."

Will spat. "Useless as ever."

Dorn charged. The others followed.

Zethrindor was too busy tearing at Madislak to pay attention to smaller foes, but they were in constant peril even so. At any moment, the two intertwined wyrms might tumble over on top of them, pulverize them with a random tail sweep or wing beat, or catch them in a flare of breath. Dorn leaped away from such threats, then, when the danger passed, lunged back into the fray and cut at whatever part of Zethrindor's shriveled, rotting form was in reach.

For all the good it did. The dracolich wasn't slowing down, and soon began to growl another spell. Dorn and his comrades attacked even harder, recklessly and relentlessly, but without disrupting the conjuration.

Seething shadow bloomed in the narrow, inconstant space between Zethrindor and the crystal dragon. For a moment, Dorn thought the undead white had simply conjured a form of armor. Then, with a pang of horror, he realized what the manifestation truly portended.

It was too late to help Madislak, grappled as he was. Dorn needed to protect his other comrades. "Jivex!" he bellowed. "Get clear!"

His butterfly wings beating quick as a hummingbird's, the faerie dragon distanced himself from the heaving knot formed by his gigantic kin. A heartbeat later, the darkness struck. Back in the plaza in the Novularonds, it had swept across the cobbles like a breaker rushing at the shore. This time it exploded up at the sky like a thunderbolt, or a tree compressing a century of growth into a single instant.

Engulfed in the column of shadow, Madislak crumbled into dust, some spilling downward, the finer particles hanging as a haze in the air. The parts of his body outside the effect—lengths of tail, feet, sections of wing—dropped and thudded on the ground.

Its work accomplished, the shaft of darkness vanished. Zethrindor leaped to his feet. His carrion flesh hung in tatters, in many places sufficiently shredded to reveal the bone beneath. The left side of his head was all naked skull, eye and ear ripped away along with the hide and muscle. Madislak, Dorn, and their allies had inflicted harm no living creature could have endured. Yet Zethrindor moved with the same fearful speed and grace as before.

Iron half leading, artificial hand poised to block, claw, and pummel, sword cocked back, Dorn planted himself in front of the dracolich's head. With Madislak dead, and even Pavel's store of spells depleted, it was obviously futile. But it was also the only thing to do, and still the only thing he wanted to do.

His comrades scrambled to place themselves on Zethrindor's flanks. The white struck at Dorn. He sprang to one side, prepared to cut at the creature's head, but the attack stopped short, while Zethrindor was still out or range. The half-golem realized it had been a feint.

One that had been intended to draw the dracolich's other foes into the distance while he was seemingly focused on Dorn. Stival took the bait. Perceiving the danger, Natali, her hair a bristling shock of white feathers, screamed, "No!" Stival stopped rushing forward, and when Zethrindor pivoted and raked at him, he was able to dodge.

Unfortunately, Stival's peril had distracted Natali from watching for threats to herself. Zethrindor's tail whipped around, smashed into her torso, and flung her through the air. She slammed down hard and lay motionless as a broken doll.

No time for sorrow or outrage on her behalf, or for anything but total concentration on the task at hand. Dorn, Will, and Pavel fought with all the teamwork and tricks that had carried them through countless combats with dangerous beasts. Stival, himself an experienced hunter and wyrm slayer, employed similar tactics. Jivex assailed Zethrindor with one magical effect after another, and whenever he saw an opening, used tooth and claw as well.

It kept them all alive for a few more heartbeats. It even allowed them to open a few more apparently inconsequential rents in the white's body. Until Zethrindor, tiring of the game perhaps, snarled a word of power.

A thunderclap boomed, the prodigious sound striking like a blow. Dorn staggered and fell. His allies did, too, all but Jivex, who tumbled crazily through the air.

Zethrindor reached to seize Will in his jaws. The halfling made some feeble effort to get up onto his hands and knees, but didn't appear to recognize the imminent threat. Nor were the others moving to protect him. The deafening bang had stunned them all.

Dorn too felt dazed and battered, but he forced himself up. Gripped his sword with both hands and cut. Maybe Zethrindor had placed too much trust in the potency of his sorcery, maybe Dorn's continued resistance caught him by surprise, for he made no effort to shift away from the blow. The blade crunched deep into his skull, on the side where Madislak had already stripped away the natural armor of scales and muscle.

Zethrindor's entire body jerked. Dorn thought he glimpsed a darkness seething up around the end of his sword and the breach in which it was embedded, as though some vile force was bleeding out. He yanked the weapon free, struck a second time, again succeeded in splintering bone.

Zethrindor floundered backward. Dorn pursued with a sudden surge of hope, until the dracolich recovered his balance and settled back into a fighting stance. His throat swelled.

Not good enough, thought Dorn. For an instant, I thought it was, but it wasn't. *I* wasn't.

Then a voice an octave deeper even than his own shouted, "You see, the small folk told the truth! The lich is weak!

Get him! Get him! Get him!"

Startled, Zethrindor twisted his head around to glare at the young, relatively slender frost giant who'd raised the shout. Probably the dracolich meant to mete out a hideous punishment, but in that same instant, another giant threw an enormous axe and embedded it in his chest.

A barrage of missiles followed, with giants, dwarves, and barbarians alike loosing arrows and flinging javelins. Then, with a bellow of hatred, they rushed in and swarmed on Zethrindor, until the dracolich nearly disappeared behind the mass of his assailants.

Dorn realized the glacier folk didn't care about the terms of his challenge to the white. They only wanted to be rid of Zethrindor, and once his opponents gave him enough trouble to convince them he was vulnerable, they'd risen up against him.

Dorn supposed that in his place, another man would be elated, but he still couldn't feel anything but hate. He tried to push his way through the press of warriors around Zethrindor, back into striking distance, but couldn't manage it. Too little strength remained in his hurt and exhausted human half.

Zethrindor started bellowing a spell, but quickly fell silent, as did the entire struggling horde of combatants. Some priest or shaman had cast a charm of quiet to keep the dracolich from using his magic.

Still, the battle raged on until Dorn started to fear that even such a horde of foes couldn't prevail against the dracolich. But then a giant wearing a breastplate carved from presumably enchanted, unmeltable ice stooped, straightened up, and raised Zethrindor's severed head high above his own. The glacier folk, or at least all those outside the field of silence, raised a thunderous cheer.

Jivex swooped down to hover beside Dorn. The faerie dragon surveyed the scene, then sniffed. "Why aren't they cheering me?" he asked. "I did all the work."

Stival kneeled beside Natali's motionless body. Despite the owl eyes and feathers, she seemed the fairest thing in the world.

"I was a fool," he said. "I should have invited you to share my bed when I had the chance. You might have said yes. By the unicorn, maybe I would have even married you, if that was what it took."

He reached to close her eyes, and froze in shock when they shifted toward his face.

"I accept your proposal," she croaked. "Now fetch a healer."

As he hurried away to find one, conflicting emotions tangled and ached in his chest. Joy to find her still alive, and anxiety that she might still succumb to her injuries if he didn't bring help quickly. Delight that she fancied him, and dismay to discover himself betrothed to a woman whose purse was as empty as his own.

But after a few strides, the dismay began to fade. Maybe her poverty didn't matter all that much. They were two of the heroes who'd destroyed Zethrindor, weren't they? That ought to earn them titles, a tract of land, and chests of gold. It was simply a matter of making sure the right people knew about it.

━━◆✺◆━━

Pavel peered up at the tableland. The glacier folk were clamoring in jubilation, but he wasn't ready to celebrate just yet, because he wasn't sure the battle was over. The surviving whites and ice drakes presumably had some way of discerning the outcome of the challenge, but wicked, faithless creatures that they were, might not honor Zethrindor's bargain.

He held his breath when the pallid reptiles soared up into the darkening sky. But instead of attacking, they flew west, and at last he too felt the urge to cheer.

Trying to swagger but pretty much hobbling instead, Will came to stand beside him and watch the departing drakes, making certain, as poor, lost Raryn would have done, that the creatures didn't double back. "Maybe," the halfling said, "they only fought because Zethrindor bullied them into it, like he did the dwarves and such. After all, Sossal was going to be his kingdom, not theirs."

"Or perhaps," Pavel replied, "they just don't like their chances anymore. Or else they're eager to reach a cult enclave and start their transformations. The important thing is, it's over."

"No thanks to you. 'Out of spells.' Pathetic." The halfling grinned, then pointed. "Look, the stars are coming out."

Taegan crept toward the cave where he and his companions had chosen to hide. From the outside, thanks to the subtle illusions Kara and Brimstone had woven, the pocket in the rock looked empty.

Perhaps, at the moment, the appearance matched the reality. If the dragons had succeeded in unlocking the elven citadel, and Raryn had already joined them inside its walls, the cave might actually be unoccupied.

But no. When Taegan skulked in far enough to penetrate the curtain of illusion, the bard, smoke drake, and dwarf all popped into view. He scarcely needed to behold their glum expressions to understand what had happened, or rather, what had not.

Anger welled up inside him. By all the powers bright and dark, it wasn't fair! He'd done what was supposedly required. Against all rational expectation, he'd succeeded in keeping the Tarterians occupied for a considerable time. Why hadn't the drakes performed their task? How difficult could it be—

He clamped down on his ire. He and his comrades had known at the onset that Kara and Brimstone, accomplished sorcerers through they were, would find it difficult to counter the enchantments of a legendary mage like Sammaster. Recriminations would be unjust, and certainly serve no purpose.

Taegan took a breath, composing himself. "I surmise," he said, "that we'll need to try again."

Brimstone sneered. "Do you imagine you can fool the Tarterians a second time? They learned from what happened today. Next time, they'll catch you before you can draw a dozen breaths."

"Not an enticing prospect," Taegan conceded. "Ergo, we need a new plan."

"I invite you to devise a feasible one," the vampire said. "Even if the Tarterians actually believe you somehow used a broken gate to leave the valley, we've stirred them up. They'll patrol more diligently. It will be all we can do to stay hidden, if, in fact, we can even manage that. We certainly have no hope of conducting lengthy experiments outside the castle."

"Nor would it matter if we could," Kara sighed. "Brimstone and I both agree, we'll never break Sammaster's ward."

Taegan arched an eyebrow. "We've journeyed a long way and overcome a fair number of obstacles just to abandon hope on the ancient elves' very doorstep."

"I know," she said, "and nobody wants to fail. But Brimstone's thirsty, frenzy's pounding at my mind, and neither of us can see any possibilities at all."

"Nor can I," said Taegan, "not as yet. But you, milady, will cling to your love of your kindred, your music, and Dorn, and you, Sir Vampire, to your hatred of Sammaster, to fend off your less agreeable impulses. Raryn and I will tighten our belts. The four of us will watch for opportunities, and even if none presents itself, wait for our allies to locate us."

Brimstone spat sulfurous smoke. "How?"

"I can't imagine. But I lack the talents of a Firefingers, or a Nexus."

"Taegan's right," said Raryn, sitting with his back against the wall and his short, burly legs outstretched, his white mane, beard, and polar bear-fur armor ghostly in the gloom. "We may fail, we may very likely die, and if so, there'll be no shame in losing against long odds. But you don't stop trying."

Kara forced a smile. "No, you don't. Please, forgive my whining."

"I didn't mean I would give up," Brimstone growled. "But neither am I inclined to deny the truth of our predicament. So I leave the posturing and prattling to the three of you." He wheeled and stalked into the darkness deeper in the cave.

Afterward, Taegan reflected that the smoke drake's parting remark had contained a measure of truth. He had been striving to feign an optimism he was far from feeling.

Because the dragons' demoralization, transitory though it probably was, had shaken him. Kara and Brimstone were creatures of exceptional courage, and far more powerful and knowledgeable about occult matter than he. If they could see no hope—

No. Enough of that. Seeking to break his somber train of thought, he grinned at Raryn. "Is there any of your delicious spadderdock remaining? I believe my exertions may actually have actually left me famished enough to choke down a bite or two."

———— ✦✦✦ ————

After months of strife, the Sossrim and glacier folk were willing to make peace, but felt no inclination to fraternize. The former camped on the ridge they'd defended at such a heavy cost, the latter, on low ground some distance back from the foot of the slope.

Mostly burned down to coals and ash, Zethrindor's remains smoldered where he'd fallen, about equally distant from each encampment. His destroyers had burned him to purge his flesh and skeleton of any lingering malignancy that might otherwise poison the earth. Or perhaps to make absolutely sure he wouldn't rise in the night.

Pavel found Dorn standing alone, staring at the pyre. Here and there, a few blue and yellow flames still danced, and some of the dragon's blackened bones maintained their shape. The air smelled of smoke, but not decay, not anymore.

"Supper's ready," Pavel said. "Stival even found some wine, the gods alone know how. He and Natali would like it if you'd drink to their betrothal."

Dorn didn't answer.

Pavel tried a new tack: "We should get an early start tomorrow. It will be difficult, but I think we can still make Thentia in time for the conclave. The Sossrim will do everything they can to help us on our way, and so will my folk, once we cross into Damara."

Still no reply.

"Talk, damn it!" Pavel exploded. "You owe me that much. There lies Kara's killer, burned to nothing, or near enough. You have your revenge. Doesn't it make a difference?"

"But did we truly destroy him?" Dorn asked. "Or is his spirit just lurking in a phylactery, awaiting rebirth?"

Pavel hesitated. "Well ... presumably the latter. But consider this: If he was one of Sammaster's newly minted dracoliches, he's been busy furthering the wizard's schemes and attacking Sossal ever since his transformation, He probably never got around to caching spare bodies near his amulet, and that likely means he'll never have the opportunity to occupy another. Imagine what it would be like to be trapped—blind, deaf, bodiless, and alone—inside a piece of jewelry for all eternity. I suspect it would be as every bit as unpleasant as dying a natural death and landing in one of the Hells."

For a moment, the hint of a smile tugged at Dorn's mouth, but then it twisted into a scowl. "That's good to hear. Still, the answer to your question is no. It doesn't truly make a difference. I thought I might feel something if I killed Zethrindor, or helped to kill him. Something big. Something that would change me. But it didn't happen."

"I understand how much you're hurting. But give yourself time."

"Are you still afraid I'll run away? Or kill myself? I told you I won't. I think about it, but I worry that dead, I'll feel just the same as I do now. Then I really won't have anything to hope for, will I?"

ELEVEN

The Feast of the Moon, the Year of Rogue Dragons

His rear and thighs aching from days of riding, mostly on mounts too large for a halfling to manage comfortably, Will trudged through Thentia, comparing the scenes that presented themselves with his memories of Midsummer in the same city.

That had been his sort of festival, everyone drinking, dancing, laughing, chasing members of the opposite sex and catching them more often than not. In contrast, the Feast of the Moon, celebrated in recognition of the honored dead and the onset of winter, was a solemn, subdued observance. The taverns closed their doors. Storytellers recited tales in which misunderstandings led to murder and suicide, young warriors perished on the battlefield, leaving their lovers to pine away, or noble kingdoms fell to orcs and plague. Folk clad in mourning sang dirges, paraded single-file through the streets with candles in their hands, and eventually fetched up in the cemeteries, where they laid offerings of food, preserved flowers, and sentimental tokens on tombs and graves.

But from Will's perspective, the biggest difference was that four months ago, Raryn, Kara, Taegan, and yes, even Brimstone had been present, and it was their absence that actually made the festival seem so depressing. That, and the sense of desperation that had descended on the seekers who still remained.

Yet even so, it was a relief when he, Dorn, Pavel, and Jivex escaped into the countryside and left the funereal proceedings behind. As before, the Watchlord's Warders guarded the approaches to the field in which the dragons and their allies were gathering. The sentries saluted the hunters as they passed.

The meeting site shined with a soft, sourceless silvery light one of the spellcasters had conjured. The glow glinted on the scales of the many dragons assembled there: Tamarand, who'd served as King Lareth's principal deputy, and challenged, dueled, and killed the mad sovereign to save his people. Nexus, yet another gold, allegedly the mightiest of all draconic wizards. Lady Havarlan, much-scarred leader of the martial fellowship of silvers known as the Talons of Justice. Azhaq, Moonwing, Llimark, Wardancer, Vingdavalac, and others, their diverse scents combining to suffuse the cool night air with a dry, complex, and rather pleasant odor.

The spellcasters of Thentia stood, unconcerned, around the feet of the colossal reptiles. There was Firefingers, a genial old grandfather of a fellow dressed in garish flame-colored garments, Scattercloak, as always muffled so thoroughly in his mantle, robes, and shadowy cowl that not an inch of skin was visible, and plump, fussy Darvin Kordeion clad all in shades of white. Her long tresses dyed their usual silver, Sureene Aumratha, high priestess of the House of the Moon, conferred softly with her proteges Baerimel Dunnath and Jannatha Goldenshield. Petite lasses who bore a familial resemblance to one another, the two sisters were mistresses of arcane magic rather than divine, but servants of the temple nonetheless.

Gareth Dragonsbane had sent his own representatives to the council. Celedon Kierney, the paladin king's foxy-faced, half-elf spymaster, welcomed Will and his companions with a smile and a wink. Scarred, hulking Drigor Bersk, probably the unlikeliest priest of mild, martyred Ilmater in all Faerûn, gave them a brusque nod far more in keeping with the grim atmosphere of the assembly as a whole.

But surely, thought Will, it can't be as bad as all that. These folk are wise. They'll think of something.

Nexus shifted his golden wings. Maybe it was the dragon's equivalent of clearing one's throat, for the others abandoned their murmuring conversations to orient on him.

"This is the situation," Nexus rumbled. "Essentially, we've made no progress since we last convened here four months ago."

Havarlan grunted. "With respect, wizard, that isn't altogether true. Working in concert with a host of allies, we metallics have found and destroyed several bastions of Sammaster's cult, enclaves which, left unchecked, would have created any number of dracoliches. We've saved many otherwise defenseless folk from drakes in the throes of frenzy, or from the secondary threats the Rage has kindled across the land."

Nexus inclined his head. "True, and I don't mean to discount such victories. But in the long run, they will mean nothing if we can't end the madness gnawing at our minds, and with time running out, we're no closer than before. We've devised the counterspell—or at least believe we have—but still have no idea where we must go to cast it."

Celedon stepped forward. "My lords and ladies, masters, I'm newly come to your deliberations. Please forgive me if I ask questions to which everyone else already knows the answers. I understand you actually have some of Sammaster's papers in your possession?"

"Written in cipher and sealed with a curse," said Scattercloak in his uninflected, androgynous, somehow artificial-sounding tenor voice. "We've managed to read a portion of them even so, but nothing that bears on the location of the elven citadel."

"We've scried for the stronghold, too," Firefingers said. "Sought its whereabouts in long-lost lore unearthed all over the continent. Dragons have flown across the northlands looking for it. All to no avail."

"Curse it," Will exclaimed, "my partners and I found the door to the place! That has to count for something."

Nexus, with his blank, luminous yellow eyes, backswept horns, and dangling barbells, gave Will a look conveying both annoyance and compassion. "I understand how hard you and your companions worked to locate that portal," he said, "and that you lost friends in the doing. But Scattercloak, Jannatha, and I have visited the site, and the gate is damaged beyond repair."

"But . . . isn't there still some kind of magical trail you can follow?"

"I'm sorry, but no."

Celedon fingered his pointed chin. "I assume you tried scrying for Brimstone and the others instead of the citadel itself?"

"Naturally!" Darvin snapped. "Do you think we'd overlook something so obvious?"

"No, good sir, I don't. But I would have been remiss if I hadn't made certain."

"I don't believe," said Firefingers, "we've overlooked anything. But I'm not yet ready to surrender. Look at the company we've assembled, dozens of human and dragon mages united in a single circle. When has there been such a formidable coven? Yet we've never pooled all our strengths and skills in a single ritual. We've been too busy running hither and yon, following up on all our various leads."

High, argent frill and quicksilver eyes shining, Azhaq said, "You're proposing a grand divination. A coordinated effort to pierce the elves' concealments."

"Yes," Firefingers replied. "It seems our best remaining hope."

"I agree," said Tamarand, "so how shall we begin? We need a structure, something to guide our individual efforts and link them into a greater whole."

"I suggest," said Firefingers, "the Great Pentacle of the Hand and Stars in conjunction with the Binder's Eighth Sign."

"A sound choice," said Nexus, and contentious as the mages of Thentia generally were, with the most powerful human warlock and dragon wizard already in agreement, for once, no one pushed for an alternative.

"In that case," said Firefingers, "I'll ask everyone to move back a fair distance. I need room."

They ceded him the greater portion of the meadow, whereupon he whispered under his breath and snapped the fingers of both hands. Streaks of blue flame exploded into being to race along the ground. Will flinched, fearing an uncontrollable grass fire, but the blaze didn't spread in the usual manner. Rather, it drew straight lines and arcs, sprang over spaces Firefingers wanted clear, defining a complex, symmetrical geometric figure further adorned with sigils and writing. Even when the design was complete, the flame, leaping no higher than the surrounding blades of grass, confined itself to the same narrow pathways, preserving the intricate form's precision.

"Now," said Firefingers, "all of you who can help, take your places."

To Will's surprise, Sureene, Drigor, and Pavel headed for the pentacle along with all the mages, two-legged and reptilian, leaving only Dorn, Jivex, and himself to wait and watch outside. Apparently even practitioners of divine magic had something to contribute to a "grand divination."

The spellcasters took care to step through gaps in the lines and curves of flame. Once everyone found the place he wanted to stand, or was supposed to, Firefingers waved his hand, and the openings sealed themselves.

"My turn," Nexus said. Instead of whispering as his human colleague had, he roared words of power at such a volume as to echo from the surrounding hills. At the end of the incantation, he spat flame.

Normally such a blast flared and died, though it might leave secondary fires burning in its wake. But Nexus's exhalation hung as a bright, seething golden cloud in the air, which gradually shaped itself into a spherical construction of arcs, lines, and glyphs somewhat resembling the design beneath it on the ground, but rendered in three dimensions instead of two.

Or maybe it was a single rune floating in the air, or a scroll without any writing on it. It flickered from one form to the next. Sometimes Will could even see multiple shapes simultaneously, a phenomenon that made a mockery of comprehensible sight and threatened to give him a headache.

"Now," said Firefingers, "let's begin."

He chanted, and one or two at a time, the other spellcasters joined in, but they didn't all recite in unison. Each had his own incantations, with their own rhythms, pitches, and peculiar inflections. The result should have been cacophony, or at least a muddled drone. Instead, all the diverse voices combined into a sort of mellifluous contrapuntal plainsong.

During the moments it was visible, the globe of fiery lines shifted. One word or symbol melted into another. A triangle, defined by radii extending through the center of the construct, vanished, and a trapezoid appeared in its place. Will could only assume the spellcasters were taking their cues from the ongoing transformations, and that was what enabled them to declaim in harmony.

Writing, dancing through changes like the structure of the sphere, began to appear on the floating scroll. The chanting grew quicker, louder, more insistent. The human spellcasters slashed their arms through mystic figures. An ivory wand in Darvin's upraised hand pulsed with radiance. Motes of shadow spun around Scattercloak like angry wasps.

A heaviness congealed in the air. Will could tell he wasn't really having difficulty breathing, but it felt like it anyway.

A fourth form appeared in the dazzling inconstancy suspended at the center of the pentacle, winking in and out of view like the globe, rune, and page. At first, it manifested so briefly and was so blurry that Will couldn't make out what it was. Gradually, though, it grew clearer.

It was a barren valley, seen from high above. Dark, snowy mountains surrounded it, and a gigantic castle stood toward one end. Dragons the color of ink, like skull wyrms but sprinkled with scales of a lighter shade, glided near the citadel.

"They've got it!" Jivex cried.

Then the illusory landscape vanished, replaced by a sphere, and despite his ignorance of magic, and difficulty discerning the details of a figure sketched in flame, Will realized that it was a different globe than before. Though he couldn't say why, it was nauseating to behold, like some heinous act of torture.

At the same instant, the feeling of weight in the air altered, too. Before, though unpleasant, it hadn't seemed especially alarming. Will had trusted that the wizards had it under control. But it was soon plain that they didn't. Even a person devoid of magical aptitude could sense it tilting out of balance, like rocks on the brink of tumbling down a mountainside and crushing the travelers below. Like rocks that *wanted* to fall.

The complex harmony of the ritual shattered as dragons howled, and humans screamed. Drigor staggered, chin dark and wet with the blood streaming from his nostrils. Baerimel doubled over vomiting. Moonwing collapsed and thrashed, argent wings and tail hammering the ground. Though stricken like everyone else, Pavel just managed to scramble clear and avoid being squashed.

The fiery orb swelled. The lines on its surface reconfigured themselves into ovals that somehow appeared to stand out from the globe, and likewise seemed larger than they should have been.

It's turned into something that's all mouths and jaws, Will thought. It's reaching out to swallow us.

Somebody needed to stop it, but the spellcasters were incapacitated. Will pulled his warsling from his belt and whipped a lead pellet at the sphere, but the missile flew right through the construct without disrupting it. He turned to Jivex, but the faerie dragon shook his head to indicate that he, too, had no notion what to do.

Then, shuddering and twitching, Nexus nonetheless manage to fix his luminous eyes on the orb. He growled a single word of power, and the sphere vanished, as did the lines of flame on the ground. The terrifying sense of malignancy enveloping the field disappeared in the same instant.

The spellcasters started shakily picking themselves up off the ground to adjust vomit-soiled and bloodstained garments, recover dropped talismans, and gingerly inspect the chewed tongues, bitten lips, and bruises sustained in their seizures and falls. All but Moonwing. The silver still lay where he'd dropped, but wasn't moving at all.

When he noticed, Azhaq lunged to his comrade's side. He peered down at the other shield dragon, then said, in a bleak, flat voice, "He's dead."

"I'm sorry," Havarlan said. "We'll remove him to a place where he can lie peacefully for the time being. But then, I think, we must continue our deliberations."

"Yes," Azhaq said. "He deserves better, but I understand."

Will supposed it was just as well they were taking a break. Brandobaris knew, most of the wizards, priests, and even dragons looked as if they needed one. Still, by the time Azhaq, Havarlan, and two other silvers came back from removing Moonwing's body, they'd managed to compose themselves. The mood, however, was even more palpably glum than before.

"What's the matter?" Will asked. "I'm sorry about Moonwing, too, but at least he didn't die for nothing. We saw the old elves' fortress, right? We actually saw it."

"We glimpsed it," Firefingers said. "But not clearly or long enough to determine its location."

"But if you did that well the first time, the next attempt is sure to work."

"Alas, no," Nexus said.

"Damn it!" said Will. "I'm tired of you people telling me that."

"No more tired," the gold replied, "than we are of saying it. But the wards are too strong. We're fortunate our initial effort to penetrate them didn't kill us all. A second would only result in further casualties."

"Cowards!" Jivex shrilled. "With the future of our people, of all the world, in jeopardy, dragons and wizards worthy of the name would try anyway!"

"I would gladly hazard my life," said Tamarand, "if I thought there was the slightest chance of it helping. So, I believe, would every one of us assembled here. But we mustn't destroy ourselves in mindless pursuit of a strategy that simply can't succeed. We must do what we've done again and again over the course of past several months, whenever a plan came to nothing: Formulate a new one."

Jivex gave a scornful sniff, but held his peace thereafter.

As threatened, the mages and drakes commenced an endless discussion too full of esoteric concepts and terminology for Will to follow. But he gleaned that no one had anything to propose that others didn't disparage as a flawed and futile waste of time.

It dampened whatever hope he had left, and bored him in the process. Eventually he sat down on the cold ground, and as Selûne progressed across the sky, and the spellcasters droned and bickered on, he found himself nodding off and jerking awake again.

Until Vingdavalac gave his wings, more yellowish than bronze-colored due to his relative youth, an irritable snap. "Is that it, then?" he demanded. "Are we beaten? Do we just go back to the havens, and sleep until we starve? At least that way, we won't run mad and commit atrocities."

"No!" said Tamarand. "I didn't rise up against Lareth merely to preside over our extinction!" He grimaced. "Not until I'm absolutely convinced of the necessity."

As the debate meandered on, Dorn, who'd stood mute and pretty much motionless since the conclave began, abruptly pivoted and stalked to Pavel's side. Will scrambled to his feet and hurried to join them.

"Figure it out," said Dorn.

Pavel gave him a quizzical look. "Surely you realize I would if I could. But our allies are some of the most learned wizards in all Faerûn. If they can't see a way . . . " He spread his hands.

"Look," said Will, "you're a fraud and an idiot, we all know that. But you claim you understand the concepts wizardry is based on, and occasionally, inexplicably, through the intercession of Lady Luck herself, I can only imagine, it's that pox-addled brain of yours that stumbles onto an idea when people far more intelligent—which is to say, most of them—are stymied. You're the one who worked out how to use Sammaster's folio, right? So don't just stand there like Blazanar's scarecrow. Earn your keep for once, and think."

"I'm trying," Pavel said. "I have been right along, and if the two of you will stop pestering me, I'll continue."

Will was sure the priest had indeed been pondering the problem. Still, after the exchange, his demeanor altered. He frowned and stared down at the ground, not at the drakes and warlocks. Will sensed that he'd stopped attending to them in order to follow where his own thoughts led.

But for a while, nothing came of it, just as nothing resulted from the wyrms and magicians rambling on and on. Probably, Will thought, because nothing could. Some dilemmas had no solutions, and this appeared to be one of them.

Then Pavel's head snapped up, and his body straightened. "I have an idea," he said, and everyone turned to peer at him.

"We're listening," said Azhaq, plainly skeptical that a mere human priest might have achieved an insight that eluded dragon sorcerers.

"First," Pavel said, "assume Brimstone made it through to the other side of the gate."

"Based on what we found inspecting the wreckage," said Nexus, "that's a highly optimistic assumption. But continue."

"Next," Pavel said, "consider that Brimstone is a vampiric drake. Supposedly, such creatures must stick close to their hoards or perish. Yet he wanders freely, and I believe I know how.

"I'm sure you all noticed the jeweled choker he wears. I think he enchanted it to embody the entire hoard. That's one of the basic principles of magic, isn't it, that a fragment maintains a fundamental identity with the whole from which it derives?"

"Yes," said Darvin, "but so what?"

"Will, Dorn, and I have been to Brimstone's cave in Impiltur. We've seen his treasure, and it fills an entire chamber. Which is to say, the hoard isn't merely a collection of coins and gems but virtually a place in its own right. By the laws of wizardry, the exact same place where he is now."

"By all the mysteries," said Nexus, "go there, and with the proper enchantments, we can open a new portal to translate us into Brimstone's presence. That's brilliant." He lowered his tapered, gleaming head in a gesture of respect.

"In theory," said Darvin, scowling. "But you said it yourself, my lord, the priest's speculations are wildly optimistic. You don't know for a fact that the collar has been made analogous to the entire horde, do you, Master Shemov?"

"No," said Pavel, "but it makes sense."

"So already," said the plump little wizard, "there's one way this scheme could go awry. We might also run afoul of more of the elf wizards' wards."

"That, I doubt," said Firefingers, scraggly white brows knitted in thought. "We know they themselves used teleportation magic to travel to and from their citadel, so it seems unlikely they left defenses in place to prevent that exact thing."

"Well . . . maybe," Darvin said. "But my gravest concern is the likelihood that Brimstone failed to reach the proper destination. If we fling ourselves after him, we might wind up nowhere at all, or on some plane inimical to life."

"Maybe we will," said Dorn. "But you folk have babbled most of the night away, and this is the only worthwhile idea anyone has come up with. So now each of us just has to decide whether he's willing to take the risk. I am."

"As am I," said Tamarand. "If it kills me, so be it. Better to die trying than to lose myself to the Rage, or waste away in my sleep."

Other dragons clamored, each declaring himself of the same mind.

"Our king," said Celedon, "sent Drigor and me to observe your endeavor and assist however we could. So, with your permission, we'll tag along."

That left the Thentian spellcasters, and from them, Will anticipated less unanimity. Though each commanded formidable magic, a number were sedentary scholars, not battle wizards inured to peril and hardship. The world as they knew it might be in jeopardy, but unlike the dragons, they weren't worried about insanity overwhelming them, and in addition to all that, they'd rarely agreed on anything in all the years he'd known them.

Yet they surprised him. Starting with Firefingers and Baerimel, each, even Darvin, albeit with a petulant, grudging air, declared himself willing to make the attempt. Maybe, after laboring to foil Sammaster's schemes for the better part of a year, they simply had to see firsthand how it would all work out in the end.

"Bless you all," said Tamarand. "Whatever befalls us, it will be an honor to meet it in such a company. Now, I suggest you small folk go home to sleep. We'll fly for Impiltur in the morning."

Jivex spat, suffusing the air with a flowery scent. "Apparently everybody just takes it for granted that I'm coming along."

"Well," said Will, "aren't you?"

"Of course!" the faerie dragon replied. "Someone of sound judgment has to lead."

TWELVE

5 Nightal, the Year of Rogue Dragons

Something had changed, but at first Taegan didn't know what.

Propped against a lump of rock, he'd been half sitting and half lying, attempting with only limited success to escape from hunger, cold, dirtiness, anxiety, and boredom into the trance-like state of vivid memory that was an elf's equivalent of slumber. Raryn lay snoring to one side. Kara's eyes were closed as well, but even so, it seemed likely she was awake, for she crooned under her breath. Brimstone was deeper in the cavern, out of view. Taegan had scarcely seen him for two days, and suspected he was keeping his distance in an effort to control his blood thirst.

Accordingly, when his intuition whispered that something was amiss, the avariel pivoted to see if Brimstone was slinking forth from his seclusion. But he wasn't, not even as a cloud of smoke and embers.

Taegan then realized what had actually snagged his attention: the alteration in Kara's singing. Before, the wordless melodies had sounded like lullabies and wistful ballads. The tune waxed louder, accelerated, assumed a driving tempo, warping into one of her battle anthems.

Taegan had never known her to sing such a song except in combat. Perhaps it was harmless, but he was leery of anything that might cause her to dwell on thoughts of violence.

"Kara?" he said.

She didn't answer, just kept singing. He repeated her name, louder this time. That prompted Raryn to open his eyes, but still failed to elicit any acknowledgment from the bard.

Was she asleep after all? Singing in the throes of a dream or nightmare? Taegan rose, walked to her, clasped her shoulder, and gave it a gentle shake.

Her eyes flew open, and the pupils were diamond-shaped. Her song became an incantation. Taegan reached to cover her mouth, but was an instant too slow. Something he couldn't see slammed him in the chest and hurled him across the chamber to crash into the opposite wall.

Kara surged to her feet, nails lengthening into talons, scales sprouting across her cheeks and brow, her moon-blond tresses shortening. Raryn scrambled to interpose himself between her and the elf.

"Don't!" he said. "Taegan's your friend. We're both your friends."

She crouched, and heart pounding, throat clogged with dread, Taegan waited for her to finish expanding and melting into dragon form. But Raryn's plea must finally have registered, for she straightened up instead. The claws dwindled, and the scales faded.

"Are you hurt?" she asked.

Taegan rose and shook out his pinions. His feathers rustled. "It doesn't appear so."

"I'm so sorry!"

"It's all right."

She glared so furiously that he wondered if she might attack again. "How can you say that? Of course it isn't 'all right!'"

"It is," Raryn said, "so long as you can rein the frenzy in."

"That won't be much longer."

"It may be long enough," Taegan said. "An opportunity could present itself at any moment. We simply have to be ready."

"So we should just keep waiting," Kara said, "for something—we can't even say what—to improve our circumstances? Wait until my mind finishes crumbling, and I slaughter the both of you? No. I'm done with that."

Taegan arched an eyebrow. "I understand your dissatisfaction with such a passive strategy, but I fail to see an alternative."

"I'm going to fight the Tarterians," she said.

"You mean, the one of you against the six of them?" Raryn said.

She nodded. "If I kill them, Brimstone can go fetch our allies. It won't matter how many maze traps he blunders into on his way through the mountains, or how long it takes him to find his way out, so long as no enemies are left to pounce on him when he reemerges."

"But you can't beat them," Raryn said.

"I fought well at the monastery, didn't I? I helped slay Malazan."

"I know," said the dwarf, "I was there, and believe me, no one respects your prowess more than I. But you didn't win your victories alone, and you can't kill six Tarterians by yourself, either. We four fighting in concert couldn't do it."

"If you're right," she said, "and I fail, the rest of you will still be safer. Because I won't be here to threaten you."

"Milady," Taegan said, "you understand your mind is under assault. So trust us when we tell you this scheme is a manifestation of the very irrationality you fear."

She smiled a nasty smile more akin to Brimstone's sneers than any expression he'd hitherto observed on her lovely face.

"If my words reveal insanity, that surely proves my point."

"Singer," Raryn said, "back at the start of the year, you hired me to be your bodyguard. I still am, even if the job has become more complicated. I can't let you leave the cave until this . . . bitter humor passes."

Kara stared into the dwarf's eyes, then sighed and shook her head. "Once again," she said, "I'm ashamed. Our predicament is difficult enough without . . . " She took a subtle step backward.

Taegan sensed she was widening the distance to improve her chances of casting a spell before they could do anything about it. "Get her!" he cried. "Knock her out!"

He beat his pinions and sprang at her. Raryn followed. She scurried backward and sang the opening notes of a charm.

Taegan punched at her jaw, and she slipped the blow. Raryn bulled into her legs, threw his arms around them, and bore her down in a tackle. Her body smacked hard on the floor, but not hard enough to stop her singing.

The final note boomed like thunder, jolting and staggering Taegan, jabbing pain into his ears, echoing between the granite walls. For a moment, he couldn't act or even think, and evidently, neither could Raryn, for Kara kicked free of his arms, leaped up, and darted for the mouth of the cave.

Taegan caught his balance, turned, and raced after her. Half deaf from the thunderclap, he faintly heard her start another song. Empty air gave birth to pale fog, concealing her willowy form. Even worse, when he plunged into the mist, grasping blindly, he found it possessed a degree of solidity, impeding him as if he were trying to push through a wall of snow.

He floundered in the stuff for another moment, until Brimstone snarled, in his soft, sibilant voice, "Are you all mad, making so much noise?" Taegan turned. Crimson eyes glowing, the dark-scaled vampiric wyrm was otherwise all but indistinguishable in the gloom.

"Kara's having a fit," said Raryn, on his feet once more and hastily taking up his axe, quiver, and bow. "She thinks she needs to fight the Tarterians all by herself, and we couldn't stop her from leaving."

Brimstone's eyes flared brighter, and the scent of burning that clung to him intensified. "That won't do," he whispered, then murmured a word of power that dissolved the mass of fog. "Climb onto my back, Raryn Snowstealer."

Taegan didn't wait for the dwarf and smoke drake to prepare themselves. He dashed out of the cave and scanned the benighted sky. Still singing, wings beating, Kara was headed out into the valley, but didn't have quite as much of a lead as he'd expected. He realized she'd required a moment to shapeshift before taking to the air.

He lashed his pinions and gave chase, rattling off his charm of quickness. Power burned and jolted through his limbs, and afterward, her wings appeared to flap more slowly. But she was still flying faster than he was.

"Kara!" he shouted. "Stop!"

It was madness to yell out in the open, where no wards existed to muffle the sound, but he didn't know what else to do.

She didn't respond.

Raryn, too, called Kara's name. Taegan glanced back. The hunter and Brimstone were flying up behind him, overtaking him, though it appeared unlikely they'd catch up with the song dragon. Brimstone whispered an incantation, power whined, and Taegan felt queasy.

A cloud of gray mist swirled into existence around Kara. Even at a distance, Taegan could smell the putrid stink of it. Kara jerked as if in pain, and her anthem caught in her throat. She dived below the vapor and wheeled back around.

For a moment, Taegan hoped that Brimstone's attack—which, though apparently aversive, had inflicted no visible wounds—had shocked Kara back to sanity. But no. She answered with a musical spell of her own. Brimstone lifted one wing high and dropped the other low, veering off, dodging, but when the song dragon's darts of azure light streaked at him, they turned in flight and pierced him anyway.

Brimstone grunted and snarled another charm. A spark hurtled at Kara, and she, too, tried unsuccessfully to dodge. The point of light flared and banged into a spherical burst of flame, searing the left side of her body. She floundered, her wings ataxic, and the smoke drake drove at her.

"What are you doing?" Raryn cried. "That could have killed her!"

"As her magic could destroy me," Brimstone said, without slowing or veering off. He had the advantage of height, and was swooping down at her. "She's lost to us now. I need to kill her before she brings the Tarterians down on us, and take her blood to keep from craving yours."

Taegan realized with a stab of horror that both dragons had succumbed to their particular compulsions. The excitement of the chase and of combat, coupled with the pain of injury, had so amplified Brimstone's thirst that it clouded his reason.

White mane streaming and tossing around his head, Raryn set the edge of his axe against Brimstone's neck. "Stop this," the ranger said, "or—"

Apparently not so stunned as she'd appeared, Kara abruptly resumed her song, beat her wings, and veered. She lifted her head, opened her jaws, and spat a sparkling, crackling flare of her breath.

The lightning infusing the vapor had little effect on Brimstone. Raryn, however, convulsed. Afterward, swaying, the dwarf continued to cling to his perch on the smoke drake's back, but that was all he could manage. He was no longer capable of threatening anyone.

Brimstone turned, compensating for Kara's attempt to dodge out from underneath him. His claws stabbed into her back, and impelled by his momentum, they plummeted together, to slam down on the floor of the valley. Old, broken bones flew up at the impact.

Raryn jumped off Brimstone and staggered away just

before the two wyrms started rolling, biting, and tearing at one another. Had he been even an instant slower, they surely would have crushed him. When clear, he collapsed to his knees, and his sides heaved. Plainly, for the moment, he had nothing more to give.

Though unscathed, Taegan felt almost as helpless. He didn't want to help Kara battle Brimstone. However demonic his fundamental nature, the vampire was an ally, and even had it been otherwise, destroying him would do nothing to restore Kara's reason.

Yet he saw no other recourse, and so, sword poised, rattling off an incantation to surround himself with phantom duplicates, he dived at the tangled, writhing drakes. Then something hissed and screeched. He leveled off and wheeled to see that the Tarterians were coming.

Someone in Lyrabar had spotted the dragons winging their way through the twilight. But either the folk in the city hadn't discerned the wyrms were metallics, or else had deemed it prudent to sound the alarm even so, for all the countless temple bells were tolling, and had been for a considerable time.

But no one had rushed forth to confront the travelers. When the drakes and their riders spiraled downward toward the hill crowned with its circle of weathered menhirs, nine standing, one fallen on its side, the landscape was otherwise deserted.

Swinging himself down off Tamarand's back—arguably a position of honor, though, grieving and guilty over Lareth's death, the gold had turned out to be just as taciturn and uncongenial a companion as Dorn—Pavel noticed that Darvin and a number of the other Thentians appeared relieved to be back on the ground. Hissing and screwing up their faces, they rubbed their thighs and hobbled stiffly around.

Firefingers, though, despite looking twice as old as any of the others, strolled briskly around inspecting the symbols carved on the standing stones. "This place was sacred to Bane," he said.

"Yes," said Pavel, "but according to Brimstone, the decent folk of Impiltur eradicated the coven long ago. These days, the circle is simply the entrance to his lair. Or at least, I hope it still is."

"If it isn't," said Havarlan, argent, much-scarred scales shining even in the evening gloom, "we'll simply have to break it open." Like most of the drakes, she crouched on the hillside, outside the ring. The space inside wasn't big enough to hold more than a couple wyrms at a time.

"Are you sure you can?" asked Will, still astride Wardancer.

Havarlan snorted, chilling the air and suffusing it with the smell of rain. "I certainly hope so. For if we can't contend with Brimstone's enchantments, we surely have no chance of countering Sammaster's magic, or that of the primordial elves."

"Well," Pavel said, "let's try it the easy way first." His bad leg aching a little—days on dragon-back had taken a toll on him as well—he strode to the center of the circle. Tamarand, Firefingers, Dorn, Scattercloak, Jivex, and Jannatha came to join him.

"Brimstone!" he shouted.

As before, for a split second, he seemed to fall, or to hurtle like an arrow through emptiness dappled with light, then the vampire's limestone cavern sprang into being around him. The cool, greenish light of the perpetual torches gleamed on coffer after overflowing coffer of coins and gems. Despite Brimstone's extended absence, the lair still smelled of smoke and sulfur.

Hovering, wings glimmering, Jivex peered about. "I'm a dragon," he said. "Why don't I have heaps of sparkly stuff?"

"I suggest," said Scattercloak, "we move. We don't want the others dropping in right on top of us."

They all hurried into a side gallery, less stuffed with

treasure than the first chamber, but still aglitter with a certain amount of overflow. The rest of their companions blinked into view, a few at a time. Once they perceived that they hadn't teleported themselves into danger, the gold and silver dragons shrank into human form, relieving what would otherwise have been claustrophobic congestion.

"Now, then," said Firefingers. "Those of us who understand portal magic will need to work in the center of the hoard. Everyone else, please, give us room."

As Pavel watched the wizards, human and dragon alike, set about their labors, Sureene, clad in silvery mail that glowed like moonlight, and made her look like a handsome warrior queen, came to stand beside him.

"Well done," she murmured.

He shrugged. "Anybody could have called out Brimstone's name."

"I mean all of it. I have a gift for you." She opened the satchel hanging over her shoulder and brought out a leather scroll case. "The divine magic version of the spell to end the Rage, scribed half a dozen times over."

"I accept it gratefully, of course, but I trust it will be truly accomplished spellcasters like Firefingers, Nexus, and you who actually make the attempt to end the curse."

"So one would expect," she said, "but then we expected the warlocks would be the ones to solve the problem of reaching the citadel, too. It's best if every spellcaster in our company possesses the means to try, and from what I understand, you've been too busy roaming around gathering vital information, rescuing kings and kingdoms, and slaughtering evil wyrms to master the actual incantation."

Was she flirting with him? It felt like it, and the gods knew, even though she was ten years older than he, he'd always fancied her. He'd just never tried to do anything about it because she'd always seemed too dignified, busy, important, and generally unavailable. He started to frame a suitably glib but modest response, then glimpsed motion at the periphery of his vision.

Will glanced surreptitiously around. Then he eased in front of an open chest, shielding it behind his body and cloak. His hand slipped toward a gold ring set with an emerald solitaire.

"Please, pardon me just a moment," Pavel said. He advanced on Will. "Leave that, insect!"

The halfling snatched his hand back. "What?"

"You know what. Leave the treasure alone. If you steal anything, you could change the hoard's essential identity, and keep the wizards from opening the gate."

"You don't know that. You just like frustrating your betters. My whole life, I've wanted to loot a dragon's lair. Now here we are, with the tenant nowhere around—"

"No one cares about your sordid predilections. Restrain yourself." Pavel turned back around, only to discover that Sureene had drifted away and stood murmuring with Baerimel and Jannatha. The moment had passed.

As he drew breath to shower Will with invective, brightness bloomed in the air above the bulk of the hoard, the soft radiance glinting on jewels and pieces of precious metal. The portal resembled a whirlpool standing on end, and likewise light refracting through a prism.

"If Brimstone happens to be flying," said Tamarand, currently wearing the shape of a slim youth with curly chestnut hair, "we could step through into empty air."

"Or something a thousand times worse," Darvin said.

The gold ignored the interruption. "Accordingly, we dragons will pass through in our true shapes, carrying our allies on our back. That way, no one will come to harm by falling. I'll go first."

Pavel supposed that meant he would, too. He headed for Tamarand, who swelled and dropped to all fours, clothing dissolving, wings erupting from his shoulder blades.

When the transformation was complete, Pavel climbed onto the dragon's back. Tamarand sprang at the luminous disk, and evidently recognizing that the gate was just large enough for him to pass through at the same time, Jivex opted to streak along beside him.

Taegan didn't know what to do. Probably, he thought, because there was no way to avert disaster.

But he could see that Kara and Brimstone were still ripping at one another as if they hadn't even noticed the advent of the Tarterians. If the six otherworldly wyrms descended on them while they were tangled together, they'd have no chance at all. Nor would Raryn, who'd struggled back to his feet, but was still only a few paces away from his draconic allies.

So Taegan decided to try to lead the Tarterians away from his friends, to give Raryn time to hide, and Kara and Brimstone a final chance to come to their senses. He flew higher, shouting and brandishing Rilitar's sword, then wheeled and raced zigzagging away from Sammaster's minions.

A blaze of breath narrowly missed him and obliterated two of his illusory twins. Beginning a charm to cloak himself in blur, he glanced back, then felt a surge of despair.

Three of the Tarterians were chasing him, but the others were spiraling down toward his allies, and despite the imminent threat, Kara and Brimstone continued battling one another. Raryn shouted to them to stop, to look, while loosing arrows at the creatures overhead. Shaft after shaft pierced the Tarterians' dark, mottled hide, but the wounds were insufficient to deter them.

With all hope lost, Taegan considered translating himself through space so he could at least die fighting in proximity to his comrades. But then the Tarterians on his tail would follow him back to Kara and the others, and though he couldn't see how it actually mattered either way, somehow he just couldn't bring himself to do it. He flew onward instead, toward the dark, snow-dappled barrier mountains.

Instinct prompted him to veer, and a bubble of shadow burst into existence beside him, almost caging him, but not quite. Unfortunately, though, his evasive maneuver turned him straight at a Tarterian that had drawn up even with him on his left flank. Until this moment, he hadn't even realized it was there.

He looked around for a ghost dragon, or one of the areas of old, decaying magic his pursuers avoided. Neither was within reach. The wyrms had him boxed in, with nowhere left to flee. Green eyes shining, the Tarterian in front of him spread its black-fanged jaws.

Then a cloud of hummingbirds popped into existence around it and jabbed at it with their needle beaks. Startled, the Tarterian spewed hammering force at them instead of Taegan, cutting a clear space through the middle of the flock but not destroying them all. The remainder continued to harass it, and it struck at them with tooth and claw.

Its distraction afforded Taegan an avenue of escape. He swung around the reptile, placing it between the other two wyrms and himself, and as he did so, Jivex's voice sounded from somewhere close at hand.

"How did you ever survive this long without me?" the faerie dragon asked.

To Pavel's relief, the gate actually had transported him, Tamarand, and Jivex to the valley they'd glimpsed before the grand divination went awry, but also into the midst of a situation so chaotic that it took him a moment or two of casting about to make any sense of it.

Exiting the portal, he and his companions found themselves on barren, bone-littered ground, with Kara and Brimstone locked in snarling combat close at hand. Three of the black, green-eyed wyrms—Tarterian dragons, if he could trust a reference he'd read as a seminary student—glided overhead.

Jivex whirled and sped away. He must have spotted something else requiring his attention. But before Pavel could determine what, one of the black, speckled wyrms overhead cocked its head back and whipped it down. Its jaws snapped open wide, and a grayish, expanding burst of breath weapon exploded from its gullet.

Tamarand lashed his pinions and leaped. The blaze of force pounded down, jolting and cracking the frozen earth, smashing crumbling skeletons, but missing its targets. All three Tarterians maneuvered, orienting themselves to strike at the gigantic gold even as he roared an incantation.

A floating circle of white radiance appeared around Tamarand's body, and a pair of sizzling lightning bolts leaped upward from the ring. Each stabbed into the belly of one of the Tarterians, and the reptiles convulsed. At the same time, the gold crouched low and shrugged, spilling Pavel to the ground.

Tamarand then leaped, beat his gleaming, leathery wings, and took to the air. A flare of Tarterian breath bashed him, made him wobble in flight, but failed to knock him down. He riposted with a blast of fire, and his assailant plummeted, its tattered wings burning like dry leaves.

Meanwhile, Wardancer sprang through the portal with Will perched at the base of her serpentine neck. The bronze looked around, then flapped her wings and climbed to join the aerial combat. Unlike Tamarand, she hadn't opted to deposit her rider on the ground first, and the halfling pulled the warsling from his belt.

Their departure left Pavel to deal with Kara and Brimstone, at least until more of his comrades emerged from the gate. As always, mere proximity to the vampire made him clench with loathing, and his instinct was to do everything in his power to help Kara destroy him. But perhaps that would be wrong. Brimstone was an ally, too, and at the moment, arguably not responsible for his actions. His exile in this desolate place had likely left him starved for blood.

Thus, instead of casting attack spells, Pavel simply evoked flares of Lathander's warm, red-gold light from his amulet. The tactic worked to a degree. Brimstone hissed, twisted his head away from the glow, and attempted to scramble backward. Unfortunately, Kara still held him gripped in her talons and coils and wouldn't release him. She simply took advantage of his temporary incapacity to inflict further harm.

"Stop!" Pavel shouted. "Let him go!"

Somewhere close at hand, Raryn bellowed the same thing. But she didn't heed them. Pavel belatedly realized both dragons were mad, the vampire with blood thirst, Kara, with the Rage, and he had no idea what to do about it.

Then Nexus was there, huge as Tamarand, so huge that even Brimstone and Kara appeared small in comparison. He declaimed a rhyme, and some unseen force seized hold of Kara, yanked her away from the smoke drake, and flung her torn, bloody body through the air. Nexus wheeled, keeping track of her, and started another incantation.

That meant it was still Pavel's job to control Brimstone. Unfortunately, fangs bared, the vampire was already pivoting back in his direction. Pavel could keep producing blazes of dawnlight, but what would happen when he'd exhausted the capability?

Then Pavel noticed the Tarterian Tamarand had burned. The dark wyrm was still on the ground, its smoking wings apparently too charred to bear it aloft once more. Its neck swayed this way and that as it sought to aim a breath or supernatural attack at the gold soaring overhead.

Pavel pointed, shouted, "Look there!" and when Brimstone failed to heed him, forced the reptile to flinch and turn with another pulse of holy light. "There's blood! Take it from an enemy, not your allies!"

Brimstone hesitated, then lashed his wings, pounced on the other dragon's back, and buried his oversized fangs in its throat. They rolled, tangled together, spat blasts of breath at one another.

Pavel thought he should help Brimstone, but peered about first, lest some menace steal up on him unnoticed.

Nexus held Kara pinned beneath him as he recited the spell to quell the Rage. Obviously, the ward she'd previously established had failed, and the gold sought to conjure a replacement. Snarling and hissing, the song dragon struggled beneath him, and Pavel recalled with dismay that supposedly, only Sammaster had achieved such mastery of the enchantment that he could impose it on an unwilling subject. Nexus must hope that, despite all appearances to the contrary, Kara wasn't wholly lost to madness.

Dorn hovered near the confrontation. Maybe he thought it would help if Kara could see him.

Meanwhile, dragons and their riders lunged one pair at a time through the portal. Some of the wyrms staggered, or crouched down shaking, as something afflicted them, and Pavel surmised that the Rage must be even stronger here near the source. But none of the metallics succumbed. They shook off their distress, then they and their human comrades threw themselves into the confrontation with the Tarterians.

Some battled close at hand, fighting the wyrms Tamarand had initially engaged. Azhaq spat pale, glittering vapor that paralyzed Brimstone's opponent but had no effect on the vampire, who then guzzled and slurped the live wyrm's blood. Gloved hands gesturing, Scattercloak murmured a rhyme, whereupon gashes split a flying Tarterian's hide.

Other dragons and their riders streaked away in the direction Jivex had gone, to confront the three Tarterians wheeling in that portion of the sky.

In both cases, the end result was the same. The guardian drakes were powerful, but so were the newcomers, who also had them outnumbered. One by one, the Tarterians fell.

Which meant no one needed any further assistance from Pavel after all. He turned back around to see how Kara, Nexus, and Dorn were faring.

The gold roared the concluding syllable of his incantation. Kara kept on thrashing. Dorn rushed in close to her head. If she snapped at him, or spat lightning, he had no hope of avoiding it.

Heedless of the danger, he placed himself before one of her glaring amethyst eyes and rested his human hand on her brow. "It's me," he said, "and you're alive. You can't let the frenzy swallow you now!"

She shuddered, then sang the same words of power Nexus had just spoken, the sound both lovely and full of anguish, or perhaps, supreme effort. Gradually, almost imperceptibly at first, she shrank back into human form. Nexus stepped back and so avoided crushing her.

When she was entirely a woman once more, Kara and Dorn embraced. She started weeping, and so did he. The latter was a sight Pavel had never seen, nor ever expected to.

Dorn and Kara slipped away from the others as soon as they could manage it discreetly. At first, they had better things to do than talk. But afterwards, as they lay twined together wrapped in their cloaks, she explained how she'd survived.

"Maybe I should have guessed," he said, playing with a lock of her moon-blond hair. "After all, I realized you'd discovered something, so maybe I should have wondered if it wasn't you and not Brimstone who woke the magic in the cobbles. But curse it all, I'd just seen you die!"

She smiled. "Did you believe only Jivex and Chatulio could conjure illusions? Perhaps I should be offended." Her levity gave way to a gentler tone: "Truly, I'm sorry my trick deceived you and caused you pain."

"Don't be sorry for something that saved your life! I just wish . . . after I watched it happen, nothing meant anything. I wouldn't be here with you now, or alive anywhere, most likely, if Pavel, Will, and even Jivex hadn't looked after me. I'm ashamed of that. You deserve a better man—"

She laid a finger across his lips. "Let's make a pact," she said. "You won't abuse yourself for all your supposed shortcomings, and I won't berate myself for my inability to withstand the Rage."

He smiled. "That sounds all right."

Kara's head turned, and after another moment, Dorn heard what she was hearing: the rhythmic scuffing of footsteps on frozen earth and rock. He'd laid his sword ready to hand, and he gripped the hilt, cast away his makeshift blanket, leaped to his feet, and assumed his fighting stance.

Carrying the new bow, axe, and harpoon his friends had brought in hopes of finding him alive, Raryn emerged from the darkness to behold his partner poised for combat, except for a total lack of clothing. The dwarf's lips quirked upward behind the shaggy white mustache, and Kara giggled.

Dorn gave her a look of mock reproach. "You can see in the dark," he said. "You could have told me who was coming."

"I wanted to," she said, "but, hero that you are, you sprang into action so quickly!"

"Sorry to intrude," Raryn said. "But Firefingers thinks the magic keeping us out of the castle is about to give way. I thought you'd want to be there." He gave them a nod, turned, and tramped back down the slope.

Shivering, Dorn pulled on his garments, and Kara did the same. They kissed once more, then descended the trail until they reached a spot affording a view of the ruined citadel.

To Dorn's eyes, the pile was mostly just a shapeless black mass in the gloom, but silvery light illuminated the vicinity of the white-walled barbican, and the dragons and smaller folk assembled there working their magic. Their chanting droned.

Kara studied the scene, then said, "Yes! Nexus and the others are breaking through."

"Then . . . we win?" It was wonderful, yet also strange to think that the year-long struggle might conclude so quietly. To realize that, here at the end, after all his battles, he'd likely just stand looking on while dragons and wizards finished the work.

"I think so," Kara said.

THIRTEEN

6 Nightal, the Year of Rogue Dragons

The ferule of his staff thumping on the ground and hard-packed earthen floors, Sammaster prowled through the Cult of the Dragon's newest stronghold, making sure all was as it should be.

He'd masked his withered skull-face with the semblance of life, and eliminated the scent of corruption wafting from his person, but even so, as he encountered his followers, many seemed nervous. Perhaps they feared he'd overheard them grumbling about the dearth of creature comforts, the long hours of arduous labor, or the surly, impatient ingratitude of the Sacred Ones for whom they toiled.

He actually sympathized with their discontents. Though a lich had little use for such amenities, he certainly recalled how the living craved tasty, plentiful food, warmth, slumber in soft beds, and diversions at the end of a hard day's work.

Unfortunately, the cult had hastily built this enclave—a palisade surrounding a collection of low, ramshackle structures with sod roofs—in the hills north of the steppeland called the Ride. Its remoteness from civilization ensured that the conspirators' enemies wouldn't discover and destroy it as they had so many others, but likewise obliged them to endure primitive conditions.

It was the inexorable progress of the Rage, however, that necessitated the lengthy, grueling work shifts. The curse kept waxing stronger, and would soon become so virulent that even Sammaster would no longer be able to suppress it in the minds of individual dragons. He had to produce enough dracoliches to fulfill Maglas's prophecy before that came to pass, because, lost to derangement, the rest of the chromatics would reject transformation thereafter.

As for the arrogance and sour humor of the reptiles—well, that was dragons for you. They were more magnificent than the very gods, but could also comport themselves like petulant, malicious, selfish children. It made sense once one realized that the even the oldest were ultimately immature and incomplete. It was only in undeath that they achieved their full potential.

So, when Sammaster caught one of his underlings flagging or shirking, he sought first to lift his spirits. To make him laugh, encourage him with praise, inspire him by describing the glorious world to come, or tempt him with promises of reward. But if such measures failed, he had no choice but resort to threats, and when even those proved insufficient, punishment.

Because the cultists simply had to keep working. Even if they were coming to hate and fear the increasingly erratic creatures to whom they'd pledged their worship. Even if their service had begun to feel like exile and slavery. Even if it turned out that the future held no reward for them but the knowledge that they'd played a part in fulfilling destiny's plan. For ultimately, that fulfillment was the only thing that mattered.

Of course, Sammaster was the person who truly bore the responsibility for creating the Faerûn to be, and sometimes, when his spiteful, envious foes thwarted one or another of his schemes, it weighed on him like a yoke of iron. Sometimes his setbacks made him feel pathetically inadequate, and he yearned to pass the burden to another. But there was no one else, and even if there had been, he actually knew it was his calling that defined and empowered him. Forsake it and his wizardry notwithstanding it, he'd revert to the hapless wretch Mystra, Alustriel, and so many others had abused and betrayed.

A roar and a crash jolted him from his meditations.

He turned. Knotted together, clawing, biting, and lashing one another with their tails, Chuth, a green drake, and Ssalangan, a white, rolled through the wreckage of the cookhouse. Cultists scurried to distance themselves from the fight. Other wyrms gathered around to watch.

Sammaster supposed it could be worse. The destruction of the kitchen with its ovens, hearth, and larder would pose a hardship to the humans who depended on them, but had the dragons demolished one of the shrines or workshops involved in the Sacred Work, their confrontation could have set the process back by tendays.

As it still might, if he didn't intervene. He flourished his staff and shouted, *"Stop!"* Magic amplified his voice into an earth-shaking boom.

The brawling dragons froze, then slunk apart, off the collapsed cookhouse and the squashed, motionless human bodies visible inside. Once again, the wyrms reminded Sammaster of children. Children caught misbehaving.

"What's this about?" he asked.

Chuth spat, suffusing the air with a noxious, stinging hint of his breath weapon. "This pale little newt claims that he, and the vermin who flew in with him, deserve the right to change before the rest of us."

"Yes," said Ssalangan. "As near as I can make out, you lot have spent the last few months lying around doing nothing.

My companions and I performed a vital service. Therefore, we've earned the right to become dracoliches first."

Sammaster wondered again precisely what Ssalangan and the other whites had accomplished, or bungled, during the course of their "vital service." The reptiles claimed they'd finished subjugating the Great Glacier for Iyraclea, losing Zethrindor and several other comrades in the doing, but were vague about the details. Sammaster suspected they were withholding information they thought would displease him.

Such perversity was frustrating, but he hadn't felt he could press too hard. He might be the architect of their destiny, but he was also, in the final analysis, their servant. Besides, a thousand other matters clamored for his attention.

Like this present bit of folly. "We've already decided in what order you drakes will undergo the ritual," he said. "The matter doesn't require further discussion."

"Curse you!" Ssalangan snarled, blood seeping from claw marks on his alabaster neck. "It isn't fair!" Other whites growled and hissed in agreement.

"I beg you to be patient," Sammaster said. "After months of preparation, we're finally ready to begin. I promise that by year's end, you'll all be dracoliches."

"I don't even want to be undead," Ssalangan grumbled, "at least not yet, not for hundreds of years. I'm only doing it because you and these miserable humans swear the frenzy's never going to end. If I thought—"

"What do you perceive when you look inside yourself?" Sammaster said. "The Rage has festered in your mind for an entire year. Is it dwindling, or growing ever stronger?"

The white grunted and turned away, unable to refute the point but also unwilling to concede it. Sammaster smiled to the limited extent that his shriveled countenance was still capable of it, then the world flared a luminous red and tolled like a colossal bell.

Or at least it did for him. No one else appeared to sense anything out of the ordinary, nor was there any reason why they should. He'd created the ward to alert only himself.

"I have to go," he said. "I'll return as soon as I can." He rattled off a charm and thumped the butt of his staff on the ground. The world shattered and remade itself in an instant.

As intended, his spell of translocation deposited him behind an arched window in one of the watchtowers overlooking the elven citadel's forward aspect. It was the destruction of his enchantment of twisted space that had triggered the mystical warning, and the folk in front of the barbican were still congratulating themselves on their success in breaching it.

They hadn't sensed his arrival, nor spotted him framed in the shadowy window, and that gave him a chance to study them. He recognized some of the metallics, like Nexus, Havarlan, and Tamarand, and had he believed that any of his enemies could ever reach this hidden, isolated place, he might have expected to encounter them here. But the rest of the motley band was an astonishment. He could see no sign of the Chosen, Harpers, or deities who'd thwarted him in the past. In their place blathered the mages of Thentia, a potential problem he'd believed he'd neutralized. A hulking warrior with two iron limbs, and a black-winged avariel. A dark wyrm with luminous red eyes—could it actually be Brimstone, who'd turned against him so long ago?

It was maddening, inconceivable, that all they'd all found their way here, through the labyrinth of perils and obfuscations he'd created to prevent it. Fury came shrieking up inside him, directed less at the intruders than at himself, a worthless dunce who'd somehow managed to fail yet again.

But no, it wasn't true. He hadn't failed, not while he himself was the final protection, still in place. He, and the minions sworn to rush to his aid, if ever the ruined castle needed defending.

Down below, his enemies, still oblivious to his presence, started organizing themselves into search parties. It gave him time to armor himself in charms of protection. Then he twisted a tarnished silver ring on his bony finger and whispered a single word.

The night blazed as if the stars were all falling at once.

With a bit of trepidation, Kara began the shift to dragon form. The Rage would grind at her more forcefully in that guise, but she thought she could bear it for as long as it would take to find and destroy the source of the curse, and her draconic prowess might prove useful if Sammaster had left still more guardians or traps inside the castle. Her wings leaped forth from her shoulders, she dropped to all fours, Dorn stepped back to give her expanding body room, then the black sky flared white.

She looked up, at luminous circles like a dozen full moons, and realized they were gates. Serpentine shadows with batlike wings appeared in the rounds, taking on definition, solidity, even as the portals faded, until the reptiles were wholly present, and the wounds in space, entirely healed.

In that first moment, she couldn't count the newcomers, though she did perceive that they had the dragons on the ground outnumbered. Nor could she identify the various species in all their diversity, especially since she'd never actually encountered most of them before, merely their descriptions, in books or recitations of esoteric lore.

But she did spot a gigantic hellfire wyrm, with bony spikes stabbing up from its head and shoulders, and the color of its scales inconstant, oozing from one shade of yellow or crimson to another as if the creature were made of flowing magma.

Also a howling dragon, long and spindly of body, with deceptively short and delicate-looking limbs. Topaz eyes dotted with minute pupils glared from its mask, and a ruff of spines encircled the back of its head.

Near the howling drake swooped a pyroclastic dragon, massively built, its hide a mottled confusion of dark patches mixed with streaks and blotches of fiery red and gold. Its wings were gray and fragile in appearance, like charred parchment.

All were wyrms native to other levels of existence, ones likewise home to fiends, malevolent deities, and the damned. Plainly, Sammaster had compelled or purchased their aid as he had that of his Tarterians and shadow dragons, and arranged for them to appear and attack if intruders unsealed the castle.

And they attacked with all the advantages of height and surprise. Commencing a battle anthem, Kara lashed her wings and sprang into the air. With a great clatter of pinions, her rogues, and the drakes who had eventually made common cause with them, followed after her.

Even as they took flight, Nexus and some of the others rattled off incantations. Celedon, Drigor, and the spellcasters of Thentia did the same. Floating shields and barriers of congealed light shimmered into existence between Sammaster's minions and their intended prey.

But not enough of them, not in time. As they dived, the lich's sentinels spat a dazzling, shrieking assortment of breath weapons, blasts of flame, lightning, and hammering sound that crisscrossed and overlapped as they hurtled down. The attacks found the gaps in the defensive enchantments and would surely have killed folk on the ground if some of the metallics hadn't deliberately placed themselves in the way. Wardancer stretched her wings wide to catch every bit of a pale burst of frost. It coated her dorsal surface in rime and made her wobble spastically in flight.

But she survived. Everyone in Kara's field of vision survived, and it was time to strike back. Wheeling, she spotted a chaos dragon—changing color repeatedly like a chameleon, only fast as the beat of a panicked heart, even the shape of its body in constant flux—within reach.

She flapped her wings and flew at it, her breath tingling and ready in her chest and throat. She opened her jaws and spat a crackling plume of vapor infused with lightning.

The flare struck the chaos dragon's flank, and it convulsed. At once, she sang words of power to evoke a stabbing shaft of the same force. Sammaster's minion struggled to swoop beneath the attack, and partially succeeded. The lightning didn't hit it in the torso as intended, but still burned a hole in each of its upraised pinions.

A pair of arrows streaked up from the ground and drove deep into the chaos drake's belly. It shuddered, wings flailing out of time with one another, and slipped down the sky until Kara was above it. She dived, talons poised to catch and pierce.

The chaos dragon's throat swelled. Its abilities fluctuated with its form, and this time it spat a stream of acid like a skull drake. Kara dodged, and the corrosive stream merely grazed the tip of one of her wings. The stuff burned, but not enough to balk her

She leveled off, seeking to shred the chaos wyrm's wings from above and streak on by. She did rip the leathery membranes, but her foe caught her hind leg in its fangs before she could fly clear, and they plummeted together.

So be it. At least she was on top, and less injured than the chaos dragon, and so the fall ought to hurt it worse than it did her. She spread her wings to make the descent a little slower, and she and her adversary tore at one another. It spat, shrouding them both in vile-smelling smoke. For a moment, she felt bewildered, empty-headed, but then her thoughts snapped back into focus. She breathed more lightning straight into the other dragon's mask and seared its left eye to molten ruin.

They crashed down hard. Bones cracked inside the chaos dragon's body, the jagged ends stabbing through its hide, but it kept fighting, and she matched it strike for strike and rake for rake. Iron talons, bastard sword, and ice-axe already bloody, Dorn and Raryn rushed to help her.

Dorn's blade sheared deep into the chaos dragon's neck. It bucked and flailed so hard that it finally broke Kara's hold on it, but then flopped helplessly onto the ground, its heaving flanks and rolling eyes the only indication it was still alive.

Its hide continued changing color, but the transformations came more slowly.

Raryn lifted his axe and smashed in the side of its skull, finishing it. Dorn turned to Kara. "Are you all right?" he asked.

She inspected her lacerated, bloody leg, charred, blistered wingtip, and the rest of the hurts the chaos wyrm had given her. They might well have killed or crippled a human, but drakes were more resilient.

"Fine," she said, then glimpsed plunging motion overhead. "Watch out!"

The three of them leaped for safety, and a pyroclastic wyrm smashed down on the patch of ground where they'd just been standing. Kara sang a spell, Dorn scrambled to place himself on their new adversary's left flank, and Raryn darted for the right.

———— ⚬⚬⚬ ————

Veiled in concealments, Sammaster watched the battle, assessing the capabilities of his foes. To say the least, they were impressive.

He'd opened the netherworld to rain annihilation on their heads. Drawn forth dragons powerful as demigods to attack with the advantages of numbers, surprise, and the high air. They should have slaughtered their targets in a matter of moments.

But it hadn't happened that way. Indeed, at this early stage of the battle, the metallics and their allies were striking back so hard as to put his otherworldly minions on the defensive. It was remarkable. Dragons like Nexus, Tamarand, and Havarlan were, of course, famous for both their natural and mystical prowess. But the Thentian spellcasters were likewise giving a decent account of themselves.

For a moment, Sammaster feared it was all going wrong, and strained to quash the feeling. Nexus and his allies were winning only because he'd been content to stand and take their measure. But he was ready to act, and the balance would quickly shift.

He would have liked to reveal himself to his foes and defy them, Mystra, and the whole sneering, lying, treacherous world. But such bravado would be imprudent. Though he had no fear of destruction, he needed to survive, to ensure that his plans came to fruition, and if all his adversaries concentrated on overwhelming him, it was just barely conceivable they might succeed. Because he wasn't as strong as he would have been if he'd known he was heading into battle. Over the past few days, he'd expended a considerable portion of his spells furthering the Sacred Work, and hadn't gotten around to preparing new ones. Summoning the Hell wyrms had drained him yet a little more.

Better, then, to lurk in the shadows. He could still dictate the outcome of the struggle. First, by supplying direction to his minions. Drawn from different realities, they lacked leaders and teamwork. They were a mob, not an army, and that was the first thing he needed to change.

He murmured, and magic carried his commands to his allies' ears, just as it constrained them to obey. Ordering one to attack and another to break off, concentrating strength where it could do the most damage and maneuvering endangered troops to safety, he shifted his wyrms around like pieces on a lanceboard. He supposed that in so doing, he had the edge over Tamarand. Standing unnoticed, he could monitor the entire conflict in a way that was impossible for the beleaguered gold.

Soon, his generalship started to make a difference, but he saw no reason to leave it at that. Though he couldn't conjure thunderbolts and the like without revealing himself, he had plenty of subtler spells in his repertoire. Magic that wouldn't burn telltale trails through the air.

He took a mouse's femur from one of pockets, whispered a charm, and snapped it in two. A huge bronze floundered in flight as some of its own bones shattered. A pyroclastic dived to blast the metallic with its blazing, bellowing breath.

Another incantation turned a young-ish silver to lifeless stone, and it plummeted toward the ground. Unfortunately, Nexus saw the danger, translated himself through space, and caught the shield drake in time to keep it from crashing down and shattering. He then restored it with a counterspell. But at least while he was busy attending to that, he wasn't hurling attacks at Sammaster's forces.

A third charm poisoned a copper wyrm's own magic, and when it attempted to cast a curse of sluggishness on an abyssal drake, the lethargy manifested in its own mind and body. The abyssal drake wheeled, seeking an advantageous position from which to attack, and the copper struggled uselessly to compensate.

Sammaster smiled, then noticed the half-golem warrior loosing an arrow. The shaft drove deep into the juncture of a howling dragon's wing and shoulder, precisely where it needed to hit to cripple the reptile's ability to fly. No longer able to flap the spasming pinion properly or extend it fully, the howling wyrm struggled to glide safely down to the ground. A brass swooped to intercept it.

In a battle like this, it was generally sensible to ignore mere archers and swordsmen as the least of the threats on the opposing side. But Sammaster had more than once noticed this particular warrior striking to considerable effect. Why allow the pest to persist when it would be so easy to neutralize him? The lich peered at the black expanse of the sky, crisscrossed with multicolored flares of dragon breath and arcane energy, seeking the proper tool for the job.

Wheeling around her blurry, constantly altering opponent and the illusory duplicates it had conjured, Havarlan murmured a charm, then beat her wings and hurled herself at the chaos drake. She'd hoped the sudden action would take it by surprise, but it tilted its wings and veered off. Its phantom twins did the same, aping its motions precisely.

Well, if she couldn't catch it napping, she'd simply have to outmaneuver it. She whipped herself around, and the chaos dragon was in front of her again. She spat her breath weapon.

Infused with the countermagic she'd just invoked, the plume of glittering vapor obliterated the illusory wyrms, aura of blur, and, she hoped, any other mystical defenses the chaos dragon might have in place. It stiffened the creature's muscles into rigidity, too, and unable to beat its pinions or shift its tail for balance, it tumbled.

She doubted her breath would paralyze the hardy chaos dragon for any length of time. In Havarlan's experience, Lady Luck favored the bold and clever, but rarely was she so generous as that. But the attack had rendered the otherworldly reptile helpless for a moment, and that was all the time a Talon of Justice needed to streak in and bury her claws in its body.

They fell together, she raked and bit at the chaos dragon, and once it recovered its mobility, it struck back. The very taste of its constantly shifting flesh and blood altered in her mouth, but somehow, always managed to be vile.

Her probing, digging talons grazed a beating heart, then lost it again, as if the chaos wyrm's constant transformations shifted even its internal organs around. She groped, found the pulsing, leathery mass once more, gripped it in her claws, and squeezed hard enough to shatter oak.

That finished the chaos dragon. She writhed free of the corpse's convulsing coils, leaped away from it, and unfurled her wings just in time to keep from crashing to earth along with it.

She skimmed along the ground, then climbed. Had she just emerged victorious from a single combat, she might have roared in exultation. But this was a clash of armies, from what she could observe, a victory for her side as a whole was anything but certain, and the truly irksome, disquieting thing was that she couldn't tell why.

Perhaps the human wizards, priests, and warriors knew,

since they weren't so much in the thick of it as she had been. She spotted a knot of them on the ground, near a huge, derelict stone battering ram left over from the siege millennia before, and spiraled down to land beside them.

"Something's wrong," she said. "The enemy has the edge again, and I don't understand why."

"Sammaster," Brimstone whispered. She turned to discover that the vampire had slipped up behind her. Blood caked his jaws, and it was likely he'd been drinking it, for his wounds were squirming and puckering shut.

"What about Sammaster?" asked Will, gore—not his own, fortunately—spattering his brigandine, warsling dangling in his hand.

"He's here," the vampire said, "directing his troops and casting the occasional spell. I'm certain of it."

"Could he hide himself so well," Havarlan asked, "that even dragons wouldn't detect him?"

Will grinned. "No offense, lady, but I'm no lich, and even I can do that when I have to."

"If he is here," Havarlan said, "we must find and attack him."

"And do something else, too," panted Pavel. At some point, he'd lost his helmet, and sweat plastered his blond hair to his brow. "Some of us need to enter the citadel, find the heart of the Rage, and destroy it, while the rest keep Sammaster and his wyrms from pursuing. I suggest we 'small folk' go in, because you metallics fight better than we do, and also because I wouldn't be surprised if the ancient elves built the interior of the place in such a way as to make it difficult for dragons to move around."

Havarlan grunted. "I don't like dividing our strength. You humans may not feel as mighty as dragons, but you're making a contribution. If you withdraw from the fight, Sammaster's forces may well overwhelm those of us who remain."

"They might do that anyway," said Scattercloak in his bland, androgynous voice. "But if we ruin the lich's plans first, then we still prevail."

"All right," Havarlan said, "but be careful. You may well encounter additional traps and guardians."

"Celedon and I," said Will, "can handle trip wires, false flooring, and the like, while the wizards turn the squamous spewers and such into cider and cheese. So let's get to it."

All the small folk who'd happened to be standing close enough to hear the plan—which was to say, Pavel, Will, Celedon, Drigor, Darvin, Scattercloak, Sureene, and Firefingers—scurried toward the mouth of the barbican. For a moment, Havarlan wanted to call them back, but resisted the impulse.

Instead, she rounded on Brimstone. "Of us all," she said, "you're the only one who actually knows Sammaster, and you're also a scrier. Can you pinpoint his location, or must we pull Nexus out of the fight?"

"I'll find him," whispered Brimstone, eyes smoldering, jeweled collar catching the ambient silver glow.

"Tell me when you do." She lashed her wings and soared upward, toward a pair of hell wyrms attacking one of her followers.

Dorn and his comrades were fighting what Kara said was an abyssal drake, a hybrid of red dragon, wyvern, and demon. Singing, wings sweeping up and down, she wheeled around it, staying beyond the range of its breath while hammering it with spells, many of them lightning in one form or another. Since abyssal drakes apparently lacked the intellect to master sorcery, it couldn't retaliate in kind.

Meanwhile, her allies assailed the otherworldly reptile from the ground. Dorn and Raryn loosed arrows. Baerimel and Jannatha blasted it with magic.

The abyssal drake dived at the humans and dwarf. Its long neck swelled and cocked, and its jaws opened. Dorn and his companions scrambled to avail themselves of what little cover existed.

The abyssal drake changed from black to red-black as it swooped into the field of silvery light. Its head whipped forward, but no stream of hellfire erupted from its mouth. Kara had evidently cast a charm to choke off its breath weapon.

It looked startled, and the bard blasted it with a dazzling, sizzling flare of her own breath. The attack charred one of its pinions, and it plummeted, jolting the earth as it slammed down.

It rolled to its feet and charged the nearest human target, who happened to be Baerimel. The temple magé froze.

Dorn dropped his bow, grabbed his hand-and-a-half sword, and lunged, interposing himself between the drake and its prey. It might run right over him, but if so, it would do it with his outstretched blade buried in its throat.

It recognized the threat, and stopped short to snap at him. He sidestepped, tore its snout with a backhand blow of his knuckle-spikes, and came back on guard. Its tail whipped around its body in a stroke that was just a blur at the periphery of his vision.

He tried to dodge, but also twisted to present the iron half of his body to the attack. The poisonous stinger struck his shoulder with a clang. It didn't breach the armor, but it staggered him.

By that time, though, Raryn had started chopping the drake's flank with his axe. Jannatha and Baerimel aimed wands at it, the former, assailing it with darts of yellow light, the latter, with a barrage of ice. The punishment kept it from pressing the attack against Dorn, and Kara plunged down on top of it, driving her claws deep into its back. She struck at its neck with her fangs.

Gripping his sword with both hands, Dorn cut repeatedly. His comrades attacked just as relentlessly, until finally, its scales a patchwork of burns and gory wounds, loops of gut hanging from a rent in its belly, the abyssal wyrm expired.

Dorn looked to Kara, crouching on top of the kill. He had to make sure she was all right, and though their adversary had scratched and bitten her, it appeared she essentially was.

She gave him what he'd come to recognize as a dragon's smile, reflecting both love and a gentle mockery of his concern.

Then her head twisted, orienting on something new, something that, until that moment, no one had perceived. "Look out!" she cried.

Pivoting toward the threat, Dorn assumed his fighting stance, iron arm extended in front of him, sword cocked behind. A dragon swooped at him. It looked like one of the shield dragons might if some disease dulled, crusted, and pitted its silvery scales with the appearance of corrosion.

It spewed a haze of fine reddish droplets. The assault had no effect on Dorn's human parts, but his artificial arm crumbled into particles of rust. His iron leg gave way beneath him, and he fell.

His natural skills buttressed with almost every bladesinger charm in his repertoire—enhancements to strength and speed, tricks to befuddle the eye and aim of an opponent—Taegan flew a zigzag course toward a pyroclastic dragon. At the moment, the creature was focused on Wardancer, but that could change in an instant.

"Now?" asked Jivex, or rather, his disembodied voice. He remained invisible as much as possible, only popping into view when he actually made an attack.

"Now," Taegan said.

Tamarand seemed to leap forth from his own veil of concealment, or perhaps a charm of teleportation, on the pyroclastic's left. The hell wyrm twisted toward the illusion, and it was even more open on the right. Taegan flew along its flank, stabbing with Rilitar's sword. The slender blade plunged deep into the reptile's flesh.

The pyroclastic twisted back in his direction, and lashing his pinions, he sought to fling himself clear. To dodge to a position that would make it awkward for the drake to strike at him.

It spat its breath weapon anyway, a blast compounded of red-hot ash and a hammering roar. The assault seared, jolted, and nearly deafened him, but he evaded all but the very fringe of it, and Jivex, vanishing once more, dodged it entirely.

Wardancer swooped over the pyroclastic and ripped with talons glimmering with enchantment. Perhaps the charm enhanced their sharpness, for the bronze's entire forefoot seemed to plunge into the hell wyrm's body, and yanked out several bloody vertebrae as she streaked on past.

Crippled, unable to flap its wings or do much of anything else, the pyroclastic plummeted. It screeched as it hurtled toward the earth.

Though plainly injured—portions of her body had a crooked look, as though bones were broken—Wardancer turned and flew in search of another combat. Taegan started to follow, then noticed what was happening on the ground. Will, Pavel, Celedon, Drigor, and several of the Thentians were running into the castle barbican.

He realized their departure from the battlefield made sense. The point of this enterprise was to extinguish the Rage. They needed to make sure they accomplished that, whatever else might happen.

The question was, should he and Jivex join the seekers, or continue fighting here? Where would they be more useful? For a heartbeat, he couldn't decide, then a howling dragon decided for him.

Skinny and purple-black, the clusters of spines on its shoulders and at the top of its neck bristling, the creature furled its narrow wings and plunged toward the courtyard at the far end of the tunnel-like gate. If it attacked the people caught in the passage by surprise, the close quarters would make it all but impossible for them to avoid its breath or magic.

Taegan extended his arm. "Grab hold!" Jivex's invisible claws clamped down on the limb, and he rattled off a spell to shift them both through space.

Scrying was commonly a lengthy process undertaken in peaceful surroundings and through the employment of a specially prepared crystal orb, mirror, or pool of water. Brimstone had only a brief time, or else success was likely to arrive too late to do any good. He needed to focus despite the distraction of the battle with all its flashes of flame and vitriol, cacophony of noise, and the nagging anxiety that one or another of the enemy would decide to attack him while he was helpless in his trance. He had only a section of weathered, dirty white castle wall to serve as his speculum.

He soon realized that under such conditions, much of the technique he'd mastered was useless. Try as he might, employing every trick of meditation he'd ever learned, he couldn't make his mind sufficiently passive, calm, and receptive.

So, unorthodox though it was, he'd attempt the opposite. Rely on passion and need instead of clarity. He wallowed in his memories of Sammaster. Recalled the false promises. The agonies of the experiments that turned him undead, robbing him of daylight, ordinary meat and drink, and countless other freedoms and pleasures the living took for granted. The final betrayal, when Sammaster decided he was unfit to inherit the world after all, and made it clear he expected him to become a groveling lackey for those who would.

Brimstone fed and prodded his hate until it burned as fiercely as he'd ever felt it, then pushed it outward to find and fasten on its object. Drowning in a sort of excruciating ecstasy, in malice that had waited centuries to achieve its final expression, he had no idea how long it took, but eventually, a gray stripe of shadow, the murky, ambiguous beginning of a vision, appeared on the chipped and pallid stone.

The rust dragon—though it was too late, Dorn recognized the creature from tales he'd heard—swooped at him with outstretched talons. He knew he ought to try and roll out of the way, but the thought seemed disconnected from his will and what remained of his body.

Baerimel's clear high voice rattled off syllables in some esoteric language. Power groaned through the air and made pebbles jitter this way and that. A plane of hovering, rippling glow shimmered into being, positioned and angled to block the rust wyrm's path to its target. Abandoning the attack, the dragon lashed its wings and climbed higher to clear the obstacle.

Raryn recited a ranger charm, then loosed an arrow that buried itself in the rust wyrm's belly all the way to the fletchings. The reptile hissed.

Jannatha assailed it with glowing darts from her wand. Pinions lashing, leaping into the air, Kara hit it with a flare of her breath.

They all hurt the creature, but not enough to stop it. It wheeled to threaten them anew, and two abyssal drakes came gliding down to help it. The odds were dismally one-sided, but still dazed and slow, Dorn didn't even try to rise and help his comrades. For what could he contribute even if he managed it?

The rust dragon turned. Dorn realized it had maneuvered to hold Kara in check and keep her from aiding the humans and dwarf on the ground. She started to countermaneuver, and the abyssal drakes furled their wings and dived.

An eerie cry sounded from elsewhere in the sky. The abyssal drakes convulsed, vomited their blazing breath prematurely—at nothing. Then they were falling, not diving, tumbling over and over as they dropped. They slammed down on the ground to lay broken and inert.

Next came a prodigious boom of a thunderclap that stunned the rust dragon and kept it from dodging when Kara spat another blast of her breath at it. That finished it, and it too fell.

At the same time, Dorn discerned who it was who had helped them. Engaged in a whirling aerial fight with at least four opponents, Nexus had nonetheless noticed his allies' peril and used his magic to succor them. He turned back around and battered one of his own foes with conjured hailstones.

Kara plunged down beside Dorn, in her haste, landing harder than usual. Raryn dashed up to him as well.

"How bad is it?" the song dragon asked.

He struggled to goad his mind into motion, so he could take stock. His arm was entirely gone. Something of his leg remained, but it was a spindly, misshapen thing, numb, and hard to bend at the knee. The iron sheathing the rest of left side, even the plates inside his brigandine and breeches, was red and grainy with rust. No protection anymore, certainly not against a dragon's fangs and claws. It seemed a bitter mockery that only his sword had come through the wyrm's assault intact.

He realized, in a dull way sure to become excruciating later on, just how bad his life was henceforth going to be. He'd spent decades hating his golem parts. They'd made him a grotesque, frightening freak. But better that than a helpless cripple.

"I . . . I'm not dying or even wounded, exactly," he said. "But . . . "

"We understand," Raryn said. "Let's get you under cover." He picked up Dorn, carried him a dozen paces, and laid him down beneath the arching ribs of a dragon who'd died thousands of years before. He then murmured a charm. Power tingled over Dorn's body, altering its colors, making it blend with the earth, bones, and shadows around it.

"Stay quiet," said the dwarf, "and nothing will bother you."

"I don't want to leave you alone," Kara said, "but—"

"Go!" he snapped. He didn't want her, Raryn, or anyone standing here pitying the broken thing he'd become.

They hovered uncertainly for another moment, then turned away to rejoin the battle. A battle that half a man could only lie and watch.

Once the gaunt, purple howling dragon swooped down into the courtyard, Taegan couldn't see it anymore. But he heard it give the eerie screech that was its breath weapon, and had no doubt it had employed it against the folk caught inside the barbican. He strained to fly even faster, and Jivex did the same.

Wind screamed, surely another conjured effect to batter Pavel, Will, and the rest, then the avariel and faerie dragon swooped over the wall and down into the bailey. The howling wyrm didn't notice them. Poised in front of the entrance to the fore-gate, it was too intent on the foes it had been attacking.

The creature's body essentially blocked Taegan's view of the passage beyond, but as best he could judge, none of his comrades was striking back at their tormentor. It seemed likely that the demonic reptile's cry and magical abilities had already incapacitated them or worse.

Then the howling wyrm lunged into the barbican. While Taegan was still too far away to divert it from its helpless prey.

Jivex hissed, stared, and a massive steel portcullis dropped down in front of the howling drake, rattling and clanking, almost close enough to clip the end of its snout. The barrier was undoubtedly one of the smaller reptile's illusions, but the dragon of Pandemonium evidently couldn't tell it. It stopped short and regarded the grille in astonishment.

"Get to the side of the gate," Jivex said, "where it won't be able to see us."

As Taegan lashed his wings and hurried to comply, a second illusion formed, directly in front of the tunnel. It was the semblance of a copper dragon with blue eyes and a gap-toothed grin, the very image of poor lost Chatulio, and with luck, when the howling wyrm turned to see who had balked it, it would assume the metallic was responsible.

Another shriek erupted from the barbican. The phantom Chatulio vanished as soon as the ripping, pounding noise swept over it. That, however, didn't stop the howling dragon from leaping out into the open at the same instant. Apparently it had intended to follow up on the breath attack immediately, with fang and talon, and had pounced before it had a chance to recognize that it was wasting its aggression on something unreal.

As a result, Taegan and Jivex were behind the confused, distracted wyrm, well positioned to assail it. The elf flew at it and thrust Rilitar's sword into its neck.

The howling dragon whipped its head around and poised it to strike at him. But before it could, Jivex appeared hovering in midair and puffed iridescent vapor at its snout.

The howling wyrm reeled drunkenly. Taking full advantage of its incapacity, Taegan drove in three more thrusts. Jivex faded back into invisibility.

Then, snarling, the howling wyrm shook off the effect of Jivex's breath. It whirled toward Taegan. The bladesinger swooped underneath its body, slashed his belly, and came up on the other side. The howling dragon hammered its wing down at him, and the stroke missed him by a hair.

Jivex lit on the infernal dragon's spine to bite and claw. The howling wyrm twisted its head around to strike back, and its small assailant whizzed away.

Terror and confusion exploded through Taegan's mind, but crying out, he denied them, and they lost their grip on him. He looked over at Jivex. His friend gave him a brusque nod to convey that he too had resisted the howling dragon's psychic attack. They attacked the hellish thing once more, Taegan cutting at it, Jivex conjuring a hood of golden dust that unfortunately failed to stick to its head.

The howling wyrm pivoted, found Taegan, and lunged at him. And kept on lunging. Taegan realized it had decided to attack one opponent, himself, relentlessly until it dispatched him. Then it would turn its attention to the other.

Snapping and clawing, the howling drake pushed him back against a wall. He tried to dodge away, but the creature spread its leathery wings to pen him in. Jivex conjured flashes to blaze and bang around its head, but failed to disorient or divert it.

The howling dragon's chest and throat swelled as its breath weapon renewed itself. Trapped right in front of the reptile's jaws, Taegan knew he was unlikely to survive the blast.

Then flares of light, flame, and jagged darkness erupted behind the howling wyrm. It screamed and whirled, seeking the source of the new attack. Peering past the drake, Taegan saw them, too. The folk the reptile had trapped in the barbican had recovered from its assault, emerged into the open, and hammered it with an assortment of spells. The magic had seared and pounded its tail and hindquarters into a raw, bleeding mess.

It started to rush Scattercloak, Sureene, and their fellows, but Taegan was faster. He flew at it and thrust his sword deep into its skull. The howling dragon fell, thrashed, and finally lay still.

Once he was certain the creature of Pandemonium was truly dead, Taegan looked around, making sure no other threat was descending on his friends or himself. None was, so he furled his pinions and set down on the ground.

"Is everyone all right?" he panted.

"Of course," Jivex replied.

Taegan regarded Will, Pavel, and the others. "What about the rest of you?"

"The wyrm's cry and other powers tore at our minds," Pavel said. "If we can spare a moment for some healing, we'll be the stronger for it."

"All right, but let's do it indoors, where we won't attract the notice of any other unfriendly dragon that happens to flap overhead." He cast about and found an arched doorway leading deeper into the castle. "This way."

Havarlan soared to join Llimark and Azhaq in their struggle with five of the enemy. But before she could climb high enough, a red-eyed shadow glided in on her flank.

"I found Sammaster," Brimstone whispered.

"Where?" she asked.

"In the top of the second tower on the wall north of the barbican."

She turned and scrutinized the structure with all her senses and arcane sensitivities. "Even now that you've told me, it seems empty to me."

"I assure you, he's there."

"Very well," she said, "I believe you."

"Then we have to attack him with as many dragons as we can. A dozen at least."

"Impossible. If we disengage so many from the fight with the hell wyrms, our defense will fail."

"If you leave Sammaster alone to do as he wishes, it will crumble faster. I know you can't perceive his influence directly, but I guarantee you, he's the reason we're losing, even with the likes of Nexus and Tamarand on our side."

"All right," she said, peering about, looking for allies she could pull from the fray while doing the least amount of damage to their chances. But the grim truth was that no one could be spared. Everyone was fighting desperately to hold Sammaster's minions in check.

Such being the case, she'd use the drakes who'd come, unquestioningly, when she called. Employing a cantrip to amplify her voice, she bellowed, "Talons! Talons of Justice! To me!"

As quickly as they were able, silvers broke away from their opponents and winged their way in her direction. Climbing in the southern quadrant of the sky, Tamarand peered at her in surprise, and no doubt, dismay. But he didn't seek to countermand her order, or waste time questioning her. Instead, his own voice magically enhanced, he directed his remaining warriors hither and yon, striving to mend the holes she'd just torn in their battle order. Meanwhile, Sammaster's troops raised a bloodcurdling clamor and drove forward.

The Talons swooped and wheeled around Havarlan and Brimstone. "What are we doing?" Azhaq asked.

"Though we can't see him, Sammaster is in that tower." Havarlan jerked her head to indicate the proper one. "We're going to assault it."

Sammaster wondered what had become of Gjellani, the howling wyrm he'd sent to slaughter the foes he'd noticed scurrying into the barbican. He hadn't expected it to take this long. Was it possible the Thentians had somehow managed to defeat the drake?

He reassured himself that even if they had, it didn't matter. The castle had other defenses. Still, it would be sloppy, reckless, to let his enemies get anywhere near the source of the Rage. If Gjellani had failed, he'd send other dragons after the Thentians. The struggle in the sky was going well enough that he could spare them.

He murmured the opening words of a charm that would afford him a view of the interior of the fore-gate and the bailey at the end of it, then noticed what Havarlan, other shield drakes, and Brimstone were doing: streaking toward the tower in which he stood. Plainly, they'd discerned his presence at last.

He considered shifting himself to another location. but since they'd found him, he wasn't certain that would shake them off his scent, and a number of the defensive wards he'd conjured were, of necessity, fused to the structure in which he stood rather than his person. Besides, he'd been itching to reveal himself and fight openly. He thumped the butt of his staff on the floor and dissolved his shroud of invisibility.

Since he had windows on all four sides, he presented a target to all the wheeling silvers at once, and several immediately bellowed spells. He willed his defenses to life, and the shield wyrms' blasts of fire, sunlight, and such frayed away to nothing a pace or so short of the spire with its high, pointed roof.

He sneered, then willed his invisible, concentric spheres of protection to expand. When the outermost came into contact with the nearest silvers, it slashed them like razor-sharp claws, and, pinions lashing, they frantically retreated.

It was too bad he could only expand the bubble out to a certain point. Otherwise, he could have enlarged it until it shredded every metallic in the valley. But no matter. He had plenty of other ways to kill them.

Brimstone dissolved into smoke and sparks, came billowing at the summit of the tower, then recoiled as Sammaster's wards wounded him even in that insubstantial state. Melting into dim translucency, a silver shifted the bulk of its substance to another level of reality, only to find the lich's defenses existed there as well. A shield drake who looked as old and powerful as Havarlan herself—a long-time foe of the Cult of the Dragon named Azhaq, if Sammaster wasn't mistaken—sought to translate himself through space, then hissed as the magic not only failed to shift him, but hurt him. Roaring words of power, Havarlan attempted a dispelling. Sammaster's mystical fortifications softened for an instant, but then flared strong as before.

He took an onion from his pocket, recited an incantation, and tore at the vegetable's layered surface. A silver screeched and flailed as strips of flesh peeled away from its body. He seared another wyrm with a downpour of acid, then sent a shadow-sword flying at a third. The blade was actually a mobile gap into the cancerous nothingness between the worlds, and when it slashed the reptile, it engulfed and obliterated it.

Meanwhile, the silvers struggled to reach him with their own spells, and failed utterly. He laughed in exultation.

Lying in the middle of the ancient dragon's skeleton, Dorn watched Sammaster's wyrms hammer his allies. It was plain that Kara and the others were losing, and he despised himself as bitterly as ever in his life for his inability to help them.

In time, however, and quite unexpectedly, a new thought came to him: He had reason to hold himself in contempt, but not for being ugly or freakish, and not because the rust dragon had crippled him anew. For surrendering to despair. After reaching the valley and finding Kara still alive, he'd vowed he'd never do it again. Yet here he slumped, wallowing in his own personal misery and self-hatred while the woman he loved, his friends, and all Faerûn were in jeopardy.

It didn't matter that he'd lost an arm. The human one could still swing a sword. Or that his metal leg was numb and withered. Other men managed to walk on peglegs, and he was at least a little better equipped than that. Or that he no longer had impervious iron sheathing half his body. Raryn, Will, and Pavel had never enjoyed such an advantage, and it didn't stop them from killing wyrms.

Dorn crawled out from under the arch of ribs, then tried to stand. The spindly, twisted remnants of the iron leg didn't immediately snap or buckle beneath his weight, so that was something, anyway. He just wished the limb had more sensation in it. He hobbled a few steps, trying to get used to it and to figure out how to keep his balance with the heavy mass of his artificial arm shorn away.

All things considered, he was in a sad state, and doubted he'd last any time at all. But all he asked of the Beastlord—no, Lathander, damn it, Pavel's god of hope—was to strike a single telling blow before some drake or other ripped him apart.

Most of the battle was still in the sky, and he couldn't shoot arrows anymore. But periodically, one or another of Sammaster's wyrms dived to the ground, and he watched for one to touch down.

"Hold up!" said Will, and the folk skulking along behind him came to a halt.

He stooped and verified that what he'd thought he'd seen on the floor was real. A glyph lay there, no doubt to discharge some form of unpleasantness when somebody stepped over it. The symbol itself was essentially invisible, but Sammaster's fingertip had smeared the dust and grime of ages when he'd written it on the sea-green marble, and the glow Pavel had conjured onto the head of his mace to light their way just barely sufficed to reveal the shape.

"Shall I dispel it?" Firefingers asked.

"No, I've got it." Will wet his finger with spit, then rubbed at the edge of the glyph, blurring it. The magic leaked out of it all at once, jabbing his digit like a bee sting and filling the corridor with a rippling burst of visual distortion.

Celedon smiled. "Nicely done."

Will shrugged. "It wasn't that hard. Neither were the other traps. I guess we've finally reached the point where Sammaster ran out of inspiration."

"Our Lady of Silver," said Sureene, "grant that you're right."

They trekked on through echoing courtyards, chambers, and hallways still resplendent with the consummate artistry and craftsmanship of the elves, but cold, dusty, and draped in thick shrouds of spider silk. Will wondered if the builders had unwittingly imported the arachnids and the bugs to feed them when they'd come to this remote and desolate place.

As Pavel had conjectured, the foes of the dragon kings seemed to have laid out the stronghold to make it difficult for wyrms to move around. Mostly, it was spacious and airy, but at certain key points, the way forward led through choke points: cramped doorways, narrow corridors, and multiple hairpin turns.

Alas, the precaution hadn't kept the dragon lords out, for here, as on the floor of the valley outside, bones lay strewn around, crunching beneath the seekers' feet if they stepped carelessly. Will could only assume the besieging force had fought its way almost to the very heart of the Rage before the last surviving elves finally stopped them.

The complex was so big, he wondered how the invaders had known which way to head. Probably they'd had magicians of Scattercloak's caliber to guide them. The faceless warlock in his shadowy cowl and layers of robe had cast a spell which, he claimed, enabled him to discern a source of extraordinary power toward the center the citadel.

So they headed where his gloved hand pointed them, with Will in the lead to look for snares, until two enormous shapes loomed out of the gloom, at which point he caught his breath and stopped short.

Ahead lay a sizable room with a high, arched ceiling. A pair of wyrms, or wyrm-like things, crouched there motionless. They were small compared to true dragons, but still huge compared to men, or, Brandobaris knew, a halfling, and they were more or less barring the way to the doorway in the far wall. Somewhere beyond that opening, light seethed and flickered, first red, then green, then violet, changing color from one heartbeat to the next.

"They aren't moving," said Jivex, hovering near Taegan, "and I don't smell them, or hear them breathing. Maybe they're dead."

"I suspect not," the avariel said. "My guess is that if the guardians are living creatures, the elves—or, conceivably, Sammaster—made them proof against the depredations of time by placing them in a state of hibernation. If they're automatons of some sort, they've no need to move around at times when nothing threatens their charge. But either way, they're likely to rouse as soon as we approach too near. Do you concur, Master Firefingers?"

"Yes," the old man said. "So let's not 'approach.' Instead, I'll teleport the lot of us right past them."

"Onto that narrow strip of floor between them and the lights?" asked Darvin, frowning.

"Since we don't know what lies beyond it, and thus have nothing better to aim for, yes."

"What if—"

"The only way to make sure we don't misstep," said Scattercloak, "is never to move at all. Wouldn't you agree?"

Darvin sighed. "I suppose."

"Then everyone gather close," said Firefingers.

He recited an incantation, and the vista in front of Will, dragon shapes included, seemed to leap at him. Then it all disintegrated into dots and blobs of light, streaking past and harmlessly through him. Then, as abruptly as it had lurched and fallen to pieces, the world remade itself, and the mysterious doorway—filled with blue radiance—yawned before him.

That close, he could feel that the flickering, inconstant light embodied a fundamental wrongness, like the unholiness infusing a pyroclastic's breath or Brimstone's very essence. It made his eyes smart, and his guts cramp. Yet he still stepped closer.

Pavel grabbed him by the shoulder. "Don't go in there, cretin. Or rather, come to think of it, do."

"Get your filthy paw off me," said Will, pushing his comrade's hand away. "I can feel it's dangerous, but after hunting for it all these months, I'm at least going to take a look at it before the counterspell blasts it to bits, or whatever it's going to do."

Apparently, everyone felt the same, for all ten of them moved forward, crowding together, leaning sideways, and craning to peer through the opening. Jivex clung upside down to the lintel to look over the heads of his larger companions.

The vault beyond the threshold was as spacious as its antechamber. The builders had inlaid an intricate pentacle in gold on the black marble floor, and used truesilver and gems to create an image of the night sky on the walls and ceiling. An enormous ruby with a streaming carnelian tail represented the King-Killer, the comet that, in times past, had served as the harbinger of the Rage.

But jewels and a mithral moon weren't the only things on the walls. Bright, fist-sized holes that Will had learned to recognize as portals pocked the ebon surfaces at irregular intervals. From the miniature gates blazed flares of power, the source of the noisome, ever-changing light shining

THE RUIN • 313

through the door. The ragged, luminous tendrils arced and whipped back and forth, burning through one section of the room, then another, but always terminating at the same point: a black amulet floating above the very center of the pentagram with a loop of chain dangling below.

"Glories of the dawn," Pavel breathed, "now I know how Sammaster did it."

"Whereas I," Taegan said, "am primarily interested in seeing you wise folk undo it. So, if you wouldn't mind—"

Something scraped on stone. The seekers spun around, to see that the wyrm-things in the antechamber were turning, too.

———— eOn ————

Dorn watched as Tamarand blasted a chaos dragon with his fiery breath. The flame withered the hell wyrm's wings, and it plummeted. Tamarand turned as if he meant to dive after it. But then a howling dragon hurtled down at him, and he lashed his wings and twisted himself around to meet that threat instead.

The chaos dragon dropped halfway down the sky, then managed to spread its blackened, shriveled wings. Maybe, despite all the holes Tamarand had burned through them, they served to slow its fall. The wyrm still smashed down hard, but then rolled to its feet and rushed foes on the ground: Raryn, Baerimel, and Jannatha.

Fast as he was able—and it didn't feel fast at all—Dorn ran to help them.

Baerimel and Jannatha shot chunks of ice and darts of light from their wands into the dragon's squirming, ever-changing countenance. Raryn threw his harpoon into the reptile's shoulder.

The chaos dragons's scales turned green where Tamarand hadn't charred them a permanent suppurating black, and hornlets sprouted over the eyes. It cocked back its head and spat poisonous vapor.

Raryn and the temple mages tried to scramble out of the way. Most likely, they all had defensive wards in place. Yet they still doubled over coughing, and the chaos dragon pounced and landed right in front of them.

For the moment, the sisters were helpless, and Dorn was still too far away. His ruddy face blistered, blue eyes bloodshot and streaming tears, Raryn straightened up, gripped his ice-axe, and attacked the chaos wyrm so savagely that it had little choice but to focus its attention on him while Jannatha and Baerimel stumbled away from it.

Raryn chopped into its forefoot. It raised the wounded leg, the scales rippling back and forth between red and blue, and stamped. The dwarf sidestepped out from underneath and hacked at the limb again. The drake lurched off balance, and he struck it a third time, like a woodsman striving to fell a tree.

But the leg wouldn't give way. The wyrm pivoted, bit, clawed, and Raryn jumped away. The chaos dragon lunged after him and drove him back.

Bellowing a war cry, Dorn raced into the distance and struck at the creature's flank. His sword plunged deep into a raw spot where Tamarand had burned away the scaly hide. The chaos dragon faltered, then whirled in his direction.

He jumped back. Sidestepped when the wyrm clawed at him. Cut, and dodged once more, fighting his own trained habits every step of the way.

He couldn't lead with the iron arm. It wasn't there anymore. He had to keep the sword in front, to threaten the drake and to parry.

Nor could he plant himself in front of the creature, trusting his armor to protect him. That wasn't there anymore, either. He had to fight like Raryn and the others: Hit the wyrm when it was striking at somebody else, and do everything possible to protect himself whenever it paid attention to him.

Maybe it was because Raryn fought superbly. Or because the chaos dragon was already hurt. But somehow, working together, the hunters both stayed alive and cut the reptile up a little more. Until one of the sisters—with his eyes on the wyrm, Dorn didn't see who—conjured a deafening shriek that tore most of the flesh from creature's skull and the top half of its neck. It flopped over onto its side to kick and flail in its death throes.

Raryn trotted around the corpse to Dorn. "Are you planning to go on fighting?" asked the dwarf.

"Yes."

"Then I've got something for you." Raryn took hold of Dorn's wrist and rattled off an incantation. For a moment, a scent of earth and greenery filled the air, and power tingled up the human's arm. Afterwards, he felt more agile, and more certain of his balance.

"Now let's kill dragons," Raryn said.

Havarlan watched in fury and grief as, one by one, Sammaster ripped and smashed her silvers out of the air. It was quite possibly the end of the Talons of Justice. She hadn't led all her followers into this terrible place, but she'd brought the best of them, the heart of the fellowship, and already the majority lay crumpled and dead on the ground.

She called out to Brimstone, who was gliding nearby. "You know the lich," she said. "How do we counter this magic? How do we reach him?"

"I don't know," the vampire said. "Perhaps if we fetch Nexus—"

"We can't! We've pulled too many warriors out of the fight with the hell drakes already. Look at the sky! What do you think would happen if either he or Tamarand withdrew?"

Sammaster conjured a dozen shadow-shapes like disembodied jaws. They shot at Azhaq, swarmed on him like angry bees, and sank their needle fangs into his scales. He roared in pain, and the lich laughed.

No more, thought Havarlan, no more of this, and she knew what she was going to attempt. She lashed her wings and flew straight at Sammaster.

She'd already discerned that concentric spheres of protection surrounded his perch. As she hurtled through the first one, pain stabbed down the length of her body from her nose to the tip of her tail.

Refusing to let it balk her, not bothering to look and see how deeply the ward had slashed her, she streaked onward. Into the second barrier.

This time, the agony pierced all the way into the core of her. Blood surged up in her throat, and her left eye went blind. Her heart juddered, and worst of all, something broke or sheared apart inside the linkage of bone and muscle controlling her pinions. They locked up, and she fell. She roared, spitting gore and bits of broken tooth, strained to shift them, and finally they flapped and bore her onward.

At the third barrier. Which she dreaded as she'd never dreaded anything before. But she was the Barb of the Talons of Justice, and duty demanded she plunge on through.

It was like being on fire, outside and in. Like becoming a being that didn't merely suffer anguish, but purely and simply *was* anguish. If she was still beating her pinions, she couldn't tell it. The sensation was lost in all-consuming pain. But maybe she was, for something—sheer momentum, conceivably—flung her at the skull-faced lich in his window.

He goggled in sudden realization of what was about to happen. Opened his mouth full of chipped and rotting teeth, no doubt to jabber a spell. But before he could, she crashed into the top of the tower like a boulder flung from a catapult.

The impact shattered Sammaster's perch and knocked him backward. He and Havarlan fell to the ground outside the castle wall amid a rain of broken stone, splintered timber, and roofing tiles.

The world faded, then jumped back into clarity. Evidently Havarlan had only lost consciousness for a moment, because everything was still the same. Sammaster was just drawing himself to his feet.

He planted himself in front of her and glared up into her face. "Die!" he snarled.

Fresh pain stabbed through her chest. She tried to claw at the lich, but her leg wouldn't move.

She took what solace she could from knowing that she'd dislodged Sammaster from his web of defenses. Perhaps her comrades could handle him from here. They'd have to, for her spasming heart gave a final lurch, then stopped.

Taegan realized he and his companions were trapped between the onrushing guardians on one side and the vault containing the heart of the Rage—where, he gathered, it was death to enter—on the other. He wondered if Darvin would take a moment to observe that he'd tried to warn them all that something like this could happen.

But the man in white didn't. Instead, like the other priests and wizards, he jabbered an incantation. Flares of booming flame, crackling lightning, and other manifestations of mystic power leaped forth to hammer the guardians.

Or rather, simply to illuminate forms made of sculpted stone and cast iron. As Taegan had suspected, they were automatons like the construct of bone he'd encountered previously, and as far as he could tell, the magic of several of the Moonsea's greatest warlocks had damaged them not a jot.

"Warriors, forward!" he shouted, and lunged at the iron golem, which radiated heat like an oven. The point of Rilitar's sword pierced its snout, and, smoke fuming from its molded nostrils, the animated statue struck at him like a serpent. He dodged and cut at its throat, but his blade bounced off.

Jivex swooped over the iron guardian and raked with his claws, striking sparks. Will darted under its belly and stabbed with his hornblade. Pavel scrambled onto its flank and pounded it with the glowing head of its mace. Meanwhile, Sureene, Celedon, and Drigor assaulted the other construct. All the weapons clanging on stone and metal raised a hideous din.

"We'll hold the things!" Taegan bellowed. "You wizards, stop the Rage!"

Scattercloak started chanting, and a moment later, Darvin did the same. Since they weren't reciting in unison, the words jumbled together in a confusing, echoing way.

Taegan hoped the counterspell was brief. He and his comrades were fighting hard, desperately, but to little apparent effect. Even enchanted weapons glanced off creatures of iron and stone as often as not, and generally just scratched or chipped them the rest of the time. While the living statues riposted with all the speed and strength of actual dragons.

Taegan dodged raking claws, slashed at his opponent's extended leg, and glimpsed motion at the periphery of his vision. The golem's head was whipping around at the end of its long neck to strike at him. He jumped back, avoiding the attack, and his opponent lunged after him. He retreated, resisting the impulse to use his wings and leave the constructs a clear path to Darvin and Scattercloak. The golem attacked faster, then faster still. It spread its wings so that he couldn't dodge past it even if he wanted to. Jivex landed on its head, bit and raked, but failed to distract it. Taegan felt a grim certainty that it was about to punch through his defense—

A flare of frost splashed across one of the golem's outstretched pinions. Taegan's muscles clenched at the sudden chill, but since the attack hadn't engulfed him, took no actual harm. The living statue, however, abruptly started moving slower than before. It was easier to evade its strikes, and cut and batter it in its turn.

Perhaps it realized as much, in whatever passed for its mind, for it attempted a different mode of attack, rearing, cocking its head back and spreading its jaws. Taegan poised himself to dodge. But Firefingers rattled off words of power, and when the flare of breath weapon exploded from the statue's mouth, the flame hooked upward to splash against the ceiling.

"Nice trick!" said Will. He darted under the statue's belly and stabbed. Gripping his glowing mace in both hands, Pavel bashed dents in its side.

"Get clear when I give the word," Firefingers said. He declaimed another incantation. "Now!"

The fighters scurried backward, and the golems lunged after them. But then, crashing and rumbling, the floor—and the ground beneath it, evidently—shattered into fragments beneath the statues' claws, and they floundered down into a pit of rubble like animals in quicksand.

Taegan grinned. Realizing the golems were more or less impervious to his magic, Firefingers had instead employed it to deny them a stable surface on which to stand. It was a clever tactic.

Scattercloak and Darvin's voices grew louder. More insistent. They'd finally reached the concluding syllables of the counterspell. Taegan turned back toward the source of the Rage to see what would happen next.

As far as he could tell, nothing. The flares of power kept on leaping from the wounds in the walls to the pendant floating in the center, exactly the same as before.

"I don't feel any different," said Jivex, hovering. "The craziness is still inside my head."

"That," spat Darvin, "is because our countermagic doesn't work! Damn it! Damn it! Damn it to Baator!"

The chunks of stone at the top of the pit crunched, groaned, and shifted as the golems started to dig their way up from the bottom.

———— ⤞∘⤝ ————

Tamarand caught an updraft, gained the high air, and dived at his foe. The wounded rust dragon tried to dodge, but he compensated and plunged his talons into its neck. They sheared through muscle and smashed vertebrae, all but beheading the creature. He released the convulsing body and let it fall.

Momentarily free of threats to his person, Tamarand then looked around to monitor the progress of the battle as a whole. Just in time to see Sammaster strike Havarlan dead.

Tamarand refused to feel shock or grief. Such emotions were for later, should he survive. For the time being, what mattered, the only thing a war leader could allow to matter, was that the silver had dislodged Sammaster from his prepared defenses.

The question was, how best to take advantage of the opening, and essentially, the answer was another impossible choice. Tamarand scarcely dared divert any more of his strength from the clash with the hell wyrms, but neither could he ignore the lich.

So, rattling off commands in his magically augmented voice, the gold divided his strength once more. The folk on the ground, and some of the metallics in the air, would assault Sammaster. Everyone else would strive to keep the otherworldly drakes from coming to their master's aid.

At least if they pushed Sammaster hard enough, he wouldn't be able to direct his troops anymore. Praying it would make a difference, wishing it were wise, invincible Lareth and not just a traitorous lieutenant in command of this desperate venture, Tamarand wheeled to attack a trio of howling dragons.

Sammaster took a moment to savor Havarlan's death throes, then turned and saw the other foes rushing to surround him, charging across the ground or swooping down from the sky. Brimstone. Azhaq. The song dragon. The two pretty sisters with their wands. The white-haired dwarf in his polar bear-fur armor, and even the maimed half-golem, still fighting despite the loss of an arm and the near-destruction of his leg.

It was the nightmare moment Sammaster could never escape. All he wanted, all he'd ever wanted, was to fulfill his destiny and create a better world. Yet time and again, a host of jealous, spiteful wretches rose up against him, to tear down whatever he tried to build. To defeat and humiliate him. To do like rats in a pack what none of them had the honor, courage, or prowess to attempt alone.

But not this time. Not if Azuth, Mystra, and all her Chosen took the field against him. This time, by the blood of every wyrm who'd ever flown, he was going to win, and in the process, annihilate Tamarand, Nexus, and all their lackeys for good and all.

He started a spell and pulled a jade circlet from a pocket inside his mantle. The song dragon hastily sang a pounding musical incantation, and flame exploded all around him. The blaze stung a little, but not enough to disrupt his own conjuring. He placed the crown on his head, and power jolted through him.

He willed himself to transform, and though he remained a thing of dead, shriveled flesh and exposed bone, everything else changed. His form expanded, fingers becoming claws, face pushing forward into reptilian jaws. Tattered, rotting wings exploded from his shoulders, and a tail writhed forth from the base of his spine.

In an instant, he was a dracolich. A dream of an undead ancient red given substance. The biggest and mightiest thing on the battlefield, his physical strength as dreadful a force as his wizardry.

Azhaq dived at him, and he spat a plume of flame. The shield dragon veered, but even a graze seared burns across half his body.

Sammaster laughed, and, relishing the snarling thunder his voice had become, commenced another charm.

———— ∞ ————

Pavel watched as Scattercloak murmured a spell and brandished a bit of quartz. Ice spread over and through the shivering rubble at the top of the pit, binding it in place as mortar held bricks.

"That might slow the golems down," the wizard said, his tenor voice emotionless as ever. "Now, I suggest that Sureene or Drigor attempt the counterspell. Perhaps the divine magic version will work where the arcane failed."

"I'll do it," said Selûne's priestess. Gazing upward as if she could see the moon through the ceiling, sweeping her mace with its crescent-shaped flanges through mystic passes, she recited the prayer. Meanwhile, the layer of ice crunched and cracked. Celedon and Firefingers murmured charms. No doubt they, too, were trying to hold the living statues down.

At the end of Sureene's recitation, Pavel conjured a glow of dawnlight, hoping it would help. It didn't. The flares of power kept right on leaping and twisting from their points of origin to the floating amulet.

"That's no good, either," said Sureene. "I'm sorry."

"If we can't do this," said Darvin, his voice shrill, "we need to clear out before the golems free themselves. Because we can't cope with them, either!"

Ignoring the mage's outburst, Will looked up at Pavel. "What was that useless bit of stupidity you tried?"

"From the start," said Pavel, "we've known Sammaster must have modified the enchantment generating the Rage. Because, in times past, it drew its power from the stars, and only woke when the King-Killer appeared in the sky. By the same token, being a creation of elven high magic, it would only obey the will of one of the *tel'Quessir*."

"I believe I understand," said Taegan. "Since the lich had to alter the mythal, the key you scholars devised doesn't fit the lock anymore."

"But why did you think a flash of sunlight would help?" Jivex asked.

"Because I think I comprehend what Sammaster did," Pavel said. "He's pulling mystical force directly from the Abyss, or possibly one of the Hells, to power the enchantment, and focusing it through his own phylactery. That was the only way he could gain control of the magic: by fusing it with his own essence. Thus, I hoped Lathander's power, which is anathema to the undead, would weaken the metaphysical structure of the magic sufficiently for our countercharm to break it apart. Because I refuse to believe our researches missed the mark entirely. Our invention just isn't as perfect as it needs to be."

"Yes," said Darvin, "and your little trick didn't tip the scales. So—"

"Please, my friend," said Firefingers, "you've fought like a hero so far. Stand fast just a few breaths longer while I attempt something else." He murmured a charm, and a floating, luminous disembodied hand shimmered into existence beside the phylactery. It tried repeatedly to take hold of the black amulet and pull it away from the center of the pentagram, but the thing kept slipping from its grasp. Then one of the seething streamers of hellfire washed over it and it crumbled from existence.

"My turn," said Will. He whirled his sling and hurled a skiprock at the phylactery. The stone hit it squarely, but bounced off without jarring it out of position. "Curse it!"

"It's possible," said Pavel, unrolling the scroll Sureene had written for him, "that part of the problem is distance. Our magic may prove more potent if the person casting it is in physical contact with the phylactery. I'll give it a try."

"What?" squawked Will. "You said it's dangerous inside the room."

"It is. The currents of force could burn and poison me. But if our friends will give me the benefit of whatever wards they have left for the casting, that may protect me."

Will shook his head. "I don't like it."

"I'm not delighted with it, either, but do you have a better notion?"

"Even if this is a good plan," Drigor said, "you aren't the most powerful cleric here."

"No, but I'm the one bound to the sun. That makes a difference dealing with the undead, just as it did on our expedition into Shadow. So I should be the one to go. Agreed?"

Drigor's scarred face twisted. "Reluctantly."

"It's settled, then. Quickly, everyone, give me your blessings and protections. By the sound of it, the golems are about to crawl up out of their hole, and then it will be your job to keep them off my back."

The stone dragon's lashing wings and ridge of spine erupted from the rubble. Taegan beat his own pinions, sprang into the air, and flew over the golem, striking it again and again with his sword. Jivex streaked after him, landed on its back, and scrabbled with his talons.

Eye glowing yellow, the statue's head burst out into the open air and twisted toward its attackers. The jaws spread wide, and the creature spewed a plume of gray vapor. Taegan tried to fling himself aside, but the breath weapon washed over him anyway.

His muscles locked, and a cold heaviness flowed through his limbs. He started to fall. No, no, he thought, I refuse this, and the malignant power lost its grip on him. His wings flapped just in time to bear him up and keep him from dropping into the churning chunks of stone on top of the pit.

He looked for Jivex, and felt a pang of horror to see that the faerie dragon, still attached to the golem's back, had become a shape of gray granite like his foe. Then, however, Jivex too shook off the petrifactive effect, his scales shimmering as he became living flesh once more. The construct struck at him, and he dodged. Its fangs clashed as they snapped shut on empty air.

Taegan cut at it and said, "Back!" He and Jivex wheeled and joined the battle line Drigor, Celedon, Sureene, and Will had formed to block the way into the heart of the Rage. Firefingers, Scattercloak, and Darvin stood behind them.

His hands a blur, Will slung skiprock after skiprock at the golems as they clambered up out of the shattered floor. "Can't somebody just sink them down to the bottom again?" he asked.

"I'm afraid not," said Firefingers. "We don't have any more of those spells ready for the casting."

"Of course you don't," the halfling said. "Here they come!" He tucked his warsling back in his belt and whipped his hornblade from its scabbard.

The golems finished their scramble up to the surface and found their footing atop the shifting rubble. Jivex conjured a troop of flying pixies to hover in front of them and jab at them with their spears, but the illusion didn't balk them. Without hesitation, they charged right through it.

That left the matter up to sword, mace, warhammer, tooth, and claw, with the wizards aiding the folk on the front line as best they could. Firefingers made the iron golem's flaming breath arc harmlessly up at the ceiling, and Scattercloak created floating shields and blasts of wind to keep the stone drake's exhalations from reaching their targets. Darvin placed one glowing wall after another in the statues' way. The barriers dissolved the moment the constructs touched them. But perhaps they slowed them down a trifle and kept them from overrunning their foes by dint of sheer bulk and momentum.

Yet the golems steadily gained ground, for all that their foes contested every inch of it. Taegan cut, ducked, slashed, and sidestepped. Jivex raked at the stone dragon's luminous eye and hurtled on, narrowly evading a snap of its jaws, then a slap of its wing. Will darted under the iron wyrm, stabbed, and darted out before it could stamp on him.

Then huge iron claws flashed out and tore Drigor's head from his shoulders. His body fell with a clank of armor.

Several heartbeats later, the stone golem's tail whipped around at Celedon. The half-elf leaped back and parried, and the combination was enough to save his life. The blow, however, snapped his sword in two. He cursed, tossed it away and snatched a dagger from his boot.

The iron wyrm raked at Sureene. The stroke failed to penetrate her mail, but it knocked her reeling, and afterward, her right arm dangled uselessly. Her comely face ashen, she shifted her mace to her off hand and advanced once more.

It was obvious to Taegan that he and his remaining comrades couldn't resist much longer. In all likelihood, they were going to die within the next few breaths, as a legion of avariels had perished in this place millennia before.

So be it. But only if their lives purchased a comparable victory. Come, on, Pavel, do it! he thought, even as he lunged at the stone wyrm's head.

Cloaked in a shimmering, multi-layered aura of protection, Pavel sprinted halfway across the vault before he started suffering ill-effects from the hellfire contaminating the air. Then, however, a bluish flare swept over him, and agony stabbed through his body. He lost his balance, collapsed convulsing, and blacked out.

He woke to the clangor of steel bashing iron and stone. Thank the Morninglord, he'd only lost consciousness for a little while. His friends were still fighting to protect them. He just hoped he was still capable of an effort worth defending.

For his throbbing tongue was raw where he'd chewed it, and his mouth tasted of blood. Worse than that, his entire body had a sickening, pulsing wrongness to it. He could feel masses swelling inside his flesh, like tumors or parasites growing.

He considered trying to heal himself. But even if it worked, the hellfire would simply poison him anew, and in any case, he couldn't spare the time. The golems might break through Will and the others at any moment.

He groped around, found his mace and Sureene's scroll, and clambered to his feet. The world tilted and spun, and he nearly fell again. He took a breath, and the vertigo partially subsided. He limped onward.

Hellfire snaked and crackled, and he was too weak and dizzy even to try to avoid the streamers anymore. They seared him, stabbed him, staggered him, and the nodules inside his body pounded like extra hearts at their touch. But they failed to knock him down as the blue one had. Perhaps Lathander was holding him up.

He hobbled the last few steps to the phylactery, and reckoning that one ought to try the simple and obvious first, bashed it with his mace. But the blow neither damaged the black pendant nor jolted it out of position.

It would have to be magic, then. He took his own amulet from around his neck and gripped it and the phylactery together in his hand. He called his deity's name, drew a blaze of purifying dawnlight from the sun symbol, and read the first trigger phrase on the parchment.

Nothing happened, and so he repeated the process.

Sammaster exulted in the impotence and degradation of his foes. He snarled an incantation, and hail hammered the two sisters. It didn't kill them, but it left them bloody and dazed, crawling on the ground like the vermin they were. A flick of his tail shattered a copper's skull. His gaze paralyzed a brass, and the "noble" metallic plummeted out of the sky.

It was glorious. Until he felt a blaze of pain. It was an insult less to the body than the spirit, and for all his erudition and long and varied experience, he'd never felt anything like it before. Yet he knew what it meant.

Some power was attacking his phylactery. Belatedly, he remembered the foes who'd run into the barbican. Repeatedly distracted, he'd never verified that Gjellani had actually disposed of them, and certainly hadn't sent any more wyrms to assist with the job. He could only assume that the wretches had somehow survived and made it all the way to the source of the Rage.

Bungler! Idiot! Playing games out here when the only thing that truly mattered was in jeopardy!

But he could still salvage the situation. All he had to do was recite the proper incantation to translate himself to the mythal. He growled the first word.

Intent on Sammaster, Dorn had momentarily lost track of Kara, but heard her cry, "Don't let him finish that spell!" Then, wings furled, she plummeted down on top of the lich and drove her talons into his spine.

Huge as she was in dragon form, she was small compared to the titanic shape Sammaster had adopted, and even her ferocious assault didn't make his recitation falter. Without missing a beat, he twisted his head around, caught her in his jaws, yanked her off him, and slammed her to the ground, where she lay unmoving.

Brimstone pounced on the lich, rending rotten, shriveled flesh with his oversized fangs. That injury did make Sammaster's recitation falter, and dead eyes glaring, he seized hold of Brimstone's collar in his foreclaws and roared a different word of power. The choker broke apart, the jeweled fragments melting even as they dropped, and the vampire dissolved along with them. For a moment, he endured as a swirl of smoke and embers, then vanished utterly.

Sammaster raised and swiveled his head, spewing fire. The blaze seared some of the metallics diving at him and forced others to veer off. Then, floating, still burning, it split and shaped itself into half a dozen bright, draconic shapes that lashed their wings and flew at one or another of his foes.

Evidently confident that none of his enemies in the air would be able to balk him, Sammaster again began the spell that had so alarmed Kara.

By that time, Dorn and Raryn had covered most of the distance to their adversary. Running on two good legs, even if they were short ones, the dwarf reached the lich first. He drove his ice-axe into Sammaster's hind leg.

Sammaster plainly perceived the stroke, because he retaliated by picking up his foot and trying to stamp on Raryn, who scrambled out from underneath. But the pain, if, in fact, that was what the mad creature felt, was insufficient to disrupt his conjuring.

Dorn rushed in cutting, ducking and dodging huge, raking talons, the sweeping, pounding tail, and hammering wings. It was insane. In his present form, Sammaster was so big that the hunters couldn't even reach his body, only his extremities, and obviously, no crippled hunter could expect to last more than heartbeat against such a fearsome quarry.

Don't think about it! Just hit and move, hit and move.

The tempo of the spell accelerated toward its conclusion. Dorn invited a strike to give himself the chance to cut at whatever part of Sammaster came hurtling at him. It turned out to be a gigantic, withered forefoot. He twisted aside, and felt the remains of his iron leg buckle. As he cut, turning his whole body into the blow, the prosthesis broke apart.

But his blade still plunged deep into the corpse-thing's limb, cleaving flesh and smashing bone. Sammaster shrieked, finally botching his incantation. As he fell, Dorn resolved to cherish the memory of that scream even as the lich tore him apart.

Pavel had read the trigger phrase four times, to no effect. But on the fifth try, the phylactery shuddered in his grip like a frenzied animal struggling to escape, then crumbled into grit and soft, tiny fragments. Their terminus lost, the flares of hellfire leaped wildly around the chamber, until the miniature portals from which they sprang exploded in a stuttering series of blasts, leaving only ragged craters in the walls.

That's it, thought Pavel. It has to be. He wanted to rejoice, but felt too sick and weary.

Besides, it wasn't entirely over. The destruction of the mythal hadn't deterred the golems. They were still striving to kill the trespassers as fiercely as before.

Pavel hefted his mace and moved to help his comrades. But as soon as he took a step, his strength failed, and he fell down vomiting blood.

Dorn looked up expecting to see the stroke that would kill him. But Sammaster wasn't moving. Or rather, he was standing in place trembling, while Raryn chopped at his leg.

A shaft of red-gold light punched a hole in Sammaster's flank from the inside. Another beam burst forth, and another, erupting from every part of his body and in all directions, until the hideous shape of rot and bone was nearly lost inside a blaze like the rising sun. The lich lifted his head and screamed, then toppled.

Right at Dorn, and even riddled with holes, there was still plenty of corpse left to squash a human. Knowing it was hopeless, he nonetheless tried to crawl, and a pair of fanged jaws snatched him up. Leaping, Kara whisked him out from under the plummeting mass.

Dorn's eyes ached as if he was going to cry. "Sammaster didn't kill you," he said. "You're alive."

She set him gently on the ground. "Better than that," she said, "I'm sane."

Will slashed at the stone dragon, and the hornblade glanced off without biting. Small wonder. In time, hammering on iron and granite dulled even an enchanted sword.

He twisted away from a talon strike. Tried to riposte but found himself too slow. He was tired, gasping, his weapon heavy in his grip, and everyone else was in the same sorry condition. The end would come quickly .

Then, abruptly, Scattercloak said, in a voice still so devoid of emotion that it took a moment for the words to register: "We've won. Fall back, gather round, and I'll translate us away."

Of necessity, Will had been focused on the enemy. Still, it seemed astonishing, unreal, that after a year of striving, Pavel had succeeded in quelling the Rage without him even noticing. As he and his surviving comrades retreated, the golems pursuing, he risked a glance to make sure his friend was hurrying to join the rest of them.

He wasn't. Instead, he lay on his belly in the center of the golden pentacle with blood around his head.

"Get up, weakling!" Will cried.

"Can't," Pavel croaked. He had gore all over his chin, too. "Finished. Worth it to be rid of you. Get out."

"Not without you!" Will scrambled toward him.

"Taegan!" said Pavel. "Stop him!"

The avariel grabbed Will and hauled him back. As he struggled to free himself, he glimpsed huge plunging shapes, leaping flame and gray vapor, the golems driving forward in a final irresistible onslaught. Then they vanished into flash and blur.

As far as Nexus was concerned, Tamarand had proved himself as brilliant a captain as Lareth. Under his leadership, the metallics had performed miracles. But sometimes even miracles were insufficient, and as their comrades plummeted from the sky, or spiraled down too sorely wounded to continue fighting, he feared this was one of them.

Then something flashed far below him on the ground. In a battle fought with sorcery and dragon breath, plenty of things blazed and flared, and he didn't know what impelled him to attend to this one. Yet he looked down just in time to witness Sammaster's demise.

Nexus started roaring out the most potent spell of banishment in his repertoire. He'd attempted it twice already without success, but with Sammaster gone, and the power of the enchantments the lich had conjured perhaps attenuated, it was worth another try.

A chaos dragon spat acid at him. A howling drake battered him with its shriek. Refusing to let the punishment balk him, he declaimed the final words of the incantation.

All across the sky, and all at once, the otherworldly dragons disappeared, cast back to the infernal realms from which their master had drawn them.

8-27 Nightal, the Year of Rogue Dragons

Grigel Ragenev dripped viscous amber poison from a glass pipette into the brew simmering in the vessel below. The task required steady hands and total concentration. The mixture had to be precise, and what made it more difficult still was that, magic being a somewhat chaotic process, one couldn't know beforehand the exact proportions, or at which moments another droplet needed to go in. Assessing the shifting colors of the elixir and the inconstant smell of the fumes, the alchemist had to make judgments as he went along.

At his back, something crashed. It startled him, his hand shook, and venom plopped into the brew. A puff of sulfurous yellow vapor revealed that the mix and thus a tenday's work were ruined.

Grigel lurched around on his stool to berate the fool who'd made the noise, but what he saw curdled his fury into anxiety. It was Ssalangan who'd knocked down the crudely made door of the hut, and who crouched glaring through the opening.

"Where," growled the white, "is Sammaster?"

"I don't know," Grigel said, his voice a little shrill. "He left without telling anyone where he was going. I'm sure he'll return as soon as he can."

"Don't count on it," Ssalangan said. "We dragons believe he fled and left you slaves behind to suffer our displeasure. As you will. But we'll hunt him down and punish him, too. We have enough displeasure to go around."

"What are you talking about?"

"The Rage, of course. It faded from our minds two days ago, but we waited to be sure it was really gone. It is. Even though you thralls swore it would never end on its own. You lied to scare us into accepting the transformation."

"No!" Grigel said. "If what you're saying is true, the First-Speaker deceived us cultists as well."

Ssalangan sneered. "I think I may actually believe you. But it doesn't matter. I'm in a bad mood, and hungry, too."

The white lunged forward, and since the doorway was merely human-sized, the wall shattered to accommodate him. Elsewhere in the compound, wyrms roared, and their worshipers screamed.

Keeping a wary eye out for ghost dragons and other hazards, Tamarand, Nexus, Azhaq, and others collected stones to build their fallen comrades' cairns. Magic would have facilitated the task, but it felt proper to toil at it with wing and claw.

Tamarand tore at a mountainside, struggling to rip out another chunk of granite. The Tarterians had fed here and so weakened the stone, but it resisted him nonetheless. Nexus set down to assist him.

"It was a great victory," the wizard said. "We mourn the fallen, but it's permissible to celebrate as well."

Tamarand grunted.

"In fact," Nexus persisted, "it was a victory worthy of a king."

"I told you already, I won't be King of Justice."

"Because you won't forgive yourself for Lareth's death. But you needed to kill him to save our entire race, perhaps all of Faerûn, and save it we did."

"That doesn't excuse treachery."

"I say it does, and it also proves the benefits of leadership."

"Lareth's leadership would have doomed us all if Karasendrieth and her rogues hadn't defied him."

Nexus sighed, warming the chill arctic air and suffusing it with a scent like incense. "Sky and stone, you're stubborn. Just think about it, will you?"

Tamarand hesitated. "I'll think about it."

———— ✦◯✦ ————

As Azhaq piled rocks atop Havarlan's body, he noticed the new scars on his legs and feet. They were as plentiful as the old ones crisscrossing the female's hide.

Though many folk considered him arrogant, even by dragon standards, he wasn't vain enough to imagine he'd grown to be Havarlan's equal. But perhaps he was silver enough to keep her dream from dying with her. To see to it that, in one form or another, the Talons of Justice lived on.

———— ✦◯✦ ————

Kara reflected that in a sense, their great endeavor had begun in an inn, and it was ending the same way. This room, however, was a private one rented for the occasion, and free of wererats.

"Back at the start," she said, "I hired some of you to help me. Obviously, we've come a long way since then, far beyond notions of pay and employment. But I still want to share what I have, as a token of my gratitude and love."

She upended her pouch and dumped the treasure clattering on a table. The coins, gems, and jewelry gleamed in the light of the fire crackling in the hearth.

Will craned on tiptoe so he could take a proper look, then, to her surprise, took only a single gold band set with a ruby. "This will do me for a keepsake. I picked up plenty on our way back through Brimstone's cave. You can give the rest of my share to a temple of Lathander." His face twisted, and he blinked.

Raryn clasped the halfling's shoulder. "He was the best of us," the ranger said.

"He was a useless charlatan!" Will spat. "But I miss him. A little."

Raryn turned to the pile and pulled out a fistful of gold and a truesilver armband set with emeralds. "I don't need much, either, where I'm headed. But I might want some."

"Are you going somewhere?" asked Dorn, sprawled on a couch, a cup of brandy in his remaining hand.

"Back to the Great Glacier. Joylin's there, with no kin left to look after her. I have to make sure she's all right. I need to see my tribe again, too, now that they've betrayed me. I don't want revenge, but I have to talk to them if I'm ever to forgive them."

"I'll tag along," said Will, "if you'll have me. I feel like doing something."

"I don't envy you a second journey on the ice," Taegan said, elegant in the new blue and scarlet suit a tailor, extravagantly rewarded, had labored day and night to finish. "Particularly at this time of year. For my part, I intend to winter savoring the luxuries of Lyrabar, and resume my forays into the wilderness come spring."

"Where will you go then?" Kara asked.

"Back to my own tribe in the Earthwood, and then to other avariel enclaves, if I can find them. I finally understand why we hide from the world. To say the least, there's no shame in it, but millennia after the chromatics gave up trying to exterminate us, there's no longer any necessity, either. Someone ought to speak to the others of that, and of the advantages of rejoining the rest of civilization."

Perched on the mantelpiece, tail dangling, Jivex snorted. "I suppose that means the Gray Forest will have to do without me for a while longer. Since it's clear you're helpless without me. Now it's my turn to choose." He lashed his wings, hurtled across the room, and landed amid the mass of gems and precious metal.

"If you'll recall," Taegan drawled, "you and I never were in Lady Kara's employ."

"It doesn't matter," she said, smiling. "Both of you, take anything you want."

After the division of the treasure came the finest meal the kitchen could provide, its best wine, and toasts to Pavel, Chatulio, Gorstag, Igan, Madislak, Drigor, and everybody else who'd given his life to end the Rage. The company traded reminiscences of their lost comrades, and after some coaxing, Kara sang her first attempt at a ballad describing the dive into Northkeep. Everyone professed to find it splendid, though to her ear, it was still a raw, unpolished thing.

Finally, one by one, the others stumbled off to seek their beds. Until only she and Dorn remained.

He sighed. "Everyone's leaving."

"As they probably should," she replied, holding his hand. "We're all tipsy."

"I don't mean now. In the days to come. I don't blame them. They have things to do, and I obviously can't follow."

"Do you believe," she asked, "they're abandoning you forever? That you'll never see them again?"

Scowling, he continued as if he hadn't heard her. "You need to go, too. Pavel *was* the best of us. You should always have been with him, not a freak like me, and now that I'm crippled again, our being together is just ridiculous. You—"

She slapped the human side of his face.

"Any more prattle like that," she said, "and you'll get another. In the first place, I would no more forsake you for possessing a maimed body than you deserted me for suffering a stricken mind. In the second, do you imagine that Nexus, Firefingers, Sureene, and the others are going to leave you like this? I don't know if they'll fit you out with iron limbs again, but they'll do something. You're one of the champions who saved dragonkind, all the world, perhaps, and a good many people love you. Stop sulking, open your eyes, and see what's real!"

His lips quirked into a smile. "I guess that sometimes, I still have a sour way of thinking."

"Then I'll have to train it out of you."

Brimstone floated in howling darkness. There was nothing to see, but he felt an invisible maelstrom whirling and churning below him. Striving to suck him down.

Though his thoughts were muddled, he sensed it was natural, probably even inevitable that he succumb to the vortex. Yet at the same time, he dreaded it, and so he resisted. Not by flapping his wings, for his body had become as diffuse and abstract a thing as his mind. By sheer will.

It was impossible to tell how long he struggled, but eventually, a point of light appeared. He strained for it, and gradually crept closer, or perhaps pulled it toward him. It became a pale, glimmering rectangle with a sparkling circle in the center, then the white glow of it was all around him, washing away the dark.

He realized he once again possessed physicality in his form of smoke and embers. The whiteness held him strait as a torturer's cage, and he probed it, seeking release. He couldn't find an opening as such, but there was a pathway, an accommodating vector, and he flowed along it.

He boiled up into frigid air. Into a valley girt with dark mountains and covered with a black and starry sky. His thoughts snapped into clarity, and he remembered this was the place where Sammaster had destroyed him.

Except, not quite. Peering down, he found a single link of his collar lying on the ground. Somehow, that one piece had survived the lich's spell of annihilation to serve as his anchor as he hung between undeath and oblivion. To enable him to clamber back into the mortal world.

He took on solid form, gashed his chest with a talon, and tucked the diamond-and-platinum link into the wound. As it healed over, he looked around.

Still wearing the dracolich form he'd assumed at the end, Sammaster—or rather, his shattered corpse—lay some yards away. Brimstone had kept the madman from translating himself away, and afterward his allies had somehow managed to slay him.

Or had they? Brimstone knew better than anyone how powerful and wily Sammaster was. Perhaps his seeming demise had been a trick. Perhaps he'd risen from this husk to assail his foes anew.

But there were cairns on the battlefield. Brimstone tumbled stones from the top of one and found a silver beneath. Only the victors could have erected the piles, and Sammaster would scarcely have bothered to give one of the metallics an honorable interment.

Still, Brimstone couldn't find it in his heart to be certain. He prowled into the citadel to seek the source of the Rage.

Golems guarded the threshold, but paid no heed to his smoky shape. Beyond, in a vault begemmed to resemble the heavens, lay the body of Pavel Shemov. Brimstone reflected that he and the sun priest would never have the final confrontation they'd both desired, then spotted a litter of black dust and fragments.

He was mystic enough to discern that he was looking at the remains of Sammaster's phylactery, which the lich had evidently integrated into the mythal, and at last he believed. He and his allies had prevailed, not merely putting an end to the Rage, but expunging its master from the world for good and all.

The realization left him feeling a strange jumble of emotions: Exultation, certainly, but annealed with regret that he hadn't witnessed Sammaster's downfall, as well as an underlying emptiness. The struggle for revenge had consumed him for much of his existence, and abruptly it was over. What was he supposed to do?

Then he sneered at his mawkish feelings, for the answer was obvious. He still thirsted for blood and power, and with a goodly number of the metallics who might have opposed him slain, and much of Faerûn still in turmoil in the aftermath of the dragon flights, it was a perfect time to strike for both. He flowed back past the golems to discover what other secrets the ruined castle held.

THE FIRST INTO BATTLE,

THEY HOLD THE LINE, THEY ARE...

THE FIGHTERS

MASTER OF CHAINS

Once he was a hero, but that was before he was nearly killed and
sold into slavery. Now he has nothing but hate and the chains of
his bondage: the only weapons he has with which to escape.

GHOSTWALKER

His first memories were of death. His second, of those who killed him.
Now he walks with specters, consumed by revenge.

SON OF THUNDER

Forgotten in a valley of the High Forest dwell the thunderbeasts,
kept secret by ancient and powerful magic. When the Zhentarim find
out about this magic, a young barbarian must defend his reptilian
brethren from those who would seize their power.

BLADESINGER

Corruption grips the heart of Rashemen in the one place they thought
it could not take root: the council of wise women who guide the people.
A half-elf bladesinger traveling north with his companions is the people's
only hope, but first, he must convince them to accept his help.

For more information visit **www.wizards.com**

HOUSE OF SERPENTS TRILOGY
By The New York Times best-selling author Lisa Smedman

VENOM'S TASTE

The Pox, a human cult whose members worship the goddess of plague and disease, begins to work the deadly will of Sibyls' Chosen. As humans throughout the city begin to transform into the freakish tainted ones, it's up to a yuan-ti halfblood to stop them all.

VIPER'S KISS

A mind-mage of growing power begins a secret journey to Sespeth. There he meets a yuan-ti halfblood who has her eyes set on the scion of house Extaminos – said to hold the fabled Circled Serpent.

VANITY'S BROOD

The merging of human and serpent may be the most dangerous betrayal of nature the Realms has ever seen. But it could also be the only thing that can bring a human slave and his yuan-ti mistress together against a common foe.

www.wizards.com

A NEW TRILOGY FROM MARGARET WEIS & TRACY HICKMAN

THE DARK CHRONICLES
Dragons of the Dwarven Depths
Volume One

Tanis, Tasslehoff, Riverwind and Raistlin
are trapped as refugees in Thorbardin, as the
draconian army closes in on the dwarven
kingdom. To save his homeland, Flint begins a
search for the Hammer of Kharas.

Available July 2006

For more information visit **www.wizards.com**

ENTER THE NEW WORLD OF

THE DREAMING DARK TRILOGY

By Keith Baker

A hundred years of war…

Kingdoms lie shattered, armies are broken, and an entire
country has been laid to waste. Now an uneasy
peace settles on the land.

Into Sharn come four battle-hardened soldiers. Tired of
blood, weary of killing, they only want a place to call home.

The shadowed City of Towers has other plans…

THE CITY OF TOWERS
Volume One

THE SHATTERED LAND
Volume Two

THE GATES OF NIGHT
Volume Three
DECEMBER 2006

For more information visit **www.wizards.com**

ENTER THE NEW WORLD OF

THE WAR~TORN

After a hundred years of fighting the war is now over, and the people
of Eberron pray it will be the Last War. An uneasy peace settles
over the continent of Khorvaire.

But what of the soldiers, warriors, nobles, spies, healers, clerics, and
wizards whose lives are forever changed by the decades of war? What
does a world without war hold for those who have known nothing
but violence? What fate lies for these, the war-torn?

THE CRIMSON TALISMAN

BOOK 1

Adrian Cole

Erethindel, the fabled Crimson Talisman. Long sought by
the forces of darkness. Long guarded in secret by one family. Now the
secret has been revealed, and only one young man can keep it safe.

THE ORB OF XORIAT

BOOK 2

Edward Bolme

The last time Xoriat, the Realm of Madness, touched the world, years of
warfare and death erupted. A new portal to the Realm of Madness has
been found — a fabled orb, long thought lost. Now it has been stolen.

IN THE CLAWS OF THE TIGER

BOOK 3

James Wyatt

BLOOD AND HONOR

BOOK 4

Graeme Davis

For more information visit **www.wizards.com**